From This Day
Forward

Books by Elswyth Thane

FICTION

RIDERS OF THE WIND

ECHO ANSWERS

HIS ELIZABETH

CLOTH OF GOLD

BOUND TO HAPPEN

QUEENS FOLLY

TRYST

REMEMBER TODAY

FROM THIS DAY FORWARD

DAWN'S EARLY LIGHT

YANKEE STRANGER

EVER AFTER

LIGHT HEART

NON-FICTION

THE TUDOR WENCH

YOUNG MR. DISRAELI

ENGLAND WAS AN ISLAND ONCE

THE BIRD WHO MADE GOOD

PLAYS

THE TUDOR WENCH

YOUNG MR. DISRAELI

From This Day Forward

ELSWYTH THANE

ÆONIAN PRESS

MATTITUCK

Republished 1976 by Special Arrangement
with Hawthorn Books, Inc.

Copyright © 1941 by Elswyth Thane

Library of Congress Cataloging in Publication Data
Thane, Elswyth, 1900-
   From this day forward.

   Reprint of the ed. published by Duell, Sloan
and Pearce, New York.
   I.   Title.
PZ3.T327Fr6   [PS3539.H143]   813'.5'2   76-18874
ISBN 0-88411-960-2

AEONIAN PRESS, INC.
Mattituck, New York 11952

Manufactured in the United States of America

From This Day
Forward

I

Lots of people believe in Destiny, and some think things Just Happen. Some are convinced that marriages are made in heaven, and others hold that the pairing of any two human beings is the result of a sort of cosmic game of farmer-in-the-dell. To some, love arrives like an avalanche coming downhill, and then again with others it would appear to be largely a process of attrition.

Maybe it would never have caught up with Elizabeth Dare if she hadn't inherited the Old Baxter Place and gone to spend the summer there, alone except for dour middle-aged Mary, who cooked for her, and Snorky, who was a Pekingese. Or maybe if she hadn't been Elizabeth Dare, but just some ordinary, commonplace woman, who wrote books, or sang opera, or performed on a trapeze. Or maybe if she had stayed asleep that August morning, instead of waking up when the first rays of the sun stretched across the Atlantic to touch the coast of Maine, where the mown green lawn of the Old Baxter Place broke up into jagged great gray rocks that staggered down all anyhow to the water's edge—

But Elizabeth Dare sat up in bed and beheld the sun arriving approximately from Cape Finisterre—which she had doubtless never heard of—and because the pink dawn light on the calm sea below her windows was exciting and strange, she wrapped herself in a velvet robe and went and sat on her feet on the cushioned window seat to watch. Not since she was a baby and yelled for her bottle had she wakened to see the sun come up—though she had been fairly close to sunrise sometimes on the other end of her day; less frequently than you might think, perhaps, for a girl who

3

was the most popular, most misunderstood, and most expensive Specialty singer in the most exclusive night clubs and musical shows in Manhattan and London. (She had never worked in Paris. She used to say she was afraid of the competition there. Nobody believed her, but it was true.)

She looked pretty nice, sitting on the window seat in the blushing light, with her feet under her, wearing blue velvet; but there was nobody to see except Snorky, who had roused at her movement in the room and was now eyeing her in astonishment with his chin hung over the edge of his basket in the corner. She was still young enough to wake up looking younger than she was, with her hair rumpled and her face washed clean of make-up. She had soft dark curls, and good bones, and knew how to carry her head, even when only Snorky was looking.

By the time the sunlight had turned yellow and warmed her upturned face through the glass she was hungry—hungry and excited and awake. And so, with a groundless feeling of stealing a march on somebody—for ten years now she had been free to do as she pleased—she hurried off to the bathroom and brushed her teeth (small, close white teeth which had had to be straightened when she was a little girl) washed her face in hot water and then cold water, slapped in a lotion, patted on powder, spent a careful minute with a lipstick, ran a brush and comb through her curls. If there had been a fire, Elizabeth Dare would have brushed her teeth, seen to her face, tidied her hair, and dressed quickly—with everything fresh from the drawer—before appearing at the top of the rescue ladder to ravish the eyes of the firemen below.

Clad now in brown English tweeds and a canary-yellow blouse and rubber-soled brogues, she went stealthily down to the kitchen and made herself a large glass of orange juice, which she drank standing on the back porch outside the open kitchen door, so that her fascinated eyes could still watch the world unfold. When the orange juice was all gone, she returned to the kitchen and wrote on the grocery-pad: *Dear Mary, I have gone for a walk, it's the*

4

most Glorious Day. Fix me a BIG breakfast. E.D. And then, putting a box half full of graham crackers under her arm, she went out confidently into the morning.

The air caught her nostrils like a new perfume. There was no wind, only freshness. Everything sparkled with dew. Bees were already at work in the garden, and a pair of white butterflies danced their foolish jigging flight above the petunia bed. The early sunlight had an almost tangible warmth, and she spread her hands to it, palms up, standing with tilted face, the line of her small throat pure as a child's, her short curls swept back by the brush, her red lips parted in her funny, pointed smile—her teeth were quite even now, but the fact that once they had not been still lent a queer charm to her smile, for the upper row curved sharply in her narrow jaw.

But you must do this oftener, she thought; you've been missing something, my girl. (There were two Elizabeth Dares, herself and the one she talked to like a Dutch uncle.) Why didn't somebody tell us mornings were like this, she thought. Imagine people *sleeping!*

And so, full of new-found virtue and orange juice, inflated into that holier-than-thou condition of the early-risen in a world of sluggards, she set off along the path which ran from the lawn away into the coarse grass at the upper edge of the rocks where they dipped to allow a small stream to enter the sea—Elizabeth Dare, feeling very strange, very excited, very *awake,* moving in a kind of bedazzled trance towards her fate.

On her right lay the rough pine groves of the Baxter acreage, cutting off the private shore line from the public road; on her left, the sea. Except close to the house, none of the land had been parked or cleared. The stream flowed brown and transparent from a pond deep in the woods, where the Baxter children, when there were any, had always gone skating in their winter holidays. The shore path had a little ford, casually built of uncut stepping-

5

stones, though a few yards farther inland the stream was narrow enough to be jumped.

In no time at all she had lost sight of the house behind her, and walked between pines and rocks, with the sea beyond. The tide was in, so there were no unfortunate smells. The water lay still and opal, with shimmering shallows. Her brown brogues turned dark with the dew, which soaked her silk-clad ankles.

Beyond the ford the path rose under her feet and dwindled towards the cliff a mile further on. A fallen log lay on the seaward side of a bramble thicket near by, which bordered a pocket-size glade, carpeted with kinnikinic and wintergreen. She turned aside and sat down on the log, which was so low that the hem of her skirt trailed in the wet leaves. She opened the box of crackers and began to munch contentedly, the shimmer of the sea in her eyes.

There was suddenly the sound as of a wild elephant amok in the thicket behind her, and something shot over her left shoulder, tangled with her outstretched feet, and landed like a stricken pine full length on the ground. At first glance there appeared to be several yards of him, but that was partly the butterfly net, which had preceded him at arm's length.

Unlike most people who fall, he neither swore nor attempted to retrieve his dignity by rising hastily and brushing things off his clothes. Instead, he raised himself on one hand and looked round to see what had tripped him.

He saw Elizabeth Dare, sitting on a log with a bitten cracker in her hand, wearing her famous expression of starry-eyed expectancy—complicated now by the element of surprise. He saw, to be brief, Elizabeth Dare.

For a moment they stared at each other in silence, she from the log, he lying where he had fallen, braced on one bent arm, his head turned over his shoulder.

"Good morning," he said politely then. "I hope I didn't hurt you."

6

"N-no," she replied, achieving an equally normal tone. "Are you all right yourself?"

"I think so." He sat up slowly, without effort—any dancer could see that he knew how to fall. "I'm sorry if I startled you," he continued with the good manners which apparently nothing could jar out of him. "I had no idea there would be anyone here."

"Naturally not," she nodded. "I never meant to trip you, either."

"I wouldn't be trespassing, would I?"

"You might. I don't know just where my boundary line is— about a quarter of a mile this side of the pond, they said."

"Oh, yes—that pond. You know, you'd better do something about that, but *quick!*"

"Do what? Why?"

"I suppose you realize you're raising the finest mosquito crop in the state of Maine down there."

"Mosquitoes! Oh, horrors, what do I do?"

"I would suggest kerosene," he said, and added, because she looked rather blank and helpless, "I'll send down a couple of kids from the Station with a can of the stuff, if you like, and they'll do it for you. Be good practice for 'em."

"Are you one of those students up at the Biological Station?" she inquired incredulously.

"Believe it or not, I'm one of the professors," he corrected gently.

"Beg pardon," she murmured, still incredulous. "W-would you like a cracker?" And further to placate him, she offered him the open box from her lap, while he recognized with delight that slight hesitation not quite amounting to a stammer which Elizabeth Dare allowed to overtake her at moments of stress, even when she was singing.

"Thanks very much." He accepted a cracker and bit into it.

For another silent moment they regarded each other with deepening interest. She saw that his eyes were gray with a dark ring around the iris, and his straight dark hair had a boyish lock which

7

escaped just forward of his left temple, and his mouth was big and generous, with deep, humorous corners. He noticed that Elizabeth Dare's candid brow was just as white by day as under the spotlight, and that her eyelashes turned up just as inquiringly. She was as real as the summer morning which formed a becoming background to the leaf-brown suit and yellow blouse with its round collar enclosing her little throat—such a little throat to house the pure, strong notes of her singing voice. All this and more he was able to observe in that brief moment before his indestructible good manners reminded him that one does not stare at a celebrity encountered socially.

"As a matter of fact," he heard himself saying as though he was rather a long way from himself, "we were going to draw lots up at the Station for the dangerous privilege of calling on you about the pond. It looks as though I've won, hands down."

"Well, that's good," Elizabeth agreed pretty vaguely, wondering what happened to his face when he really smiled. "And if you would see to it for me I'd be very grateful."

"Pleasure."

"Thank you. By the way," she went on, for he seemed to have a boundless capacity for intimate silence, "whatever it was you were chasing, you caught it." And she pointed to the butterfly net on the ground behind him, which was lively with imprisoned effort.

He removed his eyes from her face with a sort of wrench, and glanced over his shoulder with interest of another kind, alert and impersonal—the look which later on she was to classify with a capital letter as Science.

"Why, so I did," he said in pleased surprise. "Excuse me." He took a wide-mouthed cyanide bottle from the pocket of his suède jacket and laid it on the grass. With a single deft pounce he pinned down the liveliness in the net, slid his other hand under the rim, and brought out a large brown butterfly held neatly by the body between his thumb and forefinger. Its wings were quiet now. With

8

his free hand he uncorked the bottle and dropped the butterfly in. *"Anosia plexippus,"* he remarked. "Just what we wanted."

She reached out and took the bottle from his hand, and he noticed that her nails were enameled a pale, natural pink instead of blood red, and wondered if anything about her was going to prove a disappointment, and began to be afraid that nothing was. There were a couple of common white cabbage butterflies in the bottle, and an azure, pathetically small and still.

"Does that white stuff at the bottom kill them right away?" she inquired, turning the bottle in her fingers.

"The pinch on the thorax does that."

"Oh. You pinched it," she said flatly.

"Otherwise they break their wings fluttering against the glass."

"You know, you're not my idea of a professor at all," she told him suddenly, with a note of accusation in it.

"Aren't you a little behind the times?" He clasped his hands round his jack-knifed knees, contemplating her with serene gray eyes. "Nowadays professors usually remember to get their hair cut, and seldom lose their umbrellas, and even take their wives to the movies. Some of them can actually steer a woman round a dance floor without falling flat on their faces."

"And do you take your wife to the movies?" asked Elizabeth Dare, trying to look as though it didn't really matter to her what his answer was going to be.

"I would if I had a wife." His voice was very low in the spreading silence all around them. "And when I fall flat on my face there's always a good reason. Besides—" He broke off. Or rather, he just decided not to go on.

"Besides what?"

"No, I—better not."

"What were you going to say?" she pleaded.

"Well—" His gaze slid away from hers, out to sea, and his eyebrows were not level with each other, which gave him a quizzical, secretive look she found quite irresistible, so that she leaned

9

forward, watching him. "I was only trying not to say that I'd fallen for Elizabeth Dare years ago, anyway."

"How many years ago?" she demanded, her elbows on her knees, waiting for his eyes to come back to her.

"Let's see, it must have been round about 1930."

"Oh, nonsense, in 1930 you still had your milk teeth!"

He looked at her then, with a quick turn of his head, one eyebrow well aloft.

"That is probably the most insulting thing anybody has ever said to me—and lived," he remarked deliberately. "I graduated from college in 1931."

"With honors!" Again her tone held unreasonable accusation.

"Yes, and my football letter! Do you want to make anything of that?"

"No—oh, no!" She backed down hastily. "It's very nice of you to be so interested in my—career."

"You're getting to be an expensive hobby," he admitted, relaxing again before her expression of respectful gravity. "These night clubs you've gone in for lately—after half a dozen times it begins to run into money, even if I stag it."

"Half a dozen—! I'll have to get you a pass!"

"Hm-mm," he said decisively, and shook his head. "I should say—no, thanks. That wouldn't be the same thing at all."

"How do you mean?"

"Well, I don't know if I can explain—but—seeing Elizabeth Dare, on the stage or at a night club, is something very special. You have to work up to it, pick a day when you can get away from the campus, get the ticket or the table reservation in advance, check off the days on a calendar, send your evening clothes to be pressed, pack a bag, catch a train to New York, go to a hotel—and then at last you've got it, the thing you've been working up to. There she is. Singing—dancing—looking so beautiful—Elizabeth Dare, In Person." He shot her one of his clear, slanting looks with a wary edge to it, as though he half expected to surprise

10

ridicule on her face, or noncomprehension, instead of the rapt attention with which she was regarding him, her eyelashes flaring absurdly with expectancy. "If I could walk in just any night, or every night, it wouldn't be the same," he went on explaining. "It would be too easy. Elizabeth Dare shouldn't be easy. She should be hard to get to—very expensive—and too soon lost again. And believe me, on an associate professor's salary, that's what she is!"

"She's human, you know."

"Is she?" His gaze rested on her, full of a not altogether academic curiosity, and now it was she who looked out across the quiet water.

"It's not much fun for her—the way you tell it."

"She's got a world of her own, I guess. She doesn't have to pick her friends out of the front row."

"What's your name?" she asked impersonally, watching the horizon behind his head. "Since you know so much about me."

He hesitated.

"Can you take it?"

She nodded.

"My name's Rodney."

"Rodney? What's wrong with that? I thought it would be Dinwiddie, at least! What are you professor of? Butterflies?"

"Ornithology."

"Is that fish or beetles?"

"Birds."

"Oh, birds! That's not so bad! I'd like to know more about birds, myself. Why are you messing about with butterflies?"

"I don't confine myself to any one thing up here, that's why I like this place. We all mess about with whatever happens to be going on."

"Do you really like it? Teaching those brats up at the Station, I mean."

"Well, it's some satisfaction to see young people find themselves—make a false start, maybe, in the wrong subject—and then suddenly

11

orient themselves, and get off on the other foot to something that may become their life-work. Maybe that sounds—scholastic and smug," he broke off uncomfortably. "Maybe I talk too much."

"Go on," she said, spellbound. "I'm interested. Go on talking about it."

"It's hard to put these things into words, I—don't think I've ever tried before. I guess nobody ever asked me. But take a case we have up there now—a funny, homely kid, if you like, but sharp as tacks. For two years that little Jackson girl has been doing marine zoology, got good marks, seemed perfectly happy in it, was settling down nicely to Crustacea. And then suddenly, a few days ago, she saw a bird! I mean really saw one, for the first time, as a living problem. Well, she's thrown over two years of marine zoology Like That, to begin at the bottom with birds, perfectly certain that's where her real inclination lies. Now, I call that very interesting psychologically, don't you?"

"Before I answer I'd want to see what the professor of marine zoology looks like."

"Mercer? He's a nice little guy with spectacles and— Say, what did you mean by that?"

She gave him her charming, pointed smile.

"Not very bright, are you," she suggested. "Don't get around much."

"Oh, now, hold on, if you could see this Jackson kid, why, she's all sort of—"

"What *she* looks like has nothing to do with the case. Or has it?" she murmured, watching his stupefied face. "Your mouth is hanging open," she added rudely.

He became excessively reasonable, as though she was a half-wit child.

"Now, look, Mercer is a *very* brilliant man, he— Oh, no, you've got it all wrong, I never— Well, I *hope* you're wrong!" he ended lamely, remembering several incidents in a new light.

"Show me Mercer, and I'll tell you whether I'm wrong or not!"

12

"All right, come on up to the Station and see him, let's settle this thing!"

"All right, I will!"

"All right, when?"

"What's the matter with now?"

"Well, what are we waiting for?"

He rose in a single fluid movement, like a dancer, and his hand was firm and warm as he reached down to help her to her feet —perhaps forgetting that she would come up like a dancer too, facing him, her hand still in his. He was very tall, two yards and several inches of him, and she herself was tall for a woman. In another of their queer, unself-conscious pauses he stood looking down into her face, which seemed flawless in the searching light, her dark curls brushed back so you could see her small ears— until once more he remembered not to stare, and as he stepped back reluctantly their fingers parted.

He glanced round the little glade, his nose lifted to a faint stir of air.

"Do you notice that fragrance?" he said. "I can't make out what it is. Sort of a combination of several garden flowers—but there doesn't seem to be anything—"

"It might be me," she murmured, and he gave her a penetrating look, as though he could see if it was.

"Well, yes, I suppose it might be," he agreed, and bent easily from the waist to collect the net and the cyanide bottle from among the shiny wintergreen leaves. "Everybody up at the Station is going to drop dead when I walk in with you. And as a matter of fact, even if you do smell so nice, you're not exactly my idea of an actress either!"

"Well, what do you want for your money at this time of day? Something stretched out on a sofa wearing ostrich feathers?"

She saw then what happened when he really smiled.

"Not exactly. Not from you, anyway." He stood watching her as she turned back along the way she had come. "That path, as I

13

know very well, takes us out on to your front lawn. To get to the Station we go round this way."

"I've got a better idea," she said. "You have breakfast with me at the house first, and I'll drive you back."

"Would that be all right?" He was visibly tempted.

"Why not?"

"Well, I—didn't know what your arrangements might be, I—"

"There's just me and Mary the cook and Snorky the Pekingese —and nobody under the bed, if that's what you mean!"

He looked shocked.

"I didn't suppose—I mean, it's none of my business—"

"I'm hungry," she interrupted briskly. "Hurry up, and then we can tell each other the story of our lives over the second cup of coffee."

"If you can shed any light on how Elizabeth Dare got this way, I'd certainly be glad to listen," he remarked as they moved along the path in step. "You know, that's a very dangerous name you've got there—"

"Dangerous? How?"

"A man is liable to get his tongue twisted so that it comes out Elizabeth Dear before he knows where he is. I suppose most people call you that—" His voice trailed away apologetically.

"Most people call me Liz."

"Yes, I know. Liz Dear, I mean Dare."

"I was born Adair, if you must know. It was too many syllables."

"It's the same thing, really," he ruminated. "Elizabeth's Adear. It still scans."

She laughed, absurdly pleased, and they came to a place where they had to go single file, and he put her in front of him with a protective arm laid lightly round her waist for a moment—in that brief touch she felt his strength and balance and command, felt all his quiet masculinity against which one could lean so confidently, and she stumbled over her own feet with surprise at her thoughts, for she had never been a leaner. Steady, Liz, for God's

14

sake, he's only a boy, she thought—no, he's got to be thirty—well, suppose he is thirty, he's still just the young man in the front row, Liz, what's got into you?—I don't know what's got into me, but I like it, I hope it lasts, I hope— And here she stumbled again, for she very seldom talked back to herself, and when she did it was a bad sign.

"Hi," he remarked from the rear, his own unhurried footfalls inaudible. "Pick 'em up. Or do I have to carry you?"

"That would be lovely," she said over her shoulder, before Liz could stop her.

This was just as they reached the sketchy ford, where the tide stood almost level with the stepping-stones. His hands came down over her shoulders with the net and the bottle.

"Take these," he said, and automatically she obeyed.

Her feet left the ground, and she found herself very high up, held horizontally in his arms, the soft suède of his jacket against her cheek.

"Why don't you weigh something?" he inquired, but not in any spirit of criticism, and she felt him crossing the ford without apparently looking where he was going. "Give a man a real workout, there's nothing to this."

"Do put me down," she said, as soon as she had enough breath.

"What's the matter, aren't you comfortable?"

He stood still in the path to look down into her face. There was no longer any doubt that the fragrance he had noticed in the glade he now held in his arms. Taking her nonplused silence for acquiescence, he started on again, carrying her with insulting ease, not showing the least strain even in his breathing. Elizabeth knew something about condition, and her ideas about professors were getting another swift revision.

"S-somebody might s-see us," she murmured faintly, not caring if somebody did.

Instantly, however, he set her on her feet.

"Sorry," he said. "It was a crazy thing to do and I apologize."

15

"I rather liked it," she said, and turned jauntily up the path ahead of him. (Really, Liz! Well, I did like it, why not let him know? *Really, Liz—!*)

His face as he followed was very thoughtful. He had been guilty of showing off like a schoolboy—succumbing to a sudden unaccountable impulse to demonstrate his own perfect balance and co-ordination to this woman who danced and sang in a spotlight. He was strong and sure-footed because some time in the field his life, or someone else's, might depend on his being so. And something in him had rebelled at her obvious mental picture of a professor peering down a microscope in a classroom, a clumsy lummox who chased butterflies for kids to mount on insect boards. But at the same time, you couldn't say Look, girl, I've seen hell and high water in places you can't even spell, and brought back my specimens, everything I went for, and then some; I can ride anything I can get a leg over, and hit anything I can get the sights on; I can throw a man twice my weight, and I've done my five hundred hours in the air— But no, you couldn't just say things like that, out of the blue. So you pick her up bodily and carry her across a stream—sophomore stuff. And why? Not because she's Elizabeth Dare. No, not that any more. But because she's a woman who has made you feel like a schoolboy again, and so you up and act like one, all over the place. That sort of thing hasn't happened for years. That won't get you anywhere. You don't get a whole new world in the blink of an eye, you know. What have you got for Elizabeth Dare? Talking to yourself, eh? That's bad. Well, how was I to know I'd ever find her sitting on a log? And even if I did, what right has she to be just the way I wanted her to be? Say, what goes on here? You've got no time for this.

"Do you ever talk to yourself?" she asked casually, without turning round.

Startled to a standstill, he stood staring at her until she felt it and glanced back over her shoulder.

"Why did you ask that?" he demanded.

16

"Because I do. I just wondered." She stood there in the path ahead of him, waiting for his answer.

"And what do you say to yourself?" There was no derision in his level eyes.

"Well, this time I was saying to myself, Liz, I was saying, just because you saw the sunrise this morning is no reason for you to take off, I was saying—life is still the same old shoddy, imitation, second-rate, underhand proposition it was yesterday. You don't get a whole new world, I said, like a rabbit out of a hat—"

"—in the blink of an eye," he finished simultaneously, and they gazed at each other between fright and incredulity. "I said it first," he managed then.

"You mean—just now—you—"

"Yep, I've been laying down the law to myself ever since we left the ford. And we're both absolutely right, you know, there's nothing in it—for either of us." And while the words were still on his lips he knew quick panic at having read her thoughts and brutally voiced his own.

She blinked once, while his meaning went home.

"No, of course not," she agreed. "Nothing in it at all. Merely a matter of propinquity."

And she turned her back on him again, and led the way along the path towards breakfast. He followed silently, feeling rather as though he had mercifully pinched another butterfly.

II

Snorky met them at the door, the warmth of his greeting to his lady complicated by the necessity of frightening away the tall stranger by sounding like a bull mastiff. Rodney, halted in his tracks by the dreadful din, stood with the knob of the screen door still in his hand and looked down at the champion.

"My goodness me," he commented mildly. "The lions are loose!"

"Shut up, Snorky, he's a professor," said Elizabeth. *"Shut up, I say!"* she yelled, and bopped her protector with the cracker box, to no effect.

"Now, wait a minute," suggested Rodney reasonably, and laid down the net and the cyanide bottle. "This is just between us two, and we'll work it out without any help from you." He went on one knee in the middle of the rug and Snorky rushed him furiously, braking only two feet away while the walls echoed to his bull-mastiff act. "Now, look, fellah, I know how you feel, I'd do the same in your place," Rodney was saying peaceably. "But let's get together on it, you don't have to worry about me, I'm just as crazy about her as you are." Snorky left off barking, in order to look at him with surprise and some doubt. "Yes, the fact is, if ever there's any laying down of lives in her defense, just you count me in on it, that's all, because from now on there are two of us on the job to look after her. Not that you need any help, you're doin' fine, but that's no reason to throw me out of the house—is it!" His hand came out slowly, and Snorky came to meet it, and fell to licking its fingers in abject admiration.

"Well, I'll be darned!" said Elizabeth, who stood over them, watching. "He got every word you said! Between the two of you,

18

a lady would be safe anywhere." They looked up at her from the middle of the rug, Snorky pop-eyed and slavering with love, Rodney still on one knee, wearing a rather secret satisfied smile, and she retreated a couple of steps unconsciously from the impact of his serene gray gaze. "Or would that depend on what you call safe?" she wondered aloud and turned towards the dining-room, raising her voice. "Hi, Mary, put on another place, we've got a lion-tamer to breakfast!"

Mary's head came round the edge of the swing-door from the kitchen, wearing an anxious look.

"There's only strawberries and waffles," she apologized.

"Not good enough, but it'll have to do," said Elizabeth, going to the sideboard. "I'll find him a plate and tools, you dish it up."

"The berries and coffee are on the table, you can start now," said Mary, and vanished.

When Elizabeth returned to the drawing-room a minute later, the *entente* was established on the chesterfield, where Snorky was getting his stomach rubbed, wheezing with joy.

"He can be an awful nuisance if he gets a crush on you," she warned, surveying them over the back of the chesterfield.

"We understand each other," he said unsentimentally. "They're valorous little beasts, for all they look so funny."

She liked his choice of words.

"I think you're both pretty sweet," she remarked.

"Thank you," he replied gravely. "And the same to you from us."

"Aren't you hungry?"

"Mm-hm."

"Then come and get it."

"Did I hear rumors of waffles?" he inquired, following her into the dining-room, and as she paused beside her chair it slid back a few inches and then inserted itself gently behind her knees and came into place beneath her. "We don't get any high life like waffles up at the Station!"

19

He pulled out his own chair opposite her and sat down. Their eyes met smilingly across the sheen of mahogany and the glint of old silver and glass. There is an intimacy about a breakfast table, which justifies a theory to the effect that people who have had breakfast together, in any circumstances whatever, can never feel quite the same towards each other again. Breakfast is the quintessence of eating salt.

The table was exquisitely laid, with lace mats and bright china and a low centerpiece of garden flowers. The strawberries were in a crystal bowl between them, the silver coffee urn bubbled at Elizabeth's right. For the first time constraint entered their relationship. They had come too swiftly upon one of the dear realities—breakfast together in a sunny room. Because they were already so sensitive to its implications, they found themselves totally unprepared.

Elizabeth snapped off the switch of the coffee urn and poured out his coffee. Their fingers brushed as he took the cup from her, and his murmured Thank-you was a little strangled.

Snorky had followed his new god to the table and now stretched himself out with a sigh of satisfaction on a sun-warmed patch of carpet near Rodney's chair to sleep off the recent excitement. It was somehow the final touch to their sudden domesticity.

"Don't you get good food at the Station?" she inquired, breaking the silence deliberately as with a hammer, and helping herself to the strawberries.

"Oh, yes—it's very wholesome," he assured her at once.

"I'll bet it is! Try the strawberries, they are *not* from our own garden!"

"Thank you."

"I think I know what you're thinking."

"Don't you believe it, it's a lie!" he said hastily, and she laughed, and tension vanished.

"Well, then, let's say you were wondering about my being here in this house. That would be well within your rights, wouldn't it?"

20

"I suppose so," he said cautiously.

"Old Sam Baxter left it to me in his Will, did you read about that? It was in all the papers."

"Yes, as a matter of fact, I did."

"Everybody, including his widow and the Press, instantly jumped to the conclusion that Sam and I had been carrying on," she continued, pushing the handles of the cream and sugar towards him.

"Mm-hm," he encouraged her, accepting the cream.

"But *you* didn't think anything like that."

"No, of course not."

"You were quite right, too. Sam was a gay dog once, but he'd got all that out of his system long ago—before I met him."

"Mm-hm."

"That's where you say How did you meet him then?"

Rodney swallowed a mouthful of strawberries.

"How did you meet him then?" he obliged.

"In the most respectable way in the world. His son married a friend of mine. You remember the Baxter-Fenton wedding, it rocked Sherry's on its foundations! Well, I was there."

"You were one of the bridesmaids," he reminded her unexpectedly.

"Were you there too?"

"No. All I know is what I read in the papers."

"Well, anyway, you know how those things are. You stand in line for hours and shake hands with people you never saw before, and then finally you totter to a chair and somebody brings you champagne."

"And that's the last you remember till the next day."

"No such thing, who's telling this? It was Sam who brought me the champagne."

"I see. He was through with all that, but he could still pick 'em."

"Yes, and so Sam and I got talking, naturally, and I said—"

Mary came in from the kitchen and set a plate of waffles on

21

the table and picked up their empty berry dishes. Rodney's friendly eyes were lifted to her face. "Good morning," he murmured, and Mary said "Good morning, sir," and smiled at him suddenly as though he was about ten years old, and went away.

"—and I said Wasn't it hot, and he said Wasn't it, and before that wedding was over and Sherry's got back to normal, Sam had taken charge of my finances, my legal affairs, and my problematical old age. That was five years ago, and after that I never signed a contract nor invested a dollar without his advice, and I never had a row with a manager nor skipped a dividend. When Sam died last spring I felt as though I'd lost my only friend, but he had thought of everything—he'd turned over all my affairs to his partner, and he left me this house so I'd have a place to retire into. He put that in his Will, and like everything else it was misunderstood."

"It seems simple enough," he said. "What's all the fuss about?"

"There isn't any fuss. I just didn't want you to think—" She broke off. "You know, you have a strange effect on me. As a rule, the more people think the better I like it!"

"Good for business," he nodded, above his waffles. "Well, I'm glad there was somebody besides Snorky to look after you. His financial sense can't be very sound."

"And now you tell one," she said into the pause.

"I don't think I have any dark chapters to explain, I just—"

"But you haven't told me any of the important things yet—such as Who taught you your beautiful manners, and What's your favorite cocktail, and Do you go to see Marlene Dietrich's films, and Why aren't you married?"

"My Aunt Virginia. Old-fashioneds. Yes. I don't know," he answered methodically. "Now it's your turn again."

But she only sat smiling at him across the table.

"Well, come on, open up," he insisted quietly. "Who should have taught you manners?"

"My father."

22

"Cocktails?"

"Martinis. Dry."

"Dietrich?"

"Yes. I'm still trying to see how she does it."

"And why aren't you married?"

"I was."

"You *was?*" he repeated, his voice nearly cracking with astonishment. "When was that?"

"Well, it must have been round about 1930."

There was another pause then, while he retreated to the waffles.

"You're too polite to ask what happened, so I'll tell you that too," she said, and he gave her a quick upward glance and looked down again as quickly.

"You don't have to," he said. "It's none of my—"

"I know, none of your business!" Impatiently she took the words out of his mouth. "Well, it didn't last long. It was sordid and ugly and beastly, and we threw things at each other. He was a hoofer, and he couldn't stay sober, and continually got fired."

"What always beats me—" he began impulsively, and then stopped.

"Well?"

"Maybe I oughtn't to say it."

"Go on, I'd like to know something that always beats you!"

"Well, it was only that I saw your act in 1930. You were grown up then—you knew beans when the bag was open. What I can never figure out is how girls come to marry these out-and-out bums, and yet it happens every day. You weren't feeble-minded in 1930, you must have known he was a souse and got fired. I suppose the answer is Love, but I still don't get it."

"I guess I was used to bums," she said thoughtfully. "My mother before me married one—a very charming one, when he was conscious! She died when I was twelve, and after that it was my job to try and hide the bottle from him. Don't look like that, neither

23

of my drunks beat their women! I got a divorce, though, in July, 1935. Apparently you didn't read about that in the papers."

"I was in New Guinea that summer. Must have lost track of things here."

"New Guinea! What for?"

"Birds of paradise."

"Did you get them?"

"Mm-hm."

"Do you always get what you go after?"

"So far I have."

"Does your Aunt Virginia approve of your going off to places like that?"

"Not at all, but I tell her she might as well get used to it."

Mary came in with fresh waffles, and removed the empty plate. Once more his eyes were lifted confidentially to her face.

"They're wonderful," he said. "But I can't eat any more, I'm sorry to say."

"Oh, nonsense," said Mary, as though he was ten. "A big growing boy like you!"

The kitchen door swung to behind her in a silence.

"Snorky," said Rodney sadly, *sotto voce,* "they've ganged up on us. You come back to Mexico with me and forget women."

"They're always having trouble in Mexico, you'd both be killed!" Elizabeth cried.

"You sound exactly like my Aunt Virginia," he said.

"This is your Aunt Elizabeth. You know, I heard about some people who drove down there across the Border from California, and they went just a little way up into the mountains and ran into some shooting and got the fright of their lives!"

"Probably a local election. Anybody get hurt?"

"No, but they easily might have!"

"Mexicans are bad shots," he assured her, pouring syrup over a fresh waffle. "All you have to do is lie flat till it's over."

"Have you ever been shot at down there?"

24

"They weren't exactly shooting *at* me, I'd have felt safer if they had been, they can't hit a barn door."

"What happened?" she demanded, round-eyed. "Weren't you scared?"

"Sure I was scared, nobody can lie flatter than I can when the air is full of bullets!"

"But you want to go back *anyhow?*"

"Naturally. I want to go at migration time, and I want to run the whole show myself. I want to take along a couple of people I know to do the botany, I want to get a good insect man, I want to take a color camera, and I want to bring back harpy eagles alive. But the staff has to be my own choice, the schedule has to be mine, where we go, how long we stay in any one place, and so forth—which means the money has to be mine, and that's what's holding me up."

"How much money do you need?"

"Ten thousand, to do it right."

"That shouldn't be too difficult."

"Oh, I'll get it somehow, if I have to rob a bank!"

Elizabeth put her elbows on the table and her chin in her hands.

"And that's what you want to do more than anything in the world," she said thoughtfully.

"Well, yes," he admitted, as though it had been put into words for the first time. "I guess it is."

"All right. I know a bank you can rob."

He gazed at her while hope faded swiftly to doubt, embarrassment, and refusal.

"No," he said, and shook his head. "It's very good of you, but I couldn't let you—"

"Now, don't be that way, you don't know anything about it yet! It's got nothing to do with me!"

"Who, then?" he asked warily.

"Sam's partner, Andrew Blaine. The one that looks after me

25

now. He's always giving money to some museum or other, I don't see why he shouldn't give you some! You just leave it to me, I'll handle him. I can, believe it or not!"

"What are you going to do? Pick his pocket? Ten thousand isn't chicken-feed!"

"When do you want it?"

"Well, not this semester," he said, humoring her. "I couldn't get away. Not before spring."

"All right, then there's no hurry. When I get back to town I'll nick him for ten thousand if you'll promise me just one thing."

"Wait, let me guess," he said, watching her. "You want to go along."

"To Mexico?" She laughed heartily. "Not me! Whatever gave you that idea?"

He looked a little puzzled.

"Well, lots of people would."

"Look, mister, this is Liz Dare speaking. You're mixing me up with the Jackson girl, the one who suddenly saw a bird and gave up marine zoology!"

"I see. You wouldn't want to go."

"Not for another ten thousand, I wouldn't! Are you terribly disappointed in me?"

"No, of course not. Why should you want to go, it's not in your line."

"Not exactly! Snakes and bats and mosquitoes and fleas and hot tamales—to say nothing of the elections! No, thank you! But if that's what you want, I'll make Andrew give. On one condition. Promise you won't get killed."

"I think I can safely promise that," he said consideringly. "After all, I've never got killed on a trip yet."

"And you won't take any unnecessary risks."

"You sound more like Aunt Virginia every minute," he marveled. "I'll be very careful of myself, ma'am, I'll write home once a week, I'll remember to wash behind my ears, and I'll come back

26

all in one piece and under my own steam. But after all, I don't see why you should bother about—"

"Well, Andrew might just as well do some good with his money, he's got heaps and he's an awfully nice guy and he'll like you, I'm sure he will."

"Why will he?"

"Well, because—" Her beautiful hands made one of the famous Liz Dare gestures of incompetence and bewildered appeal. "—because I do," she finished lamely, and her brown eyes were very soft and shining as they met his across the breakfast table, not at all like his Aunt Virginia's, and her red mouth with its pointed smile set him wondering what it would be like to catch her laughing with a kiss—

"Well, whether I ever get the money or not," he remarked philosophically in his slow, quiet way, "it will give me an excuse to see you in New York—won't it."

"If you need one."

"Oh, I'll need one, all right. I don't exactly see myself waltzing up to you at the Flamingo Club and saying, 'This is Rodney, remember?'"

"If I may say so," she suggested, "I don't as a rule forget people I've had breakfast with."

"It does form a bond," he nodded gravely, and once more appeared to collect himself with an effort from contemplative silence. "You know, if I don't go back pretty soon they'll start dragging your pond for the body."

"We'll take the car." She rose briskly. "By the way, did we put up any money on this Mercer question?"

"No—and even after you see him, who's going to be sure anyway which of us is right?"

"The Jackson girl," said Elizabeth, preceding him towards the garage.

27

III

The Biological Station, which stood at the head of a small cove further down the coast, was originally a rich man's summer camp. It had been donated bodily by him to Science in order to release his personal exchequer from the expense of its upkeep, while at the same time preserving his *amour-propre* from the ignominy of putting it on an already drugged market. That may not make sense to anyone who has not been in a position to dispose of a luxury camp which can be enjoyed by its owner for at most thirty days out of each year. But that is the way this particular ex-millionaire ticked, and Science was duly grateful to him, and named the Station's first new species—which happened to be a form of wood louse—after him, to show its appreciation.

The main building had been converted to use by removing a few partitions, which left kitchen, dining-room and lounge on the ground floor, and the instructors' and visitors' bedrooms upstairs. On either side of it a rangy one-story wooden building had been put up, one for the student dormitories and one for the laboratory. The latter consisted largely of a roof and windows, and was full of long deal tables, camp chairs, filing cabinets, stacks of botany blotters, refrigerators, the smell of formaldehyde and ripe specimens, and the perpetual song of the little motor which pumped air and water into the aquaria. The tables were covered with a systematic litter of typewriters, microscopes, glass vials, shiny dissecting tools, artists' materials, note-books, and loose specimens dead and alive and in all stages of advanced decomposition. These last were, it is true, frowned upon by the authorities and theoretically were not

28

allowed beyond a certain age, but it is extraordinary how attached a serious-minded student can become to a dead fish whose fin-ray count appears to be leading somewhere.

The personnel of any such institution is likely to be pretty various. In this case the fifteen students were all hand-picked and winnowed, each one was there for a specific reason, there were no floaters. Both boys and girls, ranging in age from sixteen to twenty-one, wore the simplest of costumes, consisting of shirts and shorts, sweaters and slacks, or bathing-suits, and at a little distance the sexes were indistinguishable. It was a happy, uncontroversial, self-sufficient group, without complexes or inhibitions, living a life which can only be described by that awful word Wholesome.

Excited whispers in the laboratory now.

"Pst! Look what's come!"

"Hey! Rodney's got her in his hand!"

"Goshalmighty, do you see what I see?"

"Can you beat him? Just strolls in with Liz Dare in the net!"

And so on.

The big black Labrador retriever, who would go on behaving like a puppy even though he had got his growth, went caracoling down to meet them, all over smiles and eternally hopeful of a chance to lick Rodney's face.

"Down, Prince—be your age, we've got company."

"Is it your dog?" asked Elizabeth, trying to pat the sleek, heaving body which cavorted round them.

"Look out, he licks. No, he belongs to the cook's little boy. The dog's got a Peter Pan complex—he can't grow up. *Down,* you fool, behave yourself!"

A young man of average height, with a shy smile and honest blue eyes, arrived from the seaward side as they approached the laboratory, and caught Prince by the collar. In his other hand he carried casually by its middle a large and still lively herring.

"That'll do, Prince!" he said severely, bracing himself against the dog's heedless lunges.

29

"This is Charles MacDonald," said Rodney, "without whom nothing around here would function at all. He doesn't have to be told, either, that you are Miss Dare."

"How do you do?" she smiled, and ducked her head in Liz Dare's characteristic informal greeting.

"Good morning," said Charles, quite overcome. "I—guess I've got my hands full." He backed away apologetically, dragging Prince by the collar, and disappeared round the corner of the laboratory with a long backward glance.

"He's nice," remarked Elizabeth as they started on towards the steps.

"He's my right arm," Rodney admitted gravely. "Never says much. But together, we'd take on anything you can name."

"Would he go with you to Mexico?"

"I wouldn't stand a chance of going without him!"

"He must be a great comfort to your Aunt Virginia," she murmured just as they reached the door.

Thus the first clear view the occupants of the laboratory got of the two of them as they entered was just as Rodney said, looking down at her—

"Say, are you psychic?"

And she, looking up at him—

"Only now and then."

Rodney's lingering glance left her reluctantly and traveled without embarrassment from one goggle-eyed face to another round the big room. Work had frankly stopped. Everybody seemed to be holding their breath. But this looked to him an entirely natural manifestation of surprise at the blinding presence in their midst of Liz Dare.

" 'Morning, everybody," he said, theatrically casual. "Miss Dare wants to see a laboratory in action. How are we doin' today?"

"All right, I guess," said a dazed voice from somewhere.

"Well, reading from left to right, Miss Dare, may I present Millicent Long, Hubert Evans, otherwise known as Dopey, Jane Elliott,

Dr. Ford—botany—Frank Elliott, Jack White, Alice McKay, Dr. Mercer—our professor of marine zoology—Kitty Morton and—Peggy Jackson."

"How do you do?" said Elizabeth Dare, with that famous, informal duck of her head.

"How do you do?" murmured everybody politely.

"The rest of us are out in the launch making the morning haul," Rodney explained. "Well, what have we got to show a guest? Anybody got a slide under a microscope?"

"I've got some rather stale plankton," said the boy known as Dopey.

Just then Charles came in the door behind them, still carrying the fish, which was limper now, and Rodney's eye fell on him with relief.

"Charles, Miss Dare would appreciate it if we'd oil that pond for her. Will you dig up some kerosene and send out a mosquito party?"

"Sure," said Charles. "Can do." He slapped the fish down in a square white enamel pan and began to wash his hands under a tap.

"Well, I do think it's nice of you to bother," she said. "The caretaker seems to have forgotten, and your Professor Rodney said it would be good training if somebody from here did it—"

Silence fell like a brick in an atmosphere which had begun to return to normal. Eyes avoided eyes, heads bent over microscopes, pencils died in their tracks on half-written pages.

"Take Frank and Alice with you, Charles," said Rodney's quiet voice into the vacuum, "and bring back some of the pond water as is, before you muck it up with kerosene. We'll put it under a microscope and see what else she's got there besides wigglers."

"That's what I was going to ask," said Charles. "Didn't you want some of the pond water. Bring some Mason jars, kids, and I'll beg some kerosene from the kitchen and meet you round at the back.

31

Good-by, Miss Dare—hope we'll see you here again soon." He backed away, with his shy smile.

"Oh, I expect you will!" she assured him. "And thank you so much."

Well aware of an undercurrent of something, but unable to account for it in anything she had said or done, Elizabeth squinted politely down Dopey's microscope at the plankton, and listened to the diffident lecture on the drifters which he delivered in a soft southern drawl much more interesting to her ears than the actual words he was saying.

"And how are all the folks down round about Macon way?" she inquired gently in a perfect echo of his own vowels and intonations when he had finished.

"Fine, thanks! That's the best imitation Macon I ever heard!"

"Accents are my business. What are you doing 'way up here?"

"Having fun. Last year I was at a Station in Florida. This summer I wanted to work under Dr. Mercer."

"Oh, yes—" said Elizabeth sweetly, with a vague glance round, and Rodney winced where he stood beside her as she caught Mercer's eyes and somehow drew him towards her, his spectacles gleaming zealously. He was in a way a pale carbon copy of Rodney, but shorter, thinner, older, near-sighted, and humorless. "You must have quite a reputation, Dr. Mercer, if they come all the way from Georgia to Maine to sit at your feet!"

"Well, I expect it's the text-books, Miss Dare," he admitted modestly. "After a man has written as many text-books as I have, he gets a sort of following among the student body. I suppose I might claim to have my fans, as they say, just as much as you do!"

"I thought she might like to see the main building, Ralph," Rodney interposed at this point. He had never realized until now what a queer little duck Mercer was—that Very Brilliant Man.

"Oh, yes, by all means—where we foregather in the evenings." Dr. Mercer turned rather coy. "You know, Miss Dare, you really ought to come up some evening when our friend here gets going

32

on his accordion. He's pretty hot stuff!" He laid his hand on Rodney's arm in unmistakable affection, and turned back to his microscope.

"You?" cried Elizabeth, looking up at Rodney with delighted surprise. "The *accordion!*"

"Well—" he qualified miserably, "we have a sort of band here, I used to play in college, and Frank has a banjo, and there are always a couple of good voices—"

"But what fun! May I really come some time when you're playing?"

"Well, don't expect too much. Now, perhaps you'd like to go over and see the lounge—"

"Oh, yes, I do, and I must be keeping you from your work, too! Good-by, everybody, I hope you won't mind if I come again some time—"

"Oh, do—any time—delighted—" said everybody.

Rodney was holding the door open for her. She passed through it with a wave of her hand. What they could see of his face as he followed was without expression of any kind. Eyes met eyes surreptitiously, but nobody giggled. There was no need of speech. Their course was plain to all.

"Whatever we bet on Mercer, I win," said Elizabeth as soon as they were outside.

"All right, all right, what do I owe you?" he agreed hastily in a low voice, as though Mercer could hear.

"Well, let's see," she pondered, enjoying the total absence of argument now that he had apparently taken a good look at Mercer. "I think you owe me a dinner—in New York."

"Done," he said promptly. "A really bang-up dinner—white tie and tails, champagne, the Blue Danube—and you wear your pearl dog-collar."

"Nope. That's your Aunt Virginia."

"What will you wear, then?"

"Cloth-of-gold, at least!"

33

"Wonderful. I can't wait."

"Dr. Monroe," said a timid voice behind them, and Rodney turned.

" 'Morning, Eddie," he greeted the cook's little boy, who had paused bashfully in the presence of the strange lady.

"Those cedar birds you were watching," Eddie got out, standing on one leg with the effort, "they left the nest this morning."

"They did?" exclaimed Rodney with genuine interest. "Did you see them go?"

"Unh-hunh. Mr. MacDonald said to tell you."

"Thanks. Was there much excitement?"

"Quite a lot."

"I'll bet there was! I'm sorry I missed it."

Elizabeth's eyes were waiting for him.

"Dr. Monroe," she murmured, as they continued their way towards the main building. "Now I begin to get it. Rodney is your Christian name."

"I warned you."

"Yes, but I thought—" She laughed. "So that's what was the matter with them! They thought I was saying it on purpose! Why didn't you put me right the first time?"

"Well, I was on kind of a spot myself," he pointed out. "When you asked me my name I should have said Monroe. For some reason I didn't. That's a little hard to explain. Here is the lounge."

She surveyed the long, comfortable room full of chintz sofas and big chairs and a table covered with magazines.

"Where you play the accordion," she reflected.

"Now, look—"

"Oh, please let me come up some evening!"

"Sure, any time you like, but—"

"In that case I'll take myself off now, so you can get on with your day."

"It's quite a day," he said, holding the door for her again. "So far."

34

"Are you complaining?"

"No. No complaints. So far."

They came to her car in the drive, and she slid in behind the wheel. The door clicked.

"Well, good-by, Dr. Monroe, thank you for showing me round."

"Good-by, Miss Dare, thank you for coming."

She stepped on the starter.

"*Au revoir,* Rodney."

"*Au revoir,* Liz."

The car drew away from him smoothly, while his hand was still on the door.

"Why, there's Our Professor Rodney!" a falsetto voice exclaimed at a little distance behind him, and he turned warily. The mosquito party was back, coming up the hill from the garage.

Rodney exchanged a secret rueful glance with Charles and chose to ignore the remark, which had come from Frank Elliott.

"I hear the cedar birds have gone," he said, falling into step with them.

"Yes, it was quite a show," said Charles.

"If Our Professor Rodney had got in in time for breakfast this morning he would have seen them go," observed Alice, to no one in particular.

"All right, I heard you the first time," said Rodney, with something less than his usual courtesy. "Now let's forget it."

Weather-wise Charles who knew all the signs and omens, handed Alice the empty kerosene can and the Mason jar full of greenish water he was carrying.

"Here, you, take these. Leave the can at the kitchen door and say Thank-you to Mrs. Webster. Then get some of that water on a slide, I'll be right in." And lower— "Cheese it, both of you!"

The youngsters departed, smirking.

"You going up to the lab?" Charles queried casually, falling in again beside his boss.

"Yes," said Rodney, and added, not looking at him, "I might as well."

They entered together with a brisk slam of the screen door. Everywhere backs were bent over earnest labor. Rodney crossed to his own desk where the morning mail awaited him, and sat down.

"Oh, Professor Rodney," piped the Jackson girl in her reedy young voice, "did you know the cedar birds were gone?"

"Yes," Rodney replied, dangerously quiet. "I heard about it. Now, look, children, that particular joke is over. Miss Dare made a perfectly natural mistake. She knows better now. Will you drop it?"

"Well, there's no need to take my head off just because—"

"I said Drop it," Rodney reminded her, very quiet, and became absorbed in his mail.

There was a silence. Two or three people tried to catch Charles's eye, and met a blank glacial glance. Frank and Alice came in the back door with the pond water, sniffed the heavy air experimentally, and raised knowing eyebrows at each other.

Things had got back to normal by the time the launch returned about lunch time, and after the usual bustle round aquarium and refrigerator, and the usual ooh-ing and ah-ing over the catch, everybody trooped off to wash. When they reassembled round the tables, the news had been imparted.

Apparently Rodney was willing enough to talk about Liz Dare's visit so long as nobody brought up the delicate matter of her quite natural mistake. Lamentation was loud by those who had missed a sight of her.

"If she doesn't come back soon, let's send her a special invitation," proposed a lanky shock-headed boy named Tom, who sat at Rodney's table.

"Provided we can rig up something to make it worth her while," Rodney qualified good-naturedly.

IV

It rained for the next two days and Rodney, who was a mental disciplinarian as well as a believer in corporal punishment, put Liz Dare at the back of his mind and devoted himself to Jack White, a weedy youth who was writing his thesis on the Yellow-bellied Sapsucker—a subject chosen in the beginning for its tongue-twisting possibilities, now absorbing its author to the point of fanaticism.

The morning of the third day broke hot and fair. Coats and sweaters were discarded, sleeves were rolled up, everything stood open to the least stir of air from a glassy sea. At lunch time almost everybody changed to something white, and there was much talk of a swim before dinner.

In the mid-afternoon drowse a car was heard climbing the hill behind the Station. It came into the drive and stopped, and immediately all hell broke loose. High and clear above the tumult rose a sound which, though he was hearing it for the first time, Rodney recognized instantly as his own personal call to arms.

"Help!" screamed Liz Dare's voice, trained to carry well. "Rodney, come quick!" And then on a higher note of real terror—*"Rodney!"*

Almost before the peaceful silence of the laboratory had registered the scrape of his chair across its bare floor, Rodney was out of the door and Charles, as usual, was only three jumps behind him. The rest of them surged to their feet, wearing bewildered expressions, and followed.

In the middle of the path which ran towards the laboratory from the cinder drive, Elizabeth stood with Snorky held high in both

37

her hands. The mentally deficient Prince bounced frantically round her, his great jaws snapping between thunderous barks which Snorky returned with all his might, leaning out of Elizabeth's guarding clasp.

"Down, Prince, stop it! *Prince!*" yelled Rodney on the run, but while he was still a few yards away the big dog flung himself against her and she went over backwards, landing with a quick roll which gathered Snorky under the protecting curve of her body like a football. Rodney seized Prince's collar and hauled him off her, turned him over to Charles, and knelt beside Elizabeth on the ground. (Neither dog had paused for breath since the hullabaloo began, and now Charles's voice was added to the din, trying to make itself heard to Prince in chosen epithets and commands.) "Liz, are you hurt? Did he get his teeth into you?" Rodney's hands were on her anxiously, raising her against him, searching competently for blood or injury.

"No, of course not, I'm not bitten— Snorky, *be quiet!!*" She cuffed him soundly.

Rodney lifted her to her feet, and she looked up at him, still breathless, with a shaky smile. Both dogs had suddenly fallen silent, impressed at last that everybody meant business.

"Prince ought to be tied up, there's no sense to him," Rodney was saying. "But all the same, Snorky knew better," he added.

"Snorky! Well, I like that! He—"

"Snorky began it," he interrupted firmly. "He's got no business sounding off like that on another dog's territory. Here, give him to me a minute." He took the still cocky Peke out of her hands and turned to where Prince surged against Charles's weight on his collar. "Prince, that's enough—stop it." Drooling with excitement, Prince gazed up at the interloper in Rodney's hands and uttered a final hysterical bark. Snorky instantly began all over again, his little body torn by gusts of furious noise. *"Shut up!"* Rodney shouted in his ear, and Snorky paused to gaze at him with admira-

38

tion and respect. Rodney went on one knee in front of Prince, who pricked his ears and strained against Charles's hand.

"Rodney, do be careful, he could swallow Snorky in one bite," Elizabeth said nervously.

"Turn him loose, Charles," said Rodney, and Charles obeyed with a small wise smile.

Prince took a couple of steps forward and his nose was level with Snorky in Rodney's hands. Prince sniffed at Snorky inquiringly, and Snorky looked him in the eye without fear, his pink tongue visible at one side of his mouth.

"Now, believe it or not, Prince, this is a dog," Rodney was saying very quietly. "What's more, he's a friend of mine, and I expect you to be nice to him. He's got no manners, but we'll have to overlook that. O.K.?" Prince looked up at him with a worried frown and whined. Rodney laid one arm around the big dog's neck and set Snorky down on the ground. "All right, then," he concluded. "He's your guest. Show him round the place."

The two dogs touched noses amicably. Rodney stood up and they made off together side by side towards the kitchen door, Snorky gamboling through the tall grass, Prince trotting responsibly.

"Well!" said Elizabeth into the silence they left. "You know, you ought to be with a circus!"

"Who says I'm not?" he demanded, and took out his handkerchief and began to dust off the skirt of her pale blue frock. "You're sure you're all right?"

"Yes, thanks."

"Well, come over to the lounge and have a glass of something," he suggested, and glanced towards the group on the laboratory steps. "No harm done," he called to them. "Come on, Charles."

When Elizabeth had drunk a glass of sherry from the bottle Charles fetched down from Rodney's room, they all strolled back to the laboratory in order that she might view a board full of newly mounted butterflies which Alice McKay was rather puffed up about.

She and Alice became friends over the butterflies, and Frank, who always worked with Alice by a kind of thought transference, brought up the matter of an evening of song in the lounge with Elizabeth as guest of honor. Elizabeth said she'd be delighted, any time, and they set next Sunday night, which left nearly a week for preparation. Tom, just presented and still groggy, recklessly promised her a Surprise. Rodney eyed him contemplatively, aware that the thing was getting out of hand.

When he succeeded in detaching her from the student body, she went out with him to see the motor launch named *Isabel* which was moored beside its little concrete dock and boathouse in the cove.

Unreasoning happiness pervaded her as she walked with him towards the shore. Apparently she had only to find her way again into his company to feel refreshed and buoyed up and all cozy inside. The time since she had seen him last had been overcast with a dullness not wholly due to the weather, for hitherto rainy days in the old house had not bored her. She had always had the knack of solitude; and now she was tired from a winter which had required her to do a midnight stint each night at the Flamingo Club after giving a performance in a Broadway theater. So for weeks she had been content to read books from the somewhat dated Baxter library, to knit and do bits of fancy needlework and keep up a conglomerate correspondence. She slept and ate well, and felt the need of no company besides her own. Then enter Rodney, full length at her feet, and she began at once to Take Notice.

It's too soon to go back there, she thought that morning when the urge began. He'll think it very forward of you. No, he won't, he'll be pleased to see you again. Oh, so, and what makes you think that? He wants to come here, I know he does. Then wait for it—he's shy and thinks he can't come without an excuse. Well, what's your excuse? I haven't got one—yes, I have, I want to see him again. You can't very well say that when you get there. Well, why do I have to say anything, he won't ask why I've come, he's too polite—

And so it went, till about three o'clock, when she threw down a copy of *Barbary Sheep* and picked up Snorky and went out to the garage for the car. Snorky had a crush on Rodney too, and it was only fair to take him along.

Now, as she walked beside Rodney down the slope towards the boathouse, she savored her contentment defiantly. He was wearing white flannels today, and a white tennis shirt open at the neck and with the sleeves rolled up above his elbows. He looked browner than he had before, and more powerfully built for all his slenderness. A great dancing partner, she thought, lost to Science. How the man moves. Pull yourself together, Liz, you're slipping.

She surveyed the launch *Isabel* with bright, interested eyes. Its brass shone from zealous polishing and it had been scrupulously cleansed of any remains from its morning collecting trip. There was a commodious cabin, a bow-seat, and room in the stern for six or eight people on the locker-seats around the covered well of the engine. It steered by a little wheel attached to the rear wall of the cabin, within reach of the engine gears—a one-man boat.

"Who was Isabel?" she inquired, with a twinge of jealousy.

"I never knew one," he confessed. "We all sat down and tried to think of the silliest name we could find and somehow Isabel won. It reminded us of parasols and flounces and guimpes and yellow curls and a lisp. Of course some day by pure chance we're going to have a real Isabel at the Station, and that's going to be pretty funny."

"Any Isabel ought to be proud," she said. "I've never been in a boat like that. How fast can it go?"

"Speed isn't one of our requirements. Want to go for a ride?"

"I'd love to."

"All right, let's go for a ride."

He cast off the painter from an iron ring in the dock, jumped

41

aboard at the bow and stepped back along the washboard to the floor, easing the *Isabel* in against the concrete steps which were cut into the dock. Then he looked up at her and held out his hand.

"The lower step is sl—" he began, but never finished.

Elizabeth's neat white oxford came into contact with the half-dried slime on the step at the high-water line. She skidded, regained her balance, found no purchase for her other foot, and with a despairing yell cast herself bodily forward in his direction.

"Careful," he murmured as he caught her easily in his arms and landed her without a jar—very like a great dancing partner—on the floor of the boat. "You're kind of light on your feet today, aren't you," he commented mildly.

A moment more she held to his hard shoulder, while knowledge raced through her. Then she straightened.

"Golly, you're strong!" she said only. "You got my whole weight without any warning!"

"What did you expect me to do—fold up?" he queried, and started the engine.

"There's one thing I'd like to know about you." She was eyeing him with speculation.

"Shoot."

"Are you ever caught by surprise? Did you ever in your life bump into anything, or knock anything over, or drop anything?"

"Well, I was pretty well off center the other morning when we first met," he reminded her drily.

Elizabeth laughed.

"But you even *fell* with presence of mind!"

"I used to play football. You tackle pretty low, but so does Notre Dame."

She stood beside him at the wheel as they curved out across the cove into the afternoon light. The air from the sea was fresh with watery smells, the sturdy beat of the engine was a new and exhilarating sound in her ears.

42

"This is fun," she said, her curls blown back. "We're so close to the water. I believe I like boats!"

He glanced down at her sidewise, his hand lying on the wheel, his long body lounging against the cabin wall with an elbow on the roof.

"Where have you been all your life?" he asked casually.

"I went from the sidewalks of New York to the *Ile de France.* There was nothing like this on the way. Where did you live when you were little?"

"Pretty well everywhere. Montana—San Diego—Kansas City—Philadelphia—we used to go to Cape Cod every summer after that."

"You certainly got around."

"My father was a clergyman."

"No! What kind of a clergyman?"

"Episcopal. Very High. So is Aunt Virginia."

"Well, I'm damned," said Elizabeth. "Excuse me. But I couldn't be more surprised."

"Maybe your ideas of clergymen want cleaning up too."

"Evidently they do!"

"He was a very bright-eyed old bird, you know," said his son with some pride. "Not much got past him. It's too bad he had to miss you."

"And your mother?" she said, trying to work it out.

"She died when I was born. That's how I got Aunt Virginia."

"I see. Rodney, could I ask just one more question?"

"Sure, go ahead."

"Well—did you by any chance sing in the choir when you were little, wearing a round white collar and a bow under your chin?"

"I did."

"N-not the boy soprano!" she cried, delightedly.

"Mm-hm. People used to come from far and wide to hear me sing *O for the Wings of a Dove!*"

"You must have looked adorable!"

"You take the words right out of Aunt Virginia's mouth!"

43

The launch chugged on cheerfully, leaving a lovely wake in the quiet sea. The air blew soft on their faces, in a golden world all their own; a world which wore that new and burnished look it can present only to the eyes of people who—whether they are ready to admit it or not—are falling in love. Rodney surveyed it with his unclouded gaze, aware that he ought to do something to put a stop to the enchantment which had its source in the straight blue-clad figure beside him, but yielding still to the memory of the sharp thrill with which he had received the now familiar fragrance of her in his ready arms at the dock, and to an echo almost as disturbing—"Rodney, come quick!" Twice in one day she had thrown herself confidently upon his ability to do whatever was necessary for her preservation. Who saved her when he was not there? She'd done all right without him for quite a while.

"Let's go over to my place and ask Mary for some iced tea," she suggested into their companionable silence, and with a long sweet curve of her streaming wake, the *Isabel* headed for the Baxter landing.

Elizabeth basked in his comfortable acceptance of things as they were. Acutely conscious of the novelty of her own position in the life he lived, she had a subconscious apprehension that suddenly she might find herself outside it again, with the door swinging shut in her face. It left her feeling humble—Liz Dare, as grateful as an orphan for the delicious warmth and excitement of one man's mere presence within reach of her hand!· Liz, you've got it bad. What, already? What's time got to do with it? It was all over with you as soon as he spoke. *Good morning,* he said, without batting an eye. *I hope I didn't hurt you.* Well, what was there in that? I don't know, I don't know, only please God don't let me lose him now, I want him so. *Want* him? Liz, you're crazy, what would you do with him if you had him?

"I never knew before," he said out of his own thoughts while they were waiting in a couple of chairs on the veranda for Mary to bring the iced tea, "I never knew before how easy it was for

44

lotus-eating to set in. I shouldn't be here. You realize that, don't you."

"Feel as though you're playing hooky?"

"Yes, I am." His face was grave, almost troubled.

"Well, after all, I don't see why you should incarcerate yourself over there," she said, trying to sound sensible. "They're nice kids, and you're doing a great job, I can see that, even though I don't pretend to understand what it's all about. But apart from Mercer, and the botany man, and that darling Charles, you must be a little short of adult society."

"My own society has always been pretty good up to now," he observed defensively, "and adult enough, for some time past." He glanced towards her, found her eyes waiting, and his retreated again to the horizon. "I'm not sure," he went on as if to himself, "but what I'm going into my second childhood."

"So *soon?*" she murmured, watching him with a smile.

Relaxed into a cane porch chair, seemingly at his ease, he still had about him something of the woods-creature only half-tamed—wary, bright-eyed, curious to the point of boldness, but shy, ready at the first ill-timed movement of its captor to whisk into panic-stricken flight. She realized she had lured him back to the house with iced tea exactly as you lure a park squirrel, step by step, with a peanut. Deliberately, as soon as she got him to herself, she had set the bait and he had come only half willingly, tempted beyond his native caution—and now, it was almost as though he expected a trap to be sprung. She found it a very depressing idea that he should feel himself somehow delinquent, for it was her fault.

"Like your friend Mr. Baxter, I had got a lot of things out of my system before I met you," he was saying, his eyes on the water which winked and sparkled in the sunlight. "Perhaps not quite the same things—and perhaps not quite as many. He was something of an expert. But I had—graduated. I thought."

Just then Mary came out with a tray on which were things which had a cool clink and a luxurious polish.

45

"Good afternoon," he said, lifting to her his look of child-like friendliness, a look which Elizabeth knew now must be born of a lifetime's association with old, devoted servants, in that worldly clergyman's smoothly running household. She knew too, with a kind of envy, that it was an attitude of mind which nobody raised in cheap hotels and theatrical boarding-houses could ever have quite the same. Mary had been devoted to her for years, of course—but Mary and Rodney were speaking a language of their own.

"Good day, sir." Mary paused to smile down at him affectionately. "That sponge cake's still warm out of the oven. I made it for to-night's pudding, but you can cut it now."

"It looks grand," he said sincerely, and Mary departed with a backward glance.

"You seem to have made a conquest," remarked Elizabeth, pouring tea from the frosted glass pitcher into tall tumblers with ice cubes in the bottom and sprigs of fresh mint. "She gives you the food right out of my mouth. Help yourself to sugar."

"Thanks. Well, that's what I mean," he resumed his train of thought unhappily. "You see how fatally easy it would be."

"What would be?" she inquired obtusely, cutting the sponge cake.

"All this." His gesture, his slow, appreciative gaze embraced the shady veranda with its cushioned chairs, the tidy lawn with gay flowers blooming at its edges, the drowsy, peaceful sea, Mary, the sweating glass in his hand. "But chiefly—you."

"What's the matter with me?"

"You don't belong in my life," he said deliberately, and her heart began to beat heavily for she knew he was right and she didn't want to hear, "any more than I belong in yours. But each time I come here it will get more difficult for me to do without you. So I think from now on I'd better stay away."

"You mean you think I'm a bad influence," she suggested.

"I didn't say that."

"You meant it."

"All right, then, you are!" he admitted with impatience. "You're

46

a disturbing element, yes! I don't intend to fall in love with you, Liz Dare, and the only way I can keep from doing that is to see as little as possible of you—if it's not too late."

"So I'm being warned off." Her eyes, her sweet mouth, were rebellious.

"I wish you wouldn't take everything I say in the worst possible way," he objected.

"How else can I take it?" she demanded, feeling let down and baffled, with a most unwelcome inclination to cry. "I didn't ask you into my life, you fell into it—and I can't help it if you'd rather be in New Guinea than sitting on my front porch!"

"I wouldn't," he said quietly. "That's what I'm kicking about. I like it here, I don't deny that. But I haven't time. It doesn't fit in with my plans, I—"

"You mean Mexico!" she accused, nursing her grievance.

"Mexico now, something else later on. Everything about you is dead against the course I have set myself."

"All right, Ulysses, put cotton in your ears and lash yourself to the mast!"

"That's just what I intend to do." He set down his glass and rose—even in her misery her dancer's eye appreciated the long flow of his body to its full height.

"Are we quarreling?" she asked in a small voice, sitting still.

"No. The tide won't wait. We'll have to be starting back or I can't get the boat off your landing."

Together, in the intimate, boiling silence of a lovers' tiff, they went down across the lawn again to the wharf.

"You're quite sure we haven't quarreled," she prodded, watching him from a locker seat as he spun the starting wheel.

The engine missed and died. He lifted a harassed face, to find her eyes fixed on him. She looked, he thought helplessly, like a chastened child, not altogether without hope of being forgiven—an orphan child, much abused but undaunted.

"Look, Liz—will you have a heart? You don't want me—I don't

47

need you. Let's not start something we can't finish. I'm going to keep out of your way from now on, but please don't think—well, don't let's have any hard feelings."

She turned away from him, dipping her fingers into the dark water overside.

"Aren't you—taking a good deal upon yourself?" she queried.

"How do you mean?"

"To decide—for both of us—so soon."

"Liz—!" He dropped down on the locker seat beside her, and sat for a moment looking at her averted face. Then he shook his head, with doubt and regret and the old woods-wariness, though his gaze still lingered. "Oh, no," he told himself firmly. "Things just don't happen that way."

"Maybe they do." She caught at his arm with both hands, one wet from her dabbling, as he made a move towards the engine. "Wait, Rodney—I'm free, white, and twenty-one, and—I can take whatever's coming to me. But why must we go serious on ourselves all of a sudden? Maybe you'd got the wrong idea about me. Forget the girl in the spotlight. I'm no *femme fatale,* I behave myself, you're perfectly safe with me!"

"That's what you think," he said, looking down at her two hands on his arm—Liz Dare's famous talking hands, slim and white with long pink nails. He covered them both with one of his, deliberately crushing them together in his grip. "But who wants to be safe?" he added, and rose, and this time the engine started.

Neither of them spoke again till they reached the cove below the Biological Station, but it was no longer the silence of a quarrel. Elizabeth was breathing easier. The door had not closed in her face. Not yet.

She went ashore in his footsteps along the washboard with a wide step from there to the dock. The two dogs came lolloping to meet them as they approached the laboratory, and Charles appeared round the corner of the building on one of his indefatigable errands,

48

carrying a bucket of sea water in which a few small distracted fish swam busily.

"Well, they've got it all doped out," he told them. "The Queen of England never caused a bigger stir." His blue eyes rested in candid admiration on Liz Dare. "He's been promoted," he said, with a jerk of his head towards Rodney. "Now he's your chauffeur." He ambled off, down towards the shore, carrying the bucket.

"What's he talking about?" said Elizabeth, and they were hailed from the laboratory by Frank and Alice, who each held a pad and pencil and whose eyes were eager with executive enterprise.

"Oh, Miss Dare, it's all set for Sunday night!" The two youngsters advanced towards her, diffidence outweighed by enthusiasm. "We figure that if Rodney brings you over in our station wagoh, then he can take you home in it and you won't have to drive yourself back late in the evening, as it would be pretty spooky—there's no moon. And we thought if he came for you by eight o'clock, if that wouldn't be too early, it would leave us plenty of time for the program, and refreshments afterward."

"Program?" said Elizabeth, all smiles and anticipation. "Are you going to give me a show?"

"Well, kind of."

"That sounds wonderful. Please let me contribute something—ice cream—some kind of drinks—or what?"

"You give us just one song," said Frank, "and we'll call it square. Rodney can play the accompaniment on his accordion."

"All the songs you want," she agreed easily. "Eight o'clock on Sunday, then. Come on, Snorky, it's time to go home." She scooped him up out of the grass, and Rodney walked with her towards the car in the drive. "And so you're going to play my accompaniments," she murmured. "Oughtn't we to have a rehearsal?"

"No," he said. "We oughtn't."

Elizabeth tossed Snorky on to the seat and slid under the wheel with an enigmatic smile.

49

"Try and lose me, Rodney," she said softly. "Just try and do it. I've got friends at court, I have. And mind you're on time with that station wagon!"

"I get it," he said placidly. "I was wrong, as usual. So long, Snorky, I'll be seein' you!"

V

The chairs in the lounge had all been pulled round to face a cleared space at one end, at the edge of which sat Rodney and Frank, as the orchestra, and the entertainment at once got under way. There were encores for everything. But finally, turning a little towards Liz Dare, Rodney began persuasively to play the music from her latest show.

She grinned at him from her chair, and sang the number right through with him. Then as he began the next one she rose, singing, and drifted round his chair, watching his hands on the instrument, until slowly, almost imperceptibly, she was dancing.

When he came to the last bar, he went back to the first, and Liz Dare went on dancing, her eyes resting now and then on his hands, but seeming otherwise unaware of him. It was not the same dance she had done to that music in the show, but a new dipping, swaying, languorous version which imitated the lazy swell and diminuendo of the instrument between his hands—unhurried, melting, without sharp corners, her slippered feet making no sound on the bare floor, the soft full skirt of her carnation-colored dress following her long limbs in sculptured beauty.

When she had finished, with her dress in a red pool round her knees on the floor, there was an audible gasp of delight from the audience, and then yells and cheers and stamping of feet, as Liz Dare rose again and made them all a bow.

"You know you're pretty good!" she said to Rodney.

"Surprise!" he grinned.

"Well, I—"

51

"I know. Professors don't play accordions!" The instrument between his hands mocked her softly. "I was young once, don't forget."

Speechlessly she turned from him to Tom, whose tap-dance she had applauded loudly from her chair earlier in the evening.

"What are *you* doing 'way up here, you fugitive from Broadway?" she demanded.

Tom looked at her owlishly, his reddish shock of hair atoss.

"I am preparing a paper on the reaction of Echinoderms to an increase of salinity in sea water," he stated.

Elizabeth stood looking at him intently, wearing her most interrogatory, expectant expression, while she strove to make sense of what she had just heard.

"Does that mean the ocean is going to be saltier some day than it is now?" she inquired.

"Well, no, not so far as I know—that is, not—" Tom sent an appealing glance in Rodney's direction.

"Then why do you have to know—w-what they would do about it—if it isn't?" she persisted, her voice trailing away apologetically, as though to say that she knew she was being very stupid, but—

"Well, I—don't have to know—that is—it's only a form of experiment—" floundered Tom, and Dr. Mercer leaped defensively into the breach, his spectacles gleaming at her.

"The artificial increase of salinity in the water is merely in the nature of a laboratory experiment," he launched forth. "It is not, my dear lady, essential that these experiments, designed chiefly for the purpose of training the student to observe and record what he sees, should possess any practical application from—ah—from the layman's point of view. We merely endeavor—"

"B-but I don't see—"

"In other words," said Rodney, having slipped the strap of his accordion and arrived at her elbow in the nick of time, "Ralph, here, is trying not to admit out loud that an experiment doesn't have to make any sense so long as it results in a paper."

"Yes, b-but—" Elizabeth began again.

"Now, down at this end of the curio hall," Rodney continued, closing a firm grip on her arm so that she was propelled forward beside him, "it may be possible to find a tall glass with ice in it, not to mention sandwiches and cake."

"Did I s-say something?" she queried, lifting widened, anxious eyes to his face as they moved away.

"No, indeed," he assured her. "Not at all. But hereafter you just stick to dancing and leave Science to us."

Refreshments went round. Everybody was talking at once, and the atmosphere was almost drunken with good fellowship, the result of mass-relief from the unusual tension of the past few days. The time came at last when with Snorky under her arm she walked beside Rodney out to the station wagon and they began the short drive home through the pine-scented darkness.

Chatter about the party lasted them half way. Then an intimate silence overtook them. The small light on the dash reached upward to his hands on the wheel, and she found herself watching them as she had watched while he played the accordion—hands long in the finger with close, curved nails. But it was the way he used them, the economy of effort and movement—

The car stopped in her drive and he opened the door and stepped out. She waited, hugging Snorky till he squirmed, for the moment when Rodney would cross the lamps of the car on his way round to open her door—there—always hatless, he hadn't put on a coat, and the effectiveness of his dark clothes against the black velvet night was colossal. The lights picked up his face and hands, and the brown woven leather belt which nipped his narrow waist. This is it, Liz, she thought. For better or for worse, this is it—

He opened the door on her side of the car. His hand was under her arm as she stepped out. Together they mounted the veranda steps and she handed him the key. Breakfast in sunlight—and now the unlocking of a house door at the end of the day, the entering of a dimly lighted room where a fire still burned on the hearth.

"It's early yet," she said a little too lightly, bending to set Snorky down on the carpet. "Won't you come in awhile?"

When she straightened he was standing just inside the closed door, his hand still on the knob.

"Maybe you thought I wouldn't," he said, looking at her from under level brows.

"Snorky and I always have hot milk before we go to bed. I thought—"

"That's funny. So do I, when I'm at home."

"Then come along to the kitchen and have some now," she invited, preceding him to snap on lights as they went.

On the kitchen table a tray stood ready with two glasses, two napkins, and a bowl of graham crackers.

"Talk about psychic," said Elizabeth, feeling a little queer, "look what Mary's done!"

"Seems I was expected," he remarked, and leaned himself companionably against the door-jamb, watching while she got the milk out of the refrigerator and warmed it on the stove. "I could carry that," he offered when the tray was ready, and departed into the living-room with it while she put out the lights behind them.

They sat down with their glasses, each in a corner of the davenport which faced the fire, while Snorky lapped from his own dish on the hearthrug. It was Rodney who broke the perilous silence.

"You realize, of course," he remarked, "that you and I are heading for trouble in a Big Way."

"Are we?" she murmured, sipping her milk.

"There's no sense to this, and you know it as well as I do. There's no answer to it. This is one of those things that can't happen. But it's too late now. I'm in love with you, Liz, and it's playing hell with my life."

"You mean you don't want to go to Mexico after all?"

54

"Sure I want to go. Whatever gave you that idea?"

"Well, I only thought m-maybe it might have made some difference—"

"The only difference it's made so far is that I don't sleep so well at night!" he threw out unexpectedly, with a tightening of his lips.

"Well, there's no need to get sore about it—"

"I *am* sore about it! I don't want to love you, I haven't time, it doesn't fit in with my plans!"

"*Your plans*—for going off to one God-forsaken place after another till finally you get yourself killed!" she cried, hurt and indignant. "What's New Guinea got that I haven't got!"

"Birds of paradise."

"And Mexico's got fancy eagles! What do you want with 'em?"

"I want 'em to thrive, and maybe breed, in captivity. I want to know what they have against a nice zoo. I want to raise fledglings. See?"

"Prying, I call it! Prying into a poor bird's affairs!"

"Don't you ever have any legitimate curiosity yourself?"

"Yes, I have!"

"That's good! What about?"

"You!"

"Me?"

"Yes, you!" she cried angrily, for it was fast becoming a real quarrel now, as semi-humorous sparring is likely to do. "What do you do with your private life? Where do you turn when you want a little conversation, a little understanding, a little adult entertainment? Are you ever tired or sick or bored or just plain lonely? Are you ever human? Have you ever been in love?"

"Once or twice."

"With a bird of paradise!"

"No, with a woman!" he contradicted, beginning to be angry himself.

55

"But both times you won, and so here you are!"

"As a matter of fact, the only time it really mattered, I lost."

"Don't tell me any woman ever had the sense to turn you down!"

"I was going to ask her to marry me. I had what they call Intentions. But another fellow beat me to it."

"I can well believe it!"

"I felt pretty bad about it for a while," he said more quietly, ignoring that. "But it would be awkward now, wouldn't it—if she'd married me instead of the other guy—and then I'd found you sitting on that log. Because I'd have loved you just the same as I do now, which would have made things even more cock-eyed than they are—if that were possible." His quietness, his sudden return to his habitual gentle gravity, silenced her. He glanced at her briefly, and away again. "Well, now you've been and gone and done it, haven't you. You couldn't rest, could you, till you'd made me say it. So there it is, right in your lap. I'm in love with you till I can't see straight. I hope you're satisfied."

"Well!" gasped Elizabeth. "This is probably the screwiest proposal a woman ever had!"

"It's not a proposal. I said I loved you. I didn't say anything about marriage."

"*Really*, Rodney—!"

"Oh, use your brains, Liz!" he cried impatiently, and set down his glass and rose. "I can go on loving you till the cows come home, but where do I fit into your life, or you into mine? We don't match, we don't belong in the same place at the same time, we just don't *meet*, anywhere! The whole thing is—is quite impossible!"

"I see," she said in a small cold voice. "Well, if that's the way you feel about it—" She rose and set her glass down too, and crossed to the door and opened it for him. "—good night, Rodney."

He came towards her slowly, down the room.

56

"I'm sorry, Liz—I've made you angry. Maybe I've insulted you, I can't remember, but— Now, don't look like that, you know I can't take it—"

"Good night, Rodney."

He regarded her ruefully—the lovely carriage of her head, a little higher than usual now, her eyes so wide and brave in a chastening world, her full, sweet mouth and dauntless chin—

"If only you wouldn't start looking like an orphan child every time I— Oh, what's the use—!" All his resolution broke on a breath of indulgent laughter, and he kicked the door shut again as he took her into his arms.

Even while his lips descended on hers she was thinking, He's right, Liz, this won't do—just one, and then you really must get a grip on things—just one— But by then his urgency had reached her, and dizziness set in. When at last he let her go she could only collapse closer to him with her face hidden against his shoulder like a schoolgirl.

"Forgive me for trying," he was saying against the soft brown curls over her ear, while his sensitive nostrils delighted again in the nameless sweetness which always clung about her. "I knew better all along. Liz, I've never been struck by lightning before. I'm not used to it. Maybe that's why I react all wrong, I—don't—seem to—" His voice trailed away. She kept very still, her face hidden. He searched out her chin with his forefinger and turned it upward. "If I kiss you once more," he said deliberately, "I'll never be free again. I'll never know peace again, without you. Nothing I've planned to do will ever matter quite so much as it did. You'll be the first thing I think of each morning—the last thing I know each night. But don't get me wrong. Don't think I'm not going to kiss you—once more." And when he had done so, at his leisure— "Good night," he whispered, and reached backward for the knob, and with a last long smiling look at her from the threshold closed the door on himself and was gone.

Elizabeth stood there till the sound of the station wagon departing was swallowed by distance. Then she turned slowly, like a sleep-walker, picked up Snorky from the hearthrug, put out the lights one by one, and went slowly upstairs to bed, her eyes very wide and a little dazed.

He had still not asked her to marry him.

VI

So came the first night in a long, long time that Liz Dare lay awake till dawn because of a man.

At first she rather enjoyed it. But after half an hour or so of floating in a sort of vague dither, she realized that she wasn't going off to sleep very well, and attempted to assemble her mind a bit. I'll think about the party, she told herself hopefully. That will make me drop off.

Think about the party, Liz.

Well, let's see, there was Tom, who had the makings of a good dancer, and preferred Echinoderms, whatever they were, to Broadway. It seemed a pity, but one mustn't interfere. Broadway was a mug's game, he was better off in Science. At least there was a living in it for mediocrities, which was more than you could say for the Theater. And the same thing went for the girl with the red hair and the voice, who had led the quartette in a clear soprano. One was tempted to say impulsive things about radio work, but why get her hopes up when it might only mean heartbreak? Probably she was much better off with butterflies or botany or whatever it was. Botany didn't keep you hanging about in agents' offices all day, being insulted by people who were sure of their fifteen dollars a week, being pushed around by people who were more desperate than you were, waiting and waiting and *waiting* for the call that never came— Much better just to sing for fun. Botany was easier, and no doubt cleaner, and perhaps provided for your old age. There was Rodney, though, handling his accordion like a professional. If he liked, he could probably make more money with it than an associate professor ever got. It would be terrific, singing with Rodney, wouldn't it. What a furore for the Flamingo Club—Liz Dare and Rodney's accordion—

You're crazy, all he wants to do is go to Mexico. All right, he's going, isn't he? You might as well come clean with Andrew, he'll spot the whole thing anyway. You're in love with this boy, Andrew will say, his eyes all crinkled up and kind. Well, yes, Andrew, now that you mention it, I am—but you'll see why when you meet him, Andrew, and you'll be nice to him, won't you, and not try and talk him out of going, just to please me. Because he's going to Mexico now if it kills me. Even if he should get down on his knees and beg to be let off, he's going to Mexico and like it. I wouldn't feel right if he didn't. *Nothing I've planned to do will ever matter quite so much*— Don't you see, Andrew, he's got to go or else blame me for the rest of his life. But don't think I relish the prospect of three months with never a sight of him —I wonder if he writes nice letters—three whole months, not knowing where he is or what may be after him—Charles will be there—Charles won't let anything happen to him—they'd have to kill Charles first—

Think about the party, Liz.

It was fun, dancing for those kids, they're nice kids, no matter what you say, and they were darned nice to you, an outsider. I hope Rodney thought I did all right. What was all that with Mercer about experiments, I must have said something, Rodney looked sort of funny and gave me grape-juice quick. He's not good-looking, really, his mouth is too big and his chin is too long— but his eyes are like nothing you ever saw before, and his hands —his hands on the wheel coming home—

I wonder if it's the hot milk on top of the grape-juice that's keeping me awake. Idiot, it's Rodney, not indigestion, that's keeping you awake, you may as well face that. *The first thing I think of in the morning, and the last thing I know at night*— I hope you're awake too, Rodney, it would serve you right. Well, what

60

happens when I see him next? Where are we, anyway? He can't kiss a girl that way and then just say Good morning a few days hence. Or can he? I'll bet he can! Oh, Rodney, what is it you want of me? Because whatever it is, you can have it, damn you, and now you know it!

He's got to go to Mexico, though, and get it out of his system. . . .

The words had an unfortunate echo in her mind. Apparently he thought he had got women out of his system, once. Once or twice. What would they be like, the other women Rodney had loved? That one who couldn't wait, and married another man—what was she like? A woman scientist, perhaps, one that knew all about birds, maybe, a woman like those girl students up at the Station, not wearing enough clothes to be attractive, not caring if their noses peeled, letting their hair get dry and stringy, not looking after their skin and fingernails—but (it was a very big But) belonging in the same place at the same time, speaking the same language, thinking his kind of thoughts, and never, never tempting him to truancy; never, in a word, taking his mind off his work. (Well, but shouldn't a man have his mind taken off his work sometimes?) Or would it have been an Intellectual from the Literature Department, possibly a woman who wrote books and had read Chaucer and pretended to understand T. S. Eliot, but (surely it was a big But?) who didn't know how to laugh or love. (Well, obviously—*I've never been struck by lightning before,* he said.) Intellectual, or bare-legged Amazon, or the wistful kind, who was girlish and shy and gave him her cheek to kiss—? Yes, Rodney would fall for that. Or would he? Rodney knew what was what. *If I kiss you once more—*

Look, Liz, what you need is a new show. That'll take the kinks out of you, it always has before. A couple of new routines, a green leading-man, a few fights about clothes, and open in New Haven, and you'll have something to worry about! Ring up Pete in New York as soon as it's daylight and ask him how about that

61

script, and what does he think this is, a sabbatical year, and when do we start—and don't give him time to remind you how you told him if you heard a peep out of him before September first you wouldn't work for him at all, ever again. A lady can change her mind, can't she? All right, so I want to start work. Yes, *now*. Well, I can be figuring out my dances, can't I? Besides, I've got to get after Andrew about that ten thousand. Rodney's going to get a check bang in the small of the back before he's much older, and then we'll see. See what? See how he likes Mexico! Don't fool yourself, Liz, he'll say Thank-you and go. Well, of course he'll go, that's what you want, isn't it? Is it? I want Rodney, that's what I want. Go to sleep, Liz—

Sleep! She sat up in bed with an irritable bounce and turned on the light. Three o'clock.

"Snorky!" she whispered at the basket in the corner whence issued now and then a blissful wheeze. "Snorky, wake up and talk to me! Hullo. Liz can't sleep, Snorky, come over here—yes, right up on the bed—now, what are we going to do about this, suggest something! We were doin' all right as we were, we had a system, we were living our own lives and saving our money to retire on, and we asked nothin' of nobody. But along comes Rodney and *boom!* now look at us! Rodney? Why, you little son-of-a-gun, you've learned the sound of his name already! Go find Rodney! Well, I'll be darned! Hey, come out from under the bed, you won't find him there—ever."

Snorky came, backwards, dragging one of her velvet mules which he pretended had attacked him in the shadows and which he killed in the middle of the white fur rug beside the bed while she looked on, too spiritless to bop him and rescue her property.

"That's fine," she commented when the mule was quite dead and motionless, and he looked up at her for praise. "In Mexico, where Rodney likes to be, that would have been a cobra and you'd be dead by now. I'm hungry, let's go down and see what we can find to eat."

62

Pulling a warm dressing-gown about her as she went, she led the way downstairs. There were red embers still aglow on the hearth in the sitting-room, and Rodney's glass stood where he had left it. She picked it up and carried it into the kitchen with her, forgetting her own at the other end of the table, and set it down tenderly on the sink.

"Cold chicken," she said from the ice-box. "Have some? We aren't going to sleep anyway, so we may as well enjoy ourselves." She selected a drum-stick for herself and gave Snorky a bit of the liver all over lovely chicken jelly, which disappeared in no time. "And now," she said, wiping her fingers on a dish-towel, "we'll go into the library and see if Sam ever bought a book about Mexico, so we can read about all the things that might get Rodney while he's there, and bite him or sting him or crawl into his blood-stream—and then we can have really authentic nightmares!"

Sam had two books about Mexico. One was published in 1902 and the other in 1899. She carried them both back to bed with her, and eventually dozed off with the light still burning and Snorky curled up on the bed beside her, in spite of all the rules, digesting his chicken-liver with long, happy sighs.

When she roused again the sun was shining in an early sort of way, drowning out the reading-light beside her bed. Her eyes hurt when she opened them, and her neck was stiff from the extra pillow. Moaning faintly to herself, as she sometimes did on the mornings after the parties after openings, she crept out of bed and felt her way into the bathroom and turned on both taps and groped for her toothbrush.

Some time later she returned to the bedroom, bathed and brushed and powdered and lipsticked, but still a little heavy in the eye-lids. She bundled the bewildered Snorky off the bed as though he had never been invited there, and chose a soft blue shirtwaist dress from the wardrobe.

"Come on, we'll go for a drive along the cliff before breakfast. Blow the cobwebs out of our brains. How did that chicken sit with you? I could have done without mine. No, we are *not* going to see Rodney, so just relax."

She was wrong, though.

They met Rodney very unexpectedly at a crossroads in a wood about ten miles inland where he had no business to be, and riding a nervous black mare, at that. Liz Dare's gray roadster shot out of the crossroads at him, swerved with a shriek of brakes, and buried its bumper in the opposite bank. The mare, whose name was Sally, leaped into the air and came down sweating, and for the next two minutes Rodney gave as fine an exhibition of emergency horsemanship as you could wish to see. When he had succeeded more or less in convincing Sally that there were no more machines coming and that nobody had been killed—

"I'm terribly sorry," Elizabeth said from behind the wheel. "Are you all right now?"

"Yes, I'm all right," he answered with a little too much emphasis. "But you scared Sally out of a year's growth."

"What were *you* doing, coming through here at a gallop?"

"I just felt like playing Indians. Aren't you out pretty early yourself?"

"Yes, I—thought I'd drive along the cliff for a blow, and then I—just kept on going."

"Unh-hunh," he said knowingly. "I had the same sort of idea. But it doesn't do any good—does it."

"Not a bit. That's quite a horse, I didn't know you could get riding horses around here."

"At the club a couple of miles further on. It means driving over and back, but sometimes it's worth it." He swung out of the saddle and walked towards her, the bridle over his arm, Sally mincing behind him. "Good morning," he remarked, leaning his arms on the door beside the wheel, while his gaze went mercilessly over her face. "Not too good, eh? I don't know, though, blue shadows under the eyes are rather becoming to you. I didn't sleep either, if that's any satisfaction."

"I'm not asking for satisfaction," she said, enduring his scrutiny at close range with a conscious effort. "If a woman gets kissed it's her own fault—usually. Look, Rodney, let's say the grape-juice went to our heads, or something. I don't want this to get out of hand any more than you do. I've got a new show going on in September. Any day now I'll have to go back to start work on it. You know what's the matter with us, don't you—propinquity."

"I prefer to call it by a shorter and easier name," he said, his eyes on her face.

"Call it whatever you like six months from now," she suggested.

"Thanks, I will. Is that a date?"

Too late, she sensed in him unmistakable withdrawal. She had done it now—in her effort, her stupid, instinctive, feminine effort to save her face under his all-seeing gaze, she had struck a note which made last night's kiss seem a trivial incident in the life of Liz Dare the actress, whereas it had shaken Elizabeth the woman to her foundations. Too hastily she plunged again, and went wrong again.

"Oh, I'll be seeing you long before then," she said. "There's a little matter of a check from Andrew Blaine."

"Forget it."

"Indeed I won't forget it, it was a promise!" Liz Dare the benefactress. It was getting worse all the time. If only she could get away quickly before she said anything more—or before she burst into tears of sheer anguish on that broad tweed shoulder. "The next thing is whether I can get myself out of here," she said, and stepped on the starter.

He stood back away from the car, and Sally shook her head and danced at the sound of the motor.

"You're not stuck," he said. "Fortunately there's no ditch."

The car moved smoothly in reverse, out into the road. Damn. Nothing to do now but drive away, with this awful sort of gap between them, unless—

Rodney had mounted again, and sat looking down at her from

65

Sally's back. He rode a cowboy saddle with long stirrups and a high pommel.

"Rodney—" She leaned towards him across the door, swallowing her pride and her defenses, blue shadows under her eyes in the pitiless light. "Don't let me fool you. Don't take any notice of the act, Rodney. You were right the first time. I didn't sleep. That's why I'm such a fiend this morning, maybe."

He edged Sally in close to the running-board and set his forefinger under Elizabeth's chin.

"I know," he said. "Try not to run into anything more and break your neck before you get home, won't you. It's bad enough to be haunted by you while you're still alive."

"Rodney, I—"

"I'll see you again before you leave for New York," he said, and gave Sally her head and was gone, back along the road he had come.

Elizabeth drove home slowly, deep in thought, feeling leaden inside, tearful, upset, thwarted, adrift—feminine. All right, she had warned him. She would go back to New York at once. Well, in a week's time. If he hadn't come by next Saturday she would simply drive over to the Station and there in front of everybody she would hold out her hand to him and say, Well, good-by, Rodney, nice to have known you, I'm leaving for New York in the morning. There wasn't much he could do about that, was there!

Stop it, Liz, you're thinking like an actress. You're not an actress any more, you're just a woman that's fallen in love, and you don't know how to behave. You've been struck by lightning, Liz—or was it a truck? Anyway, stop thrashing around and give the anaesthetic a chance. You'll live, if you're careful.

Work is what we want. Back into the old practice clothes and a muck sweat. Soft, that's what you are. Delusions of grandeur, with all this time on your hands. You're forgetting you're a clown, Liz, first and last a clown, you sing for your supper. Next time he sits in the front row he'll be disappointed. Oh, he will, will he.

66

At ten o'clock she rang up Pete at his office in New York and berated him for forgetting she was alive, for not caring whether she ever had another show or not, for holding out the script on her, and for never making a friendly sound from one month's end to the next.

When she paused for breath Pete said wait a minute, he'd fallen over backwards and struck his head on a blunt instrument, but he was coming round nicely, thanks, and wasn't she ashamed to start drinking so early in the day. There then ensued a long, expensive, and extremely intelligent conversation about the new show, and it ended with her saying she would be at his office exactly one week from Now, which in turn left Pete saying over and over as he hung up, What a gal, What a gal.

Well, that's that, she thought, with some satisfaction. Now what do we do till Saturday? Wait for Rodney, of course. What else? I'll tell you what else. A nice stiff workout each morning!

It was Friday before he came.

Elizabeth was lying on her stomach on a rug laid down in the sun on the front lawn where it sloped towards the shore above the petunia bed. She was wearing practice clothes, blue cotton slacks and shirt, with a blue ribbon holding her dark curls behind her ears, and she was reading the script of the new show, which had not arrived till Thursday morning's mail. Snorky lay on the grass beside her, cherishing his rubber bone.

A car came into her drive and stopped. Its door slammed. Elizabeth lay still and held her breath. There had been so many false alarms, which always proved to be the butcher or the man about the oil stove.

Then Snorky, too full for utterance, turned himself into a silent brown streak across the lawn towards Rodney, who paused, bent his knees, and held up both hands as though about to make a drop-kick—Snorky took a flying leap at his chest and was of course safely caught and held.

67

Elizabeth rose from the rug and came towards them slowly, trying by will power to control her heart action, wearing that expression of mixed apology and anticipation which Rodney called her orphan-face. His gray eyes, wide open in the brilliant light reflected from the sea, were more demoralizing than ever in his tanned face.

"I may as well resign," she said as she came up to him. "Snorky has belonged to you, bag and baggage, ever since he first laid eyes on you." (That makes both of us, she thought. Shut up, Liz.)

"Good afternoon," said Rodney politely, and added without further preamble— "I have come to ask Snorky for your hand in marriage."

She stood there in the sunlight, blinking at him, while it went home.

"Rodney—does anybody ever know, from day to day, what you're going to do next?"

"Not any more," he said, as it seemed apologetically. "Not since the lightning struck. I'm still finding bits of myself scattered all over the place. The fact is, even now I'm not quite all here."

"Well, bring what there is of you over here and sit down."

He set Snorky on his feet in the grass beside the rug and then faced her gravely, clasping his hands around one knee to keep from laying hold of her; waiting, with an inquiring lift to one eyebrow, for her further reactions to the purpose of his visit. Elizabeth perversely looked out to sea and remained silent.

"You seemed surprised," he mentioned gently, "at what I suppose we can call my Offer."

"Well, after the telling-off I got Sunday night when I apparently misunderstood you—"

"You wouldn't agree to forget that?"

"Well, I—"

"Otherwise I shall be apologizing about Sunday night for the rest of my life—which seems to me an awful waste of time."

"You said—"

"I know exactly what I said," he interrupted without raising his voice. "I remember what you said too, and I haven't forgotten how you looked, either, standing there by the door. Now—would it help any if I got up and came in all over again, or can we just go on from here?"

She looked at him rebelliously, out of the corners of her eyes, sitting very straight on the rug.

"Go on, enjoy yourself," he invited her with resignation. "I'm eating crow—I'm groveling, I think is the word, in the dust at your feet. The sooner you can bring yourself to pass sentence, the better I'll like it."

"Rodney, do you *really* want to marry me?"

"No," he said at once, as though that much should have been obvious. "Of course not! What a silly question! I can't live without you, that's all. Especially when you go and tie your hair back with a blue ribbon."

She gave him her adorable pointed smile. Just at this moment Snorky bustled on to the rug between them, carrying his rubber bone, which he laid down at Rodney's knee and then stood gazing up, wheezing with self-sacrifice, his pink tongue hanging.

"His little All," said Elizabeth softly. "Rodney, that's very touching. He's giving you his bone."

"Thanks very much," said Rodney, with a brief glance at it. "Liz, haven't you had enough fun now? Isn't it about time you let bygones be bygones—when there's so much ahead?"

"I wonder just what is ahead." She looked at him directly, holding on to herself with an effort. "Suppose I just caved in this minute, and said Yes—what becomes of us?"

"I don't blame you for asking," he admitted, his grave eyes on her face. "It's a thing you've got a right to know in advance, if possible—as much as anybody ever knows in advance what's going to happen in a marriage. I've given some thought to it myself during the past few days, strange as that may seem—and I've come to the conclusion that I Don't Know. But the funny part is, I find I don't seem to care. Well, I mean—"

"That other woman—the one who got tired of waiting for you to ask her—what was she like?"

"Has that got any particular bearing on—"

"Yes, it has. You must have had some sort of life in view with her. You must have visualized some sort of—routine. What was it like?"

"Just the usual sort of thing, I suppose. A small house near the campus, with a maid and a cook—somebody cheerful to come home to at night—somebody beautiful across the table—somebody sweet to wake up with—" You could see him gather himself together to go on, his mouth tightening at the corners. "Even a few years ago I could—afford a wife in such circumstances. I have—something besides my salary, from my father's estate, most of which went to Aunt Virginia during her lifetime—"

"Where did she come into your plans—a few years ago?"

"She isn't the kind to move in on a newly married couple. She would either have stayed on in the house we have now, or she might have gone to New York to live her own life, I don't know, it never—got that far. Marcia would have fitted into the University routine quite easily, she was very young and—"

"Marcia?" repeated Elizabeth, and crinkled her nose. "Was that her name? Was she one of your students?"

"Oh, Lord, no, she was Bryn Mawr."

"Oh-h, I see! 'One of *those!*" Elizabeth nodded her ribboned head with a world of meaning. "Was she really beautiful?"

"Now, look, Liz—" he was beginning dangerously, when Snorky, guarding the bone, let out an anguished yelp because he could no longer bear to be ignored by both his deities. "Shut up," said Rodney irritably, for it was no time to interrupt him.

"He wants you to throw his bone," Elizabeth explained. "He'll go on like that till you do," she added with some satisfaction.

Rodney picked up the bone and made it disappear up his sleeve,

70

and showed Snorky his empty hands. Barking hysterically, Snorky began a frantic hunt in the rug around the edges of Rodney who after watching him a moment produced the bone, apparently out of Elizabeth's hair, and showed it to him. Snorky sat up and begged for it—his own idea. Without visible annoyance, but with a great deal of quiet determination, Rodney rose, took Snorky in one hand and the bone in the other, carried them both up to the veranda and put them down on the other side of the screen door, and returned to the rug.

"What sort of man did she marry?" Elizabeth resumed with interest. "Do you see her often? Has he made her happy, do you think?"

"How should I know, I've never laid eyes on him, he could be the Ahkund of Swat for all I care now!"

"You mean you've never—"

"*No,* I've never seen her since she married him, which was about two years ago!"

"Why, Rodney, you're shouting at me," she said, looking pleased.

"You keep on like this and I'll strike you," he warned, and sat down quite close to her and laid hold of the arm which supported her, running his fingers down it to the hand which rested on the rug between them. "I'm the first to concede one thing," he said. "The life I lead is nothing to offer you. It would have been little enough for somebody like Marcia, who had her own family to go back to when I was away if she didn't want to go along. More often than not, it would be impossible for a woman to go along even if she wanted to. I realized even then that my holidays and sabbaticals ought to belong to my—family if I had one, but they won't, you know. I'll always have to go wherever I can whenever I get the chance. After I lost Marcia to a man who sits in an office all day every day, I—well, I made up my mind not to marry, because I could see that no woman would be satisfied with my kind of goings on—unless she loved me enough to—to—"

"To be satisfied with crumbs."

"Well, I only thought—that is, I hoped that since you had your own work, something to do when we are separated—you might not find it too much of a bore—"

"Sounds like an ideal arrangement, doesn't it! Whenever you feel the urge to go to Mexico, I do a new show and everybody's happy!"

"Well, perhaps not ideal, but—it's the way I am, I guess," he admitted.

Elizabeth sat still—so still that he could see the little pulse that beat in her throat while he waited. He had no way of knowing what went on in her mind during those few seconds which seemed to each of them endless. He could not guess from her hands, so quiet under his, or from her delicious profile, which was all he could see, that Liz Dare was fighting the battle of her life against all her impulses. There was no visible sign of the sudden click in her mind, like the click of the tumblers under the sensitive fingertips of a Jimmy Valentine, telling him that the combination of the safe is his, if only— Patience, Liz, don't rush it. This is your whole life, Liz, your life or else nothing at all. That Marcia, maybe she wasn't so dumb as she looks. Better no Rodney at all, than mere snippets of him now and then, when he has nothing better to do, eh, Marcia? Perhaps you're right, at that. But where does one find the courage to let him go, and how does it feel to cut the heart right out of your body, Marcia, does it heal after a couple of years? Ah, but I'm stronger than you were, Marcia, I can do it alone! I'll start a new show, instead of marrying the Ahkund of Swat. You had the right idea, Marcia, but you didn't have the follow-through. Double or quits, Marcia, those are brave words you've taught me, but godalmighty, girl, you've got to do it alone, you've got to be around when he comes to, you've got to be able to take a little punishment, you've got to see it through— all the way through. Well, here I go, Marcia, wish me better luck than you had!

"No, Rodney, it isn't good enough," she said.

There was a long silence.

"I was afraid of that," he said finally, with an unself-conscious humility which was very nearly the end of her.

"Rodney—I've told you before—Liz Dare is human."

"Mm-hm," he agreed at once. "But not human enough."

"Rodney—"

"Oh, I've tried to think she was," he assured her, locking his hands round his knees. "I've tried to imagine her living in a University town, going to faculty teas—my own personal, private bird of paradise among the dull little earnest brown house wrens some of the other professors no older than I am have got for wives. Or sitting beside me at the village movie theater, holding hands like a couple of love-sick sophomores—and going home after the show to a dark, warm house to which I carry the key, and having hot milk together in the kitchen before we go upstairs to bed. And then I'd say to myself, You're out of your head, I'd say. What is there in that for Liz Dare, I'd say. A man when he marries likes to think he can contribute something she's never had before. But comes Christmas, for instance, and what do you give her? A mink coat? She's got two already. A diamond wrist watch? She's wearing one."

"Rodney, please don't—"

"There's nothing anybody can give Liz Dare, I'd tell myself, except more of what's she's got—or a good deal less."

"Unless it's love."

"Oh, *that!*" he said disparagingly. "They sweep great gobs of that off her doorstep each morning! Now, I've got to be getting back to the Station, we're entertaining a couple of visiting firemen from Harvard, and Charles has bet me I can't get a drink into them before dinner."

"Rodney, you must listen to me!" She caught his arm, preventing him from rising. "What about that dark warm house when you're not in it? What about my going upstairs to bed not knowing within several hundred miles where you are, or even if you're

73

alive or dead? I'm not your Aunt Virginia, and neither was Marcia! Your faculty teas don't scare me, even if I'm not from Bryn Mawr! But those empty days and nights while you're racketing around God-only-knows-where enj-joying yourself and risking your silly neck do scare me! Because I *am* in love with you, Rodney Monroe, but before I throw up my hands and go down for the third time, what guarantee do I get that I won't be the college widow after the first year?"

"Liz, say that again—you *are* in—"

"In love with you, yes, but where does that get us so long as you've got this Cortez-complex about Mexico and all the rest of it? It's no good looking at me like that, all dazed and happy, have you heard one word I'm saying?"

"Yes, but—surely you wouldn't want to turn me into one of those arm-chair scientists who sit back and pull their specimens out of moth-balls!"

"I guess if I marry you, I want you to live to a ripe old age," she said.

"Well, I will! If only you'd get rid of this crazy notion that I'm always in danger when I'm in the field! The only field-man who has hairbreadth escapes or gets bitten by snakes or falls on his head is a bad field-man. And I'm a good one. If you don't believe it, come with me to Mexico and see for yourself!"

"The Eagle's Mate! Oh, no, not me! I'm not the type!"

"But it's all so simple, Liz, it's such fun!"

"*No*. That's out. I don't go with you. Anywhere. I know better."

"All right, so it's out," he said amiably. "*Now* what are we fighting about?"

His eyes were on her, laughing and kind and compelling. It looked so easy. It would be such fun—while it lasted. Steady, Liz. She pointed to the script, open on the rug beside him.

"Do you see that? That's my new show. We start on Monday, and open before Thanksgiving. But by that time you'll have

74

Andrew's check for ten thousand dollars and Mexico. That's Life, Rodney. That's the way you want it, and that's the way you're going to get it. But we don't have to say Good-by forever—provided you get back alive, of course! You can still see Liz Dare from the front row, but with this difference—now you have to take her out to supper after the show!" She rose in a single flash of movement and stood looking down at him with her charming, pointed smile. "Why marry the gal, Rodney? Just look me up whenever you're in town!"

He came to his feet too, at that, and his voice was dangerously quiet as he said—

"You know better than that."

But she struck again, all her claws out, because she felt humiliated, felt she had abased herself all for nothing, to a man who could have kissed her into submission even now, only he wouldn't try.

"A girl might as well marry a sailor!" she cried, defying his sense of the proprieties again with relish. "You'd better stick to maiden aunts, Rodney, they get used to it!"

He was keeping his temper with a visible effort.

"You know perfectly well that there would be months—sometimes years—when I never went anywhere that you couldn't go if you liked."

"After you've finished with Mexico!" she jibed.

"I have no immediate prospect of going to Mexico," he told her patiently.

"Oh, yes, you have!" she said between her teeth. "You're going to Mexico before you're a year older, if it's the last thing I do!"

"In that case, I suppose I should say Thank-you," he said, in polite and formal tones. "Good-by, Liz."

He held out his hand. Slowly hers came into it. He stooped and laid his lips against her fingers, and then walked away across the grass to where the station wagon waited in the drive.

She stood where she was and watched while he started the engine and drove away, without a backward look or a wave of his hand. Then she went into the house and buried her face against Snorky's soft mane and cried real tears—the first in a long, long time that she had shed because of any man.

VII

The course of a theatrical production, like that of true love, is never smooth. When Elizabeth got back to town she found that the new show had developed leading-man trouble and was indefinitely held up. After a couple of stormy sessions in Pete's office, she resigned herself to waiting till Hollywood could be made to disgorge any one of the only three leading-men who were good enough to keep up with Liz Dare, and rang up Andrew Blaine.

The following day she lunched with him at India House, a ceremony she always enjoyed, first because the food was pretty special, second because the service made her feel like a queen, and third because though Andrew Blaine might be in his sixties he was still the handsomest man in Wall Street. He had white hair, and enough of it; knowing, ice-blue eyes with little laugh-wrinkles all around them; a clipped mustache; and two deep lines, also from laughter, in his lean cheeks. His chin was square, with a slight cleft in it. His figure was thirtyish at most. Widowered for the past ten years, he was every hostess's dream of the Extra Man, and an escort to be prayed for by any female over twenty.

Elizabeth, who knew she had the inside track with him, touched her sherry glass to his and watched him with satisfaction over the brim as she sipped. Andrew, for his part, observed that her fabulous eyelashes rayed upward in something more than her usual look of trustful, innocent anticipation.

"Now, then," he began as soon as the serious work of ordering lunch had been done, and the waiter had taken away the big menu cards, "suppose you tell me what it is you've been up to."

"Why, Andrew, aren't you clever, how did you know there's anything?"

"You've ~~got~~ cream on your whiskers, Liz, and you're purring like a Packard. Confess."

"Well, first of all, I want ten thousand dollars."

Andrew raised his eyebrows.

"Those sables have come over you again," he said.

"Nope. No sables this time. It's a trip to Mexico."

Andrew's brows went still higher.

"You mean you want me to *buy* you Mexico?" he inquired.

"I wouldn't have the place as a gift! It's for somebody else."

"Mm-hm," he said suspiciously. "Perhaps you'd better begin at the beginning."

"Well, to go 'way back—did you know there was a Biological Station on the shore not far from Sam's place in Maine?"

"Vaguely," he said. "Yes, so there is. Cartwright's camp, it was."

"Well, I got sort of interested in it. It was a nice crowd, really. One night they gave a party for me."

"Mm-hm," said Andrew suspiciously.

"There was a man there who studies birds, I forget the word for it. And more than anything else in the world he wants to go to Mexico to catch eagles. And finally I decided it would serve him right if he d-damned well had to go and do it!"

"I dare say it would. But why should it cost me money?"

Elizabeth said if that was the way he felt about it, she would use her own money and say no more about it.

"You can't," said Andrew with some satisfaction. "Not without my consent. Not any more than you could buy sables with your own money unless I approve. As I've told you before, it would be a pleasure to me to provide the sables myself. But I don't think I'd get much fun out of sending an unknown ornithologist to Mexico just because you feel vindictive towards him."

Elizabeth said he was pretty nice.

"How nice?" he queried, watching her.

Elizabeth said as a matter of fact he had asked her to marry him.

"So you send him to Mexico," Andrew commented. "It seems a bit drastic."

"I guess I haven't made myself clear," she said unwillingly. "He's —we're—I'm in love with him."

Andrew shook his head regretfully. The deep lines in his lean cheeks were deeper.

"It's still not clear," he murmured.

"If you could see him, Andrew— He's several yards tall, and his mouth is too big, and his hair is thick and straight, and he doesn't put stuff on it, and his eyes have a dark ring around the iris, that means something special, I read somewhere, and—and he was a choir boy when he was little."

"Very comprehensive," said Andrew, nodding. "I see it all now. All except one thing. How much does he know about birds?"

"That's not a fair question, how could I tell? But you could, couldn't you, if you met him?"

"Well, not instantly," he admitted. "Does he know you're tackling me about this Mexican trip?"

"Yes, but he doesn't believe you'll come across."

"He's quite right," said Andrew gently. "Are you going to eat that, or would you like something else?"

"This is lovely, I am eating it. And you've misunderstood. He didn't ask me to ask you."

"Naturally not. You don't as a rule fall for stupid men."

"Oh, please don't be like this!" she entreated. "I'm not a fool, I do know something about men by now, and this one is—is the one I want to marry."

"Then where does Mexico come in? As a bribe?"

"No. As a purgative."

Andrew jumped.

"My dear Liz—!"

"He's got this trip on his mind. He won't be happy till he's done

79

it. But if he goes and gets it out of his system, maybe then I'll stand a chance. That sounds perfectly terrible, and of course I wouldn't want him to know I think that way, but—it's no good pretending to you that it's sheer altruism or that I've got any sudden urge to contribute to Science, you always find me out in the end. I don't give a hoot about his eagles, but I am in love with Rodney Monroe, and if he can't settle down until he's—"

"*Who?*" Andrew's soup spoon had stopped half way to his mouth, his blue eyes were suddenly very much in focus on her face.

"Rodney Monroe, the man I'm—"

"Well, why didn't you say so?" he remarked, and laid down his spoon and gave her his whole attention. "Mexico, is it! How much does he want?"

"Ten thousand. Do you *know* him?"

"No, but I'd like to. Can you arrange that?"

"But that's what I've been talking about all this time!"

"Now, let's start all over again," said Andrew sanely. "It's Rodney Monroe that wants to go to Mexico."

"Yes."

"Your ex-choir boy."

"Yes!"

"The one you're in love with."

"*Yes!*"

"Extraordinary," said Andrew, and picked up his spoon. "When does he want the money?"

"You mean you're going to give it to him?"

"Of course. Are you sure that's enough?"

Elizabeth was looking utterly bewildered.

"Andrew, I don't understand. There was nothing doing at all, and then as soon as I said his name you—"

"It happens to be one of the biggest names in American ornithology."

"*Rodney?*"

80

"Monroe." His eyes crinkled up in his smile. "And I asked if your—protegé knew anything about birds! Has he got a sense of humor? Would he know that's funny?"

"B-but I didn't know—"

"You wouldn't," he said pityingly. "You're only in love with him. You wouldn't know that he's written a book on migration that begins where all the others leave off. You wouldn't know—"

"A *text*-book?"

He gave her a patient look.

"I said a *book*. But you wouldn't understand one word in ten, so don't rush out and buy it." He looked at her again, penetratingly, as though seeing her in a new light. "It makes less sense than ever now. What does Rodney Monroe think of you? Oh, yes—he wants to marry you."

"Well, he doesn't, really, it's only that he can't live without me— he says."

"I can see how that might be," he said, his eyes on her face. "Liz, are you serious about this?"

"I think, if I lose him now I'll just want to die."

"Extraordinary," said Andrew again. "Are you going to Mexico with him, then?"

"My God, no! We had a sort of fight about that. In fact, we fought practically every time we met."

"Doesn't let you have it all your own way, eh! That's good."

"The way we left it, he was going to Mexico and I wasn't going to marry him at any price. But I will, when he gets back, if he asks me again. You'll make sure that he does get back, won't you."

Andrew said he should think Rodney Monroe could take care of himself by now.

"But he must have the best possible equipment—g-guns, and things."

"Naturally, I'll see to that. Well, hurry up, produce him, let's get going on this thing!"

"I haven't got him up my sleeve, Andrew! He's still in Maine, at the Station."

"How soon can you get him here?"

"I suppose if I wired him you wanted to see him, he'd come tomorrow."

"Then wire him. Say I've been wanting to meet him ever since I read his book."

"He'll be surprised. I was."

Andrew said it didn't follow.

"He never even mentioned the book to me!" she marveled.

Andrew said he could well believe it.

"Tell me some more about him," she entreated.

"Darling Liz, you know him. I don't. You're in love with him. I've never set eyes on him. How can I—"

"But I don't know anything *about* him. What's he *done,* to be so famous?"

"Well, he went to New Guinea with Rogers and Sturgis after—"

"After birds of paradise! I know!"

Andrew looked at her inquiringly, and she added—

"He did mention that. We had a sort of a fight about it. Go on."

"I think after that he went to Guiana to get moving-pictures of hoatzins. He—"

"Of what?"

"It's a kind of bird," he explained kindly. "They won't live in captivity. You have to go where they are."

"Where's that?"

"Guiana."

"I thought that was a French prison."

"If he does marry you, Liz, he's crazy, and I mean to tell him so!"

"He's trying not to," she said humbly. "Go on about him."

"Now it's your turn," said Andrew a little exhaustedly.

"Well—" There was a dreamy pause.

"And I don't mean just the color of his eyes," said Andrew.

"He knows he can do anything he likes with me," she confessed. "But on the very last day we had another fight and I said he was going to Mexico if it was the last thing I did. So then he got very polite the way he does when he's angry—he has lovely manners, his Aunt Virginia brought him up—got very polite, and said Thank-you coldly and kissed my hand and went away without another *word,* and I had to come back to town."

"Liz, if you don't show me this man before the week is out I shall die of curiosity! Are you *sure* it's Rodney Monroe you're talking about? I suppose there couldn't be two of them?"

"He isn't anything like what you'd expect a professor of orna—orna—"

"Ornithology."

"—ornithology would be."

"Obviously," said Andrew. "Wire him tonight. Ask him to come down at once. Tell him I can't stand the suspense. Will you give the dinner or shall I?"

"I will. And I think on second thought if you don't mind I'd better write him a letter instead of wiring. I'll need more words, you see, because we—well, we weren't exactly speaking to each other when I left."

"You're wonderful, Liz," said Andrew sincerely, almost with awe. "A man may be feeling all his years—there's a war on—the market has gone to hell—life is perilous, and the world is stale and sick and sad. Then you walk in, and instantly the angels sing! I shall tell him that too."

VIII

"*Dear Rodney*—" wrote Liz Dare that evening in her round, legible hand on the thick square white paper which carried her Central Park South address and telephone number.

Then she sat for a long time biting the pen and gazing at the blank sheet of paper in front of her. *Dear* Rodney, I've done it, she thought, and now I'm frightened. Not just that you may break your one and only neck in Mexico. Not even that you may meet up with a transcendent *señorita* and forget me forever. But frightened of time, Rodney, and perspective—six months from now, a year from now, when you get back. And maybe of your work, that means so much to you. I'd think nothing of giving up my job in favor of that warm little house near the campus, and holding hands in a movie, and coming home to hot milk in the kitchen— If I married you, I wouldn't want to go on singing at night clubs for a mob of frustrated tired businessmen and their overfed wives and what-nots, when I could be at home in bed with—with a good book, Rodney. I've earned my living just as long as you have. Longer. And I like it. I like a spotlight, and people putting their hands together at the end of a song, and people saying That's Liz Dare, when I go somewhere for lunch or dinner. But I'd give it up like a shot, for you. Wouldn't that entitle me to your holidays and sabbaticals? Apparently not.

So you can't live without me, Rodney, she thought—but only when you have time, only when it wouldn't interfere with migration. Well, I won't fight the birds for you, all the rest of my life. We're going to settle this first and last and get it over. And if I

84

lose, why, I've still got my health and my Public. But no heart. You've done that to me. It won't be so much fun now, without you. Nothing will ever be so much fun again, without you. That doesn't make sense, when I've seen you just four times in my life. Lightning only strikes once. Once is enough. The other three times didn't count, you had me without them. Andrew says I won't understand your book. Well, maybe I would. Birds go south for the winter, anybody knows that. Very sensible of them. What is there in that to write a book about? Andrew is very impressed with you, I can see that. You're something pretty special, aren't you. Nobody tells me anything—

Dear Rodney [she wrote]

Today I had lunch with Andrew Blaine, and to my intense surprise he knows all about you and has read your book and wants to know you and says can I arrange it. Can I?

The idea would be for you to come down at once and I'll give a dinner. Just a few people. So will you please wire me when? Today is Wednesday, and you may not get this till Friday, bother, there's the week-end, and it's hard to get people then. Well, how about Monday or Tuesday of next week? Andrew said wire you tonight, but I thought I could explain better in a letter. Andrew says yours is one of the biggest names in American ornathology. You probably knew this already, but I didn't. Why didn't you say you had written a book?

Snorky sends love.

Liz

On Friday morning Elizabeth's bedside phone rang at a quarter to nine. At first she tried to turn over and ignore it, but it kept on. Mary's niece, who as parlormaid completed Elizabeth's staff in town, and whose name was Gertrude, opened the bedroom door quietly and looked in.

"Answer it and tell 'em to go to hell," said Elizabeth, muffled in the pillow. "Everybody I'd want to talk to knows better."

Gertrude's soft voice began coping with the telephone. Then—

"It's Long Distance," she said. "Will you speak to them now, or shall I tell them to call later?"

"Tell 'em— Long Distance!" Elizabeth sat up dazedly, and then grabbed the phone out of Gertrude's hand. *"Rodney!"* she yelled into it, and an amused female voice said, "One moment, please."

After the usual formalities his voice did come down the wire, and her heart stopped dead, turned over, and then began to hurry.

"Liz, this is the craziest letter I ever got from anybody. What does it mean?"

"Means what it says," she got out, sitting up in bed with her elbows on her knees, holding on to the phone with both hands lest he go away again and leave her. (Gertrude closed the window, laid a soft knitted jacket round Elizabeth's shoulders, and went out and pulled the door shut carefully behind her; and then pelted through the drawing-room and dining-room to tell Mary in the kitchen that everything was all right now, Somebody had rung up on Long Distance and Missy was very pleased, even though it waked her.) "Means we want you to come to dinner on Monday," said Elizabeth, and laid her forehead against the cool mouthpiece of the phone in an effort to get closer to him.

"Yes, I know, but not *next* Monday, the Station doesn't close for another two weeks, and after that I have to—"

"But, Rodney, it's only for the night, can't you get away?"

"No!" he said, with laughter in it. "You're crazy, I can't just—"

"But Andrew wants to talk to you."

"That's very nice, but—"

"He's going to give you the money, but he wants to know when you start and exactly where you're going, and all that sort of thing."

There was a moment's silence at the other end. Then Rodney spoke, very quietly.

"Now—wait—just—one—minute," he said. "Did you say—"

86

"It's all *fixed,* Rodney, all you have to do is come and get it!"

"The—not the whole ten thousand!"

"Andrew never does things by halves."

Rodney could be heard then at the other end shouting for Charles. Other voices took it up distantly. Then his came again, rather breathlessly, speaking to somebody near by.

"It—looks as though we're going to Mexico," he said.

"Yippee!" said Charles distinctly.

"Liz, look—Charles and I don't want to get drunk all for nothing. Did Blaine say in so many words that he'd give us the money?"

"Well, it was very funny about that," she explained, getting more awake now. "I didn't happen to mention your name at first, and he wasn't a bit interested. Finally it sort of came out in the course of the argument that I was talking about Rodney Monroe, and then he perked right up and said How much and When and Was that enough. All he seems to want in return is the pleasure of your acquaintance. So will you please come down on Monday and—"

"No, I can't do that," he said firmly. "If he really means it he won't change his mind in three weeks' time, and—"

"Three weeks!"

"That's the best I can do, Liz, I have to—"

"Charles can look after things up there."

"Liz, will you use that beautiful thing on the end of your neck you call a head? I run this place. I can't leave. Blaine will understand that if you don't. Present my compliments and say I will be in New York three weeks from tomorrow if he wants to see me then. Or shall I write to him? It seems like taking a good deal for granted, but—"

"Why does it? The money's yours, if you ever get round to collect it!"

"I'll get round. I'll get round to thank you for it, too. When I see you."

"I hadn't anything to do with it. You can thank that fellow named Rodney Monroe. I never heard of him, but Andrew had."

"You will," he promised. "Just wait for it. You will. In about three weeks' time."

"Rodney—are you *really* pleased?"

"I'll tell you more about that too, when I get a chance."

"Thrrree minutes," said a brisk female voice.

"Go away!" said Rodney's. "Liz, are you still there?"

"Yes, Rodney."

"You remember that bet I lost?"

"About Mercer."

"I'll settle that too, while I'm there."

"Dinner. Just us, somewhere."

"Absolutely. You said something about cloth-of-gold."

"You'll get it," she assured him. "Hi, Snorky, guess who! Come say Hullo to Rodney. Yes, it's *Rodney!* He knows your name, isn't that intelligent of him? Come on, Snorky, right up on the bed this once—now, speak to Rodney! Speak!"

Snorky yapped excitedly.

"Hiya," said Rodney. "Liz, what was that about bed, did I wake you?"

"Well, sort of."

"Where were you last night?"

"None of your business."

"I get it. You wait."

"What'll I tell Andrew?"

"Tell him Three weeks from tomorrow. And the same to you! Oh, by the way, Liz—for your information, ornithology is spelt with an *i.*"

His receiver clicked on the hook.

Three weeks! Well, what did I tell you, she thought, he'll stay there till the Station closes, and after that he'll go and enroll the Freshman class and write out its exercises. And then, if he happens to think of it, he'll get round to you, Liz Dare, and not before. That's Rodney. Would you have him any different? *Yes!*

Gertrude, apparently suspecting that there would be no more sleep that morning, opened the door softly and came in with a tall glass of hot water tinged with lemon juice. She set it down on the bedside table and went into the bathroom and turned on the taps.

Gertrude was the perfect maid, in that she never asked questions. She never said "Will you have your bath now?" If the odds were in favor of it, she turned on the taps, and if she had guessed wrong —which seldom happened as she was very nearly clairvoyant—you simply yelled at her and she cheerfully turned them off again. She brought you your hot water without being asked, and if you didn't want it yet you could let it sit there till it got cold and cheerfully she'd bring you another. She brought in the mail with the morning paper as soon as you woke up, because usually you wanted it then, but if you didn't take any notice of it she would dig it out of the bedclothes for you later on when you were ready for it, or else you'd find it in a neat pile by your plate; and if necessary it pursued you, still silently and in a neat pile, to the middle of your desk-blotter. Except in rare domestic crises, Gertrude practically never spoke unless she was spoken to; which made her invaluable to an employer who was continually going over lines in her head or listening to the elusive rhythm of a new step in her mind's ear. It was even more convenient if you were in love, because it made it possible for you to go on thinking about Rodney and his unpredictable, enthralling perversities till you nearly went mad.

This morning Elizabeth heard the bath water with resignation, and sat up against her pillows in the knitted bed-jacket and sipped her hot water, looking sleepy and happy and adrift. The mail was brought, and with it a package. When Gertrude had cut the string for her, Elizabeth unwrapped a brand-new jacketed copy of a rather hefty volume entitled, simply enough, *Bird Migration,* and underneath it in smaller type the name of the author, which was, believe it or not, Rodney Monroe. Andrew's card fell out, and on it he had written: *Here it is. Read it. I dare you. A.*

Maybe you think I won't, she thought. Every word. Still sipping her hot water, she turned the pages lovingly, for this was part of Rodney. There were maps, with little dotted lines. There was an Appendix—horrid thought—and a Bibliography and an Index. No pictures.

Anyway, it was very comfortable to have something that was Rodney on one's bedside table. Even the telephone, having brought his voice into the room, shone now with a new luster.

Three weeks isn't really a very long time, unless you're in love with a man at the far end of it. Then the days can develop a certain lag.

Elizabeth bought rather more clothes than she needed, because she kept on seeing another dress that Rodney might like better than the one before. He would be in town two days, apparently. There would be her dinner on Saturday night for Andrew to meet him, and then there was all day Sunday, and then there was Rodney's dinner on Sunday night, which was the most important part. The cloth-of-gold gown, intricately draped, very exclusive, every bit as expensive as it looked, and weighing roughly a ton, was in her clothes cupboard a week ahead of time.

Elizabeth, who liked to break in a new gown once or twice in a quiet way before its official début, had decided against the usual procedure this time. The gold gown was for Rodney, when he paid his foolish debt about Mercer, and no one was to see it before he did.

She put it on one evening at home, and while Snorky watched critically from his basket in the corner of the bedroom, she stood in front of the full-length mirrors, and walked and turned and walked again, sat down and rose and sat again, tried a few dance steps, pinched up the fabric here, pulled at it there (knowing that it was perfect and needed no alteration) lifted its hem to survey her new gold slippers, tried another pair with higher heels, decided to use the new pair anyway, turned out her jewel-case—that gold-link bracelet—no, too green—ended by rejecting everything in it because the gown itself scorned any further adornment. She put her hair up on top of her head, and rejected that in favor of the way he was used to—spent nearly an hour choosing the exact shade of powder and lipstick required—went back to the mirror routine: sit, rise, walk, turn, walk, sit, rise, walk—just there, on the shoulder—too much fullness?—perhaps not—how about half an inch off the length in front?—no—well, maybe it was good enough—maybe he'd like it—

Apparently he didn't write letters. Elizabeth, who did, had half expected some sort of follow-up to the telephone conversation, but Rodney appeared to regard the whole thing as settled, for no further comment came from him—which was pretty exasperating. After a week of eagerly ripping open every envelope addressed in a strange handwriting which arrived in her mail, Elizabeth gave him up entirely. Maybe he was afraid of compromising himself if he laid pen to paper. Cautious man, wasn't he.

"I've got the Daltons and Caroline Jones coming to dinner," she told Andrew on the phone on the third Monday. "And Stanley the publisher, and you and Minnie and Rodney and me."

"Splendid," said Andrew. Minnie was his sister, whom everybody loved, and Caroline Jones was beautiful and blond.

"That makes us eight," Elizabeth went on. "I'm going to sit between you and Rodney, and I'll give you Caroline on your left, just to show him, and put May Dalton on his other hand. She won't know anything about birds either! Then Stanley, and Alan Dalton across, and Minnie opposite to me. Is that all right?"

"Seems to be perfect."

"In the meantime, will you please take me out to dinner on Wednesday or Thursday so I can rehearse my dress? It's new."

"Delighted," he said, for he prized these requests very highly. "What color is it?"

"White. With silver."

"I like you in white. I like you anyway. Let's make it Wednesday. I'll be there at seven-thirty."

"Andrew, you're a great comfort. I wish he behaved as well as you do!"

"Probably if I were his age I shouldn't be behaving at all well myself. You must give a man a certain amount of line," said Andrew, "after he feels the first jerk of the hook. He's bound to head for deep water."

"What a perfectly horrid way to put it!"

"Remember to take up the slack as you get it," he cautioned, "but be sure to give him time to tire. If you hurry him he may panic and tear out the hook at considerable injury to himself, and get away from you forever."

"He's not a trout, Andrew!"

"More like a marlin, probably. They can put up quite a fight. When you're ready for the gaff, let me know."

"He's not like a fish at all! I don't care for your figures of speech!"

"What *is* he like, Liz?"

"He's Rodney. There isn't one at the zoo."

"Probably doesn't do well in captivity."

"Andrew, I don't think I like you today. You're full of nasty innuendoes."

"Darling Liz, I regard this Monroe with legitimate suspicion. Either he's a superman or else he wants stamping on. I'll decide when I see him."

"Presumably he *will* be here on Saturday, but he hasn't said so again. Have you heard from him?"

"Not a sound."

"Sometimes in the middle of the night I wonder if I can be wrong, Andrew. Maybe I ought to call the whole thing off right now. Maybe I shouldn't have asked those other people. What's he

92

going to look like in evening dress? Will he know to *wear* evening dress? I didn't tell him. He didn't ask. Maybe—"

"Nonsense," said Andrew soothingly. "What about his Aunt Virginia?"

"Think I can count on her for a white tie?"

"I think so."

"Perhaps you're right. Well—till Wednesday, Andrew."

Five endless days till Saturday, though. You'd think Rodney was Santa Claus. Well, maybe he was. . . .

IX

On Saturday morning there was a telegram with her mail.

ARRIVING NEW YORK SIX-THIRTY PM WILL CALL YOU FROM THE
UNIVERSITY CLUB LOVE

RODNEY

Love. That's not very cautious. Watch your step, Rodney.

That white dress, now—will it do? Maybe the blue one— No, Stanley has seen it. The hell with Stanley, Rodney hasn't. No, I think the white. Six-thirty P.M. Hours and hours away. Why did I wake up so early? I know, I'll skip round to Elizabeth Arden and let 'em give me the works. That takes up time.

And so six-thirty came at last. Well, give him time to get to the Club from the train, Liz. Andrew's living there now too. They'll probably pass each other in the lobby—foyer—lounge—whatever the University Club calls whatever it's got—and not know each other. Except if Andrew sees anything that tall with a bag he might suspect— Oh, thank God, there he is!

"Hullo," said Rodney intimately, down the telephone. "What time is dinner?"

"Eight o'clock."

"Dinner jacket or tails?"

"Which did you bring?"

"I brought both, what do you suppose?"

"Tails," she said faintly.

"You haven't forgotten about our other dinner tomorrow night?"

"No, I kept it open."

94

"It's not open any more, it's taken. How's Snorky?"

"He's fine."

"Well, how are you?"

"I'm all right, thanks."

"You sound sort of orphaned again. Have I done something wrong?"

"I expect I'll feel better when I see you."

"I know what it is, you've got stage-fright," he said unexpectedly. "So have I. Give me a cocktail quick when I get there."

"Old-fashioned."

"Anything. But make it strong. Unless I can count on that I'll probably arrive reeking of liquor from the bar here."

"Red or white wine at dinner?"

"Red wine, the exact color of your lipstick. By the way, I've been wanting to ask you—why doesn't it come off?"

"Well, how do you know it doesn't, Dr. Monroe?"

"I know by my white handkerchief when I got home that night after the party. Next question, please."

"Does everybody else's lipstick come off on you?"

"Ow!" said Rodney inelegantly. "I asked for that one! And there's another thing. Do you still smell of flowers?"

"I've aged in the past three weeks," she admitted, "but I don't think I've changed in any of the essentials."

"That's good. I think I feel a little better now, don't you? Of course there's going to be an awful moment when I come in the door and you have to shake hands—I presume you will shake hands?—instead of casting yourself round my neck with a whoop of joy. Right then is when I want that cocktail."

"Maybe I'd better just hand it to you as you enter."

"That's an idea."

"We're talking awful nonsense, Rodney!"

"I know we are. People in our delicate condition always do."

"Did you talk awful nonsense to Marcia when you—"

"Just for that I'll hang up on you. Now." And he did so.

95

"Well!" said Elizabeth aloud speechlessly, and went off to take her bath.

She was still in it when the telephone rang again, about five minutes later. Gertrude answered it. There wasn't any argument from Gertrude. She laid down the receiver at once and went to the bathroom door and tapped on it.

"Dr. Monroe is on the telephone," she said.

"Damn," said Elizabeth. "All right, say I'm coming." She swished up out of the fragrant water and wrapped herself in a terry-cloth robe and trotted out to the phone. "What's the matter now?" she demanded.

"Nothing's the matter. I only thought, wouldn't it be better if I came a little before eight o'clock and sort of got it over?"

"*No!*" she shouted. "It would be much worse!"

"All right, all right," he murmured placatingly. "I was only thinking—"

"Don't think!" she advised him. "I'm trying not to!"

"Can you make it?" he queried with interest.

"Rodney, darling, go away, will you, I'm in the bath. Or I was!"

And this time it was Elizabeth who hung up, leaving him to contemplate with a fatuous smile the very domestic sound of his dismissal.

Andrew arrived first, as was his established privilege. Then the Daltons. Then Stanley, bringing Caroline Jones. Then Minnie. They were all terribly punctual. When the bell rang again it simply had to be Rodney.

The Awful Moment had come. He was giving his hat to Gertrude in the little foyer. (Gertrude would put it down anywhere and run to the kitchen for the cocktails.) Then he was crossing the threshold towards her, and automatically she went forward with her hand out, the perfect hostess, all in white, unruffled, dignified, serene— God help you, Liz, she was thinking, if ever you had any scraps of sense about him, they're all to-hell-and-gone now!

96

Rodney looked (and there is only one word for it) Magnificent. His white tie was a miracle of perfection, his white waistcoat hugged his narrow middle, his flat shirt-front held two pearl studs, his thick straight hair shone with brushing, there was no lock at all—he looked scrubbed and shaved and tailored and turned out. He looked the way Royalty ought to look.

Andrew glanced from him to Elizabeth and back again. If he had not been Andrew, his jaw would have sagged. His sister Minnie shamelessly nudged his elbow.

Seated on Elizabeth's right at dinner, Rodney took stock deliberately of his surroundings. This was her life, her home, and these were her friends. That long white drawing-room with windows above the Park, a room lit by shaded white lamps, upholstered in white leather and satin, modern, spacious, soft, and expensive, with mirrors and open bookshelves and a built-in radio cabinet and a wood fire—that was Liz Dare. The dining-room, pale robin's-egg blue, with the glint of mahogany and crystal—the dinner-table, agleam with silver and candlelight and delicate china, waited on by the deft little maid in black and white—Liz herself, looking no less than an angel, looking so calm and sleek and sure and unembarrassed (only he knew better)—it was all as he had been able to anticipate it, only a little more so. Andrew Blaine was unquestionably all right. He liked Andrew. The others, too, every one of them, could just as well have been found in his Aunt Virginia's drawing-room. He would not have minded if they couldn't have, but he was conscious of a slight relief, he was not sure from what.

Perhaps he was relieved that there was nothing theatrical about the company—only about the situation in which he found himself. To these people, who were Liz's friends, he was the outsider, the bird of another feather. He himself was the one undergoing inspection. How much did Andrew know? Probably All. And Miss Caroline Jones, whose eyes were everywhere, by no means regarded him, Rodney, with indifference. (It is impossible not to sense these things, when one is six-feet-three and knows how to wear one's

97

clothes, and has no wife to protect one.) In vain in the sight of the Bird, is the net of the Fowler displayed—or words to that effect, as regards Miss Caroline Jones. With Liz, now, there was no net. Apparently. Or if there was, one wouldn't care, one would just walk into Liz's net and scream for her to come and collect what was hers. Who was this Stanley? Very off-hand around here. Good-looking brute, too. Women were supposed to like 'em prematurely gray like that. Doubtless considered Distinguished-looking. Took it Big. Obviously well-known to the maid. Is that so. All right, maid, you wait.

And all this time he had been listening and replying to May Dalton on the subject of winters in Florida, and making sense too; for he had been there himself one winter, and had almost frozen to death.

When the soup and the fish soufflé had gone, Elizabeth turned to him for the first time.

"How's darling Charles?" she said.

"Flourishing. He sent his regards."

"Thank you. Give him my love."

"I *will* not!" said Rodney, and a large silver platter of squabs came down between them. "My, my," he said, dealing with it, "Mary has regular' let herself go on this meal!"

"She knew you were coming tonight, and this is her idea of how you ought to be fed."

"They're very elegant victuals. Please present my compliments to the cook," he added, lifting that limpid, friendly gaze to Gertrude's face.

"Present 'em yourself," said Elizabeth. "She'd love it."

"May I? Thanks. What's *her* name?" he inquired as Gertrude moved away with the squabs.

"Gertrude. She's Mary's niece."

"Does she answer the phone when you're in the bath?"

"Always. Anything else you'd like to know about my household?"

"Well, while I'm checking up, where's Snorky?"

98

"Shut up in my bedroom. Parties of more than four people always excite him."

"Maybe Mary would let me have a word with him while I'm in the kitchen."

"Mary would let you have anything you want around here."

"Well, that's something to start with."

When Elizabeth was arranging her table, she had felt safer to put Rodney next to her than to abandon him to Caroline or Minnie at the other end of the table. Now she was not so sure. The easy, inaudible intimacy of his conversation was beginning to tell on her. His grave, unembarrassed eyes rested on her so openly, so—honestly. She began to have a horrible feeling that she hadn't fooled anybody for a single minute. Or was that just her own guilty conscience?

Her chief reason for placing Snorky incommunicado was his infatuation for Rodney. Snorky had always taken Stanley and even Andrew in his stride. His passionate worship of Rodney was bound to cause comment, and even give rise to false impressions. After all, Snorky had seen Rodney only four times. (Once was enough.)

Therefore when the time came to leave the men at the table with their coffee and liqueurs, a distinct relief mingled with her natural regret that it was necessary to let Rodney out of her sight for any part of the time embraced by his visit to New York. But this opportunity for him to talk to Andrew man to man was perhaps the main purpose of that visit. Her chin was a little high as she rose and herded the other women into the drawing-room and closed the glass doors behind them. There you are, Rodney. Go to it. If you don't get that check now it's not my fault.

"My dear!" said Caroline Jones as soon as the doors were shut. "Where *did* you get him? And *where* does he keep himself?"

"Who? Oh, the Monroe man. He wanted to meet Andrew. Something about going to Mexico. He's a professor of ornithology."

"Of what?" said everybody.

"Birds," Elizabeth explained, looking superior. "He wrote a book about them. Andrew's read it."

"A professor!" said May Dalton, and giggled. "You'd never suspect it, with that look in his eye! Is he married?"

"He doesn't seem to be," said Elizabeth. "Cigarette?"

"Thanks. My goodness, if I'd known he was so learned I would have been afraid of him. As it was, I had a wonderful time!"

"If that's what professors are like nowadays, I don't wonder all the girls want to go to college," remarked Minnie Blaine, who was a dear, with soft gray hair and a pretty face. "In my day they all seemed to be like the one in *Little Women*."

"I wonder if I could get him to come and talk to the Garden Club," said May. "Does he lecture about birds?"

"I haven't the faintest idea," said Elizabeth, trying not to sound cold. "Why don't you ask him?"

"I think I will!"

"You'd better be quick, then. I understand he's off for Mexico in the spring."

"But how exciting!" said Caroline. "I've always wanted to go to a fiesta!"

"How about a slight case of gunplay on the side?" queried Elizabeth. "Would you care for that too?"

"With him to protect me? I'd adore it!" cried Caroline, and crowed with laughter.

It was idiots like Caroline, Elizabeth perceived contemptuously, that had got him into a state of mind where he thought everybody would instantly want to go with him. Well, maybe for a change he would appreciate somebody who hated the mere idea.

Gertrude brought the coffee, and while they drank it Elizabeth tried to explain why she was not starting the new show immediately. When Gertrude came in for the empty cups they all rose and trailed down the passage to Elizabeth's bedroom to powder their noses, and when they returned to the drawing-room somebody left the bedroom door open. They were no more than seated again when Snorky bustled down the passage, cast about the room a minute, and then planted himself in front of the dining-room doors and began to bark.

Elizabeth made a hasty movement towards him, but Rodney was nearer the door. It opened from the other side, and Rodney was seen to greet Snorky affectionately before it closed again, with Snorky in the dining-room.

Elizabeth thought she noticed a look of speculation in three pairs of feminine eyes.

"Rodney rescued him from a ferocious big Labrador up in Maine," she said casually, "and ever since then Snorky has simply worshiped him."

On the other side of the doors Rodney was saying—

"There was a big Labrador up at the Station and Snorky nearly ate him alive. They'll tackle anything, these Pekes, regardless of size." He sat down with Snorky on his lap, and resumed his conversation, and his brandy.

In the drawing-room—

"Is Rodney his Christian name?" said Caroline with interest. "How nice. I wonder if he'd come to supper tomorrow night. It's buffet."

"He's only down for this evening, to meet Andrew," said Elizabeth brazenly. "He's taking the morning train back, I think."

"What a pity. Perhaps he'd stay over if I asked him."

"Try it and see," suggested Elizabeth, and this time she did sound definitely cold.

The evening wore on, and the men were conscienceless about returning to the drawing-room—a thing which did not as a rule occur at Elizabeth's dinner-parties. She managed to get the conversation off Rodney Monroe and keep it off, but it was inclined to languish.

Finally the glass doors opened again and the men filtered through, looking pleased with life and full of good food and drink. Rodney and Andrew loitered last, still talking together, pausing just over the threshold while Andrew finished the story he was illustrating with gestures, and appeared to draw a map with his toe on the carpet, and Rodney watched absorbedly. Snorky, looking rather smug, was under Rodney's arm.

When at last they drifted, still talking, within earshot, Elizabeth said ring for Gertrude to shut Snorky up again if he was being a nuisance.

"He's doin' all right," said Rodney, and set the little dog down on the floor. "Let him have his fun."

Snorky stood about aimlessly for a minute or two, and then bundled off down the passage towards the bedroom. Elizabeth saw him go with relief.

But not for long. Only too soon Snorky was back again with his bone, which he deposited on the carpet at Rodney's feet and began to bark. It was Rodney, by now, who was telling Andrew a story with gestures, and not interrupting himself at all he squatted on his heels, possessed himself of the bone, and made it disappear. Snorky danced up and down in front of him and had hysterics.

"Snorky, shut up!" said Elizabeth. "Do stop, Rodney, you'll drive him nuts with that trick!"

Rodney produced the bone, apparently out of Andrew's trouser-leg, palmed it, and stood up. Snorky went off again into excited barking. It was impossible to hear yourself think.

"Snorky, *be quiet!!*" commanded Elizabeth, and bopped him behind. "What *is* the matter with you!"

"I'm afraid he's tight," said Rodney guiltily. "He had the last drop of my brandy."

"Oh, Rodney, how could you! He'll be sick!"

"I'm sorry, Liz, I had no idea it would go to his head like this," he apologized. "I had a pet monkey once who could drink me right under the table."

Liz. She felt that register with the witnesses of what was somehow taking on the aspect of a domestic brawl.

"I suppose the monkey died of delirium tremens!" she said.

"It died of old age," he contradicted. "Come on, you little souse, let's go find Mary." Something very like a snicker escaped him as Snorky eluded his hand and backed away, barking for his bone. "Tight as a hoot-owl!" Rodney said, and captured Snorky on the second try and straightened with him in his hands. "I'll get Mary to bed him down. I want to thank her for that dinner anyway." And carrying Snorky, he departed kitchenwards with all the ease and assurance of a homing pigeon.

Mary. She felt that register too, with the now enthralled audience. He called her servants by name. He knew his way around the apartment. He got Snorky drunk, and then said "I'm sorry, Liz," on that easy intimate note. She was compromised, that's what she was.

Somehow the evening never quite jelled again. Soon after Rodney returned from the kitchen Elizabeth found herself alone at last with him and Andrew, and said she thought they'd better all have a slight brandy-and-soda. She went to the tray which Gertrude had placed on the coffee table in front of the fire and began to mix them, remarking as she did so—

"Well, Rodney, between you and Snorky my reputation isn't worth the paper it's printed on!"

"What have I done now?" he inquired.

Elizabeth came towards them, a glass in each hand. She gave one to Andrew and shoved the other at Rodney.

"What has he done now!" she said bitterly, and turned away for her own glass.

Rodney could be seen casting his mind back.

"But you said at dinner I could go and speak to Mary," he pointed out.

"Oh, sure, I asked for it! *And* I got it!" She raised her glass at him. "Here's to Liz Dare, I hear she's got off with a college professor, I *wonder* what they find to talk about!"

"Well, I offered to make an honest woman of you, and you turned me down," he reminded her, and while she was still speech-

103

less he glanced at Andrew, who sat in a corner of the davenport with his brandy-and-soda, enjoying himself immensely. "All right, Liz—before witnesses: Are you going to marry me before or after I make this trip? It's almost four months till I start, and I'll be away about three. That's a lot of time to waste."

"Look how long I've lived without you up to now!" she said, wishing he wouldn't stand on the hearthrug with his back to the fire and a glass in his hand, looking as though he belonged there. "I guess I can manage somehow, till you get back—"

"Does that mean that when I get back you *will*—"

"*No!* I never said that! Besides, how do I know you'll get back, from a place like Mexico!"

"Oh, Mexico's out," he said airily. "I'm going farther south now —in Central America."

She looked from one to the other with apprehension. Andrew buried himself quickly in his glass.

"Why?" she demanded. "What have you two been hatching behind my back?"

"The fact is, Mexico is too safe and civilized," Rodney explained, watching her from the hearthrug. "I'm going down where it's really wild, and things pop out at you from behind every tree."

"Who s-suggested Central America?" demanded Elizabeth, both frightened and angry. "Whose idea was that? Yours, Andrew?"

"Mr. Blaine knows a house I can get," Rodney continued, "down on the West coast, for headquarters. It belonged to a planter who got some horrible tropical disease and came up here and died of it. The house has stood empty ever since, and is probably full of scorpions and vampire bats and snakes, but I can get it very cheap."

"Andrew, how dare you send him to a place like that? There must be lots of better houses, and I read about a man who died of being bitten by a vampire! Andrew, why do you encourage him—"

"Honey, I was fooling," said Rodney quietly. "Don't fall for it."

It was the first time he had called her anything but Liz, and he

104

had chosen to do it in front of Andrew. She swallowed the unexpected endearment almost visibly, like Snorky asking for More.

"You mean it won't be any more dangerous than Mexico would be?"

"Of course not. Much more comfortable than anything I had thought of, and just as good, if not better, for what I want to do. It's a little farther to go, but now that I don't have to worry about money that doesn't matter."

"By the way," said Andrew, "when do you want the money?"

"Listen to him, Liz," Rodney said reverently. "That is the most beautiful arrangement of human sounds I ever heard. When do I want the money! I'd like to get Charles started on the color camera as soon as possible, sir. He'll want to do some experimenting with that part of the equipment."

"Then suppose I send you the first five thousand right away, and the rest whenever you want it."

"Thank you. Would you like to see Charles? He'll be coming down to New York very soon."

"By all means. Have him ring me up when he gets here."

"Look at Liz," said Rodney, amused. "The orphan child! All right, we're through now. Be nice to us for five minutes, and then we'll go away and let you get some sleep."

"I was wondering about Snorky," she said.

"Maybe I'd better have a look. Where will I find him?" Rodney set down his glass on the mantel.

"In my bedroom. Straight down the passage and to the left."

Rodney left them, matter-of-factly disappearing in the direction of her bedroom. Elizabeth looked at Andrew.

"Well?" she said softly.

"Hang on to him, Liz. It's a very rare bird."

"You do like him, then."

"More than I can say."

"But, Andrew, we don't *belong* together, we—it doesn't—"

"Follow your heart, Liz. It's in his pocket."

105

"How do I know he won't smash it?"

"Maybe he will. But you can't get it back now—can you?"

Smiling his secret smile, Rodney entered Elizabeth's bedroom, his light step soundless on the thick carpet. By the time he had reached Snorky's basket in the corner, his trained eye had memorized most of his surroundings—the long, black windows framing the spangling lights of the Park vista—the shifting crystal dazzle of the dressing-table, the sheen of many mirrors, the gleaming chaise-longue with its folded pink coverlet, the 'square white bed with curving satin edges—and through a half-open door a bathroom touched with pink. Here too, that nameless fragrance which was Liz Dare was stronger than he had ever caught it before.

He bent over the slumbering Snorky, who did not rouse under his gentle hand, and then straightened and allowed his 'gaze to travel once more over the room. Darling Liz, this is where you were when I phoned, this is where you will go to sleep tonight— On the table by the bed, beside the white telephone, under the white lamp, lay his own book on migration. He went over and picked it up. A marker had been left three quarters of the way through. His smile deepened. He left the room with the book in his hand.

"Look what I found on her bedside table!" he said, as he re-entered the drawing-room.

"I gave it to her," said Andrew. "I dared her to read it!"

"I am reading it," she told them with dignity. "I don't know why you should both assume it was miles beyond me. There's one thing I don't understand, though. Of course I haven't finished it yet, but there is one thing that doesn't seem to me to be quite clear, so far."

"Maybe I was saving that for the end," suggested Rodney. "What wasn't quite clear?"

"Well—you won't laugh at me?" she stipulated. "I suppose it's quite simple really, and I'm just being stupid."

106

Oh, no, they assured her, such a supposition was quite impossible.

"Well, it's only—why don't the birds ever get *lost?*"

They looked at each other over her head. Then Andrew hid behind his glass.

"Shall we tell her?" murmured Rodney, who had no glass to hide behind.

"Do you. think we'd better?" asked Andrew anxiously.

"You tell her," said Rodney. "You've known her longer than I have."

"No, you tell her," insisted Andrew. "She wouldn't believe me."

"Say, what is this?" Elizabeth demanded. "I ask a simple question—"

"She asks a simple question!" Rodney exclaimed, and came and sat down on the arm of her chair and took one of her hands in his. "The fact is," he said tenderly, "you have hit the nail bang on its ~~silly~~ head. We don't know."

"You don't—! Oh, come, now, Rodney, that's absurd, you can't fool me, you wrote a book about it! You must know!"

"Very well," he sighed. "Instinct."

"But that's just a word!" she objected. ";That doesn't *explain* anything! You've got to do better than that!"

Rodney turned to catch Andrew's eyes.

"The woman *thinks!*" he marveled. "You keep on like this, Liz, and the first thing you know you'll see why I'm going on the trip!"

"You mean you might find out how they do it?"

"Well, not all in one blaze of light," he qualified, and rose from the arm of her chair. "I'll be seeing Rogers in the morning, sir— thought I'd go up and have a look at that bird."

"I might go with you," said Andrew, rising also. "Suppose I drive you up there, about ten o'clock."

"Up where?" queried Elizabeth jealously.

"The Zoo. Want to go along?"

107

"Not at ten in the morning!"

"I thought not! Good night, Liz." Andrew took her by the elbows and kissed her cheek, as was his established privilege. "Thank you for another delightful evening."

She followed them out into the foyer, and Rodney stood looking down at her, his hat in his hand.

"Good night, Liz. I'll phone you in the morning." His forefinger rested a moment beneath her tilted chin. "What time do you wake up?"

"If you can get any sense out of her before noon," said Andrew, "you're a better man than I am!"

"Good night," said Rodney again, confidentially, and they were gone.

X

When the telephone bell first cut across her consciousness the next morning, Elizabeth knew without opening her eyes who it would be, and reached for the receiver blindly and applied it to the ear which was not buried in the pillow.

"Hullo," she mumbled, wishing Gertrude would come in and shut the window, which Gertrude immediately did.

"Good morning," said Rodney. "Is this too early?"

"How early is it?"

"It's nine o'clock. Aren't you up yet?"

"Listen, Rodney, you might as well get used to the idea, I'm *never* up at nine o'clock!"

"I remember once you were. Twice in fact."

"I know! And look what happened!"

"You met me. Both times."

"So now I've learned my lesson. Now I stay in bed till noon!"

"I see," he said, amused. "That's an awful big bed you sleep in, Liz. Aren't you ever lonesome?"

"What a thing to ask a girl at nine in the morning!"

"I'll ask you again at nine this evening. How would that be?"

"Rodney, do you always wake up as bright as this?"

"What do you mean, wake up? I had breakfast an hour ago!"

"Come have another breakfast with me here about an hour after we hang up. About ten-fifteen."

"By ten-fifteen I'll be on the way to the Zoo with Blaine."

"Must you go?"

"You heard me say I would, last night."

"He'd let you off."

"I can't let myself off. I wrote Rogers I'd be there this morning."

"Oh, why can't I hate you and be done with all this!" she wailed.

"Try," he said. "Try real hard. How far do you get with it?"

"Will you be back in time for lunch?"

"Yes, I'm lunching with Dr. Andrews, he—"

"That's fine!" she said cordially. "In that case you wouldn't be interested in having lunch with me. That's just dandy!"

"Well, you see, he gave up his week-end in the country on my account, and—"

"That's Big of him!"

"Well, yes, it is, you see there's a man just back from Costa Rica who—"

"Oh, *all right,* Rodney, I suppose you're taking tea with an Eskimo and dining with a Hottentot!"

"Not exactly. I'm dining with you."

"Are you sure about that?" she asked dangerously.

"I said dinner three weeks ago, and I meant dinner. Seven o'clock this evening, black tie. Liz—are you there?"

"No, I don't think I am," she said slowly, and hung up on him.

Rodney stared at the dead receiver in his hand, and then with one eyebrow cocked he picked up his hat and fled along the passage to Andrew's room.

"I seem to have put my foot in it," he said, and gave Andrew the gist of his conversation with Elizabeth. "She's furious. She hung up on me. She doesn't seem to realize that when I haven't been in New York for months there are people I have to see—especially with a thing like this trip coming on. I never said I'd see her before dinner time today. I'm a little out of my depth, sir. What do I do now?"

Andrew pondered a minute.

"Call her back on my phone," he said.

"I—don't think she's speaking to me."

"She's had time to cool off. I'll talk to her myself if you like."

110

Rodney sat down obediently at Andrew's telephone and called Elizabeth's number. Gertrude answered. There was a pause. Then—

"Miss Dare says she will speak to you at seven o'clock this evening," said Gertrude unhappily.

"I told you," said Rodney to Andrew. "She won't come to the phone."

Andrew took it out of Rodney's hand.

"Gertrude. This is Mr. Blaine. Find out if Miss Elizabeth will speak to me."

Another pause, while they looked at each other with the mutual guilt which overtakes grown males who find themselves on the wrong end of female perversity.

Then came Elizabeth's voice, so pitched as to be plainly audible to Rodney through the receiver which Andrew held.

"Whatever you're going to say, Andrew, *no!* Take little Rodney to the Zoo and let him watch the monkeys and listen to the lions roar. Then give him a Fiji Islander for lunch, and take him to the movies, or to *church,* for all I care, but keep him out of my sight till seven o'clock if you don't want his throat cut!"

They both winced as her receiver banged on the cradle, and then they sat shaking their heads at each other.

"It looks pretty bad," said Rodney.

"She's spoilt," said Andrew philosophically, never having run afoul of it himself before. "You must expect that with Liz. People like Stanley have spoilt her."

"Yes, that reminds me, who is this Stanley?"

"He's a publisher."

"What else?"

"Seems to have a lot of spare time. You must remember that Liz is used to queening it. A man like yourself with a mind of his own is bound to be in for some fireworks. But don't let her scare you. Don't give in to her too much."

"Give in to her! I couldn't, even if I wanted to! I suppose I

111

should have left more time for her today—lunch or something—but to tell the truth, I never thought about it, I had a lot of things to see to, and—anyway, I'd no idea she'd get mad at me like that, I—"

"My boy," said Andrew, and the lines in his lean cheeks were very deep, "the time to worry is when Liz *doesn't* get mad if you don't take her to lunch!"

"I guess you're right," said Rodney, with a reluctant grin.

They set out together for the Zoo.

About five that afternoon the house telephone rang in Elizabeth's apartment, and Andrew said he was downstairs and could he come up. Elizabeth said he could.

He found her in a very fetching house-coat, dark brown velvet with a golden silk panel let into the front. The day had turned cold and wet, and she was drinking China tea in front of a wood fire with some knitting in her hands and the radio bringing a symphony orchestra into the room. It was as pretty a picture as you could wish to see, and Andrew surveyed it with appreciation as he entered.

"Tea's just come in," she greeted him, and lifted up her cheek for his kiss. "Have some?"

"Please."

"It was nice of you to come and keep me company in my—bereavement," she said. "Ring the bell for another cup, darling."

But Gertrude was already in the room with another cup in her hand.

"Liz, I won't have you bullying that man," said Andrew, sitting down with his tea on the other end of the davenport.

"Did he burst into tears?" she inquired with interest.

"He did not."

"Was he angry?"

"Not visibly."

"Didn't he react at all?"

112

"In a—bewildered sort of way. Do you really want to know why he didn't leave more time for you today? He never thought of it."

"Next time he will!"

"You're up against something, Liz. That's a real man you've got there, not a stuffed shirt."

"So what?" murmured Elizabeth, knitting very fast.

"So you look out. Why do you suppose he hasn't married long before now? Because half a dozen other women before you have fumbled it, that's why. Don't think nobody else has tried, Liz. Don't think he isn't woman-conscious. There's nothing wrong with him, you're not the first woman in his life. Do you know why all the others lost him?"

"Well, at least one of them married somebody else because she got tired waiting for Rodney to propose, but I've no complaints along that line."

"Much against my principles, I am giving free advice today," said Andrew. "It may never happen again. Are you listening?"

"Yes, Andrew, why *did* all the others lose him?"

"Vanity."

"I don't think I follow."

Andrew sighed.

"When I realize I'm doing all I know to pitch you into Rodney Monroe's arms," he said, "I am aghast. I adore you, Liz. I have dreaded the day when you might marry again. I was selfish enough almost to hope it might never come. But I seem to have changed my mind."

"Why—Andrew—" The knitting-needles were quiet now.

"I changed it last night, before I left here. It was still changed this morning, when he came into my room to say he had got a little out of his depth with you. Liz, you owe him an apology. Not in so many words, that would only embarrass him. But see that you treat him right when he comes tonight."

"How the masculine element does stick together!" she marveled, for from Andrew this was treason.

113

"Stop it, Liz. Tell me truthfully, Are you in love with him?"

"You know I am. I told you at lunch that day."

"Then learn humility. Go down on your knees and thank God for him. Get rid, right now, of any idea of punishing him for daring to live his own life today. A woman has not begun to love," said Andrew a little didactically, "until first she has made herself humble, until mentally she has put his slippers to warm before the fire and set a lighted candle in the window. Unless you can be grateful that Rodney Monroe is taking you to dinner tonight, instead of holding it against him that he didn't take you to lunch as well—you aren't worth his trouble."

"Well, really, Andrew!" But it was rather a subdued voice she protested in. "That's as much as to say I have no rights at all!"

"Rights? There are no rights in love!" he cried impatiently. "There are only privileges. You are the woman he comes to at the end of the day. What more can you ask?"

"But, Andrew, I don't—think—I—" She was almost inaudible now.

"You have wit and charm and beauty, and something else there is no word for," he went on remorselessly. "What good is all that to you unless it is for him? And what good is it to him if it is all hedged round with a shopworn routine of whims and clichés and childish squabbles? I am a jealous man, Liz, and I prize our friendship more than you can ever know. If it were Stanley or Dick Mason or some one of those blighters, I'd sit back and let you muck it up any way you chose and never lift a finger to put things right. But it's Rodney Monroe. That's why I'm here, to say to you—The time is short, even when you're young. Don't waste any of it. Give him the surprise of his life when he comes here tonight. Forget the act, Liz. Be yourself. Nothing else is good enough for him."

"You know what will happen if I do that?"

"I think so."

"And have I your blessing on that as well?"

114

Andrew stood up, looking a little tired. She rose too, and laid the knitting aside, and gave him both her hands, along with an apologetic sort of smile.

"Wouldn't it be a funny thing," he said, "if I knew him better than you do?" Then he kissed her on both cheeks, and left her. At the door he turned. "Never tell him I was here," he said, and went.

XI

Thus it came about that when Rodney rang Elizabeth's doorbell at seven o'clock that evening, he expected almost anything but what he got.

The first thing that happened to him was Gertrude, who opened the door with a bright smile, and received his hat in reverent hands. The next thing he encountered was an empty drawing-room, festively lighted, but devoid of even Snorky's welcoming presence. Rodney sat down, rather warily, on the end of the davenport in front of the fire. Going to keep him waiting. He knew all about that one. He was not prepared, however, for the prompt arrival of a superb-looking Old-fashioned on Gertrude's silver tray.

"Miss Elizabeth was kept on the telephone," said Gertrude in her soft voice. "She'll be in soon."

"Thank you," said Rodney, reaching for the cocktail, which he felt a distinct need of.

Next appeared Snorky, pelting down the passage to sit at his idol's feet, pink tongue hanging.

"Hullo," said Rodney, and raised his glass. "How about you and me getting drunk together when she's finished telling me where I head in?"

Lastly came Elizabeth herself, who, so far from being kept on the telephone, had been standing for the past few minutes in front of a mirror in the gold gown trying to get the shake out of her knees before her entrance; a more than usually beautiful Liz, if possible; smiling, composed, and friendly, not even wearing an orphan-face—with that touching, expectant flare to her eyelashes.

116

"Hullo, Rodney," she said meekly, and as he unfolded from the davenport to meet her she laid down the fur wrap she carried and came straight up to him and gave him her hand.

His incredulous eyes went from her upturned face to the intricate dress she wore.

"By golly, it *is* cloth-of-gold!" he said.

"I promised you it would be. I always keep my promises."

"Then promise now to love me always," he said, and was overheard by Gertrude, who was coming in with Elizabeth's Martini on the tray and a plate of canapés in her other hand.

Elizabeth touched her glass to his.

"Here's to Always," she said, and drank.

Rodney, who was still waiting for the catch in all this, began to look a little dazed.

"No scrap?" he ventured cautiously.

"No scrap."

"Well, thank God for that, I thought you were sore at me!"

"I was. You woke me up at nine in the morning and then left me with the whole day on my hands. But now the day is gone, and you're here, so—hooray."

"Liz," he said, "every time I see you, you make less sense than any other woman I ever saw before. Maybe that's why I get crazier about you all the time."

"Do you, Rodney?" Her eyes were innocent and pleased.

"Let's go gay," he said. "Or maybe you think a professor doesn't know how."

"Well—how gay?"

"As gay as it's possible to go on a Sunday night in a black tie. You know, that gown calls for something much more special than what I had in mind."

"What did you have in mind? Now, please, never mind the dress—let's do whatever it was you thought of!"

"Well, I thought we'd start with dinner at the St. Regis and a couple of dances. O.K.?"

117

"O.K."

"Then, if you don't like the way I dance, or if we run out of anything to talk about, I was going to suggest that I know where there's a Dietrich film, and we might get in in time for the last show. I sort of go for her."

"You're sure I don't remind you of her?"

"Quite sure," he grinned.

"All right, then, we'll see it."

"Liz, you're kind of fun. I just thought I'd mention it."

"Let's see what you say by the end of the evening."

"Now, at nine o'clock I mustn't forget to ask you—"

"Hand me that wrap and let's go to the St. Regis."

"Yes'm, that's just what I was going to do."

Take notice of a man the waiters adore at sight. He's got something. Liz Dare had seldom been seated and served with more punctilio and solicitude and flourish than was commanded by the unaggressive presence of Rodney at the St. Regis.

"Have you got ideas?" he inquired as the menus were put into their hands, "or will you leave this to me?"

"Gladly," she said, and laid down the card at once, and thought— All right, Rodney. Do your stuff.

The meal which followed maintained his prestige with the staff and delighted her critical palate. Rodney knew his way around a menu, that was plain. Dry champagne, too. Nice and dry. Chalk up another one for Aunt Virginia.

After that, Elizabeth was hardly surprised that he danced like something straight from heaven, with a subtle lag in tempo that you have to be born with. He had also a trick of cutting through an open space on the floor which twice turned her head over her right shoulder, when he said gently, "I can see where we're going, Miss Dare, just relax." The slow waltz finished her off entirely. By the end of it she was nestled against him in a sort of blissful coma.

"Well, I finally got you tamed," he remarked as they reached

118

the table and he slid her chair under her. "I thought I never would."

"How was I to know you'd dance like something I've always dreamed about?"

"Do you know now?"

"You're wonderful!"

"Don't forget," he said matter-of-factly.

"Rodney. Tell me the story of your life."

"What, *now?*" he queried, looking shocked. "With the salad and cheese coming in? Liz, there's a time and a place for everything!"

She sat looking at him, well, *gloating* at him, her elbows on the table and her chin in her hands, while the waiter hovered devoutly above him, serving the salad.

"When were you born?" she asked with seeming irrelevance when the waiter had gone.

"You couldn't do it in your head," he said. "I've been thirty-two for several months now."

"Oh, God, are you as young as *that?*"

"I'll be gray around the ears soon enough if this goes on," he told her moodily. "I've an idea you can age a man pretty rapidly. And how about yourself, grandma, which side were you on in the Civil War?"

"Well, it's only fair to tell you, I've been twenty-nine for several years now."

"That's a nice age," he remarked thoughtfully. "Maybe I should have stopped there myself."

"Don't you care?"

"All I really care about," he said, "is the water that has run under bridges since 1930 when I first saw you, singing that one little number at the Winter Garden. Why I didn't get busy right then, I can't think."

"You were still in school!"

119

"And you were already married. So what. So we've wasted a lot of time. Let's dance this."

If you really danced with Rodney it was impossible to talk to him at the same time. They returned to the table to drink their coffee, and the bill arrived at the lift of his eyelid, and he said—

"Now, I don't want to hurry you, but—"

The film was at a modest re-run theater on a side street—one of the little dark ones. Rodney slipped off her wrap and laid it expertly round her shoulders, and all in the same movement took possession of her hand—also expertly and without pinning her arm to the arm of the seat between them; but Elizabeth had not had her hand held in a movie for a long, long time, and therefore did not fully appreciate his skill in that respect.

She surrendered her fingers to his clasp with a sense of complete unreality. This is me, Liz Dare, she thought, sitting in a third-rate movie house having my hand held, and I like it. It's second childhood, that's what it is.

She was very silent in the cab going home, even after he had with his usual presence of mind closed the glass between them and the driver.

"Tired?" he said, and she shook her head. "Cold? Sleepy? Bored? I give up."

"I'm happy," she murmured. "You might have known it by sight."

"Spell it," he suggested, and took her hand again.

"It's the nicest evening I've ever had, Rodney."

"Well, thanks," he said, and held her fingers briefly against his lips. "Considering some of the evenings you must have had, that is a real compliment to me. What's so special about tonight? Name three, I dare you."

"Tall, dark, and handsome—able to order a meal—able to get round a dance floor—and on top of all that, I think you're the *kindest* creature I ever knew."

"Let's see, now. Tall, yes, I admit that. Dark—your eyes are

120

brown and mine are sort of gray. Handsome—maybe you'd better look again where the light is better. It doesn't take any particular amount of imagination to order a meal like that, beef if it is properly cooked is still the best food in any language. One of the things they taught me at college was not to fall over my own feet while the dance-band was playing or while I was carrying the ball. As for the last part—do people usually kick you downstairs?"

"Mentally, at least verbally, quite often."

He pondered this.

"Oh, well, I don't think I have the makings of a wife-beater," he decided, it seemed with regret.

"Pity," said Elizabeth.

"It is too bad. Because I've an idea you're going to need it now and then."

"I'm not going to marry you, you know."

"You're not," he said. "So I'm going to have trouble with you about that. I thought maybe by now—"

"Don't argue, Rodney, please! You know it's better not. Besides —I'm older than you are."

"Is *that* what's on your mind!" he exclaimed, enlightened.

"That's what settles it," she sighed, and the cab stopped in front of her address.

"We'll go into what settles it when we get upstairs."

Once more he fitted her key into a door, and they entered a warm, lighted room. A tray with whiskey and soda and glasses and an ice-bucket was on the table.

"You can have hot milk if you'd rather," she offered. "I'm going to." She rang the bell.

"All right, I will. I'm cold sober now, I might as well stay that way while we figure things out. Let me take that." He laid competent hands on the fur wrap on her shoulders.

"I'll go tell 'em in the kitchen you want milk, else we'll only get—one glass—between us—" Her voice faded away breathlessly, for she had caught his eyes. His hands were still on her shoulders.

121

"Here we go again," he whispered, and kissed her. "It's been too long—much too long," he said then. "Come here, I want another." He took it.

"Look out, Rodney, I've rung the bell!"

"I'll teach you to ring bells!" he muttered, and lifted her off her feet and sat down with her on his lap in a big chair.

"Rodney, she'll bring the milk!"

"Let her, she might as well get used to this!"

With a little sound, half laugh, half sob, she nestled against his shoulder.

"You make it so difficult for me to be sane and sensible and do the right thing for you!"

"I'm the one that's being sane," he pointed out. "I'm the one that knows we're licked. We can't dodge this, Liz—any more than we can dodge tomorrow's sunrise. You wouldn't know about that, though, you probably never saw one."

"I saw one once."

"I'll show you sunrises," he promised, his lips in her hair.

It was Mary who brought the hot milk, because Gertrude had not yet got back from the movies. Rodney looked up at her without any embarrassment, while Elizabeth, who until now had managed to keep her private life out of the servants' view, buried her face against him like an ostrich and pretended she wasn't there at all.

"Good evening, Mary," said Rodney politely. "Just set it down. Don't congratulate me yet, but I think I'm making progress."

Mary gave him her indulgent smile, put the tray down on the coffee-table near by, and left the room.

"Oddly enough," said Rodney, "there are two glasses of hot milk. Liz—? Liz, for the love of God, you're not *crying!*" He pushed back her hair. His fingers touched her cheek and came away wet. "Is that my fault? I never meant to make you cry." He found her chin and turned it upward. Her eyes were swimming, her cheeks shone in the lamplight, her lips were unsteady. He felt now as

122

though he had struck the orphan child with a baseball bat. "Honey, whatever it is, I never meant to, I'll never do it again, I'm sorry, I apologize, I grovel, I'm lower than a snake's belly, only tell me why you're crying!" He took out his handkerchief and began to dry her. Even in her anguish, she noticed that he knew enough to *pat* a woman dry instead of scrubbing her make-up all over her face. (Who taught him that?) Gratefully she offered herself to his dexterous handkerchief. But more tears came as fast as he mopped them up, and her breath quivered sharply through her open lips. "You're very beautiful when you're half drowned, but all the same I'd feel better if you'd stop now," he said. "Is there any way to turn off the tap?"

"R-Rodney—"

"Yes, my darling. Tell me."

Instantly she was flooded again.

"You m-mustn't say things like that! Here I am t-trying to pull myself together so we can drink the m-milk before it gets cold, and you call me d-darling *for the first time!*" she wailed, and hid herself again in his shirt-front.

"All right, go ahead and howl," he said philosophically, and slid down in the chair and crossed his legs underneath her so that she would be more comfortable (who taught him that? not Aunt Virginia) and held her so close that her sobs shook them both. "That's the stuff. Get it out of your system."

Gratitude of an abysmal nature contributed to her collapse. A man who didn't get angry, or bored, or derisive, if you cried? A man who didn't go out and bang the door? A man, moreover, who was content to make you comfortable while you did it, content to wait till you came round, content to let you be a fool in your own way while his milk cooled on the table? Oh, Rodney, you are the *kindest* creature! Completely undone by the luxury of his behavior, she held to him convulsively and howled.

"There," he said, when the storm at last had spent itself. "That

123

was quite a cry. You'll feel better now. Handkerchief?" He put it in her groping hand.

"I'm so sorry, Rodney, I never meant to d-drench you."

"Maybe I had it coming to me," he remarked with equanimity. "Think nothing of it." She felt his balance shift under her in the chair as he reached a long arm for the milk. "Have some of this. Neat."

"I'm not drunk, Rodney, honest."

"Who said you were? Here."

Like a child, she drank while he held the glass.

"It didn't get so c-cold, after all."

He drank from the same glass.

"How would it be if I put a little whiskey in it?" he asked.

"You can't reach the whiskey from here," she said, and nestled.

"True," he agreed. "It's better without."

They shared the milk, until the glass was empty, and Elizabeth drew a long sigh of exhaustion.

"I must be getting heavy," she said. "I guess I can stand up to things now."

"I'm still waiting to know what happened." He made no move to oust her.

"I'll tell you exactly what happened. I was trying to get myself screwed up to send you away Forever, and you were so sweet to me—"

"Was that what you were trying to do? I wondered. It didn't seem to work, did it!"

"But, Rodney, I—"

"Liz, wait. Sit still and listen to me." He laid his cheek against hers. "Let's do it the hard way. Let's get married now—before I go."

She was suddenly so still she hardly seemed to breathe. It wasn't any use any more, she was thinking. There was something in knowing when you were licked. We were both wrong, Marcia. When it's Rodney you take what there is to have and are grateful.

124

Go down on your knees and thank God for him, Andrew said. He said something else, too. The time is short, he said, even when you're young. Already they had wasted ten years. Be yourself, Liz—

Rodney was looking down at her.

"No argument?" he whispered.

"Whatever you want—whenever you want it." Her eyes met his, and he knew what she meant, and smiled before he kissed her.

"Well, now we're getting some place," he said a few minutes later. "Let's see, now—watch me try to think, this ought to be good!—I can't get down here again till Wednesday afternoon. We can get the license hocus-pocus over then, and have dinner together. And on Saturday I can get here before noon, and we can be married and have the week-end somewhere. That's all a college professor is entitled to for a honeymoon. What's the matter? Is Saturday too soon for you?"

She shook her head. She was looking a little puzzled.

"Do you want to be married in church," he went on gravely, "or do you prefer the City Hall?"

"City Hall will do," she answered, dazed.

"Got your divorce papers handy? You may have to show 'em."

"Walter's dead now," she told him, feeling in a trance.

"Then you won't need 'em," he decided matter-of-factly. "Hadn't we better ask Blaine to give you away at the wedding?"

She nodded, speechlessly.

"Let him do the rest of the thinking for us, then, that's all I'm good for—at the moment. Liz, darling, I'll make you happy somehow, and I promise *never* to kick you downstairs! And now," he added a few minutes later, "would you mind if I did have that whiskey?" Quite firmly, with no further foolishness, he put her off his lap and rose and poured out a stiff drink. "How about you?"

"No, thanks." She came and knelt on the davenport, watching him at the tray.

"You're so quiet," he said, as the soda fizzed into his glass. "Are you having regrets already?"

125

"I was just thinking—that nothing I've got is quite good enough for you."

It was the first time she had ever seen him even for a moment nonplused. He hesitated, the glass half way to his lips, thrown right out of his stride.

"If you say that again in a week's time, I'll deal with it," he said. "Not tonight." With his eyes on hers over the brim of his glass he drank deeply. Then he looked at his watch. "I'm taking myself out of here. Now."

"Rodney—"

"I know. Don't say it." He set down the glass with a little click of finality.

"I was only going to say that you might get the license tomorrow morning if—"

"I've got a faculty meeting tomorrow morning."

"Is that terribly important?"

"I have to be there. My leave of absence for the spring term will come up."

"I'd—forgotten about that," she said faintly.

"I hadn't. That's why Saturday. Among other things." He came to her, set his forefinger under her chin, kissed her lightly, and set her free. "Good night. I'll be here on Wednesday, early in the afternoon."

She followed to the doorway of the drawing-room, watching while he picked up his hat.

"Now, behave yourself," he said. "I'm going. Oh, all right—one more."

When the door had closed behind him she put out the lights in the drawing-room and went thoughtfully down the· passage towards a bath and bed. Well, Snorky, he's ours, won't you be pleased!

Again she stood before a mirror and looked at herself in the gold gown. So you're going to be married, Liz. Six days from now. And you said you never would. You said Anything But That.

126

You meant it, too. But that was before Rodney. It may be a funny thing, but Andrew knew him better than you did! Well, how was I to know there was anybody like Rodney? Look at—well, look at a lot of other people. Stanley, for instance, or Dick Mason—or Walter, for that matter, who married you how long ago—yes, take a good look at Walter, a week before he married you! Rodney needn't ever know how that was. Rodney needn't know how stupid you were when you were young. Young? When was I ever young? I wonder if Walter really was as drunk as I thought he was, that time—I wonder— Stop it, Liz. You've forgotten that. That never happened to you at all. That was two other fellows—

Wake up, Snorky, he's going to marry us, did you hear? We're going to live with him, now, there's going to come a time when a door doesn't close behind him. Live with him where? We didn't get that far. What about Aunt Virginia? I never thought about her. How about that week-end honeymoon, will it be here or—where? A lot of things seem to have slipped our minds. Well, a woman does sort of like to know where her honeymoon is going to be. Look who's talking, what sort of honeymoon did you have last time? That wasn't exactly Niagara Falls! Oh, forget it, can't you—

Wherever Rodney is, it will be a honeymoon. Well, yes, there's no getting round that. What you meant to say is, so long as Rodney is there you don't care where you are. Atlantic City. That's a bit crowded with memories, isn't it? There are lots of places up the Hudson. He'll think of something. You've got somebody to think for you now. *I can see where we're going, Miss Dare—*

Godalmighty, what about the show? Pete will be fit to be tied. Andrew will have to Handle It. Of course I might still do the show in the spring, while Rodney is migrating. Where will I be then, I wonder. Will I keep this place on? I'd better. What becomes of Mary and Gertrude? Liz, you can't do it. Oh, can't I!

Wednesday will fix it. Dinner on Wednesday. Then we'll know. Go to bed, Liz, you're all in. It's an awful big bed you sleep in. All right, Rodney, I'll be lonesome—

XII

So resigned had she become to his habits of non-communication that on Tuesday morning she had opened his letter before she realized that the small, neat handwriting (with tidy tails to the y's and the t's tidily crossed and the margin as straight as though it had been ruled) was Rodney's. It had already lain around for half an hour with the rest of her mail while she read the paper and drank her orange juice in bed.

My Dearest [it began]

This, in case it doesn't turn out the way I mean it to, is a love letter. I haven't had much practice.

First of all, we forgot about asking Aunt Virginia to the wedding. I have remedied this—hastily. She'll never feel we're legally married unless she sees it done, especially as you're an actress, which is something we've never had in the family before. But don't get the idea that Aunt Virginia has any objection. On the contrary, she's like me, she can't wait.

There is one thing, though. Aunt Virginia is the daughter and the sister of a clergyman, and I am a clergyman's son—and the moral of that is, we don't get by with a City Hall ceremony. Aunt Virginia is willing to settle for the Church of the Transfiguration, and to save me time on Wednesday she has already written to make the arrangements. If possible, we will use the chapel. So think round now among your friends and decide if there's anyone else you want there besides Blaine. His sister was kind of nice, I thought. I shall bring Charles with me, of course, now's his chance to be Best Man with a flower in his buttonhole.

128

Also, I must remember to write down on Wednesday the names of your father and mother, and your own middle name—mine's Bagehot, by the way—for the notices which Aunt Virginia is preparing for the newspapers. And she has just now put her head around the door and said What about the announcements, meaning the ones to be engraved and sent out by mail, I suppose. I replied, with my usual presence of mind, that if anybody knew What about them, she did. And she said Blarney, and went away.

Now, see what you think of this. Aunt Virginia has a farm in Connecticut, and when I say farm I mean farm, an old white house with a porch, under old elm trees, full of old furniture, and the oldest local inhabitant to take care of it. It has what are called Modern Conveniences, but no furbelows. It's about three hours' drive from New York—less from here. We could be there by mid-afternoon on Saturday and we'd have to leave after dinner on Sunday evening. But we'd have it all to ourselves—except for the oldest inhabitant, who is a very good cook—and that has certain advantages over Atlantic City. (I'm sorry there isn't really time for Niagara Falls.) It's only a suggestion, maybe you've thought of a place you'd like better, but I'm trying not to spring all this on you without any warning on Wednesday, when I arrive with a list as long as your arm of things Aunt Virginia has thought of. (You'll find a letter from her in the same mail, I believe.)

I knew this wasn't going to turn out well as a love letter, so far it sounds more like a questionnaire. But there's one thing more to go into. You've never seen this house. Aunt Virginia and I have lived in it for five years, and I've got sort of used to it, but she says it may seem very pokey to my new, forgive me, bird of paradise. Do you want to come up and see it before Saturday? (I have just been in and had a look at the guest room, and I must say I got a very queer feeling where my stomach used to be.) Otherwise, I shall simply bring you here on Sunday evening and carry you over the threshold in the regulation cave-man style. Aunt Virginia, being the soul of tact and discretion, plans to remain in New

129

York indefinitely, she says, and hear some music. She is a solitary drinker when it comes to symphony concerts. Will you want to bring your own maid, that's another question which has come up. We have two.

It is getting more complicated by the minute, I'd better stop now. There is a good deal in favor of a desert island, isn't there.

That's all I have to say until Wednesday. Except this: I shall love you till I die.

Rodney

When she had read it twice through, Elizabeth lay back against the pillows feeling distinctly shaken. Snorky, who had been sitting patiently on the floor beside her slippers for a long time waiting to be spoken to, couldn't bear it any longer and jumped up on the bed and approached Rodney's letter where it lay on the coverlet between her hands. Elizabeth snatched it away from him as though he could read, folded it, and put it back in its envelope. Then she sifted the pile for Aunt Virginia's.

My dear Elizabeth—

I have just heard a rumor to the effect that Rodney has taken leave of his senses and plans to be married on Saturday. Because he is such a clam, I was barely aware that he was acquainted with you, although a picture of you, cut from a magazine, has adorned his bureau in a silver frame for years. Or am I giving something away?

He doesn't have to tell me that you are beautiful, but I am glad to learn that you are pretty sweet. He will be good to you, my dear, because there isn't a malicious bone in his body. Just go on being sweet to him, that's all I ask. And try to love me a little, for I am prepared to do as much for you.

Sincerely,
Aunt Virginia

When Elizabeth had read this one through twice over too, she reached for the telephone.

130

"Andrew, I've let myself in for a great deal more than we ever dreamed," she began in an awed voice. "First of all, Rodney's middle name is B-a-g-e-h-o-t. How do you say it?"

"*Baj*jut."

"That's wonderful. 'His moth-ah was a *Baj*jut.' I suppose that's why we've got to be married at the Church of the Transfiguration, and there are going to be engraved announcements sent out, and who do I want to ask to the wedding?"

"Whom," said Andrew.

"Yes, and he's arriving here on Wednesday with a questionnaire as long as my arm. Andrew, I'm from the wrong side of the tracks, I don't know what to do about all this."

"Would Minnie be of any use to you? She'll be back on Friday."

"Gosh, yes, I'm beginning to think I don't even know the Facts of Life! But it's tomorrow I've got to see him."

"Well, why worry, if he knows what to do? Now, don't panic, Liz, just bring him along to my office as I told you yesterday. I've spoken to the City Clerk and he's willing to make out the license in his private office, which allows you to dodge the Press boys in the big room, and he'll give you time to get out of the building before he files it."

"Well, that helps. You know, Andrew, I don't think it's even occurred to him yet that he's marrying a notorious character, and as for this church ceremony, it's *fatal,* they're sure to spot me now—"

"That will give Aunt Virginia something to think about, won't it!"

"I feel like a keg of dynamite just before it blows up in baby's face," she said.

"I'll tell Minnie you want to have tea with her on Friday and go into things, shall I?"

"Yes, please, and ask her to stand by me at the wedding. He says we'll use the chapel, whatever that means."

"Because it's smaller, I expect."

131

"Oh. I thought maybe it was Higher. No first night was ever like this! I'm right off my feed already."

"I'll tell you something, Liz. So is he."

Andrew was a great comfort.

He was a comfort even to the self-possessed Rodney when it came to getting the license. It was after three on Wednesday when Rodney arrived at Elizabeth's apartment, and Andrew's car and driver were already waiting at the curb. Elizabeth, feeling very gone inside, had been walking up and down the floor with her hat on. She opened the door to him herself.

"I'm late," he said unnecessarily. "Traffic's terrible. Aren't you going to kiss me, or am I on a diet?"

She kissed him.

"Andrew's sent his car for us," she said, as soon as she could. "We're to pick him up at his office. He's going with us, so the City Clerk will make out the license in his private office."

"That's fine. What's the hurry?"

"The Bureau closes at four. Do you want this license or don't you?"

"I certainly do. What a wonderful hat! I did say I loved you, didn't I. All right, where's your coat?" He put her into it, and she started for the door. "I never did see anybody in such a hurry to get married," he murmured.

"Well, it was your idea in the first place." She paused with her hand on the inside of the door. "And if you mean to do it this week we have to start now, that's all. I don't want to rush you into anything."

"Let's start now," he said.

In the car on the way down town he put a small square box into her hand and said—

"Maybe the City Clerk would think better of us if you wear a ring while you sign your life away."

She opened it on a big aquamarine, exquisitely cut and set— which was pretty subtle of him.

132

"Oh, *Rodney—!*" she got out, before her throat closed and her eyes filled.

"The question is, does it fit." He pulled off her glove, slid the ring on to her finger and kissed it into place.

"Rodney, I never had an engagement ring b-before. I think I'm going to cry."

"What, *again?*" But his eyes were kind.

With the co-operation of his friend the City Clerk, Andrew saw them through the License Bureau and got them out the back way and down the stairs and into his car.

The drive up town, through traffic and a misty rain, was slow. Instead of dropping Andrew off at the Club they persuaded him to come back to Elizabeth's apartment for a drink. By the time the car drew up outside the building where she lived a half dozen men in raincoats with cameras or folded newspapers in their hands had gathered round the end of the awning.

"Oh-oh," said Elizabeth, spotting them first. "Rodney, meet the Press! Keep smiling, no matter what they say, never answer back, stick close to mother, and don't by any chance bolt for the door."

The car stopped, the doorman stepped forward, the cameras went up into action like a sort of salute, Andrew stepped out and turned to give Elizabeth his hand as she followed.

"Hullo, boys, that was quick work!" she said quietly, and paused with one foot on the step while the flash bulbs blazed.

"Attagirl, Liz!"

"When's the wedding, Miss Dare?"

"Give us a *beeg* smile, Liz!"

"Where did you get him, Liz?"

"Boys, this is Dr. Monroe," she said calmly, as Rodney joined her on the pavement. "Treat him just the way you would me!" And she gave them her delightful, ~~painted~~ smile.

The bulbs flashed again, and she started towards the door, linked to Rodney's arm on one side and Andrew's on the other. As they crossed the sidewalk—

133

"When's the wedding, Liz?"

"Not for weeks. I'll let you know."

"When's the new show?"

"In the spring. We've got leading-man trouble."

"Sure you won't go domestic on us now?"

"Why would I do that?"

"Where did you meet him, Liz?"

"Up in Maine—summer vacation—love at first sight—you can say I am ver-ee, ver-ee happy. Now, run along, boys, see you at the wedding!"

The glass doors swung to behind them.

"Well, that's that!" said Andrew with relief.

"Could have been worse. I'm sorry, Rodney, these things will happen."

"They like you," he said, thinking it over in the elevator. "They're all for you, Liz—why should I kick?"

"They'd better be for me, I've spent half my time wiping their noses for years!"

"They'll be down on you if we do dodge them on Saturday," said Andrew.

"Every man for himself," she reminded him. "Dodging the Press, if you can do it, is all just good clean fun and no holds barred!"

A wood fire burned in the drawing-room, and the lights were on in the drizzly twilight. She left them alone together and went to remove her hat, returning in a remarkably short time wearing a blue velvet house-coat whose highlights matched the new ring. A few minutes later Gertrude came in with glasses on a tray and hot canapés.

"It's pretty early to start drinking," said Elizabeth, "but it's a dretful night outside for man or beast. Andrew, God bless you— we'd never have made it without you. Stand by us, won't you!"

"Forevermore," he said rather solemnly, and they drank to it.

When he had gone Rodney and Elizabeth sat down on the davenport and talked their own brand of nonsense for a while.

134

Then Rodney appeared suddenly to recollect himself and took a folded paper out of an inner pocket. It was a list, in his tidy handwriting.

"Now, while I am still more or less conscious," he began, "we'd better write down the answers."

"Do I have to hold up my right hand and swear?"

"Yes. Middle name of the bride?"

"So far as I know, I haven't got one."

Elizabeth Adair, he wrote.

"Father's name?"

"Jack. Well, maybe John."

He wrote *John.*

"Mother's name was Bessie," she continued. "No, I suppose it must have been Elizabeth to begin with."

He wrote *Elizabeth.*

"Where did they live?"

"In their trunk. I was born there."

"Shall I say 'of New York City?'"

"You might as well."

"What was Walter's other name?"

"Trent. Does that have to go in?"

"It seems to be customary, in the newspaper notices, to mention former marriages if any, at the end. When did he die?"

"About two years ago. I only happened to see it in the paper because it got a quarter column. 'Found dead.' One of those things."

Rodney wrote *Trent—d. two years ago.*

"Now, about the At Home card," he said. "Shall I put my own address on it, assuming that you will be willing to live there, at least for a time? And are you coming up to look it over before Saturday? Aunt Virginia suggested you might come back with me tonight."

"Rodney, I'd rather not. Would she mind awfully?"

"Of course not. Just as you like."

"Please, it's only that I can't walk into Aunt Virginia's home

135

like a prospective t-tenant inspecting something that's for rent!"

"She'll understand that, I think. I'll use my address, then, for the card. Maybe when I get back from this trip we can find a place you'd like better."

"Why wouldn't I like this one? Rodney, can't you see—why should I care if it's this house or a house two blocks down the street, so long as you're in it too? What does it matter to me if the front door opens east, west, north, or south, so long as you walk in at the end of the day?"

His eyes rested on her thoughtfully for a moment. Then he said—

"It's difficult for me to concentrate when you say things like that. And I have to concentrate—a little longer." He crossed off *Visit* on the list. "Now, about the farm—do you want to go up there on Saturday?"

"Yes. I think it sounds perfect."

"Then I'll bring the car down." He crossed off *Honeymoon. Rings,* which came next, was already crossed off. "Aunt Virginia thinks we ought to have lunch before we start. The wedding's set for noon, by the way."

"I don't know where the Church of the Transfiguration is," she said, "but I'm quite willing to be married in it so long as you're there to hold my hand."

He glanced at her humorously under his eyebrows.

"It is doubtless better known to you, my Heathen Bride, as the Little Church Around the Corner."

"Oh, that!" she cried, enlightened. "Dorothy Clark was married there. I was bridesmaid."

"Then you know where you are. Aunt Virginia suggested the Colony Club for luncheon."

Elizabeth suppressed an impulse to say She Would.

"Let's let Andrew give us all lunch at Minnie's house in Beekman Place and we'll dodge the camera boys," she said instead.

"Very well, lunch in Beekman Place, and we can leave in the car from there." He crossed off *Luncheon.*

136

"Rodney, you wrote something about Aunt Virginia's staying on in New York for a while. Why wouldn't it be a good idea if she lived here in my apartment? She could just move in as I move out, and Mary and Gertrude could look after her. Would she care for that?"

Rodney said he didn't see why not.

"Then I'll write a note and ask her. You can take it back with you."

"And that means, I gather, that you don't intend to bring Gertrude with you." He crossed off *Maid*.

"I want to bring Snorky, though."

"Naturally. I wouldn't have you as a gift without him. No others of your female friends coming to the wedding besides Blaine's sister?"

"No, I—don't think of anybody." She had found she was strangely shy of her wedding as regards people like Caroline Jones.

"That makes two corsages—Aunt Virginia and Miss Blaine," he said, accepting her decision without comment. "Three buttonholes —Charles and Blaine and me. And your bouquet. Any special requirements about that?"

"My dress is sort of a funny blue."

"I think roses," said Rodney, giving it deep thought. "There's a cream-colored kind, if I can find it. Thorley's may know. Will you like me in a white carnation, do you think, or will I look like a floor-walker? Now, stop it, Liz—stop it—" He got out his handkerchief.

"I n-never had a bouquet before—"

"Don't you want one this time?"

"Oh, *yes*, but—"

"Then stop crying! I never knew such a drippy bride as I've got! Here—look—here's your wedding-ring. Anything to distract your mind! But you'll have to give it back to me tonight so I can get it engraved inside."

137

"W-what are you going to put?"

"Don't you wish you knew? Maybe just our initials and the date. Maybe I've thought of something better. Does it fit? Now, don't tell me you didn't have a wedding-ring before!"

"It wasn't engraved," she said, gazing reverently through a blur at the chased white gold circlet he had laid in the palm of her hand. "And it always came off black on my finger."

Quite suddenly, quite blindingly, Rodney saw everything—saw past the luxurious dazzle of Liz Dare in her white apartment above the Park to a forlorn dancing kid who had stumbled into marriage with someone who was never sober, who never had any money, who married her with a cheap ring and no flowers, who only stood for something sordid and ugly and beastly, and who came to an ambiguous end; something that should never have happened to her—something that had left scars—something she must be made to forget as quickly as possible, for the orphan-look was real, and not a thing to be joked about ever again. Quite suddenly he reached for her, gathered her all anyhow into his arms, her face smothered against his shoulder, his buried in her hair.

"Liz, I'm not always as stupid as this—I told you I couldn't see straight. Well, now I can. I've been lying awake nights wondering how I had the nerve to marry Liz Dare—wondering how I could ever give her anything she hadn't already got too much of—"

"I tried to tell you what you could g-give her, and you said—"

"I said a lot of things I wish I hadn't. It was what they call a defense mechanism. Every time I tried to say the other things, the real things, I was afraid some other guy had said them to you first—and better. I couldn't seem to think of any new ones."

"Oh, but you did! In your letter. At the end. I've read it a dozen times, just to make sure it was there."

You could see that he remembered what it was. *I shall love you till I die.* The written words ran voicelessly through both their minds, as he sat looking down at her face against his shoulder.

"Dinner is served," said Gertrude softly from the doorway.

XIII

Doubtless because she was used to queening it, Elizabeth was able to take a college town in her stride. By Christmas time, even most of the wives liked her. She made mistakes, of course, but Rodney, whose own life had never been encircled by academic habit, was unperturbed by them. Snorky too, walking the campus as though he could lick several times his weight in wildcats, soon had everything in his department under control.

So it all came true, and they held hands in the village movie, and came home afterwards to a warm house to which Rodney carried the key. The house which Rodney had lived in for five years with Aunt Virginia had taken on, as houses must, something of their own personality. Although the drawing-room chintz was a little faded by now, the rooms were spacious and full of sunlight and warmth and books, the servants were middle-aged and smiling, the china and silver were old and exquisite, and the beds were large and comfortable.

"Are you happy?" Rodney would demand anxiously, at more or less frequent intervals. "Are you sure you're not bored up here in the backwoods? Shall we go down to New York next Saturday on a regular bender?"

But somehow the bender never came off. It was weeks before Elizabeth was able to elucidate to herself the secret of her pervading happiness. There was Rodney, of course, more charming each day, more fantastically considerate than any man had a right to be, more fun than any human being she had ever known. But even when Rodney had gone for the day, when she was left with hours to herself, the warm, beaming, exultant happiness did not abate. She seemed to stand back and *see* herself being happy, and marvel at her own capacity for contentment.

At last it dawned on her. Leisure. A gentle routine. Companionship. Cherishing. For the first time since she could remember, somebody else was writing the checks, earning the roof over her head, paying for the food which came to the table. If she did nothing for the rest of time, it would go on like this, because Rodney regarded it as his responsibility—he would have said his privilege—to feed and clothe and house her, while she did nothing but adorn his life.

She read ravenously, from a well-stocked family library—classics she had never known, books Rodney had loved as a child, new books she ordered as they came out. She made things for the house as diligently as a schoolgirl with a hope-chest—she had always loved to do needlework—initialing new linen absorbedly, re-covering worn sofa cushions with her own neat *gros-point*. After having left her own housekeeping wholly to Mary for years, she learned housekeeping now from the friendly, willing Anna and Theresa whom Aunt Virginia had trained in Rodney's ways and preferences. She had gone domestic in a big way, and she loved it.

Rodney, whose home had heretofore run itself behind his back without calling his attention to itself, was intrigued with her embellishments of his domestic scene. He was always an observant creature, and he always took an interest. Domesticity was a new game which they both played with childlike zest, down to the last embroidered guest-towel.

She found with astonishment that except for the things she bought for the house she had nothing to spend money on besides postage stamps, cosmetics, and the hairdresser. The New York rent, which she insisted was no affair of Aunt Virginia's, was paid as usual out of her account with Andrew's firm, and she wrote the checks for Mary's and Gertrude's wages herself. The rest of her income piled up in the bank. She had all the clothes she could use

140

for some time to come. The monthly bills went to Rodney's desk and were dealt with by him without comment.

She had no idea what his income was, except that he had more than his professor's salary, but he seemed entirely serene about it. He had scaled his living to what he could afford. He knew approximately what his expenses would be. If the butcher's bill fluctuated a few dollars upward, there was no crisis; if a plumber's bill turned up unexpectedly, there was no panic.

Something of all this got into a letter to Andrew, along with a vague surmise as to why, if finances were so easy here, a thing like the trip to Mexico was so out of reach. Andrew cleared that up. Rodney and Aunt Virginia probably lived on an income, paid quarterly, and doubtless diminished in recent years. They used it as it came, for their gracious way of living. To finance a trip besides was impossible without touching their capital, which they were right not to do. Andrew seemed to feel that she might have worked this out for herself, and reminded her of their own perennial deadlock about the sables which he would not allow her to buy out of her investments.

Cherishing. It was the most beautiful word in the language. It was the most wonderful sensation in the world, to know that the four bright walls you called home were yours by ancient dower right, by the civilized custom and masculine habit of mind which says that a wife shall be kept secure. To have and to hold, to love and to cherish. There were women who took these things for granted. But not Liz Dare.

"Rodney, why shouldn't I pay the household expenses?" she said once at the end of the month.

"First tell me why you should," he said.

That settled that.

"Am I costing you more than Aunt Virginia did?" she asked on another occasion.

"No, are you trying to?" he inquired with interest.

You couldn't do anything with him.

After Christmas, preparations for the trip began to take on a rather relentless aspect. Charles was busier than a bird-dog. Things came out of storage, and things arrived from shops, and most of them accumulated in Rodney's study across from the drawing-room, where he did his tutoring. Elizabeth never entered it without a feeling of awe mixed with amusement. My husband, the professor. Books lined its walls to the ceiling. It had a flat-topped desk at which he made up his lecture-notes and corrected his examination papers under a green-shaded student lamp. In the corner near the window there was a plain oak table with a book rack and another lamp, where a student might sit all day unmolested, making free use of the books from the open shelves. Because of the bookshelves there was little wall space left for pictures, but in a corner between two windows Rodney had hung his Senior football group, a portrait of his father, an air-view of the Andes so vast it made you shiver, and a motto lettered in Old English on brown art paper with a red and gold initial. This last he had treasured in his sight ever since he had purchased it himself at the age of fourteen. It read: *He is free who lives as he chooses.* EPICTETUS, *Discourses,* Bk. IV.

Now the prospective personnel for the trip began to be interviewed in the study, and sometimes afterwards were invited to meals. There was a solemn, youngish man named Skinner, who wore spectacles and exactly fitted Elizabeth's mental picture of a Dinwiddie. Even Rodney admitted that Skinner caricatured the mythical professor, Type A-1, but explained that he knew all about tropical insects and that was why he was going along. Frank Elliott was going too, as Charles's handy man, and Alice McKay came down from Smith one week-end to hear all about it. Elizabeth presided at luncheon, and heard Alice's voluble enthusiasm for Central America in all its aspects with a slight skepticism. Alice said enviously over and over again what a wonderful opportunity it was for Frank, and how lucky he was to be able to get away—and then was openly astonished and incredulous to learn that Elizabeth, who could get away, actually was not going.

After that Elizabeth's manner towards Alice was just the least little bit in the world reserved. If Rodney didn't expect her to go, what business was it of Alice McKay's? She implied—rather too sweetly—that this was going to be a trip where wives might be somewhat out of place, and Alice said, "But Mrs. Guerber's going!" and then looked at Rodney as though she might have given something away.

"Who is Mrs. Guerber?" inquired Elizabeth into an unmistakable pause, and everybody seemed to be waiting for Rodney to reply.

Rodney, who by now had begun to have his typhoid inoculations and looked a little heavy around the eyes as a consequence, said that Mrs. Guerber was the wife of Dr. Guerber, who was one of the best botanists there was and who had collected all over the world.

"What's she like?" inquired Elizabeth then—in almost any other circumstances an entirely harmless question, which somehow turned out to be, as she uttered it, the wrong thing to ask.

"She is small and leathery and pig-eyed, and has straight iron-gray hair which was hacked off with a butcher-knife," said Rodney explicitly. "She always wears mussy brown clothes and closely resembles a titmouse, except that she speaks with a strong European accent."

"W-what good will she be on the trip?" asked Elizabeth, and everybody waited for Rodney to go on.

"She is, or was, a professional nurse, for one thing," he went on. "And she knows, I suspect, almost as much about botany as her husband does. She has followed him clean round the world on his collecting trips, and is said to have saved his life single-handed on five separate occasions."

"Obviously the sort of woman you should have married yourself," said Elizabeth, and her chin was a little too high. "Guerber sounds German to me."

"They're Austrians," said Charles, looking at his plate.

"Well, in that case, let's ask them to lunch one day," Elizabeth suggested, and found Skinner eyeing her balefully through his spectacles and knew he was having the quite colossal nerve to pity Rodney for having married her.

"We will," said Rodney quietly. "They arrive from Washington some time next week."

The Guerbers came to lunch, and Mrs. Guerber was even as Rodney had said, a titmouse dressed in mussy brown. Dr. Guerber was bony and near-sighted, with a moth-eaten mustache which wanted trimming and gray hair which had been born *en brosse* no matter how he tried to disguise the fact now. He was animated and eager and rather touching, Elizabeth thought, in his open gratitude apparently for just being treated like a human being. His eyes rested often on his wife, who sat small and silent over her plate, rarely looking at anybody. The Guerbers ate slowly; that is, they tried not to hurry, but when each course ended their plates were scraped piteously clean. Elizabeth, always a scrupulous hostess, took a second helping of everything as it came, but the Guerbers steadfastly refused, with downcast eyes. Except the coffee. They each had two cups of that, in shameless greediness, and they drank it noisily, with long, rapturous sippings.

"Well, you see how it is," said Rodney when the Guerbers had gone. "Charles has found them decent lodgings, but they'll have to eat here now and then, until we go."

Elizabeth was looking bewildered.

"Rodney, are they *hungry?*"

"I expect they're starving," he said point-blank. "It doesn't matter to them—much—because they have managed not to be separated. But it makes you feel kind of sick."

"I don't—I didn't understand—" She was still looking bewildered. "I thought Austrians were gay, charming people—"

144

"Not any more. Oh, good God, Liz, can't you *see?*" cried Rodney, who almost never swore, but typhoid inoculations always told on him terribly and he had for several days been something less than himself. "Are you blind, Liz, must you have it *diagrammed?* Sure they're Germans, but if Germans want to say they're Austrians these days, who can blame them? Guerber is half a Jew, and his wife is what Hitler calls Aryan. I saw them in Germany in 1932. I saw their home, bare and clean and childless, but very precious to them. I had a letter of introduction from one of my professors here who had known them in India before 1914, and had entertained them in Washington in 1924. He always said no naturalist's education was complete until he knew the Guerbers, and before I'd finished drinking coffee with them that day in Jena I knew what he meant. Because of Hitler, they went to Vienna, and you know what happened there. So they went to Prague. In 1938 I found them in London, living in one room, a garret with no heat in it. They were hungry then, too, but they still served a kind of coffee."

"Rodney, I'm sorry, I only meant—"

"There was a Smithsonian man traveling with me that time, and he got all steamed up about them. Somehow or other after we got back he fixed things in Washington, and we sent them their passage money. They've taken out their papers here, and we all have to find them bits of work to do, like translating things we don't really want, because they won't take money for nothing, and still they're hungry!"

"But isn't there some way—"

"His flower-paintings are the most exquisite things you ever saw, but who wants flower-paintings these days? They were in Costa Rica on their wedding-trip round the world in 1909, and he's beside himself with joy about going to the tropics again. I don't think she cares any more. All she cares about now is to be with him, wherever he is, because he's all she's got left. Together they can still remember happiness, and all the happiness there is

145

for them is what they can remember! So now you know about the Guerbers!" He went into his study and closed the door behind him.

Elizabeth stood looking at the closed door a long minute. It was the first time anything like that had happened in their marriage, and it was not just the inoculations. She went and sat down in the drawing-room with a magazine on her lap, waiting for the study door to open, if it ever did open again.

Pretty soon Charles came in from the street, with his arms full of parcels, and started for the study. Elizabeth ran out to intercept him in the hall, motioning him away from the study into the drawing-room behind her. He came, looking mystified.

"How do I get the Guerbers on the phone?" she demanded.

Still more mystified, he wrote it down for her.

"Don't say anything about it to Rodney," she told him.

It was the wrong thing to tell Charles. He looked at her with a puzzled frown.

"Why?" he said.

"He's angry with me about the Guerbers. I guess I was pretty stupid, but I think I know a way to help them."

"It's none of my business, but I'd leave it lay if I were you," suggested Charles.

"I'll show Rodney I'm not as dumb as I look!"

"Are you sure you want to?" he queried unhappily. "He'll get over it, you know. He feels rotten—these inoculations are hell and damnation. We're all pretty snappish right now, he took my head clean off this morning, I haven't seen it since."

"What did *you* do?" she inquired, interested.

"I forgot something. It might have been serious, but it isn't."

"Did he swear at you? He swore at me," she said, with the gruesome pride of one who exhibits rival sores.

"Look, Liz, give us a break. Me, I've got a vaccination for sale cheap. With Rodney, it's the typhoid germs they're pumping into

146

him. It'll all blow over before we start. Don't hold anything against him now."

"Trust you to be on Rodney's side!" she cried bitterly.

"It's a good place to be," he said, and ambled off to the study with his parcels.

Dr. Guerber became incoherent with gratitude and excitement when she asked him on the telephone to bring some of his flower-paintings and show them to her. Within an incredibly short time he and his wife were back again, and he knelt on the carpet to open a shabby black portfolio.

His paintings were in water-color on sheets of smooth paper about ten inches by twelve. He handed them up to her one by one, and even her untutored eye could see that each was a miracle of skill and patience in its sheer beauty of line and color, and its intricacy of delicate detail. Mrs. Guerber sat silently watching, as shapeless as a rag doll dumped down in her chair, her strange, opaque eyes going from her husband's eager face to the long white hands of the woman who held his paintings. Each time Elizabeth's smiling glance tried to include her she retreated still further into herself, seeming sullen and shy and out of it.

Elizabeth, who had in the beginning only meant to be kind, and intended to make some of her friends pay generously for flower-paintings, was quite carried away by them now that she saw them, and said they must go into a book at once and she knew just the publisher to do it. And perhaps, she suggested, Dr. Guerber would be willing to write a page or so about each flower, so that ignorant people like herself could better appreciate it, could know where it grew and how he had found it and what its most pronounceable name was. Dr. Guerber was enchanted with this idea. In Germany before Hitler he had published many books, and always he had dreamed of a book in English, which he really wrote very well, much better as he spoke it, a book to be published in America, with his name on it—

"But you mustn't be too technical about this one," she warned him. "These pictures are so lovely that anyone can understand them, and anyone would want to own them. So you must keep it easy."

"But so easy as for a child, I will keep it!" he agreed, boiling with his unquenchable enthusiasm. "With each flower, see, I will put some small anecdote, some little adventure that befell me while I quested it—yes?"

"Yes!" nodded Elizabeth. "That's exactly what I mean! Will you let me take these up to New York to show to this man I know will publish them?"

Some of the light went out of his face, and he glanced uneasily at his wife, who met his eyes with her unblinking opaque gaze.

"They are all I have," he said haltingly, as though ashamed, and opened his empty hands. "I can never replace them—I have lost so much—I—forgive me, I never let them leave me now—"

"I know exactly how you feel," she said quickly. "And you're quite right, of course. But wouldn't you just let me put them in my car tomorrow, drive straight to New York with them, show them to him in his private office, and drive back with them the same afternoon?"

Again his eyes sought his wife's, and Elizabeth thought she saw the faintest sign of negation pass from her to him. The light left his face a little further.

"My wife and I—" he began.

"Hullo, what's going on here?" Rodney's quiet voice spoke from the doorway.

It was Dr. Guerber who tried, incoherent in his eagerness, to explain to Rodney what Elizabeth wished to do. Rodney looked at her inquiringly.

"Stanley will go crazy about these," she said. "I want to take them to him. If I know anything about Stanley, Dr. Guerber will get a contract for the book's publication before you go. Stanley works fast."

"I have tried to make clear to your wife," Dr. Guerber took

148

it up ruefully, "how these are but remnants of all I once had. If I lose them I have nothing to show for all my years of toil—so it is only that I hesitate—"

"They would be perfectly safe, I assure you of that," said Rodney. "The only thing is, Liz, it would be a very expensive book to get out, and few publishers nowadays are in the mood to—"

Elizabeth found Dr. Guerber's eyes fixed on her in an agony of hope and anxiety. Her chin went up.

"Stanley doesn't insist on making a lot of money on every book he does. If ever he sets eyes on these things he won't rest till he's published them. He would pay well, and everybody can use a little extra money these days."

"Yes, yes, I would be so glad to—" Dr. Guerber burst out, and checked himself with another glance at his wife's impassive face.

"Well, all right, there's no harm in trying, is there!" Rodney decided cheerfully, and Mrs. Guerber's gaze shifted to rest on him in dumb acceptance of his edict. (Like a dog, thought Elizabeth involuntarily. She looks at Rodney like a dog, worshiping and—patient.) "Charles can drive you down tomorrow, Liz, when he goes to see about the camera," Rodney was saying. "You'll be back in time for dinner, and if the Guerbers will dine here they can take the paintings home with them. Will that do?" he asked, and looked directly at Mrs. Guerber.

"You are very kind," she said, and her eyes fell before his, to her hands which were knotted in her lap.

When once more Rodney and Elizabeth were alone while the Guerbers receded from their front door—

"I'm sorry you got his hopes up again," he said. "I've already sent him to every publisher I know, with the same result—very beautiful, too expensive to reproduce, and No-thank-you."

"Maybe you weren't in a position to blackmail any of your publishing friends," she suggested, her chin still a little high.

"Well, no, I wasn't," he admitted, and gave her a long, speculative look. "It seems you have the advantage of me there." He

149

turned away towards the stairs. "Something tells me I'm going to lie down before dinner. This arm has left me no peace all day."

"Rodney."

He paused on the bottom step of the wide, curving staircase, looking back at her, his hand on the newel-post. His slender height, the weary turn of his long body on the stair, the heavy look around his eyelids, caught at her heart.

"Rodney, have we quarreled about the Guerbers?"

"I don't think so," he said reflectively. "It would be pretty silly, wouldn't it, to quarrel about anything so harmless as the Guerbers! In fact, it would be pretty silly to quarrel about anything at all, with the time getting so short."

Smiling, he held out one arm to her in tender invitation, and she went to him swiftly, and they climbed the stairs together, step by step, with their arms around each other's waists.

When she entered Stanley's office the next day, carrying the portfolio, he made no bones about being glad to see her. One of those men who prize their bachelorhood above all the wealth of Ind, he nevertheless had entertained hopes, of one kind or another, regarding Liz Dare for a long time now. Like most of her friends he had no doubt whatever that Rodney Monroe was only a phase, and that she would come back to them eventually if not a lot sooner. Liz Dare a professor's wife? Liz Dare retire? Don't make me laugh.

He received her, therefore, with the liveliest interest and a resounding kiss. Now, he thought, we shall see how the wind blows.

Elizabeth, after that kiss, came straight to the point. She undid the shabby portfolio in the middle of Stanley's mahogany desk, and produced the paintings. A little puzzled, but always willing to oblige, Stanley removed his gaze from her face—he had never seen her look so well—and obediently turned his attention to the portfolio's contents. Once there, however, it was riveted. There was nothing like them in this country. They had an eighteenth

150

century charm and delicacy. If they were scientifically accurate as well, why complain, but their *charm*—their microscopic daintiness —their *touch*—! Yes, indeed, they must be made into a book. Yes, indeed, he was the man to do it.

"Oh, *darling,* I knew you wouldn't let me down!" she cried, and threw her arms around his neck and hugged him.

Instantly all his antennae were alert. Something going on here?

"Did you doubt me?" he reproached her, feeling his way.

"Rodney didn't think you'd touch it. He'd already tried some cheap-skate publisher or other who said it was too expensive a job."

"It is. But it's worth doing all the same."

"That's what I *told* him!" she crowed.

"Am I putting my oar into some sort of private brawl?" he asked hopefully.

"We-ell—" She looked at him under her lashes. Stanley was a very old friend, and Rodney was behaving badly. "I am trying to prove something," she admitted.

"So the professor can be wrong," he observed, watching her with satisfaction.

"Oh, we didn't *quarrel,* exactly, we never do that any more, but I—I just thought I'd show him!" she ended defiantly.

"G'ad to be of assistance," murmured Stanley with a presumptuous smile.

"Rodney isn't quite himself these days—you see, they're off for Central America soon, and he's being shot full of typhoid germs, and that makes him cross."

"You aren't going with him?" He pretended to be surprised.

"Oh, Lord, no, do you think I'm crazy?"

"I was only asking," he apologized. "And what becomes of you while the professor is away?"

She saw now what she had laid herself open to with a mind like Stanley's, which she had once likened to a sewer, and she sat looking at him silently a moment, baffled and defensive.

151

"Now, don't get any wrong ideas," she said firmly. "I'll probably do the show while he's away."

"I see," said Stanley.

"You do not, you don't see anything of the kind! Surely two intelligent people like Rodney and me can be separated for three months without one of them heading for Reno!"

"When we come to look back on this conversation a few months hence," he said, "I hope you will remember that it was you who mentioned Reno and not me."

"I *didn't*, I only said—"

"Well, somebody did," he reminded her softly.

They eyed each other, she resentful, while he smiled.

"Now, look," she said with slow emphasis. "I'm crazy about Rodney. I always have been since the first time I laid eyes on him, and I always will be."

"You must be," he assented, smiling. "I've never seen you look so beautiful, and that comes of love, they tell me, I wouldn't know. But is it any reason to kick your old friends in the teeth? Haven't I got a right to be glad you'll be in town again, so we can see something of you now and then? I've missed you, Liz. Is that a sin?"

"Have you, really?" She smiled back at him, mollified.

"Are you surprised?"

"Well, I was never the only woman in your life!"

"I never said you were, my dear. But there is no one, I find, who can take your place in it."

"That's very well put," she smiled.

"Come home, Liz. All is forgiven."

"Thanks, maybe I will. Can I have a check for Dr. Guerber?"

And so she arrived back in time for dinner with the portfolio safe and a letter from Stanley offering Dr. Guerber three hundred dollars advance and a contract for signature before he left—provided he was willing to supply within the next six months not less than two hundred nor more than four hundred words of text (in English) for each painting.

Dr. Guerber was at once beside himself with enthusiasm.

"Three hundred dollars! But with that I can pay something of what I owe, I can buy my wife a dress, I can have my raincoat, we can have *coffee,* we can—we can— Oh, but of course, a story to each flower, it will be so simple! My notes—my diaries—all are gone!" He showed his open, empty hands. "But it will be so easy to remember—my wife and I between us can remember more than will be necessary—it is all we really do now, for recreation, is remember—" He turned to the silent woman who sat with hooded eyes, her hands knotted together in her lap. "Ernestine, my darrling, are you speechless? Can you not say to Mrs. Monroe one word of thanks for what she has done—"

Mrs. Guerber's quiet eyelids lifted. She looked at Elizabeth without expression, listless, unillumined by any of her husband's joy.

"You are very kind," she said.

"Oh, don't thank me, thank Rodney! If he hadn't happened to mention the paintings I might never have known about them."

Mrs. Guerber spoke again, almost harshly.

"We thank Dr. Monroe as we thank God—in our prayers," she said.

XIV

As the time before departure grew still shorter, Rodney worked harder and later, returning to his study in the evenings after dinner; and though he left the door open, though he was in and out and spoke to her as he passed, and smiled, and sometimes dropped a kiss on her wistful upturned face, it was plain that except for infrequent intervals his mind was not on his wife. Her sense of desolation grew day by day. Not even the prospect of returning to New York and starting rehearsals, and being made much of by people like Pete and Andrew—and Stanley—and Aunt Virginia, consoled her. Rodney was going away. And Rodney was the sun. Day by day, too, she grew to envy Mrs. Guerber, who wanted nothing any more except to be wherever her husband was. . . .

One evening Elizabeth came to the door of the study about ten o'clock, and he looked up at her with an absent smile and said—

"This can't be much fun for you."

He had had his third typhoid injection only that day, and his smallpox vaccination had taken with a vengeance. His eyes were bright with fever, and the boyish lock was down across his temple.

Encouraged by his smile, she smiled back, and drifted into the room and stood idly turning over the pamphlets and abstracts which always accumulated in a wire basket on one corner of the vast desk. Everybody who ever published a scientific paper seemed to send it to Rodney, whether it had anything to do with birds or not—and most of them seemed to have been written by Dinwiddies like Skinner. Those which had not to do with birds usually carried a pen-and-ink inscription across the cover by the author, who had once gone somewhere with Rodney, or been to school with him, or to him. Sometimes the titles indicated what seemed to her a disturbing trend of thought on Rodney's part, such as an apparently treasured copy of a report on an *Expedition Ornithologique en Indochine Française*—never mind about Indochine Française, Rodney. Sometimes they were pretty funny, like *The Starling's Family Life and Behavior* by a peeping-Tom who had given them a glass-sided nest and then discovered, with surprise, that in all duties associated with the raising of the brood the ♂ was quite as attentive and industrious as the ♀ ; it developed also that young starlings are house-broken by their parents at a very early age. Elizabeth got quite fascinated by that one. *The Occurrence of Vestigial Claws on the Wings of Birds* proved to be quite as dull as it sounded, and *Hearing in Insects* (inscribed) failed to live up to the possibilities in its title.

Rodney went on writing, his aching head propped on his left hand. He hadn't even asked her to sit down, or what time it was. He seemed oblivious to her presence, which was not a thing to be encouraged any more than notes on Indochine Française. Elizabeth went on digging in the wire basket, and finally turned up what brought involuntary laughter, and Rodney gave her a rather patient glance of inquiry. She held the fat paper-bound treatise so that he could see its title. *The Present Status of the Musk-Ox,* it read.

"That was written by a fellow I knew in London," he said, as though in extenuation. "He sent it to me."

"Well, how *does* the Musk-Ox rate these days?" she asked. "And with whom?"

"Oh, all right, very funny," he agreed, and his eyes returned to the typewritten pages in front of him. "I haven't read it, I couldn't say." But he was smiling.

Further encouraged, Elizabeth came round the desk and inserted herself between it and the arm of his chair and sat down on his lap. She was not really a little woman, with her length of limb, but she was so flexible that she could instantly become lap-size. Rodney laid down his pencil and pushed back his chair and crossed his legs underneath her. With one of her nestling movements she pressed her cheek against the hollow of his shoulder and tucked her fingers round his tie.

"Rodney."

"Yes, my darling, you have a very thin time, you don't have to tell me. It's just the way it always is with trips."

"Rodney, I give in. I can't bear it. I want to go with you."

She noticed that first of all his arms tightened instinctively around her. Then he said—

"Well, great Scott, Liz, it's about time you said so!"

"I am saying so. I can get ready. I've got riding-clothes and lots of slacks and things. Will it be awfully hot?"

"It will. Hotter than hades."

"Then I'll just buy a lot of wash-silk tennis-dresses. Presumably I can get washing done down there?"

"Presumably. Are you sure this isn't just because you can't bear to let me out of your sight?"

"What else would it be?"

"Liz, you're hopeless. I don't even know if I could manage it at the last minute this way. What will Blaine say?"

"Andrew will see how it is." (The time is short, said Andrew, even when you're young.) "What is there to manage? I'll just pack up and go."

"Well, for one thing, you'd have to start your inoculations to-morrow, there's barely time for them. I always have mine early so I'm over it before the last few days when everything seems to come up at once."

"Do I have to have them? I'm perfectly healthy, and I was vaccinated only three years ago before I went to France."

"Charles and I are perfectly healthy too, but we have them all the same. And a three-year-old vaccination won't do. Anybody who doesn't have fresh inoculations doesn't go. That's flat."

"All right, all right, anything you say! Unless you don't want me," she added perversely.

"Of course I want you, but you said you wouldn't go, and that was that."

"I've changed my mind."

"That's fine. What about the show?"

"I haven't signed a contract yet."

"You're an unscrupulous woman, aren't you!" he said admiringly. "I'll talk to Charles, and see what he says."

"I thought you were boss around here."

"None of that, now. Charles is my right arm, don't forget. It's very bad luck to go against one of his premonitions."

"Charles won't want me."

"What makes you think that?"

"They don't approve of me—any of your followers. They think I'm a bad influence."

"You are," he smiled. "But I can take it, I guess."

"Don't you mind what they think?"

"Why should we mind? It's none of their business what I do with my private life." He laid his cheek against hers with a quick, possessive movement. "Oh, thank God, Liz, I wanted you to come —I wanted it so bad I thought I'd die!"

"Why, R-Rodney, I never dreamed—"

"Three whole months without a sight of you," he whispered. "What do you think I'm made of?"

"I don't know," she answered slowly. "I don't know what you're made of. I wish I did. Rodney, why don't you *say* what you want, and then you'll get it! You mouse around the house wearing that poker-face of yours—how do I know what goes on inside you?"

"I love you. That's what goes on inside me. Twenty-four hours a day, seven days a week. Believe it or not."

"I didn't think it mattered much if I didn't go, so long as you had Charles and the birds."

"You smell different from either Charles or the birds," he said, and drew a long breath.

"Rodney, your face is so hot. Are you running a temperature?"

"I certainly am. That last shot is a daisy!"

"Can't you stop work now? Let's celebrate because I'm not going to be left behind. There's a fire in the drawing-room. Let's have our hot milk in there, and reminisce about that night up in Maine when you wouldn't ask me to marry you."

"I'm going to put this carcase of mine to bed pretty soon. Right now it's nothing but the scene of civil war, arson, and mob-rule. The worst should be over by tomorrow. Then, as soon as we sail I start in with quinine, and that makes me slightly deaf for a few days, you'll have to shout."

"Is it worth it?"

"Is what worth what?"

"Is the trip worth what you go through first?"

"Invariably."

"Will I think so too?"

"I hope so. But it has me worried."

"You'll be there," she said, nestling. "So long as I'm with you, I won't mind a little civil war."

When Charles entered the study the following morning Rodney looked up at him warily and said—

"Are you feeling fairly strong today?"

"I guess so. What's the bad news?"

"Maybe you'd better be sitting down when I tell you this."

Charles stopped short in his tracks. He hadn't actually gone white, but he looked as though he might.

"The trip's off!" he said hopelessly, and collapsed into the nearest chair.

158

"Wrong. Liz wants to go with us."

There were a lot of things Charles might have said. He got them all into a thin, speechless whistle between his front teeth.

"Maybe I'm crazy to want to take her," Rodney admitted. "Maybe it's entirely the wrong thing to do. But I find the flesh is very weak. So if you think we could possibly manage—"

"O.K.," said Charles cheerfully. "Can do." He would have said the same—with just about as much enthusiasm—if Rodney had mentioned that seriously, no fooling, he wanted a couple of planets, say Jupiter and Venus, to use for shirt-studs.

"Now, look," said Rodney. "If there's any real reason why it would be better not—"

"She'll have to start her shots today."

"I know. Charles, if there's anything on your mind—"

"Nothing's on my mind, son, except her transportation, her bedding, her mosquito-canopy, her inoculations, her passport, her emergency stuff, and a half dozen other things. I've got to get at it, that's all. Shall I ring up the doctor now and make her appointment?"

"Please. And, Charles—I don't think we'll regret it."

"Nobody's going to regret it," said Charles, busy at the dial of the telephone, "except Mrs. Guerber."

"How do you mean—about Mrs. Guerber?"

"They aren't even sisters under the skin," said Charles. "Dr. Brown's office? I want to make an appointment for Mrs. Monroe to come for inoculations—" etc.

Before long, Elizabeth put her head around the door and looked at Charles wistfully.

"'Morning," said Charles, and grinned.

"All right, you can come with us," said Rodney, and his eyes were pleased and proud as they rested on her. "On one condition, which is—no matter what happens, you're to do exactly what you're told to do as fast as you can and talk afterwards. If that

159

is fully understood, we undertake between us to get you back here all in one piece. Now come in and take a chair and write down all the things you have to do today. You're going to be pretty busy from now on."

XV

It was fun to go down to New York and shop prodigally for tropical wear. Rodney said the nights might be cool, and that she wouldn't want evening dresses—but lots of simple little things like those tennis-frocks she mentioned. He said to get big hats. He advised riding-clothes of the coolest material possible. He said to take three months' supply of all her toiletries, because she wouldn't be able to get her sort of things there. He said to get something for sunburn, and asked if she had dark glasses. And he suggested that she do her shopping at once, before the inoculations got to work. Then, with the expression of one who watches his youngest set out for the first day of school, he saw her off for what she still called Town.

Her eyes were misty as the train pulled out of the little station, for she was to have dinner at the apartment with Aunt Virginia and spend the night in the guest room there, and already she was lonesome for him. He grows on you so, she thought dismally as the cinder tracks slid by. He grows *into* you, like roots. Leaving him even for two days is like having a tooth pulled. To love anyone like this is slavery. I never thought I had it in me to love anyone like this. What have I done to Aunt Virginia? How does she live without him, when she's used to seeing him every day!

She arrived at the apartment therefore a little before dinner time in a state of abject apology, with a taxi full of boxes and bundles. She was warmly received by Gertrude and Mary and Aunt Virginia, and she noted again with a shock how Rodney would look if he were fifty and a spinster. Aunt Virginia was tall

161

and rangy, with a generous mouth and a long chin—and her eyes were as young and uncompromising as Rodney's own. It made you homesick for him just to look at her.

Arrangements for Snorky to live at the apartment while Elizabeth was in Central America were discussed. Aunt Virginia was charmed, and Elizabeth wondered if Snorky would find solace in the resemblance to Rodney. Then she said, over a glass of sherry in front of the fire—

"Sometimes I wonder how you can ever forgive me for marrying Rodney."

"I sometimes wonder myself," said Aunt Virginia frankly. "But on the other hand, I'd never have forgiven you if you'd turned him down."

"That's a comfort," said Elizabeth.

"When I think how I've hated all the other women in his life —!" Aunt Virginia ruminated, turning her glass against the light, and shook her head profoundly at her own recollections.

"Have there been a *lot* of other women?" ventured Elizabeth, and Aunt Virginia rolled a speculative eye at her.

"I can't say that Rodney has ever been what you could call a misogynist," she remarked. "When he was a little boy and went to dancing-school he punched another little boy's nose because of a little girl with red hair, and it's sort of gone on developing along those lines ever since."

"I see," said Elizabeth, amused.

"Oh, yes, you can laugh now, but it was very awkward at the time! Of course the little girl was to blame, she had asked Rodney to cut in."

"Naturally. What happened?"

"His father dealt with it, man to man, in the study," said Aunt Virginia philosophically. "I was never present at those sessions in the study. Mind you, women always made his father's life a burden!"

"Why didn't he marry again?"

"Because not to was the hard way, I always thought. And also, I suspect, because he enjoyed the chase. As Rodney always has too, till he met you."

"How did they lose him—all the others?"

"That's putting it the wrong way round," said Aunt Virginia. "The question is, How did you land him?"

"We fought an awful lot," said Elizabeth uncertainly.

"Ah!" cried Aunt Virginia. "That's very interesting! Some of them tried too hard to please him. I remember one we called sweet-Alice-Ben-Bolt—you know the type—"

> "'She wept with delight when you gave her a smile,
> And trembled with fear at your frown,'"

Elizabeth sang at once, through her nose.

"Precisely. She brought out all the worst in him. Why, I've seen him deliberately *glower* at her, all for nothing, till she was nearly out of her mind, and then he'd appear to forgive her for something she had never done in the first place!"

Elizabeth giggled.

"And there was one named Marcia," she prompted.

"Ah, well, that wasn't even funny," admitted Aunt Virginia, sipping her sherry. "That was one of our larger lunacies. Marcia was a brute of a blonde. She led him on, and then married another man. Did he tell you about that?"

"He mentioned her once. Bryn Mawr!" she added significantly, and made a face.

"I'm Bryn Mawr myself, it wasn't their fault," said Aunt Virginia. "That girl was just born a snob. Would you believe it, she thought she was too good for him!"

"Oh, she did, did she!"

"She used to come for week-ends," Aunt Virginia went on. "Football games, and such. There was something about her, the minute she walked in the door the whole house began to look

163

sullen and drab and cheerless. Even the silver turned dull, and the fires always smoked. It made you think, it really did."

"Did Rodney notice?"

"He notices everything. But to him, it only meant that the place really wasn't good enough for her. She *humbled* him. It was awful! More sherry?"

"Thanks, I will."

"I can tell you, Marcia was pretty bad while she lasted," said Aunt Virginia, pouring out another glass of sherry each. "He *moped*. Pray God you never see him do it! Like a sick bird, sitting on one leg with its feathers all rumpled—"

"What do you think he saw in her?"

"She was a born tart as well as a born snob. Before the French Revolution she would have been *maîtresse en titre*. We needn't even pretend that Rodney didn't know better. But he'd been going through a dull patch, and tartiness was right up his alley. I doubt very much if I can tell you anything about Men," said Aunt Virginia, cocking an eyebrow at her nephew's wife and looking extraordinarily like him, "but don't get any sort of idea that Rodney isn't one, will you!"

"No," said Elizabeth meekly. "But he's such a *nice* one!"

"They can all be very tiresome when they try. Rodney was asking for it, and he very nearly got it. That railroad king, or whatever he was, came along just in time. If Marcia had married Rodney and then he'd met you, we'd have had a nice mess."

"That's funny." Elizabeth stared at her. "He said something like that himself."

"He's fairly intelligent for a man, if I do say it as shouldn't. Doubtless even Rodney realized that Marcia's bag of tricks wouldn't have lasted him six months, and he knows he's in love with you. I hate to think what I'd have gone through with him if he'd lost *you!*"

"He did his best to lose me! I practically rammed myself down his throat. You never saw anybody so cagey as he was!"

"The burnt child," said Aunt Virginia. "That Marcia business must have left him feeling as though he'd been pulled through a hedge backwards. There's nothing to this rebound theory with Rodney. He always takes awhile to convalesce." She sipped her sherry meditatively. "I could see I was up against something new as soon as he got back from Maine, but I couldn't tell what. When Rodney's simply out on the tiles, I may say, he's a joy to have around the house—oh, very gay indeed! Well, it wasn't that. Nor it wasn't that *Noli-me-tangere* Marcia-look either. He was very sweet and very quiet—I could see that he was thinking hard."

"Didn't he say anything about me?" asked Elizabeth, enthralled, for failing Rodney's actual presence as the day drew in, the next best thing was to hear about him, and Aunt Virginia knew more about him than anybody in the world.

"Not very much, and that should have warned me. But somehow I never suspected you till he got back from New York."

"And did you hate me—when he told you?"

"I was looking at him, my dear. Six Marcias could never have made him look the way one Elizabeth did." Aunt Virginia finished her sherry and rose.

"Oh, now, darling, *don't* stop just as you're coming to the best part!" Elizabeth entreated her. "How did he look? Tell me how he looked!"

"He looked as though somebody had turned on an arc light inside him," said Aunt Virginia. "They call it Love. One more glass of that stuff, and I'll start telling you all the bright things he said when he was a baby. Show me what you bought. I love bundles."

As was to be expected, the inoculations laid Elizabeth low, and her packing was done in a haze of general debility, with occasional highlights of headache and flashes of fever. Rodney, who by now had assimilated most of his germs, was helpful and con-

165

siderate, and assured her that it would pass by the time they reached Los Angeles.

Her last typhoid injection came on the morning of their departure, and made the train journey a further misery. Rodney took a drawing-room, and Elizabeth, who had always dearly loved trains, sat all day in a corner by the window, drooping, while Rodney checked over lists and made notes and totted up bills in preoccupied silence. (Charles had been sent on ahead three days before with Frank as his aide, to collect things at Los Angeles, where a lot of their supplies were to be waiting.) Every now and then a meal was served on a folding table in front of her, and she ate listlessly whatever she could of it. Every now and then when the train stopped long enough Rodney made her put on her coat and walked her up and down the platform. Every now and then the Guerbers or Skinner, who were in the Pullman just behind, would look in at her—invariably just as she had got off into a semi-comfortable doze—and she would say she felt a little better, thanks, and they would go away again. Thus the time passed somehow, and on the morning they arrived at Los Angeles she did, to her surprise, feel a little better.

They were to sail on a fruit boat from Los Angeles, where another bird man, named Sturgis, was to join them. He had been in New Guinea with Rodney in 1935, and was said to have very sound ideas about keeping harpy eagles alive in captivity.

They spent two days at the Ambassador, during which time Elizabeth further revived, though still falling short of her usual enjoyment of life. And then, the morning they sailed, Rodney said it was time to start her quinine. With a rather piteous look she swallowed the first capsule and put the box in her hand-bag. Every morning before breakfast was the best time, said Rodney. Regularly, like brushing your teeth. Don't forget, now.

The boat was clean, but that was about all. It was a small freighter, and the amenities of its passenger space were subject to the convenience of the cargo, largely bananas, it was designed to carry. The cabins were tiny, with one chintz-curtained bunk above the other, and on the rail of each of these was fastened a suggestive little bracket with a cardboard container inside. There was a narrow cushioned sofa along the opposite wall under the port-hole, one wicker chair, a basin with running water, a cupboard beneath it, and a wardrobe like an upended coffin.

"But, Rodney, there's no bath!" cried Elizabeth incredulously, and he looked up at her from the floor where he knelt stowing luggage under the bunk.

"This is a fruit boat," he said. "Not the *Ile de France*. Should I have mentioned it sooner?"

Less than half a dozen people besides themselves completed the passenger list, and dinner the first night out was quite jolly. There was something about Rodney now that she had never seen before. He was quiet, self-contained, outwardly just as usual—but inside him something was singing. Frank rollicked with excitement, for it was his first ocean voyage, and even Skinner beamed behind his spectacles. Dr. Guerber was pathetically intoxicated at the idea of going somewhere without having been forced to flee, and with the certain knowledge that he would be *persona grata* when he got there—and the tropics at that! He kept patting his wife's passive hands, knotted as always in her lap—if only she'd knit or something, thought Elizabeth, her own white fingers occupied after dinner by a needlepoint bell-pull for the house at home, a wad of colored wools in her lap.

Sturgis, a stoutish, friendly man with a strong, mellifluous voice, knew Central America well and called it God-forsaken, at the same time smiling a pleased sort of smile because he was going back to it. But several times during the evening Rodney would look at Charles and Charles would look at Rodney and there would pass between them such a glow of deep and wordless satisfaction, such a wealth of ancient understanding that Elizabeth, watching, felt left out and lonely. Rodney and Charles were in some seventh heaven of their own, composed of sea air, the swish

167

of white water below the rail, the gentle creak of timber, the pot-pourri of ship smells—Rodney and Charles were Going Places.

By the second morning at sea her ears were queer from the quinine and the wind was rising. Soon after lunch Rodney missed her from the lounge and went down to their cabin. She was lying on her bunk, which was the lower one, looking crumpled and small.

"I know just how you feel," he said. "And we may as well face it, there's a storm blowing up. The best thing you can do is go to bed with a bottle of champagne. Want some help about getting there?"

"I'm not seasick," she said indignantly. "It's that damned quinine!"

"Yep, it's nasty stuff," he agreed. "It's better than malaria, and that's about all you can say for it." He laid an inquiring hand on her silken ankle, and then took off her shoes and rubbed her feet in his warm hands. "There's no sense in getting chilly," he said. "Where's your hot-water bottle?"

"I don't know. In the big suit case. I'll be all right pretty soon."

Rodney laid a blanket across her feet and went after the hot-water bottle. When he found it he rang for the stewardess and asked her to fill it.

"Come on, Liz," he said, then. "You're going to be put to bed. Which will you have, the stewardess or me?"

"You."

Her flesh was cold when he touched her.

"Now you *have* done it," he murmured. "Why didn't you pull the blanket over you when you lay down? Sit up just a minute, can you, while I— That's it. Now the bed-jacket, it's got long sleeves. There we are."

"I've never been s-seasick in my life!" she said vaingloriously, and the boat gave a derisive lurch. "Oh, *Rodney*—!"

The bracket with its little cardboard container was conveniently placed, and Rodney held her head in commiserating silence.

The hot-water bottle came, and was put where it would do the most good. Champagne came, of a sort, and seemed to help a little. Rodney was a good sailor, of course. Good? He was perfect! He and Charles and Mrs. Guerber were the only passengers to appear in the dining-room. Elizabeth lived on champagne and bits of cold chicken breast, and the quinine which Rodney handed her before he went down to breakfast. His tact and his sympathy never flagged, and she, from whom even self-respect eventually departed, wondered drearily if he would ever think her beautiful again, and decided that anyway it was too late now to fall back on the stewardess. Besides, Rodney was the best nurse she had ever had.

She lost all track of time, but at last there was a night when Rodney, coming down to bed, announced that with any luck they would be blown into Manzanillo, the first stop, early the next morning.

When she woke, the boat was still heaving gently but the engines were slowed down. Pretty soon Rodney came in, smelling of wind and spray, and said he thought it would be a good thing if she made a real effort and went up on deck awhile, and did she want some help.

Elizabeth sat up willingly enough, and then said she did want some help. Rodney washed her face with a hot cloth and then a cold one—found her clothes and put her into them—tied her shoes and held a hand-mirror while she used a lipstick and powder-puff.

"You're awfully good to me," she mumbled at some point during his ministrations. "Just like a m-mother."

"What was that?" he queried. "Other foot, now. You've still got two, believe it or not."

"Rodney, are you sure you aren't sick of the sight of me forever?" she mumbled, and leaned against him while he used a comb on her rumpled curls. "Are you sure you wouldn't rather just drop me overboard and say no more about it?"

"Since when have you been delirious?" he inquired. "Here's your coat. Come along top side and look at Manzanillo. 'Tisn't much of a place, but the sun is shining and the sky is blue and the air is nice and warm. Frank has seen his first palm-tree, and just think! there are real live pelicans out fishing for their breakfast!"

XVI

The port of Santa Rosa was typical of a dozen others along the coast south of Manzanillo, which is in Mexico, and north of Panama—and it was only a little worse than most of them. It presented a strip of scraggy waterfront, with palm trees all askew; a huddle of corrugated iron shacks which were warehouses, at the shoreward end of a rickety pier on stilts; a muddle of thatched dobe huts, crawling with unclothed children, poultry, and pigs. Behind the town rose the jungle-clad slope of the inevitable volcano, with the inevitable smoke-cloud above it.

From the waterfront you traversed an unsavory, stifling alley where starveling dogs elbowed the big black vultures for garbage on the local dumping-ground, and thus you came to the broad Avenida and the grass-grown cobbles and tipsy lamp-posts of the Plaza. Here the palms and purple bougainvillea in the Parque round the gimcrack bandstand were powdered with the same fine volcanic dust which stirred at every footfall. Here the white plaster façade of the mission church on one side faced the police station and the Hotel Europa on the other. The flat-fronted houses, seldom more than one story high because of earthquakes, and pock-marked with bullet holes from some forgotten revolution, cast no shade in the mid-afternoon heat. Occasionally a massive door stood open so that from the glare of the street glimpses could be had into dusty, flowery patios with dribbling fountains and sad caged birds. There was no American consul, and not even an International Club. The nearest fruit-company hospital was nine miles away at Santo Tomas. The theater was closed up tight,

171

recognizable by a couple of tattered posters from the last show, long since departed. The only entertainment now was the Sunday night Plaza concert and parade.

A half-breed policeman in a ragged blue uniform with a revolver sagging in the holster at his belt leaned against the wall of the jail, his bare feet crossed, while he watched a trio of dirty children teasing a loaded pack-mule, whose master was attending to some business inside the police station. A pair of drooling oxen plodded along, urged on by a pointed stick in the hand of a half-grown Indian boy, an empty wooden cart clattering behind. There was everywhere the heavy, constant, not unpleasant smell of coffee, over-ripe fruit, fish, greasy cooking, and Indian.

Mr. Phipps, agent of the fruit company at Santo Tomas, had come down to meet them and turn over possession of the house which Andrew had arranged for them to occupy. He was a small, wilted, anxious man, obviously awed by his responsibilities. The unexpected sight of Liz Dare, exquisite in white silk and a wide hat, carrying a practical but decorative parasol, completely floored him. You could see his mind conducting a frantic inventory of the house she was to live in, and finding very little to comfort him.

Under Mr. Phipps's diffident guidance they went straight from the dock to the Hotel Europa with their hand luggage, and Rodney ordered dinner and a night's lodging for them all. The hotel was a square white building with little iron balconies outside the windows on the second or top floor, and a large, well-tended patio full of flowers. On the way to it, the cobbles under Elizabeth's white-shod feet, the walls of the houses on either side, shimmered and swayed before her eyes in the fierce heat of a tropic afternoon. There was a trickle of perspiration between her shoulder blades, and a soaking strip two inches wide beneath her belt. Sturgis mopped himself regularly, Skinner shone pinkly with a new sunburn, Frank was gaily dripping at every pore, and the Guerbers agreed that they had forgotten how hot it could be down here—

172

but Charles and Rodney seemed unimpaired; seemed, in fact, not to notice anything unusual in the temperature. Elizabeth decided that Rodney looked as though he had been born in white ducks and a solar topi.

When the arrangements had been made at the hotel, Mr. Phipps put Rodney, Charles, and Elizabeth into a dilapidated open touring-car with hot black leather seats and a ragged canvas top, and drove them along the rutted road which led from the Avenida up the side of the hill behind the town to the Casa Paraiso.

It was a little used road, as not much lay beyond the house except a few native farms and a huddle or two of thatched huts claiming to be villages. Just outside the town was a graveyard full of white plaster tombs, with a garbage pit at the edge of it where vultures swarmed. The fact that there was almost no traffic had no effect on Pedro's use of the horn, which he blew with indiscriminate zest for ox-carts, children, dogs, chickens, or merely an empty hairpin curve. The surface of the road was more like that of an abandoned stream-bed, and the zigzagging course it took often passed the same hut three times at different levels. Most of the brightly dressed Indian women at the roadside were or had been comely, they were all barefoot and all seemed to be in advanced stages of pregnancy, while with the most glorious ease they carried a baby on their backs and a loaded basket on their heads.

But as the car climbed, the staggering beauty of the tropics set in. Purple bougainvillea, flamboyant lilies, scented jasmine, were lively with humming-birds and the lazy beat of papilio wings. There were breadfruit and calabash trees, and the strange, spiky beauty of pawpaws. Macaws and parrokeets, which one never thought of as flying free, looked down complacently from the trees they called home. And the air grew perceptibly cooler as they climbed, for the house was knowingly placed at the upper boundary of the acres it commanded.

The Casa Paraiso had been built some years ago by an enterprising American who sank a fortune in his belief that there was a much larger fortune to be made by growing bananas and cacao. Came the blight, for which there is still no adequate remedy, and the bananas all died, and the cacao showed no profit. So one day he simply left his hacienda Paradise—walked out, with only a suitcase, and took the northbound boat back to the States, and died soon after he got there, as much of a broken heart as anything else. His estate, to which there were no longer any heirs, and which he had placed in Andrew's hands, by that time consisted solely of the derelict Casa Paraiso, with its solid mahogany doors and partitions, its tiled floors, its deep-set grilled windows looking out above the ravaged acres of banana plants which covered the slope below, its spacious high-ceilinged rooms, most of them still only half furnished, and its overgrown patio. The house remained exactly as he left it, except for the effects of time and earthquake shocks, which had cracked a wall here and there, and shaken down some plaster, and smashed the crockery. The rugs and hangings had molded and discolored with the procession of the rainy seasons. The fountain in the patio had ceased to flow. But some of the orchids which the doting owner had hoped to grow there still flourished untended.

Mr. Phipps, who had been his admiring friend, was both excited and dismayed to receive the letter from Andrew requesting that the Casa Paraiso be opened, cleaned, and put in order for the use of Dr. Monroe and a party of seven, who would bring their own bedding and supplies. The letter asked also that servants be found and recommended on Dr. Monroe's arrival.

Mr. Phipps had found it saddening to enter the house again and see the wreck it had become. But in pursuit of his instructions from New York, he scrupulously supervised and harangued and criticized while a couple of Indian women, aided by an aged Negro foreman who had never left the place, turned it out room by room, swept up the fallen plaster, let in the hot dry-season air, and shook their heads over the marks of mold and insect life

174

on its furnishings. Things literally came apart in their hands. But the house itself stood firm, and was soon made weather-proof again, its cooking-stove in repair, its laundry ready to function, its water supply tested and approved.

Beyond the garage and stables, which surrounded a small patio of their own, the road petered out immediately into a mere mule-track which wound away upwards past the ruins of an ancient dobe village which had been destroyed by an earthquake in 1892. The car passed through an open gate with carved mahogany doors heavy enough to withstand a siege, in a white archway dripping purple bougainvillea. Elizabeth stepped out rather limply, and Charles just behind her said, "I'm going to like this!"

Then the two Indian women, comely, with innocent, sleepy eyes, dressed in new, brightly colored, shapeless clothes, presented themselves shyly as the Señora's staff. The Señora smiled her best at them, and they smiled back at her reverently, for they had never seen anything so beautiful in their lives unless it was the Madonna in her festival robes. Rodney spoke to them in his informal Spanish, and they tore their eyes away from the face of the Señora long enough to reply politely to him, and at once resumed their un-blinking contemplation of the vision in white which he had brought with him.

Carmela was a very good cook, Mr. Phipps was explaining, and Antonina would "assist." He added that there was also a Negro, remnant of the grand banana days, a gaunt great man from Jamaica, no longer quite right in the head, perhaps, but entirely gentle and possessed still of remarkable strength. He lived in one of the deserted workmen's huts down the slope, and cultivated his own garden patch, which fed him. Mr. Phipps suggested that the old black would be useful to clear the patio and make it bloom again, if that were desired, and anyway he was able to lift and carry. His name? Everyone had forgotten. He answered now just to Jamaica. Rodney said that he would like to see the man, and Antonina was sent to fetch him.

175

The colonnade of the patio had a red tiled roof supported by mahogany posts at the outer edge of its tiled floor. The strangled fountain in the center of the large unroofed part was shallow and tazza-shaped, with a raised curb. Once there had been some sort of pattern, with tiled paths and a lawn with a graceful iron bench shaded by a pepper tree. Now giant geraniums, magnolia, outsize ferns, unpruned rose-bushes, jasmine, tuberoses, and unbelievable wild orchids climbed and rambled and overhung. Little orange and cypress and fig trees, once formalized, had outgrown their pottery urns, cracking the sides wide open with the thrust and bulge of their confined roots. The low, dense shade of an avocado tree darkened one corner, killing out all bloom beneath it. It was an orgy of crowding, untrammeled tropical fruition.

The kitchen and laundry were at the far end from the *sala* and the bedrooms, screened by a pleached lantana whose growth had now passed all bounds. The cooking-stove was built into the outer wall of the house under the shade of the patio roof. Little lizards darted along the tiled floor and sunned themselves at the edge of what had once been lawn. A tanager sang its heart out in the top of the pepper tree.

"Well!" said Elizabeth, as they stood surveying it all from the shadow of the colonnade. "It looks exactly like Hollywood's idea of what a neglected patio would look like!" And then she took a surprised step backwards as Antonina reappeared with the Negro known as Jamaica.

He was clad in a dirty loin-cloth, a wide sombrero, and a friendly, unembarrassed smile. He was as tall as Rodney, and had magnificent shoulders, and he met your eye with a simple dignity all his own. Rodney looked him over and said in his casual, unemphatic way—

"Good afternoon."

"Good afternoon, sir."

"I hear you're something of a gardener," Rodney suggested.

"Formerly I was, in the old days," said Jamaica slowly, as though

176

his English speech came rustily, its original soft British modulations intact. "Anything from orchids to bananas—I used to have what you might call a Way with them, sir."

"Do you think anything can be done for the patio now?" Rodney inquired, and it was plain that in those few brief moments he had made up his mind about the man. "It's pretty well run riot."

Jamaica surveyed the dusty, rambling vegetation sadly, seeing the patio as it once had been, as it was meant to be.

"Well, sir, someone needs to take a *machete* to it first of all," he said thoughtfully. "But there is still a good deal here that is worth saving."

"Suppose I put you in charge," said Rodney. "Do you want to take it on?"

The old Negro looked at him with incredulous gratitude, but no servility.

"Are you giving me a job, sir?"

"That's right—head gardener. It looks like a lot of work, but it's all yours."

"Thank you, sir." Jamaica straightened, took on a visible inch of self-respect, but he was trembling with eagerness and seemed dazed by his good fortune. "I—never thought to have a job again, sir."

"Well, go to it, you've got one now!" said Rodney cheerfully. "There must be some tools somewhere. You see what you can find, and let me know what else you need."

"I know where—thank you, sir—I know where the tools used to be kept in the old days—" His forefinger rose vaguely to the brim of his hat and he turned away towards the kitchen end of the patio, like a man walking in his sleep. When he had gone a few steps he hesitated and looked back at Rodney. "Might I—speak with you *privately*, sir?"

Rodney went to him, and was seen to nod gravely to some request, and then rejoined the others.

"Are you really going to turn that ogre loose here with a

machete?" Elizabeth whispered. "We'll all be murdered in our beds! What did he say to you?"

"He asked me to buy him some trousers, and take it out of his first week's wages. Which shall be done."

They had already decided that owing to customs and transportation difficulties, and to the quick tropical nightfall, there was no possibility of sleeping that night at the Casa Paraiso. It was nearly dinner time when they arrived back at the hotel.

Elizabeth blinked a little when she entered the room in which she was expected to sleep, but Rodney after a swift and knowing investigation said that it was remarkably clean, and that she could hang things up safely. Still looking somewhat dubious all to herself—even the three-a-day of her childhood had shown her nothing quite like this—Elizabeth laid the fitted tray of her dressing-case on the bureau without taking anything out of it, and perched her hat gingerly on a corner of the mirror.

The heat in the bare-walled whitewashed room seemed very nearly a tangible thing that you could stir with your fingers like water. Elizabeth peeled off the white silk dress which had been sticking to her again ever since they left the Casa Paraiso, splashed cold water about recklessly—the house had a bathroom, anyway, with a real porcelain tub—did her face over, put on another white silk dress over dry underthings, and was ready for dinner. Rodney too washed his face and changed his shirt, but seemed not to have perspired at all on his tidy white ducks. He paused just inside their door on the way out, and laid his arm around her waist.

"Honey, the worst is over now. Tomorrow you'll begin to enjoy yourself. I promise."

Elizabeth said she was sorry she had been such a nuisance so far.

"I don't know," he remarked, with one of his slanting looks, "you're pretty fascinating to me, even when you're seasick. It must be Love!"

The rest of the party was assembled under the rhythmic creak

178

of a large ceiling fan in the bar, along with Mr. Phipps whom Rodney had invited to join them at dinner. A fairly unanimous vote was cast for Tom Collins. The drinks when they arrived after a slight delay were something less than they might have been, owing to a breakdown of the ice-machine in the hotel, but everybody drank them thirstily in the devitalizing heat, while a coppery sun slid down the sky towards a slick, heaving sea.

Mr. Phipps seemed restless. Two or three times he rose, glass in hand, and drifted to the door or the window which looked on the baking Plaza, and then drifted back. After one of these excursions he nodded silently at Sturgis, who said cheerfully, "Well, perhaps you're right," and mopped himself, and then found Rodney's eyes upon him and began to tell a rather pointless story about a man he had last seen in Panama.

There wasn't a fan in the dining-room, only flies. The tablecloth was spotted and the silverware a little slimy. There were two bamboo bird-cages with a dejected, mangy-looking mocking-bird sulking in each. The waiter wore his shirt outside, and no shoes, and shone with sweat as he bustled to and fro in his touching zeal to serve them. (Rodney always had the same effect on waiters. As a race, they collectively ran their legs off for him.)

Elizabeth, who would have sold her soul by now for a lettuce-clad American fruit-salad fresh from the cracked ice, worked away conscientiously at the greasy plate full of chicken and rice and red peppers before her.

"The Señora feels the heat?" the waiter inquired solicitously, thus calling attention to her shortcomings, when he came to take away her plate and found most of the generous helping still there.

"Well, perhaps a little—just at first," she admitted, apologetically, and he clucked a commiserating tongue.

"Any time now we will catch it," he said significantly. "Always I can tell!"

"Catch what?" said Elizabeth blankly, and Rodney's quiet voice overlapped her.

179

"How about some fruit?" he was saying to the waiter. "How about some mangoes?"

"Ah, yes, mangoes!" cried the waiter intelligently. "But certainly, *señor*—mangoes we have!" He padded away, kitchenwards.

While they were drinking the thick black coffee sweetened with brown sugar, and waiting for the mangoes, a dull rumbling began somewhere back of beyond and seemed to roll towards them, increasing as it came.

"Thunder!" said Elizabeth, listening.

"Here we go again!" said Mr. Phipps simultaneously, and pushed back his chair.

"Is it *really?*" cried Frank, looking excited and pleased, for the coffee cups had shivered in the saucers on the table, and in the kitchen something fell and broke.

The Guerbers were on their feet, Skinner's chair went over backwards as he rose. Rodney's hand closed hard on Elizabeth's wrist as he too rose, pulling her up at the same time.

"Come on," he said briefly. "Earthquake."

"*Earthquake!*" she repeated on an incredulous squeak.

"Now, don't get scared, they have them all the time down here— little ones that don't amount to much. You just run out into the open till it's over."

The rumbling was considerably louder as they emerged into the Plaza, and it didn't sound so much like thunder any more. There was a sort of rending sound along with it, two sharp reports like distant blowouts, and then a bumping from underneath as though a cosmic trunk was going down a staircase in hell.

Elizabeth stumbled sharply on the cobbles and caught at Rodney's arm, and her knees were wobbly and her tongue was dry, because earthquakes were things that killed people and burned down whole cities—she had never envisioned little earthquakes that didn't amount to much. Some tiles rattled off a roof across the Plaza and she knew by her dizziness that the ground beneath her

180

moved, not all in one piece like the deck of a ship, but heavily, like something live disturbed in its sleep.

"R-Rodney—!"

"It won't last long," he said soothingly.

From the buildings all round the Plaza people were trickling out, looking up at the volcano and calling to one another. Night fell visibly, as though someone had dropped a snuffer on the setting sun, and the air was dusty and had an acrid taste. Somebody else, with great presence of mind, threw the switch at the power-house which controlled the street lighting, and lamp-posts showed murkily in the gritty darkness. There was a sullen red glow in the sky from the volcano above the town.

"There's the padre," said Rodney. "Let's go and speak to him."

Coming across the dimly lit Plaza towards them was the priest— an enormous man, with a front too impressive to be called a stomach. A ragged child trotted beside him, holding to his cassock. With a single shrewd glance at Rodney, who was just then passing under a lamp-post, the priest changed his course and sang out a cheery Good-evening in English, and extended a cordial hand.

"I am Father Joseph," he continued, as though there was nothing at all unusual in the circumstances which surrounded their meeting. "I presume you are of the Casa Paraiso party?"

"My name is Monroe," said Rodney, in the same key, shaking hands. "This is my wife. It's her first earthquake," he added.

"Good evening, *señora*." The priest turned merry eyes full of understanding on the white-clad figure which clung to Rodney's arm while she offered her other hand. "It is alarming at first, I know. But we get used to it down here."

As he spoke, the ground grumbled again and tiles fell with a crash from the roof of the hotel behind them. Somewhere a woman screamed, and the child crowded closer against the priest's legs, peering up at the strangers. Then, with no further warning, all the lights went out.

"Oh-oh," said Rodney calmly in the eerie darkness which some-

181

how tasted more strongly now of brimstone. "There goes the power-plant!"

"Always!" the priest's rich voice replied without apparent concern. "On the slightest excuse, our electricity breaks down!" The ground was rocking again under their feet, and the child whimpered in the dark, and the priest spoke to it reassuringly in Spanish. "This shock *is* more severe than usual, I shall have injuries to deal with, I am afraid. People lose their heads," he regretted. "They run into things, they *invite* disaster! And then they come to me to be mended."

"If you need any help with your first aid, let me know," said Rodney, and Elizabeth, pressed against his side with his quiet fingers holding hers, marveled again at how he took things in his stride, at how nothing startled or upset him—this fantastic conversation going politely on between him and the priest while the darkness all round them rumbled and shook and tasted of cinders, and roofs fell and people screamed, and the child clasped Father Joseph's knees and felt itself safe. "My kit is not unpacked yet," Rodney was saying, "but I might be of some use myself, and I have an experienced nurse with me as well."

"Always scalp wounds, and smashed toes, and a few broken bones," sighed the priest. "There is a doctor in town, of course—a very competent doctor, trained in the States—but the people come to me, instead of to him. For one thing, they are used to me—and for another, I do not charge them anything! I think the worst is over now, but there may be some confusion at the hotel, at least till the lights come on again. If you and your wife would care to come along to my house—just there by the church—I can give the Señora a chair and some candles, at least!"

"Thanks very much," said Rodney, "but we—"

"I have been looking forward to your arrival," the priest went on in his charming, almost unaccented English. "Naturally I did not expect our first meeting to be quite like this! But in any case,

182

my house is now more than ever at your disposal—" The sentence had a wistful lift.

"Thank you," said Rodney. "Charles!"

"Yep, I'm here," said Charles's voice out of the blackness near by.

"Go dig out some flashlights. There's one in the brief-case up in my room. We're going down to the dock. Where's Mrs. Guerber?"

"I'm here, Doctor."

"I want you and Liz to go over to the padre's house for a while. Perhaps you can help him if there's anyone hurt. The rest of us are going down to see to the stuff, in case there's a wave."

"Yes, Doctor." Mrs. Guerber materialized beside them.

"But, R-Rodney—" implored Elizabeth, holding to him.

"I won't be long," he said, detaching her fingers. "It's all right now. You stick to the padre till I get back. Come on, Charles—"

"All right, hurry up!" yelled Charles from a little distance.

"Coming!"

Rodney was gone from her, enveloped at once in the thick dark. The noise had stopped now, and an eerie wind sprang up, rustling the dry palm leaves and foliage in the Parque. Here and there in the houses candles began to show, or a lantern. The cobbles underfoot were once more behaving as cobbles should.

"There's Maria, watching for us," said the priest, and looking towards the white glimmer of the church, Elizabeth saw a light in the doorway to the left of it, where an old Indian woman stood holding a candle stub and peering out, the tiny flame flickering behind her shielding fingers. "She has no fear for herself, but always she is frightened lest something will have dropped on me!" the priest continued with amusement, and called out to the woman in Spanish as they all moved towards her.

Elizabeth sat in a corner of the padre's little parlor, sipping a glass of his excellent wine and listening while he and Mrs. Guerber reminisced about earthquakes they had known. Then a few casualties began to arrive.

Kettles of hot water were brought by Maria, and more candles

183

for a better light; rolls of bandages and absorbent cotton appeared, there was a strong smell of antiseptic, a baby cried and cried. Mrs. Guerber, on her knees on the sheet which Maria had spread over the floor, was silent and efficient, bathing, stitching, soothing, behaving exactly as though she wore a starched white uniform. Elizabeth, sitting useless and forgotten in her corner, had grown a large inferiority complex—for if she offered to help she would only be waved aside, as she knew very well, and so why expose oneself to humiliation?—when she became aware of a pair of eyes which regarded her steadily from the floor near her feet.

A scrawny little Indian boy of perhaps ten, with a fresh white bandage at a somewhat rakish angle round his head, like an irreverent turban, was squatted there, gazing up at her.

"Hullo," she said, and smiled at him.

The boy smiled back.

"What's your name?" she asked, grateful for someone who did not appear to regard her as beneath contempt.

The child murmured something in Spanish and was then overcome by shyness.

"I'm Liz," she continued informally. "Who are you? Come over here by me." She held out her hand, and the boy rose and approached her warily. "Liz," she repeated, pointing to herself. "You say it. Go on—say it! *Liz.*"

"Leess," said the boy at a venture, and giggled apologetically.

"That's it! Now tell me *your* name," she pleaded.

He murmured something, his eyes caught by the flash of the big aquamarine on her third finger. She let him look at it, and he touched it timidly with one grubby fingertip, and smiled up into her face. Elizabeth fished about in her white leather hand-bag and pulled out a tiny smelling-salts bottle of cut crystal with a gold top. She unscrewed the cap and held the bottle under her own nose, sniffed, and made a funny face. Then she held it under his nose and they laughed together when he too sniffed and made a very funny face. She put the cap back on, and laid the bottle in his hand.

184

"You can have that," she said. "Just to remember me by. Don't lose it, now!"

Stupefied with delight, he fumbled again at the cap, and she showed him how it worked, and again they sniffed, and laughed together.

There was the sound of a woman's sobbing at the door, and Elizabeth turned quickly. Rodney stood there, holding the limp body of a two-year-old child in his arms. His coat was gone. His white trousers and shirt, even his face, were smeared with dirt and ashes, and bloodstains showed where the child lay against him. The sobbing came from a barefoot woman in a bright ragged dress at his side. Blood trickled from a cut at the edge of her black hair, and she held the wrist of her right arm in the other hand. But it was not from pain that she wept, but for the child.

Mrs. Guerber went to him and held out capable hands for the thing he carried.

"The child is dead," he said without moving. "Father, this is for you. The woman's arm is broken, and nobody seems to know where the doctor is. There's been quite a fire down on the waterfront."

Father Joseph took the child's body and spoke in Spanish to the sobbing mother. She followed him from the room.

Rodney looked about him, then, rather wearily.

"Hullo," he said to Elizabeth, and his eyes went on past her to Mrs. Guerber who was tidying up, with Maria's assistance. Most of the injured had gone home, though one or two still sat about as though waiting for something. "Things are better down there now," he said. "Fortunately the wave didn't amount to much. Charles and the rest are still grubbing round. Our stuff's all right. The lights will come on soon, I hear. Can I do anything?"

"It is nothing," said Mrs. Guerber. "We are nearly finished here. There was nothing very bad."

Rodney looked back at Elizabeth.

"Who's your small friend?" he asked, and smiled at the boy who still stood close beside her.

185

"Ask him his name, Rodney, I can't make him understand. He's sweet, can't we do something for him?"

There was an interchange of soft Spanish between Rodney and the bashful little boy, who showed the crystal bottle with pride and then hid it jealously in his hands for fear he might not be allowed to keep it. Elizabeth saw that Rodney was amused and at the same time pleased with her.

"His name is Vicente," he said. "And he has fallen in love with you. But you know that already, I don't have to tell you."

Elizabeth was at once acutely conscious of Mrs. Guerber's unhumorous presence, and wished he hadn't said it.

Father Joseph returned with the injured woman, and they made a splint for her arm and a bandage for her head, while she went on sobbing drearily to herself. Rodney, on his knees beside her, wrapping the bandage, gave the priest an account of the state of the waterfront. Then the woman was led away by Maria, and the room was cleared, except for Vicente, squatting near Elizabeth's feet. When Father Joseph questioned him with a hint of severity, Vicente looked up mutely at his angel, and Elizabeth patted his shoulder and said that he was a friend of hers, and Father Joseph let him stay.

Charles arrived then, to say that everything was under control, and the others had gone back to the hotel to wash up. So far as he knew, only the child had been killed. And even as he made his comforting report, the electric lights suddenly came on again with an effect of restoring everything to normal.

Father Joseph heaved a sigh of relief and looked round for the bottle of wine, and bustled off to find more glasses, in Maria's absence. Remarkably little had been broken in the kitchen, he announced on his return. The walls of his house were very thick, nearly as thick as those of the church.

Elizabeth sat quietly, feeling as though a nightmare was over. An earthquake, her first, had come and gone. Because of it, she had acquired a new *cabellero* named Vicente, Rodney and Charles

186

had each ruined a suit of clothes, and somewhere a woman ~~still~~ wept for a dead child. And yet here they all were, drinking wine in a tidy room, electric-lighted, exactly as though nothing out of the way had occurred—not even talking about earthquakes any more. It was like waking from a bad dream, yes—but this dream was real, and could happen again.

She glanced at Rodney, relaxed into his chair, a fragile glass in his long fingers, his face easy and smiling—but with a smudge across one cheek, and those dark, dreadful stains on his white clothes. She glanced at Mrs. Guerber, remote and silent and composed, on the edge of things; at Charles, whose glass was already empty; at Vicente, turning the crystal bottle against the light, his hurt forgotten in rapture; at the priest, who was telling Rodney about his collection of insects. None of it seemed quite real, though. It was such bad theater. Psychologically it was all wrong. More evidence of disaster should remain.

Even while she thought it, Father Joseph left his chair and went eagerly to a cupboard and brought out two large square boxes with glass tops. Inside them were rows of insects on long pins, beetles in one, butterflies in the other. Each separate specimen had a label, minutely lettered.

Rodney and Charles bent above the boxes, admiring the things on pins, seeming very impressed, and said that Skinner must come and see them. Father Joseph beamed with pride, for never in his life before had he had an opportunity to converse like this with actual scientists, with men whose lives were spent at what was to him only a fascinating hobby; men who could appreciate the attraction such a hobby could possess for a busy person like himself.

"But some of the beetles are beautiful!" Elizabeth discovered with surprise. "I never knew before that beetles could be as lovely as that. Those iridescent ones in the corner—what are they?"

"They are dung beetles," said Father Joseph simply. "It is a thing to contemplate, is it not, *señora*? The lovely ones are the dung beetles. Nature makes one very thoughtful."

187

XVII

Elizabeth found it difficult to get to sleep in a hard bed she didn't trust, surrounded by white plaster walls she no longer had confidence in. (Rodney slept at once, of course. It was perhaps the one really infuriating thing he did—to sleep like a baby whenever the need overtook him.) She was wakened from exhausted unconsciousness early the next morning by the jangle of bells from the church across the Plaza.

For a while she lay still with her eyes shut, hoping the noise would stop. When it finally did, other noise took its place—the rattle of wooden ox-carts over the cobbles, the babel of uninhibited native voices raised in tropical cries and laughter and controversy, the yapping of a tethered dog, the squawk-squawk of a tame parrot in a near by patio. There were smells, too, enough to wake the dead—the dominant, cheerful smell of coffee, plus a whiff of fresh-caught fish, a whisper of garlic, a touch of stale frying-fat, a *soupçon* of manure—and then, without a footfall to herald it, there was the familiar smell of Rodney's shaving-soap and fresh linen, as he bent over her and laid his lips against her cheek.

"Up," he said softly. "This is our busy day. I'm going down to the dock now with Charles and get things under way. You be ready for breakfast when I get back."

She stirred drowsily and locked her arms behind his neck so that his weight eased down on the edge of the bed. He was all shaved and brushed and dressed and ready for the street, and as usual he had done it without any bustle or banging about.

"What time is it?" she asked vaguely.

188

"I hate to tell you. But if you want to get out of here before it turns really hot you'd better get a move on."

"I dreamed there was an earthquake."

"That makes two. We had one before we went to bed."

Her eyes came open then, and she regarded him dazedly, remembering.

"Will there be earthquakes up at Casa Paraiso?"

"Little ones, I expect, now and then. Maybe not another for months, you never can tell."

"Rodney, what kind of a place have you brought me to?"

"You'll like it up there," he said, and smiled, and kissed her lightly, and started to rise, but her arms pinioned him.

"How long will you be away?"

"Till breakfast." There was no dalliance in him this morning. He removed her arms gently from behind his neck. "Don't you dare go back to sleep again!"

The door closed behind him and his sun-helmet and his smile.

Perhaps he was going to be a little less enchanting, a little more like other men, when he was bossing a trip, she thought, lying still while her eyes traced a long zigzag crack across the white wall behind the bureau. Oh, well—margin for error. Not even Rodney could be perfect all the time, three hundred and sixty-five days in the year. That crack in the wall—it was a fresh one—it hadn't been there yesterday when they first came into the room—

She sat up hastily, and grabbed for her slippers.

She was dressed, but still pottering with her powder-puff and comb when he returned. He forgot to kiss her. He closed her dressing-case with such despatch that he left her comb outside and had to drop it into his coat pocket. He stood with the doorknob in his hand while she put on her hat. Decidedly a little less Rodney than usual. He had a lot on his mind, of course—

There was a fine layer of dust, which was really volcanic ash, over everything you touched, but everybody in the dining-room was congratulating themselves and each other that the volcano had

189

not been roused to real activity, that the wave had done no damage, and that there had not been one of the usual torrential storms, to follow what was cheerfully alluded to by Mr. Phipps as a right smart shock of earthquake.

Mr. Phipps, who was waiting around for the bus which was to take him back to Santo Tomas, said that it was a lovely Central American day—and Elizabeth went to the door of the hotel and stood looking out. At that hour of the morning the heat was not intense, the blue sky was full of billowy white clouds—and black vultures—the golden sun shone divinely without glare, and there was the singing of an infant school in the house next the church. In the Plaza, a gang of eight ragged prisoners in chains were languidly piling débris into a wheelbarrow and pretending to sweep up, while their almost equally ragged guards—four of them, barefoot, each wearing the remnants of a uniform—sat on the curb and played cards, their rifles pointing any which way, their laughter loud and carefree.

Rodney joined her at the door, carrying some magazines they had read on the boat and a couple of new novels.

"Is it all right with you if I give these to the padre?" he said. "He's crazy for something to read."

"Will he like those?" she asked dubiously, for it was a very miscellaneous collection.

"He'll love them. Want to come with me and see?"

She crossed the Plaza at his side. Old Maria opened the door to them and ushered them into the little parlor, and disappeared. The infant voices ceased, and Father Joseph stood on the threshold, beaming. His eyes went straight to the bright newsprint in Rodney's hands, and he could hardly tear his gaze away again.

"Well, well," he said cordially. "I hope the Señora is none the worse for last night?"

She smiled at him angelically and said she had quite recovered, thanks.

Then Rodney proffered the magazines and books, and the priest

190

took them from him almost with a snatch, he was so eager to examine his treasure.

"But this is very thoughtful of you," he murmured, his fat fingers caressing the gay jackets and patting the cover of a film magazine. "I have not seen anything like this since—oh, since donkey's years! See, this is the last American magazine I have had—" He opened a drawer in his ancient mahogany desk and took out of it a dreary, tattered copy of *Esquire* from the preceding year. Half its width had been soaked in sea water, and the pages were brittle as he turned them. "You perhaps know this magazine?" he queried innocently, looking from Elizabeth to Rodney.

Rodney said Yes, but they didn't see it very often.

"It cheers me up sometimes—it cheers me," said Father Joseph, and found the page he sought. "Perhaps you didn't see this one?" He pointed to a black-and-white cartoon.

Rodney looked, and laughed. Elizabeth peeked past his shoulder and her eyes widened. It *was* funny. But how did Father Joseph know that it was?

The priest put *Esquire* tenderly back into the drawer and stroked his new magazines again.

"What a feast!" he gloated. "What a temptation to idleness! I am more grateful than I can say, for such a temptation!" His gaze sought Rodney's face with a kind of humble dignity. "There is not much I can offer— But of course you read scientific German?" And when Rodney nodded, he went to a little book-case across the room and took out a volume and blew the dust off the top of it. "I have here—I do not know if it is rare—an old German book about the tropical birds of prey—I do not know if you would care—"

"May I borrow it?" said Rodney.

"I am honored," said Father Joseph, infinitely pleased.

Elizabeth suspected, as they crossed the Plaza again towards the hotel, that Rodney had taken the book out of sheer good manners to increase the padre's self-esteem. Touched by the pathetic little library, she wanted to send to Los Angeles for dozens of books instantly and present them all to Father Joseph, wanted to take out subscriptions in his name to *Esquire* and all its friends and relations, if that was what he liked—but Rodney restrained her.

"We'll leave him a lot of our books when we go," he said. "Don't swamp him. What I gave him just now will last him quite a while."

"But that's *niggardly!*" she cried, all afire with good will. "Please make out a list of what he'd really like and let me order them by the next boat!"

"All right, Lady Bountiful," said Rodney affectionately. "But you'll only drive him crazy, he hasn't much time to read."

"Time. He's got nothing else *but,* in a place like this!"

"All right, all right," said Rodney, smiling.

Breakfast consisted of *tortillas,* prunes, and coffee. Elizabeth ate the prunes and drank the coffee. The flowers in the hotel patio seemed brighter than on the previous evening, and the blooms which had opened that morning were not yet coated with dust.

Towards the end of the meal Dr. Guerber lifted his nose and sniffed appreciatively.

"There is some sort of fragrance here," he said. "I cannot make out what it is." And he sniffed again, towards the patio.

"It's not out there," said Rodney, wearing an expressionless sort of expression. "It's over here by me."

Dr. Guerber looked at him, mistrusting his own understanding of English, which was after all very reliable.

"The fragrance," Rodney explained. "It's Liz. I thought it was a new flower once myself, but don't let her fool you. It's just Liz."

"Charming," said Dr. Guerber, sniffing. "There is lilac in it, I think—yes, and jasmine—and possibly freesia—"

"Wrong," said Elizabeth. "No freesia. They're soapy."

"No freesia," he agreed, sniffing. "Possibly heliotrope. What else?"

192

"Ah!" she said mysteriously, sipping her coffee. "Wouldn't you like to know!"

Dr. Guerber chortled delightedly at this badinage, and wagged a playful forefinger at her.

"I and the humming-birds!" he said. "If always you smell so goot, we will follow you in droves!"

There was a slight pause, during which everyone but her husband became aware how unamused Mrs. Guerber was. Rodney pushed back his chair.

"Well," he said. "I think, Charles—"

"Rodney, will you please buy me those birds?" Elizabeth demanded unexpectedly.

"What birds?"

She pointed at the bamboo cages where the two disheveled mocking-birds moped on their dirty perches. Everyone waited to see what Rodney would do.

"Why do you want them?" he asked. "They aren't long for this world."

"I want to set them free."

"Why?" he asked patiently. "They'll only die a little sooner if you do."

"But, Rodney, look at them! I can't stand it. What are you made of?"

Rodney rose with his usual leisurely grace, and the others left their chairs also, only too willingly and filled with hopes of escape.

"Everybody get their luggage downstairs now," he said. "The cars will be here soon. Charles, you and Frank go back down to the dock and watch the loading."

The company dispersed, which left Rodney standing over Elizabeth at the table. His eyes rested on her thoughtfully. They were Rodney's eyes still, but not those of her pampering lover. She felt herself outside again, as she had in the beginning—outside looking in at the different world he inhabited. The door was closing again in her face. On this busy morning, full of what were to him

193

customary, absorbing affairs, such as the directing of native porters, the handling of delicate luggage full of instruments, the establishment of a new base in the field, she was the one thing too many. She should never have come. She could only be in the way here. Perhaps he would cease to love her at all, if this went on, whereas if she had stayed behind and he had had a chance to miss her—

"Maybe I shouldn't have m-mentioned it," she murmured wretchedly, looking at him with a wide, tragic, pleading gaze—her orphan-face again, but she couldn't help that.

"One of the first things one has to learn in the Latin tropics," he informed her kindly, rather as though addressing a recalcitrant class-room, "is that there is no S.P.C.A. And then one has to realize that it is no good trying to start a private S.P.C.A. of one's own."

"I'm sorry, Rodney—"

"The birds are not being ill-treated, you know," he went on, making a visible effort to be reasonable. "They're probably fed and watered at quite regular intervals. I'll buy them if you wish, and kill them, because the condition of their feet is hopeless. But the next time we come here, there will be two more."

"I'll try to f-forget it," she mumbled, avoiding his eyes.

"They'll be just about as well off if you do," he said, and drew back her chair as she got to her feet, and handed her her forgotten hand-bag from the table. "We must go and say good-by to Mr. Phipps."

Seated with Rodney and Mrs. Guerber on the hot black leather upholstery of the open car, Sturgis in front with Pedro the driver, Elizabeth emerged slowly from the coma of despair which Rodney's disapproval always induced in her, and began to wonder how soon she could get a bath in that lovely porcelain tub in the Casa Paraiso's bathroom. There was nothing like a bath, after all, to take the bitterness out of life. Rodney never laid things up against

194

her, that was something. And pretty soon she would be able really to forget about the birds.

Charles, Frank, Skinner, and Dr. Guerber had remained behind to see the loaded pack-mules on their way before following in the second car. Rodney's party were to start settling in meanwhile, with the hand luggage they had brought.

Jamaica, who must never have stopped working since they last saw him the day before, had got the fountain going again, so that the sound of its cool dribble filled the patio. He had begun to clear the end nearest the bedrooms, trimming back the overgrown, trailing greenery to reveal unsuspected glories of hidden bloom—a climbing yellow rose, half smothered, had come to light, camellias and carnations, and a fig-tree, once beautifully pleached and about to be disciplined again. On their arrival Rodney handed the old Negro a paper parcel which was received with dignified thanks, and soon Jamaica reappeared in clean blue and white striped trousers and a singlet, and resumed his *machete* outside the open door of the room where Elizabeth was disposing the contents of her dressing-case.

The house itself was really lovely, with its hooded fireplaces, its delicate grilles at all the windows cutting a sharp pattern of shadow on walls and floors in the bright sunlight, and its colored tiles everywhere, even in the risers of the wide steps which placed the rooms on different levels. What had been the *sala* would be the laboratory, furnished with the knock-down deal tables and folding camp chairs and carpentered shelves of field-work. A smaller room, intended by the builder for the library, would be used as a sitting-room and library combined—only a few of its waiting shelves were filled, mainly with cheap, moldy, cockroach-gnawed volumes of dated fiction and detective stories. Extra furniture brought in when the *sala* was cleared for action made it both comfortable and impressive.

The bedrooms were in a row along the most decorative side of the patio, each opening on to it with a tall slatted door, each with a high grilled window in the opposite wall. Rodney and Elizabeth had the big one in the corner next to the *sala* and the bathroom, then came Charles and Sturgis, then Frank and Skinner, and the Guerbers at the far end. Owing to one of Charles's premonitions, they had brought camp bedsteads as well as mattresses, bedding, and mosquito-canopies, but some of the fine mahogany four-post beds already in the rooms proved to be usable, and were shifted about, two to a room. There were great carved wardrobes and chests of drawers in the rooms as well. Even the straight chairs were heavy and beautiful in shining mahogany. By assembling the furniture scattered throughout the house, there was plenty for the use of eight people, and the dining-room, apparently finished first, was full of stateliness and charm in the old Spanish style.

Thus Elizabeth found herself in a setting both picturesque and comfortable. There is no more graceful line than the drape of white mosquito-netting above a big bed, no more becoming background than the gleam of old mahogany in a shadowed room with faded burgundy hangings, no style of furniture better calculated to frame feminine beauty than dark Spanish massiveness. Elizabeth, moving daintily about her new home with her springing step, wearing her simple white silk frocks, was a sight which Andrew deserved to see. Even Rodney, in the midst of his unpacking, twice told her with a catch of his breath to just stand still and let him look. "Are you sure you didn't have a Spanish grandmother?" he inquired at last, and she replied (although with gratification) that the only grandmother she'd ever heard much about was Irish. Rodney said that would do. And added that he could well believe it.

A few days after their arrival Rodney was going round with fresh quinine rations for everybody, and picked up the box on Elizabeth's bedside table to replenish its supply. He found it far from empty, and he froze there, the box in his hand.

"Liz, what about this quinine?"

"Well, I—"

"You've not been taking it."

"Well, it made me feel so awful, and I—"

"When did you stop?"

"On the boat. After Manzanillo. It was so wonderful to feel *right* again, I just couldn't bear to—" She faded out apprehensively.

In an awful silence Rodney filled a glass with water from the bedside thermos and came towards her with glass and box like an avenging angel with a fiery sword.

"Take one now," he said, his voice flat with surcharged calm, and she saw with astonishment that he was angrier than she had ever known him to be before. "I don't know what to say to you about this," he went on while she obediently swallowed the quinine, and he took the glass from her again and smacked it down on the tray. "Perhaps it will penetrate if I say that I ought to send you back to New York by the first boat."

"B-but, Rodney—"

"Nobody is going to be a bit surprised if you do get malaria and become a general nuisance," he said bitingly. "I was the one who thought you had the brains to come on this trip and prove yourself a responsible human being who has come of age. I was the one who trusted you to obey orders and do what was expected of you. Well, I was wrong! And nobody can feel a bigger fool than I do!"

"Oh, Rodney, I didn't know—"

"You knew I told you to take one of those things every morning like clockwork! It would serve you right if you did get fever now, but I hope you don't, for the sake of the rest of us. For my own sake, if you like! Because if you don't, maybe nobody else will have to know you skipped your quinine because you had a better idea, and I won't have to be ashamed of my wife!"

"*Really,* Rodney—!"

He was gone from their room, lightfooted as always, but in literally a towering rage.

Well, that blew over, after a while, and she didn't show any signs of fever, though she felt crushed and apologetic for days.

Rodney when he cooled down admitted grudgingly that since she had had several doses to begin with, the gap might not amount to anything.

It was an unfamiliar and difficult routine which confronted Liz Dare. For instance, you had to shake your clothes out and tip up your shoes each morning lest scorpions had crawled into them during the night. And while Rodney explained more than once that to a person in good condition a scorpion's bite was not a whole lot worse than a bad bee sting, Elizabeth had a violent, unreasoning horror of actually finding one of the beasts lurking in something she might have worn.

There was the morning when Rodney had gone on to breakfast and left her still dressing, and a scorpion did run out across the floor and she threw the heavy water-pitcher of the china chamber set at it and screamed and screamed till Rodney arrived on the run, to find the pitcher in pieces on the floor and the scorpion—also damaged—lying in a pool of water, while Elizabeth cowered in the middle of the bed with her feet under her and her hands in front of her face. Patiently he sorted her out from the mosquito-netting, put on her shoes for her, and led her away to a cup of coffee, giving orders to the staring Antonina to sweep up the pitcher and the dead scorpion and make a thorough search, because the Señora was unaccustomed to wild life in her bedroom.

She was afraid of snakes too. Not willfully, nor from any exhibitionism. She had never been required to meet snakes socially before, and she was honestly and deeply afraid of them, 'way down into her involuntary reflexes, so that she dropped things and screamed for Rodney if she saw one. It was useless to try to explain to her the difference between venomous snakes and harmless ones. None of them had legs, they were all silent and furtive and terrifying, much worse than lizards, which were bad enough. Once Rodney attempted to use psychology, and drew her attention to the scales on a bird's legs—she liked birds, didn't she?—and he explained how their feathers were once scales on a prehistoric lizard.

198

She listened enthusiastically—it was her first real glimpse of the tremendous riddle of evolution—and the next time she saw a snake she screamed for Rodney. Lizards did not rise much in her estimation, either. But they were not, as a rule, slimy-looking, and at least they ran instead of wriggling. Rodney replied to this casuistry that snakes had legs too, vestigial ones, inside, which ran like anything whenever the snake crawled, and Elizabeth patted his cheek in front of everybody and said there was a Limit.

They had brought along an automatic refrigerator, run by the same little dynamo which supplied them with electric light and which lived in a repaired hut down the slope. After she had found dead specimens of one kind or another in it several times, cozily alongside the alligator-pears for lunch and the ice for the Planters' Punches, Elizabeth never opened it again, preferring not to know. She decided too that it was better not to know what went on in the kitchen whence emerged the excellent food which Carmela devised for them from what were to her strange and exotic supplies, such as dehydrated fruits and vegetables, dried milk, and boxed cereals. Carmela's *tortillas* became a *specialité de la maison,* small and delicate and piping hot; and her *frijoles,* fried a crusty brown beneath a secret sauce, had to be tasted to be believed. The Casa Paraiso lived high, there was no doubt about that. And the Guerbers were beginning to get caught up on their coffee drinking, which they still did noisily, with the rapt concentration of a religious rite.

The hours the expedition kept were an agony of self-adjustment to Elizabeth. Early breakfast was an obvious necessity, to catch the cool of the day. Early bedtime logically followed. But never since she was born in a tank-town on the Orpheum Circuit had Liz Dare been expected to turn out the light in cold blood and go to sleep before midnight. At the Casa Paraiso the electric light went off at the main every night at eleven, when Charles, unable to hold his eyes open any longer, would take a pocket torch and go down the slope and turn off the dynamo till morning. After eleven, if the Casa Paraiso desired light it used candles or oil lamps. Reading in bed was further complicated by the mosquito-canopies and a fear of fire from the candle-flame. And Elizabeth, accustomed also in later years to a delicious dawdling over her bath and cold cream and hair-brush night and morning, found herself cramped on one side by people who wanted to go to sleep and on the other by the breakfast bell. She was too proud to ask for a tray in bed if Rodney wouldn't offer it—even had sleep been possible in the mornings, which she soon realized it wouldn't be.

And so each midnight found her lying awake in the dark, separated by two ghostly mosquito-canopies from the motionless, soundless, but comfortingly warm creature which was Rodney asleep. (He was always so quiet about it that twice during the first month of their marriage she had waked him up by trying to make sure that he wasn't suddenly and mysteriously dead.) Things moved in the patio, though, outside their open door and under the brilliant tropical stars. Things moved there all night long, with rustlings and whisperings and nameless little scamperings. And there were small, melancholy insects which sang like treble cicadas, and large bumbling insects which droned and thumped, and moths which flittered softly, and bats which swooped and darted, chasing the moths. And there was a big bird—she was sure it was big, though Rodney said it was just a goatsucker—which asked over and over again, brusquely, "Who-are-you?" and wouldn't take No for an answer.

Then, about dawn, came the parrots, screaming across the sky in droves to their feeding grounds, near which they were too improvident and too inconsiderate to sleep. Then Carmela—or Antonina—began to make the *tortillas,* which meant an endless, monotonous slapping and patting and slap-slapping in the kitchen, accompanied by happy talk and laughter which strove with only intermittent success not to be heard across the patio. Then Jamaica arrived and began to chop and snip. Then the rich, strong smell of coffee drifted across the morning air. Then people began going

200

to the bathroom. Then the kettles of hot water for shaving were set down outside each door with a cheerful clatter. Then Rodney was moving quietly about on his lawful occasions, and there were soft Rodney-sounds—toothbrush, water being poured into the wash-bowl, the scrape of a razor, the stealthy tug at a drawer which stuck, military brushes—"Come on, Liz, you'll never make it."

I don't care, she thought one morning, with her eyes still shut. Right now I don't care if I never make it, what do you think of that? Suppose I said so, right out. Would there be a row? Suppose I said I'd like breakfast *brought* to me from now on, would you disown me forever? I wouldn't give Mrs. Guerber the satisfaction, though. That woman hates me. She has a contempt for me. She thinks I'm frivolous and useless and bad for you and beneath your notice. I'm beneath Dr. Guerber's notice too, but he hasn't noticed it yet. Watch yourself, Liz, there's no good creating a Situation just because you could if you wanted to. The poor man is starved for a little beauty, that's all. Beauty and fun. Somebody to make jokes with, he loves to laugh. The way he feels about me is no worse in its way than the simply *abject* way she is about Rodney. Maybe she thinks it's maternal, the way she feels about Rodney. Yah. No woman feels maternal about any man unless he's her son. I wonder if I thought that up myself—

"Liz—your water's getting cold."

There was a time, she thought, when you kissed me to wake me up, instead of yelling at me like a drill-sergeant. I *will* say that. My God, I *did* say it!

Her eyes flew open. Rodney stood there by the bureau, a brush in each hand, looking at her in surprise. He laid down the brushes and came and pushed back the mosquito-netting and sat down on the edge of the bed.

"What's the matter?" he said quietly. "Aren't you happy here at all?"

She reached past him for the glass of hot water which some time

201

ago he had set on her bedside table, and he reached to put it into her hand, halfway.

"Oh, I don't know, Rodney," she said vaguely, sipping. "Maybe I shouldn't have come. Or maybe the honeymoon's just Over. I've heard of such things."

"Liz, for the love of God—!" Rodney, who almost never swore, was aghast.

Just at that moment Charles passed their open door, whistling, on his way to breakfast. His eyes, of course, were straight ahead, but Rodney glanced over his shoulder instinctively.

"That's one of the things that's the matter," she pointed out at once. "We can't say two sentences to each other that can't be heard or seen by several other people! I was raised in the theater, where there is supposed to be no privacy—but no theater can touch this for a gold-fish bowl!"

"You can't ever expect much privacy in the field," he said patiently. "Everybody just gets on with their lives and nobody takes any notice."

"We aren't getting on with our lives," she murmured, sipping, while a lump rose in her throat.

There was quite a pause. Then—

"Do you want to go home?" he asked.

"I suppose I might as well. It would be better for you and the birds if I did. I'm no good to you here."

"What makes you think that?"

"I do everything wrong. I'm ignorant and idle and I only put people's backs up. Mrs. Guerber hates me, and Skinner is so sorry for you it sticks out of his ears."

"Suppose you try being sorry for Mrs. Guerber," he suggested. "And I don't mean because she's a refugee. I mean because she's so jealous of you."

"Oh, Rodney, it's too fantastic! What on earth would I want with her poor little weed of a man!"

"Her man has nothing to do with it," he said surprisingly. "It's yours that's making the trouble. Now, don't get me wrong! You are young and beautiful, and I am besottedly in love with you for anyone to see. That is what they call Romance, in any language. From her point of view, you own the world, you've got everything, and so far as she can see you've done nothing to deserve it, any more than the nearest orchid. She has worked and starved and suffered and grown old—and she has nothing. And she hadn't anything much to begin with—not love, as we know it, nor creature comforts we take for granted, nor the satisfaction of a job well done and paid for—not even the child which was her right. I don't as a rule preach before breakfast, but give the woman a break, Liz."

She was silent a moment, sipping.

"All right, you're pretty smart, aren't you," she said meekly, at last. "Do you know as much about birds as you do about people? And why does Skinner run to spread his cloak under my feet every time he sees me coming?"

"Well, that's pretty simple too," he said, and grinned. "Skinner is one of your Dinwiddies, all right. To you, he's just something that crawls out when you turn over a stone, but—"

Again there were footsteps along the tiled floor of the patio outside their open door, and she grabbed his arm and his voice died away guiltily. It was Sturgis, eyes front, on his way to breakfast.

"Well, you do see what I mean!" she remarked.

Rodney rose and shut the slatted door. Privacy was even then only an illusion, of course.

"—but even a Dinwiddie has feelings," he continued, returning to the bedside, and setting down her empty glass for her. "Skinner's feelings are all tied up in knots, but they're there, all the same. Women scare the living daylights out of him, especially you, and so he fancies himself as a woman-hater. He may outgrow it, or he may turn into something really queer. Why should you worry about that?"

She lay against the pillow, looking up at him.

203

"What I worry about is us."

"What seems to be wrong with us?"

"I don't know."

There was another pause.

"Do you want to go home?" he asked again.

Her eyes filled.

"Oh, Rodney, I don't as a rule cry before breakfast—"

He leaned forward and slid both his arms beneath her shoulders where she lay. She tried to turn her face aside and his was laid against it.

"Tell me," he whispered.

"You don't *n-need* me here—" she gasped, fighting tears and feeling foolish while she said it.

"I need you every breath I draw," he said. "Shall I recite it each morning with your glass of hot water?"

"Then I n-needn't go home?"

"Fool," he whispered, and kissed her, and the breakfast bell rang. "Now look what you've done," he said without moving. "By the time you've got yourself together we'll all be ready to leave the table. Shall I send you something on a tray?"

At that her arms tightened stranglingly round his neck for an instant—not because at last she could have breakfast on a tray, but because at last he had thought to suggest it, and so she didn't want it any more.

"I'll hurry fast," she promised. "If I don't get there before you've finished, don't wait around."

"Feel better now?" he insisted, lingering, and she nodded against the pillow. "You mustn't brood about things, Liz—it's fatal. If I get absent-minded, sock me, I can take it! But don't for God's sake suffer in silence, that's grounds for divorce. Slippers?" He turned them upside down and then handed them to her, and went off to breakfast.

XVIII

The domestic air was considerably cleared after that, though the lack of anything like a domestic atmosphere still irked her. Everything stood open all the time. Even the bathroom (which was very large and grand and accoutered in rose-colored porcelain, with a high grilled window in the outer wall and a solid mahogany door on to the patio) gave one a feeling in its spaciousness that there also one lacked privacy—which was of course an hallucination.

The long hot days slid by, into long nights brilliant with stars. Sometimes in the evenings Rodney would get out the accordion and Elizabeth would sing—their repertoire was large and varied, old songs, new songs, French songs, Spanish songs—almost anything their spellbound audience demanded of them. Request numbers included everything from *On, Wisconsin* for Frank to *Holy Night* for Dr. Guerber, who asked for it suddenly and with diffidence, and listened to it (minus a few of its words) with tears which finally spilled over and shone on his cheeks, while his wife looked on stolidly, from her corner. "It has been so long," he apologized, and blew his nose loudly. "Perhaps it is better to forget—after so long." Rodney's tactful instrument slid easily into a Strauss waltz. "Dance, Liz," he commanded softly, and she stepped out into the middle of the room in one of her little white silk frocks which ended just below her knees and left her slim arms bare, and danced for them a simple improvisation in waltz-time till Dr. Guerber's foot was tapping again.

Sometimes Rodney was broody and preoccupied, sometimes he was for no traceable reason more rollicking than she had ever seen him. Once on a scented moonlight night as they strolled about the patio, he kissed her, out of sheer exuberance, long and hard. And Mrs. Guerber, who was on her way to the bathroom in a dressing-gown and slippers, saw, and Rodney swore under his breath, and never kissed her in the patio again, moon or no moon. But always Elizabeth was aware that he lived in a deep, abiding happiness which had nothing to do with her—at least, she alone had never been able to create it for him. Rodney enjoyed every minute of his days and nights, breathed in satisfaction with the tropic air, absorbed some nameless delight through his very pores. Charles was the same. And in a newer, more excited way, so was Frank.

Elizabeth, gingerly sampling what was to her an entirely gratuitous experience, failed to become an addict. On the contrary, she began surreptitiously to mark off on a hidden calendar the slow march of days towards the time of their departure from the Casa Paraiso. Meanwhile she occupied herself conscientiously, striving never to seem idle or bored, and accepting gratefully the time Rodney spared for her whenever he thought about it.

Elizabeth didn't know, and nobody was going to tell her, that the parent harpy eagle has a wing spread of about seven feet, and its claws are twice as large and powerful as those of any other bird of prey. It nests in the tallest trees of the jungle forest, or on rock ledges on the more inaccessible cliffs. It objects, naturally, to having its nest disturbed. There are never more than two young to a nest, and their own mothers couldn't call them beautiful.

To reach them, if one is not an eagle oneself, one ought to be half Indian and half *chasseur alpin*. Rodney was depending largely on ropes, balance, tenacity, and luck, with racing goggles to protect his eyes. It was a nice tough assignment, and even if they got the fledglings down safely there was the so-far unsolved problem of diet and exercise in captivity. That was where Sturgis came in.

Five nests with eggs were located and marked on successive

camping trips into the jungle with an Indian guide. Once found, they were frequently inspected for the date of hatching and the progress of the brood. Sturgis was fussy about the exact age of his protégés when they were delivered to him. They must be left with the parent birds long enough to get the right start in life, but not long enough for the change to be too great a shock to their infant sensibilities. None of it made much sense to anybody but Sturgis and Rodney.

Besides the trips Rodney made out into the jungle with Charles and the guide, on horseback, he sometimes went into Santa Rosa in the ramshackle touring-car on mail days or to send a cable. Usually the car was driven by Pedro the handy man, who also acted as interpreter and cared for the horses. Elizabeth didn't much like spending a night at the Hotel Europa, but once she went along to see the Sunday night parade in the Plaza while the band played. Mr. Phipps came over by bus from Santo Tomas to have dinner with them, and then they all joined the strolling populace in the counter-clockwise stream round the bandstand where the marimbas twanged exquisite rhythms sadly.

Elizabeth lagged and stopped at the edge of the stream. Rodney, who was of course instantly aware that she had fallen behind, pretended not to notice, and glanced back over his shoulder. She was standing beside two little boys at the curb. Their bare brown feet were executing an odd, formal dance-step on the cobbles. Their bodies hardly moved, only their eyes and their feet, treading out the precise and intricate measure. Elizabeth watched, her dancer's heart keeping time, though her narrow white-shod feet were still.

One of the little boys was Vicente. The other, a year smaller, was his brother Amadeo, and Amadeo sang the words of the song softly to himself, as he danced. The marimbas stopped, and so the dance stopped too, and Vicente smiled up at her. The music began again at once, but Vicente stood still, smiling at his angel, who spoke to him in a language he could not understand.

Rodney turned back.

"What's this?" he inquired gently. "Dancing lessons?"

"Oh, Rodney, please ask him to do it again! I must learn that step, it's wonderful, and very tricky!"

Rodney requested an encore, and Vicente and his brother, with a murmured comment, went again into their dance.

"He says this is a different one," Rodney explained.

Elizabeth's eyes followed the bare brown feet, her ears strove jealously with Amadeo's crooning Spanish. Slowly her own feet began to shift, ever so little, with his, and she was humming.

"Listen to it," she implored Rodney. "Listen hard! You can pick these up on the accordion. Maybe we can write them down. This is the real stuff, Rodney, I'd like to take it back with me."

"O.K., let's buy Vicente," he said, falling in at once with the idea.

And this, in a manner of speaking, was done. When they returned next morning to the Casa Paraiso, both Vicente and Amadeo were in the front seat beside Pedro, both looking a little overdressed in new blue and white striped overalls. Between them was their father's ancient guitar, with which he had courted their mother. Amadeo took after his father, who was in the band. Amadeo could play chords on a guitar to accompany his crooning songs, and his memory for endless repetitious verses was infallible. Their mother was only too pleased that they should emigrate, for a time, to the Casa Paraiso household, as she had had four more sons since Amadeo, and only prayed that the next baby—now well on the way—might be a girl, so that there would be some hope of help with the housework.

Nominally, Vicente and Amadeo were to be assistant gardeners under orders to Jamaica. But much of the time their tools lay idle while on the shady side of the patio they patiently went over their steps for the Señora, and Amadeo repeated to her all the verses he knew while she learned them blindly by rote.

It was a cheerful sound to accompany such monotonous business as changing the blotters on pressed botany specimens, or even painting the portrait of an orchid, and Dr. Guerber loved it, and sometimes joined them in a bumbling humming a little off key. Skinner, whose work was often close and tiring, and who always felt the heat, found their extraneous noise very hard to bear. To Rodney also it was a distraction, yes, but a pleasant one, and Frank shamelessly hung about to watch, neglecting his chores. Mrs. Guerber watched too, but furtively and without expression, from behind her slatted bedroom door or around corners.

Came a great day when Rodney brought out his accordion and settled himself in a chair tilted back against one of the mahogany posts which supported the patio roof, and gave his attention to catching Amadeo's tunes as Elizabeth sang them to him in her funny parrot Spanish, which caused him (and Amadeo) considerable amusement. But once in the middle of a song he suddenly stopped everything—

"Hey, hey, hey!" he said, looking alarmed. "Don't sing that to anybody who knows Spanish!" And he spoke severely to Amadeo, who hung his head and grinned.

"What's the matter?" demanded Elizabeth, poised to go on.

"They're not seemly words," said Rodney, and laughter lurked behind his eyes. "This wants looking into!"

Thereafter Amadeo sang him all the songs straight through, and when the words wouldn't do, Rodney substituted new ones which would.

Andrew had presented her with a small kodak and a supply of films when she left New York—the kind of kodak that you simply point at something and push the button down, and the next time you point it you push the button up again, and so on. "It's so simple, she can't possibly go wrong with it," Andrew had said to Rodney, with that slightly patronizing air they adopted towards her when they were together, as though (much as they loved her) she was a little half-witted. Therefore it was pretty exciting when Charles got round to develop the first roll, along with his own film-packs, and there were actually pictures on it that she had taken herself.

209

Proudly she mailed prints off to Andrew and set about taking more. A good many of them were pictures of Rodney, often unaware of the camera, busy about his mysterious pursuits. Then she undertook to get pictures which would give Andrew some idea of the Casa Paraiso, and several of these proved to be quite lovely; and when Charles said the one of Rodney and Jamaica in the patio with the tazza-fountain beyond was good enough to be enlarged she felt as though she had been knighted. Charles found it a little difficult to conceive that while you were in process of becoming Liz Dare there wasn't much time for kodaks, and once you had got to be Liz Dare there was somehow still less, and that therefore taking pictures of your very own was a real thrill; much more of a thrill than posing for his color film with flowers and specimens, but she did that too with endless patience and good humor.

Andrew had often spoken of Mayan remains, which he took an interest in, and she now found herself in their vicinity. Well, that was Something. So when Dr. Guerber reported one day at lunch that there was what appeared to be a calendar stone in fair condition only a hundred yards up the mule-track beyond the house, and much less than that distance into the jungle on the left, Elizabeth was at once ambitious to photograph it for Andrew. Dr. Guerber said he had driven a stick into the ground beside the track to mark the place where you turned off, in case anyone was interested. He said he would be pleased to show her the stone, whenever she wanted to take its picture, and she thanked him, with Mrs. Guerber's opaque eyes upon them, and made up her mind to slip off that afternoon when he wasn't looking, and avoid complications.

She found the stick, upright at the edge of the track, and went left into the undergrowth, with a wary eye for snakes. It was the first time she had ever been so far from the house alone, and she felt very adventurous. She would say nothing about the picture of the stone until Charles developed the roll, and then they would

210

all see, with surprise, that she had been out by herself and got it, without a word to anybody.

She came suddenly upon the stone, rising above a tangle of ferns and creepers. Close beside it stood one of the moth-eaten little undersized local horses, its bridle trailing. And on the ground, half hidden in the tall fern, lay an unpleasant-looking man of very mixed blood with a revolver in his hand, and it was pointed towards her.

Elizabeth stopped dead and went cold. The man's face relaxed into a grin, and he said something in Spanish and got to his feet and swept off his hat in a wide gesture of gallantry which nearly over-balanced him, and she saw then that as well as being ragged and dirty and unshaven and massively built, he was very drunk. She began to back away from him towards where she had left the track, and he said something more and tucked the gun into its holster and advanced upon her with what were obviously the friendliest feelings in the world. Elizabeth screamed once and her hand flew up instinctively to her mouth. As it did so, his eyes caught the flash of the big aquamarine on her third finger.

His face changed again, and he reached for her.

Rodney, at work at his table in the *sala,* raised his head sharply and listened. Charles, who sat beside him, looked up inquiringly.

"I thought I heard Liz in the road," said Rodney, and rose and started for the door. "Until she can tell her snakes apart, I'd just as soon she was afraid of them all!"

As he emerged from the house into the mule-track the familiar cry came again from up the hill—

"Rodney! *Come quick!* RODNEY!!"

He broke into a run.

Guided by what became a continuous, wordless screaming, he plunged into the undergrowth and came upon the struggle. He was, of course, unarmed. His quick eyes saw the Colt .45 in its holster, saw that the man was drunk, saw that with Elizabeth

211

fighting and twisting in his arms the chance of getting a decisive hold on him at the first try was remote. Rodney stood still and spoke in biting Spanish, requesting the fellow, in effect, to take his filthy hairy paws off his (Rodney's) wife and be quick about it.

Elizabeth's captor, being very drunk indeed on a potent native brew of the *aguardiente* species, swung round to face him with her still pinioned in his hold, and made a flattering comment on Rodney's taste in wives, at the same time passing a glance like an insolent hand down her body. Rodney, whose eyes had gone oddly bright and narrow, repeated his request in still plainer language, with references to the man's immediate family connections—he swore much more freely in Spanish than in his mother tongue—and the man, being perhaps hypersensitive about his relations, drew the .45.

Rodney moved then, it was impossible to see quite how. Elizabeth felt the impact, heard the gun go off once harmlessly above their heads, was dragged down with them, rolled clear, and sat up dazedly to see them locked together on the ground. It was then that she showed real presence of mind. She began to yell for Charles.

At the same time she looked round for any kind of weapon, and seized a jagged chunk of rock. Rodney's voice came to her, panting, but calm.

"Stand back, Liz—don't try to help—if you love me!"

Their hands were gripped together on the gun. Elizabeth stood above them, yelling for Charles, and saw with horror that slowly, surely, with deliberate intent, Rodney was forcing the gun back between their bodies. A few seconds more they rolled and strained and grunted, the gun between them. Then it went off again, and just as it did so Charles and Frank crashed on to the scene, white-faced.

Rodney wriggled out from under and sat up, disheveled, ground-stained, and breathless. Elizabeth dropped to her knees beside him, sobbing in a tearless sort of way while her hands touched his face, pushed back his hair, felt his shoulders, counted his arms and legs, which were all there, and no blood ran.

"I'm all right, Liz—don't howl—I'm not hurt—"

Charles was bending over the motionless stranger, whose fingers still gripped his own gun.

"I'm afraid you've killed him, son," said Charles quietly.

"That's what I meant to do," said Rodney just as quietly, and their eyes met across the body.

"Naturally," said Charles then, with a slight effort, and added—"But what do we do with it now?"

"Couldn't we just say nothing?" suggested Frank. "He doesn't look like a general favorite to me. D'ya think he'd be missed?"

"Now, now, no shenanigans," said Charles quickly, on a warning note. "The shots could be heard at the house." Again his anxious eyes sought Rodney's face.

"Well," said Rodney, getting rather stiffly to his feet and brushing himself off, "let's take him into town and present him to the police with our compliments. The chances are that nobody loves him—much."

"The main thing is going to be to keep you out of the hoosegow while they assess the damage," worried Charles.

"We'll try what ready cash can do about that," Rodney said. "You boys drag him on to his horse, I've had enough of him. Come on, Liz—" He reached down a helping hand to where she still knelt at his feet, looking up at him with wide, scared eyes.

"I called you and you came," she said flatly. "He might have k-killed you— Oh, *Rodney*—!"

He caught her just as she tipped sidewise into a fine Victorian faint.

And so, after standing her ground with a rock in her fist, she was ignominiously carried home after all, and laid out on her bed, and had to be brought round with brandy.

XIX

That's what I meant to do. The words ticked in her mind as she sat between Rodney and Charles in the front seat of the touring-car on the way down to the police station at Santa Rosa. Charles drove. And in the back seat, decently wrapped in a horse-blanket, was the body of the man Rodney had killed because he meant to. Not in anger, not just in self-defense—but with deliberate intention. The dead man's own finger had been on the trigger—underneath Rodney's. But it was still murder.

And she—who had had some idea of cracking the man's skull with a rock in case Rodney was getting the worst of it—she had only just stopped short of murder herself! She had been ready to kill, with her own hands, with all the strength she had—to save Rodney. But Rodney hadn't killed just to save himself. *That's what I meant to do.* He had given himself away, hadn't he, to all of them who heard him. It was because of her.

She knew it in every blackening bruise left by the dead man's hands, in the sick release from terror which still surged through her in receding waves—and in the protective curve of Rodney's shoulder against hers as he sat sidewise between her and the car door, with his arm along the back of the seat behind her. If Rodney had not been at his desk that day, instead of out on the mountainside with Charles, anything might have happened to her. Because he was there, he was guilty of murder in a strange and savage country—but surely even here a man who killed in defense of his wife would go free? That was their story, already agreed on, and in its essentials it was certainly true. But there was

214

more to it than that, and all three of them knew it. The man had been more or less under control, Charles was on the way, the gun was still in the clear—and it was because of some leering words in Spanish, because he had held her defenseless in Rodney's sight, that he died. *That's what I meant to do.* Each time the words sent a shiver of primitive excitement through her civilized nerves.

What kind of man was this, that she had married? It was still Rodney, after all, who was so kind, so gentle, so quiet—so implacable. She stared down dizzily at his lean brown hand as it lay palm upwards in his lap, cradling her own wrist where the big black-and-blue blotches were coming out on the tender skin—his right hand—it was his left which had pressed the dead man's finger on the trigger—

"Rodney, I th-think I'm going to be sick—"

"Stop the car, Charles," he said calmly.

Charles tramped on all the pedals, bringing the car to a standstill, and they both sat looking down at her sympathetically while she fought off nausea. When things steadied she found she was gripping Rodney's hand till her nails bit in, and he endured it without comment.

"Let's get out a minute," he was saying. "Let's walk a little way."

He opened the door. Guided by his compelling hands, she stepped down weakly into the road and fell into step with him, while Charles followed along behind them in low gear.

"Rodney, you did it on purpose."

"They can't prove that."

"But you meant to kill him. You said so."

"Mm-hm. Well, how about you with that rock? You weren't by any chance aiming it at me, were you?"

"I thought you were in danger."

"You thought right. For about five long seconds he had me on toast—just before I spoke to you—and he missed his chance." They walked on slowly, his arm around her waist. "You don't like having an assassin for a husband, is that it?" he queried, touching as

215

he often did on the sore spot in her mind. "Honey, he'd lived long enough. You—or the next woman. And it might have been Carmela or Antonina—and she'd have been found dead. You wouldn't have preferred that, would you—just to keep my hands clean? Oh, hell, why dress it up?" he broke off unexpectedly. "He mauled you and I killed him. They won't hang me down here for that!"

Her throat was tight. She walked on beside him in silence. This was Rodney—who said so little of love in words, who could forget for hours on end that she existed, until in his own good time he was ready to forget Science for a while—this baffling, intricate, enslaving creature who had married her—

"And you," he continued, "you're up against it, aren't you! Will you get used to the idea, do you think, or does it seem to you bad taste to love me now?"

His eyes were smiling down at her. It seemed impossible that he should look so exactly the same, so completely *Rodney,* with that Thing in the back of the car. She knew that he understood without speech from her everything that had passed through her mind since that shot was fired. Murderer or no, he was Rodney and she belonged to him and she was glad. She melted against his side, within the hard circle of his arm.

"It's a funny thing," she said. "I thought I was civilized—but suddenly I could kiss your hands."

"Not here," he said gravely. "All right, Charles."

He helped her back into the car.

Santa Rosa had not finished its siesta, and the streets were almost empty when Charles stopped the car in front of the police station. The three of them got out and went in.

A young man with greasy hair and sleepy eyes emerged from a back room and regarded them haughtily. His gold-braided coat was unbuttoned, revealing linen far from fresh and a furry chest. His boots had not been polished for weeks.

Rodney explained in his easy Spanish that his wife had been attacked not a hundred yards from her home by a drunken out-

216

law; that hearing her screams he himself had gone to her rescue; that as soon as he appeared the outlaw had pulled a gun on him, which in the ensuing struggle had gone off and (unfortunately) slain its owner; and that the body was outside in their car, and would someone kindly send out and collect it.

The young man in gold braid, who had been temporarily paralyzed by the recital, came to life and clicked his tongue in distress. Then he shouted until a pair of heavy-eyed policemen appeared, also very unbuttoned, and commanded them to go and bring in the carcase they would find in the back of the Señor's car. And very reluctantly they shuffled out the door to do so.

Meanwhile Father Joseph had happened along in the street, and had recognized the Casa Paraiso car, with the unmistakable bundle in the back set, around which flies buzzed. Incredulously lifting a corner of the horse-blanket, he beheld, still incredulously, the face of the corpse.

He stood back and watched the two policemen lug the blanket-wrapped bundle into the police station. Then he followed them to just outside the door, where he flattened himself—so far as that was possible—against the wall, and indulged in a little Jesuitical eavesdropping.

He heard the heavy bump of the body on the floor and knew that then the blanket was being stripped back, while the Señora, no doubt, looked the other way. He heard the Señor Doctor call attention to the fact that from the condition of the wound it was plain that the gun had gone off between them at very close range in the struggle, and that it was the dead man's own gun, and not one in the Señor's possession. He heard Señor MacDonald point out that one had only to look at the marks on the Señora's wrists to see the sort of thing she had been subjected to, and Father Joseph knew the solicitous pleasure with which the gold-braided *Commandante* would inspect the Señora's wrists. Passports were produced, there was mention of the nearest American consul, and then, cutting across the Spanish curlicues of officialdom—

217

"How much?" demanded the Señor Doctor crisply in the same tongue.

There was naturally some official reluctance expressed at so hasty a settlement of so grave a matter—there was also some official delicacy about naming an official price—which was finally fixed at forty American dollars.

Very soon after that, Rodney, Charles, and Elizabeth emerged from the police station to find Father Joseph standing just outside, against the bulletin-board to which were affixed the notices of local interest—Lost and Found, fiesta dates, traveling entertainments when there were any, band concerts, and so forth. Father Joseph ignored Rodney's polite greeting with a knowing smile, and pointed silently to a placard on the notice-board which offered in plain bold type a reward, amounting to forty American dollars, for one Juan Bolivar, so-called, dead or alive, wanted for the murder of a policeman and the theft of his gun, along with jail-break and sundry other misdeeds.

Rodney read the placard in a single angry glance, and looked at Father Joseph inquiringly. Father Joseph nodded.

"You're dead sure about this," said Rodney.

Father Joseph nodded.

"Please come in with me," said Rodney, and ripped the placard from the notice-board and retraced his steps into the police station. The *Commandante* was just indicating to the policemen that the body of Juan Bolivar, so-called, might be removed from the presence, and he looked round suspiciously as Rodney entered, followed by the priest, with Charles and Elizabeth behind. Rodney slapped the placard down on the desk and said that he would have his forty dollars back, *muy pronto*. When it was not immediately forthcoming, he added a blistering comment to the effect that he didn't so much mind doing the local constabulary's dirty work and mopping up the local bad man free, *gracias,* for nothing, but that he did object to being fined for taking what were after all merely the sanitary precautions which the local constabu-

218

lary were too (and here followed several well-chosen adjectives from a language rich in opprobrium) to attend to themselves; and that he laid no claim to the reward, as forty dollars all at one time had probably never before been seen on the premises, and for all he cared never would be again, once the money he had deposited a few minutes before was duly returned to him, which it would be. Now. He held out his hand.

Under the accusing eyes of the Church, the young man in gold braid, looking more paralyzed than ever, put a feeble hand into his pocket and brought out the money. Rodney took it from him and clapped it into Father Joseph's astonished palm.

"For your poor," he said briefly, and stalked out to the car.

The swift tropic darkness fell as Charles headed the car again towards the Casa Paraiso. They were very silent. Elizabeth sat between them, her hat off, nodding with exhaustion against Rodney's shoulder, as they ground noisily up the hill behind the town.

They ate a belated dinner while the others gathered round the table to hear the rest of the story of Juan Bolivar, so-called. Sturgis was much amused by it. His plain pudding-face broke all up into chuckles, and his rather nondescript blue eyes rested on Rodney with a fatherly pride and affection.

After dinner Elizabeth went into the library with some needlework and turned on the radio. She was sitting there alone when Sturgis came in, and said he wanted a detective story to read, and pottered along the shelves. "Something nice and tame," he said. "Life's too exciting around here."

Elizabeth smiled, and picked through the pile of bright wools in her lap, trying to match a green by lamplight.

"You're all so pleased with him you can't contain yourselves," she said. "Does any man ever get too old for playing Indians?"

"I couldn't say yet," said Sturgis. "I'm only sixty-one." He glanced at her shrewdly across the room. "Give you kind of a funny feeling?" he queried with unexpected kindliness.

"I'm afraid it does," she admitted, still smiling. "I thought I was

219

going to be sick in the car going down. Rodney was awfully nice about it. He always is, when I disgrace him."

"In this case, he had no room to be otherwise. Rodney lost his lunch."

"Wha-at?" She stared at him incredulously.

"In the bathroom, right after he brought you round. Maybe I shouldn't have mentioned it," he said, his round face crinkled and benign.

"Well, I—I think I'm glad you did," she said gropingly.

"I thought perhaps you would be. And I knew he'd never tell you himself."

Their eyes met. In silence they exchanged a small, intimate smile over Rodney, who had killed a man and then been sick in the bathroom. Somehow, to Elizabeth it made all the difference.

"I suppose one always does chuck the bunny after the first one," said Sturgis confidentially. "I know I did!"

"You!" she cried, wide-eyed. Sturgis too? she thought in bewilderment. This round-faced, stodgy, benevolent-looking man—*too?*

"It was years ago, out in India," he said reminiscently. "I was hunting Impeyan pheasants then. Fellow kept rolling rocks down on us. Killed one of my bearers. Finally I got tired of it. I went after him and I got him. I was sick as a dog afterwards. I couldn't have been more than twenty-five at the time. Rodney's been lucky —so far. It was bound to happen to him, sooner or later. I told him next time wouldn't be so bad."

"N-next time—? You mean—you—"

"Four," he said gently. "Things happen, you know—and you have no choice. I don't mean you ever get used to it."

Just then the news broadcast began, and Rodney came in from the laboratory to hear it, still looking exactly like Rodney. But now she knew. Rodney had lost his lunch.

When the news of the war was finished—

220

"Well, anyway, I'm getting my hand in," said Rodney. "Too bad he wasn't a German, he was acting kind of like one." He rose and turned the dial till it landed on a rumba, where he left it.

"German or no German, how does it feel now to be one up?" Sturgis queried, cocking a searching eye at him.

"Feels better, thanks," said Rodney, and went over to Elizabeth and laid back the neck of her blouse to where the scrape of dirty fingernails on the white flesh had been well painted with iodine. The appearance of it seemed to satisfy him. "Yep, it feels better all the time," he said, cupping his hand briefly under her chin. "Sturgis, I don't want to make a mollycoddle of her—but how about a rule that hereafter she never goes out alone?"

"Might keep your score down," said Sturgis judicially.

"What's bogey on this hole, anyway?"

"Four," said Elizabeth unexpectedly. "But it can be done in one —I hope."

Sturgis, having accomplished what he came for, remembered his detective story. Rodney cautioned him against bad dreams, and he departed with a book under his arm.

"Rodney, he's a darling!" she said in an awed whisper.

"I thought you'd notice that eventually," he smiled, and wisely forebore to ask what Sturgis had been saying. He came and sat down beside her and smoothed out the needlework between her hands to look at it. "Very nice," he said. "You ought to have a better light for this. I'll ask Charles to bring in a goose-neck lamp from the lab."

His grave gaze was bent on the tapestry piece he held, he rubbed his thumb lightly across her neat stitches—it was the last small necessity to his mental digestion of his day, to find her with a pile of bright wools in her lap, stitching a new cover for the seat of a Chippendale chair at home. She was safe, she wasn't having hysterics, and she was his—his first by right of conquest, and now by a peculiarly satisfying form of jungle law. He felt

221

suddenly tired to the point of exhaustion, but—and this was some-how her doing—strangely at peace.

"Rodney—" Her lips were close to his ear. "I'm crazy about you!"

"You don't say," he murmured, gratified, and kissed her reck-lessly, just as Charles came in to say that he was going down to turn off the lights now.

XX

I want to go home, she thought, lying awake that night while Rodney slept. I mustn't say so, I mustn't let anybody know—they might think I'm afraid. I am. I want to get out of here. I want to get Rodney away. He might have been killed. They might have put him in jail. They might even—

Oh, God, I want to go home, where Aunt Virginia is, and Snorky. I want my own house again, with hot milk in the kitchen before we go to bed, and no mosquito-netting after. I want to be able to say whatever I like without having to whisper for fear someone will hear. I want my own bathroom, and a hairdresser. I want to go wherever I like without having to watch where I step, and without a bodyguard. I want to see Rodney in a white tie, and go dancing with him at the St. Regis. I want him to myself, once in a while. *I want to go home!*

Tomorrow I can count up the days again with a calendar, she thought, listening to a new sort of scrabbling in the patio—(one would think she had heard them all by now). And on Thursday we get newspapers and mail. I wonder what Pete's doing. Never mind Pete, you've retired, Liz, you married a professor, remember? Little did you think, that morning he fell over you in Maine—! We'll have next summer there, that's something—only this time he will live at my place and drive over to the Station each day— and back home each night. Well, that's worth waiting for, isn't it! Remember that morning you woke up at dawn—the last time you ever woke up without Rodney on your mind—the last time you ever will. . . .

Heigh-ho, those were the days! You were free, then, free as a bird—well, as a sparrow, Liz. You lived your own life, then, the way you like it, in peace and comfort—and a good deal of emptiness. Anyway, you thought you lived. You thought you were happy, you thought you liked to be free. *He is free who lives as he chooses.* According to Epictetus, Rodney's still free—always will be. I'm the one who is captive. Kiss your chains, Liz. Kiss, if necessary, the rod. But not for long now. The time's almost up. They think they can get the fledglings next week. Home by the end of the month, maybe. Home to my own bathtub, thank God. And never again for Liz. Never, *never,* NEVER again!

I said I wasn't cut out for this sort of thing. I told him I was no Eagle's Mate. I wasn't even going to try. And now look. Well, I asked for it. I didn't have to come. It was all settled the other way, and I had to go and change things. I wanted to come, I really did. And some of it hasn't been so bad. This house has great beauty, in its way—sharp sunlight, bright color. The people are sweet—Carmela is worth keeping forever, and Vicente and Father Joseph—and poor little Mr. Phipps. Darlings. Besides, I've been with Rodney, I've seen him every day, I've watched him when he didn't even know I was looking, and I've learned things about him—things I wouldn't be without. He's different here. It's a complex creature I've married, men aren't as simple as you'd think. Rodney seems simple, and then he goes and does something haywire, and you realize you haven't solved him at all. I used to think men were a lot of wooden Indians with about three ideas amongst 'em—but not Rodney.

I'll be glad when it's over, all right, but at the same time I'm glad I came. It was worth doing—once. I can see now how much it means to him, even if I can't see why. It ought to mean more to me, I suppose—take the music I've learned from Amadeo— you can't get that sort of thing without coming after it. If Pete ever got his eye on those kids— They're better off where they are, though. Broadway is a mug's game, I'm well out of it. I'm not homesick for Broadway, I'm only homesick for home. Rodney offered to let me go home, that day—but I think it would have broken his heart if I had. I wonder why that is. I wonder why he wants me here, when all I do is be a bother. I wonder what he gets out of it, really. It isn't marriage.

Well, what is marriage? We're together. That's marriage, I suppose. Mutual experience. And little things like tonight, promising me that lamp. He liked me to be doing needlework tonight. He liked the feel of it—he must have remembered it was for the chair in the hall—he must have thought about home—he must have sensed a background, a continuity— *I need you every breath I draw.* That wasn't just a pretty speech, he meant that. I wonder if Rodney is ever lonely, just like other people, deep down inside where your guts are, where ordinary human contacts can't reach, so that you feel all hollow and afraid, and there's nobody to talk to. That feeling hasn't caught up with me much, since I've known Rodney —he stands between it and me. I can remember nights when there was only Snorky to hold it off—never mind that, Liz, we're through with all that since Rodney took charge. Yes, but I wonder if he ever gets tired of being competent and strong and imperturbable and poker-faced and—all those magnificent things he is. I wonder if he ever just wants to crawl into a hole and pull the hole in after him, the way I do. I wonder— Liz, you've got something. Maybe Rodney isn't so all-fired self-contained as he seems!

But this is heresy. All right, then, but how come he lost his lunch? Sturgis knew Rodney wouldn't tell me that. Sturgis was trying to make me see that Rodney isn't a superman. I'd have fought him if he'd said so, he knew that. But Sturgis meant me to go on thinking. Sturgis meant me to know that Rodney needed something tonight that I could give him—and it dawns on me several hours too late. You're a great help, Liz, that's what you are! But what could I have said? Charles came in and—when we got to our room Rodney had a grip on things again, he didn't seem to need any help. There wasn't time. There never is time, the way we live here, somebody always comes around the corner, how can I— Rodney, what did you want? How did I fail you? I didn't mean to, I didn't know there was anything I could do— *You* are the wise one, Rodney, you should know what's best for us. If only you'd *tell* me what you want. . . .

And so at last she slept, with tears on her cheeks, never guessing that he had had all he wanted from her when he saw her fingers steady on the needle, and her confident, unclouded innocence of the turmoil inside him—to say nothing of that whisper close to his ear.

When she clung to him next morning, with the soft moth-kisses of her orphan-ways, he feared that she was apologizing for being the involuntary cause of his blooding, and decided on a form of mental hygiene which he put into effect at once.

He and Charles, on one of their scouting trips after nests, had come upon a Mayan relic of considerable size—a tall, three-sided stone stairway decorated with hieroglyphs, which rose above the clogging jungle growth with steps the size of bleacher seats and came to an abrupt end in mid-air. Jasmine fronds clothed it in perfume, which drew the humming-birds; orchids, lantana, and giant fern grew round it; great jungle trees towered above it, where shy toucans and raucous parrots perched and monkeys chattered. The light was never very good. But the noonday sun came through in shifting golden spangles and a picture then with one of the better cameras was possible. He suggested that they make a picnic, just the two of them, taking their lunch, and photograph the stair for Andrew.

Because it meant a whole day of his undivided company, Elizabeth was delighted, and he noted with relief that she showed no fear of the jungle after her encounter of the day before. He did not grasp the fact that it would never occur to her, even now, to question her own safety so long as he was with her. He himself knew that if she had not been alone, Bolivar, so-called, would have passed by or lain low with no more than an appreciative glance. Her own tacit acceptance of the same fact surprised him, because he was never aware how his mere presence was to her a guarantee of immunity to anything from bees to Bolivars. She had a simple, unreasoning conviction that if Rodney was beside her even venomous snakes slunk off in harmless confusion.

They set out soon after breakfast on two of the under-sized, patient horses of the country, lunch and the camera in their saddle-bags. The stairway lay beyond the ruined village several miles up the half-obliterated track which dwindled fast above the Casa Paraiso. It was not far enough to require the presence of a guide, and Elizabeth's eyes were bright and her heart was light as Charles waved them off and returned to his private concerns in the dark-room he had established in a corner of the laundry. They would eat their lunch on the stair, and return at their leisure before dark. Rodney was hers again, for a whole day. She could say whatever she liked to him, and no one could hear. If he kissed her—if!— Mrs. Guerber wouldn't see. Life was sweet, and she was glad she had come to Central America.

Rodney's conscience smote him as he observed her touching happiness. It took very little to make her happy. He should have thought of doing something like this sooner. He should have realized before now how much an occasional day off with him would mean to her. He had neglected her heartlessly, he was a selfish brute, and anyway he had never seen her lovelier—she had pushed her hair all up inside the crown of her immense sombrero because of the heat, she sat her pony easily, long-legged as a boy, her arms were slim and brown— Well, God bless Bolivar, wherever he was! Without him, they might never have embarked on this delicious day.

They passed the ruined village on their right and wound up-ward, through heat which even at that altitude was like cotton wool. The track was shaded by an arch of jungle green which grew so low and lavishly that they had to dismount every now and then to force their way through it, though only the week

227

before Jamaica had been up with his *machete* to cut away the tangle.

"It's like being ant-size," said Elizabeth, lifting her face to where the tree-tops would be if one could have seen them. "If you were an ant in tall grass you'd feel like this!"

"Remember when Alice drank 'Drink Me' and began to shrink?" he said. "It's about time I read *Alice* again."

"I remember when I read *Alice*," she remarked, and he glanced quickly at her face, which wore the closed-up, defensive look recollection of her childhood always brought. It was a tract of time in her life as dark as Africa to him. He was in a way jealous of it, and he always somehow dreaded to hear.

"When was that?" he queried, for at the same time he could never bear not to encourage any reminiscence of hers which would help him to comprehend and so eliminate those things he meant her ,to forget, with him.

"It was Christmas in a hotel in some little dump in Minnesota, and we were practically snowbound, and I had a sore throat. Mother had bought a doll and a book for my presents, because we were working and she felt flush. I named the doll Dolores and the book was *Alice in Wonderland*. But father had forgotten to buy anything for mother, and then he said Christmas was all nonsense anyhow for people like us, and stamped out and didn't come back for hours. So that's how I read *Alice*. I began it so as not to hear him and mother quarreling, and after he went I read it to a sort of *obbligato* of mother crying on the bed, and finally it was invaded by the usual jitters that father wouldn't turn up in time for the act. But he always did turn up in time for the act, drunk or sober, I will say that for him. As far as I can remember, I haven't seen *Alice* since, I don't know what became of the book."

There was a pause.

"I'll lend you mine when we get back home," he said into it, with a matter-of-factness he did not feel.

"Tell about yours."

228

"Mine was a birthday present, I think. I couldn't have been very old, because I remember sitting on Aunt Virginia's lap while she read it to me on a rainy day. I even remember the dress she had on—it was a sort of wine-colored velvet—I can still feel it against my face when I think of Alice. Of course I've read the book a good many times to myself since then, but it still sounds like Aunt Virginia."

"You must have been an awfully nice little boy," she said wistfully.

"If I wasn't nice I got told about it—plenty."

"Did she spank you?"

"Dad caned me. Regularly. For the good of my soul. He caned Charles too, because Charles hadn't got a father to do it."

"I expect that's why you both grew up to be so irresistible."

"I expect so."

They rode on slowly, ducking under creeper festoons and sagging branches, through heat that brushed their shining faces like visible steam, accompanied by the smell of pony-sweat and damp leather and flowers—scent that lay in heavy accumulated strata on the thick, sluggish air they breathed.

"Isn't it still!" she said.

He didn't answer at once, and she turned to look at him. His eyes under the brim of his sun-helmet were clear and cool—and searching. He glanced up into the branches above them, which were very empty, suddenly, of the flutter and chatter which usually went on there.

"It's hotter up here too," she commented a minute later. "Is that because we're getting nearer the crater?"

"We aren't as near as that." He twisted in the saddle and looked back down the trail behind them. "No," he said then, as though in answer to his own thoughts. "There's an open space up ahead, just before we come to the stair. We may as well go on."

"If we were at home I'd say there was a storm coming," she remarked. "You feel it sort of tight in your chest."

"It's only a little farther," he said, "and then we'll have a cool drink and some food before we start back."

Soon after that the track, though it was now hardly worthy the name, came out abruptly on to an old landslip, which had carried away all the big trees and left great rocks tossed about which still stuck out above the undergrowth of giant fern and lantana and coffee-bushes. For the space of a hundred yards or so it was overhung by the sheer face of the cliff from which the ground had once broken away. Then it plunged again into the green tunnel, and there was the stair before them, jungle-clad, ageless, and mysterious.

They dismounted and drank pineapple juice from a thermos, and Rodney said they had better get the pictures first of all. They scraped away foliage and moss and made detail photographs of one of the steps. Then they photographed each other sitting on the great blocks of stone, and then they had lunch, using the step above them as a table, though it was too high.

But the picnic seemed to be not entirely a success. Rodney glanced up now and then into the trees above them, where that strange, empty stillness prevailed. He was a little quiet himself. Elizabeth wondered if he was already regretting the time he had sacrificed to her amusement, and some of the bloom went off her happiness. She ceased trying to entertain him, and began rather forlornly to pack up the lunch box again. They had barely finished eating, but Rodney rose at once and said they had better be starting back. She acquiesced drearily, and went on packing up. It was no good trying to compete with the birds. Rodney in the field was not Rodney in love. She might have known.

His hands came down into her blurred vision, assisting her fumblings.

"I hate to cut short our time like this," he was saying. "But the fact is, I don't like the looks of things. I want to get you back to the house."

"Looks of things?" she repeated, startled, and as she spoke there was a low distant rumble somewhere under their feet.

"I thought so!" he said with dreadful satisfaction. "Earthquake!"

"W-what had we better do?"

"I was counting on that landslip as open ground, but I didn't realize there was so much overhang. It might come down again. Still, we'd better run for the edge of it—" The rumbling came again, louder, and there was a rocking, heaving motion with it, and then the apocryphal trunk began to bump down the subterranean stairs again. The horses jerked up their heads and Rodney caught the bridles. "Come on, Liz—it's all right, don't be scared. Never mind the lunch box."

She scrambled down the two lowest steps and caught the hand he was holding out to her. After they had gone a little way she tugged away from him and turned back.

"The camera!" she cried. "I forgot it!"

A rending sound like the end of the world drowned out his voice as he called after her. The earth beneath her feet twisted and shivered and wrenched until she staggered helplessly, and looking up she saw a great tree leaning towards her—while she stared, fascinated, suspended in time, it seemed to move downwards in slow-motion, cutting a swath through the creepers and air-plants which draped it and its fellows as it came—then something struck her hard between the shoulder blades and she fell forward on her face simultaneously with the resounding crash of the tree on the ground just behind her.

For a mon ent she lay there, deep in yielding fern, wondering why Rodney did not come and pick her up. Something lay across the lower part of her body. She raised herself cautiously and looked round. The shielding weight was Rodney.

He had thrown her clear, but the trunk of the tree had caught him just at the knees, pinning him to the ground. Dazed, holding her breath, she crawled out from under him. He lay perfectly

231

still, face down in the fern, his arms still spread protectively on either side of her. There was a thrashing in the branches of the fallen tree further along—one of the horses was down, entangled in wreckage. The other had disappeared.

Even the earth was quiet again, while she crouched there trying to take it in. Nothing moved in the empty branches above her, except the ghostly fingers of a little wind which came and went. Then the sun faded out, and all the world turned gray-green and sinister, and there was the taste of brimstone on her tongue. The ground beneath her gave a last silent shudder, and that was all.

"Rodney!" Her hands were on him, frantic, pleading, futile. Where did you feel to know if they were dead? How did you bring them round without brandy or cold water if they had fainted? How did you tell if bones were broken? What did you do if bones were broken? What *could* you do, if Rodney could not even speak to you? *"Rodney!"* she sobbed, and thought she could feel his heart still beating, though he made no move, no flicker of life, between her shaking hands.

It was a calamity she had never conceived in her wildest nightmares, that he should not answer when she yelled. Rodney was like the sun, he might be under a cloud, he might be on the other side of the world, but he was *there,* he would come back, he was still warm and bright and comforting if you could get to him, because without him the world would shrivel and die. Desperately she fought off the kind of panic that turns into madness and stampede, fought to get her hands steady and keep her teeth from chattering, fought for shreds of self-control to think with, to do whatever had to be done to save Rodney.

You can't go to pieces now, you've got to bring Charles here.

That was the first lucid idea she had had in an unrecorded aeon of time. She recognized it as lucid, with prayerful relief. Charles. Yes, of course, Charles must come. Charles wouldn't let him die. Charles would know what to do.

She sat back on her heels, both hands pressed to her temples, forcing her numb brain to think again. No use to call Rodney now, he couldn't hear. No use to try to move him, with the trunk of the tree pinning him down. That was the first thing, then—to shift the tree. But when she had tugged with hopeless, straining muscles at the pitiless weight she realized that that wasn't making any sense, and desisted. Nothing could be done without Charles. The thing was to get Charles on the job as quickly as possible.

She went to where the horse lay, further along among the branches, its saddle knocked askew. She caught the bridle and pulled, and said brisk, encouraging things, but the horse only thrashed about feebly with starting, frenzied eyes, and then its head fell back and blood ran out of its mouth and it died. So that wasn't any good either. She stood a moment staring at it without compassion, and then dropped the bridle and went and sat down again by Rodney, holding her head and trying to think clearly.

To get to Charles one would have to follow the trail back to the Casa Paraiso on foot. That would take time, of course, but it could be done. It meant leaving Rodney here, alone and helpless, for hours. It meant that he might come to and think she had deserted him, or that she too was hurt somewhere out of his sight. Suppose more trees fell while she was gone—suppose the volcano above them really burst—suppose— It was the only way, though. If she just sat there beside him, like Casabianca on the burning deck, he might die before help came. Charles knew approximately where they were. But Charles might not begin to worry about them before nightfall when they didn't show up. Knowing Rodney, Charles would assume that they were safe. Knowing Rodney, it was as much as Charles's life was worth to assume otherwise.

But I can't just walk away and leave him here, she thought —brace up, Liz, you've got to do it—I can't, *I can't*—would you rather watch him die, then?—no, no, I'll go, only—you're wasting

233

time, Liz—but if he should come to and find me gone he'll go crazy—you can leave him a message—

Rodney always carried a small note-book and pencil in his hip-pocket for bird-notes. She dug them out and wrote: *I've gone to bring Charles. Don't be frightened, we'll be back before dark.* She tore out the page and tucked it into his fingers. She bent over him, touching his hair, his cheek—he was so still—don't be frightened—that was a pretty silly thing to say to him—Rodney, I don't know any other way. . . .

Feeling numb and dizzy and queer, though the ground was quiet under her feet, she set off along the green tunnel of the trail, stumbling a little, trying not to hurry and use up all her strength at the beginning—and was confronted suddenly by chaos. The overhanging cliff had come down the mountainside, bringing everything with it. Where the trail had been was now just a mass of rock and bruised foliage, with flowers sticking out of raw dirt, and tree-trunks thrown about like matches. There was nothing to follow. She was cut off. And Charles, when he came to find them, was cut off. He wouldn't even know where to look for them.

The completeness of the catastrophe steadied instead of demoralizing her. She was on her own now. It was up to her. If she caved in now there was no hope at all for Rodney. Well, she wasn't going to cave in. Oh, no, you don't! she told the trackless waste between Rodney and rescue. Over my dead body!

This was Liz Dare talking, the Liz who had beaten her way up from the three-a-day to the Flamingo Club, from that snowbound dump in Minnesota to white and crystal luxury above Central Park. Soft, am I! We'll see about that!

She stood a moment, rejecting any romantic idea that love alone could guide her back to Rodney once she had crossed the featureless jumble of broken terrain ahead. No, the way back would have to be marked somehow, as she went. The trail they had come by must begin again somewhere, if only it could be picked up beyond the landslip. After all, if you kept on going down hill, you had to arrive somewhere, and once you could glimpse the ocean you had your bearings. Ignorance of the task ahead of her contributed to her courage. Ignorance and rage. She might be no pioneer woman, no intrepid female hunter, no leathery globe-trotter, no Mrs. Guerber, if you like, but by God the earthquake hadn't been born that could take Rodney away from her!

Let's see, now, you blazed a trail with an ax, or you—yes, you tied things on to things, to guide you back. Bits of handkerchief, bits of—no scarf—no petticoat—nothing much to spare—Rodney had a handkerchief—and there were napkins in the lunch-box. She turned back to where Rodney lay—he was just the same—collected his handkerchief and necktie and the note-book, found the lunch-box and took the napkins and waxed paper—stooped again above Rodney to get the pen-knife out of his pocket in order to slit the cloth into little strips—and with a last long look at him started off again through the murky jungle light. Her watch had stopped when she fell, but she knew it was about midday. Something had happened to her wrist when she fell, too. It was very stiff and had begun to swell, so that the watch-bracelet was cutting into it. She took off the watch and put it into her pocket. The swollen wrist was just one more insult. She ignored it furiously.

The going was unutterably bad. She slipped between tree-trunks which lay with their roots in the air, and she caught her feet in streamers of vine. Soft, spongy earth gave way beneath her, rocks rolled perilously towards her, branches whipped her face, thorn-bushes tore her clothes. She struggled on, panting, sobbing, swear-ing; pausing every now and then to tie a bit of rag on to some outstanding bush or branch, each in sight of the one before, but as far apart as she dared make them. The sky above her, when she could see it, was low and leaden, and filled with flying ash, and a howling wind was coming up.

But when she had covered what seemed endless miles of hope-

235

less crawling and climbing and sliding she saw with a gasp of satisfaction the sea stretched out below. So at least she was still on the right side of the mountain. She scrambled up a slanting log and stood there, braced against the gale, searching minutely with her eyes at the far edge of the landslip for the broken end of the track which had once led across its path. At last she thought she saw it—a sort of hole—but everything looked different without the sun—to gamble on that sort of hole in the green tangle meant a drastic change in the direction she had set herself—a sharper descent than she felt was right. She hesitated, glancing back along the way she had come. If I make a sharp turn downwards here, I must remember to turn sharp up when I come back with Charles, she thought. Ripping at the fabric with the pen-knife, wincing savagely from the pain of her sprained wrist, she fastened a piece of Rodney's necktie to a bare branch-end beside her and made the downhill turn. She was running out of markers.

It was farther than she could believe to the edge of the landslip and that nebulous hole in the green where the trail should begin again. Once she paused to work clumsily with the pen-knife until she had hacked out a sleeve of her shirt to cut into strips—her swollen wrist made the business of tying them painful and exasperating. She was too tired now to be angry any more. The tide of fury which had carried her well along on this impossible journey had receded and left only a dogged resolve.

It was the trail.

She stumbled into it, sobbing with relief, just as the tropic storm broke in a roar of rain and a leaping curtain of lightning and a thrashing wind. For a long time she clung to a friendly tree-trunk and tried to breathe. She was instantly soaked, of course—soaked and suffocated and blinded with rain. She had found the trail, but there was still a long way to go. Her left arm was drumming with pain, her body was a mass of bruises, her hands were torn and bleeding. And now there was lightning, and she was afraid of lightning.

236

She hid her face against the tree and heard herself calling Rodney's name in an ecstasy of foolish terror. But that wasn't any good any more. Rodney lay very still, face down, back there in the fern. . . . *I shall love you till I die,* he said, between the lightning flashes, and she lifted her head incredulously to listen. It was as though for a moment he had stood beside her. The storm crashed and pounded around her, while she listened. But I *heard* him, she thought, and forgot to flinch as lightning danced across her sight. I must be going mad—I *heard* him—

Then she was making her way along the trail without knowing how, while the rain beat down. The quake had been here too, for there were new obstructions to be climbed over and crawled round. The horse could never have made it—but how will we ever get him down without a horse?—Charles will know—Charles won't let him die—

She tripped and fell on her hands and knees in the mud, and stayed there, just as she was, her hair streaming around her face. I can't get up. I can't go on. Suppose the earthquake hit the Casa Paraiso too—suppose the house just isn't there any more—suppose it has slid right down the mountain on top of the town and the town has slid into the sea—suppose I can't find Charles— I can't go on—

She pulled her hands out of the mud, one at a time, and watched the rain wash them clean of the rich black earth which ran up her bare arms in thick dribbles. Rodney's aquamarine on her third finger was washed into view, with the slim wedding band above it, nearest her heart— *From this day forward,* it said inside, with their initials and the date, not of their marriage but of their meeting—

She caught at a hanging vine and it bore her weight as she dragged herself up, and then it snapped viciously in her hand so that she staggered backwards. She plodded on again, swaying drunkenly, and holding to things at the side of the trail. The mud sucked at her shoes with every squelching step, the rain beat down.

The next time she fell she lay there, at the end of caring, while only the pounding rain kept her from fading into unconsciousness, until finally she heard him again, as though he bent above her— "I, Rodney," he was saying, "take thee, Elizabeth—" She sat up groggily, and found herself in a slimy pool beside the track, which was now just a rivulet of mud. "—to my wedded wife," Rodney was saying. "—to have and to hold, from this day forward—to love and to cherish—" She got to her feet again, sliding and splashing onward in the mud of the trail. "I, Elizabeth," she repeated obediently, "take thee, Rodney—to my wedded husband—to have and to hold—"

That day in the church—how tall he was, with the white carnation in his buttonhole—how grave—but not nervous, the way she was—Rodney was used to churches—her hand was trembling when she held it out for the ring, but his was warm and steady—Rodney at his wedding looked somehow like a choir boy still. That first evening at the farm—he carried the bags upstairs and then left me with the most sublime tact, to hang my things away—we both changed into country clothes—when I went down to find him, tea was waiting in front of the fire—Rodney couldn't eat anything—I think that was when Rodney had stage-fright—I didn't —not after I got out of the church. Then we went for a walk in the dusk before dinner—there was a little path cut through the woods to a pond, where some ducks lived—and Rodney showed me the tree-stump where a chickadee had nested last spring—it was so low you could look right in—he said the bird wasn't afraid —well, not of him, anyway. We ate dinner, all right, both of us— it was broiled steak and mashed potatoes—and home-made ice-cream—you didn't mind Mrs. Wilkins coming in and out, she was so old, and she knew all about it—it was Rodney she looked at when she said Good-night to us—I wonder what she was remembering. The fire burned down while we sat there after dinner on the chesterfield—it was like a desert island after all—we had the world to ourselves till tomorrow, nobody could get at us, there were no trains to catch—he was wearing a rough tweed coat that scratched my cheek—I stood on the bottom step and watched him put out the lights in the living-room before we went upstairs —in the dark—

I'm down again in the mud—I wonder how long I've been lying here—get up, Liz, it can't be far now—daylight's going fast —no, it can't be, it's still mid-afternoon—I do believe the rain is stopping—you can't find the bits of rag after nightfall—get up, I say—there we are, back on our legs again—legs still there, Liz, now put one in front of the other—that's the girl, one in front of the other—

The next night he brought you home to Aunt Virginia's house, and carried you across the threshold—it was very late, because we sat so long after dinner at the farm—we got drowsy in front of the fire, and how we hated to start out on that cold drive instead of— "This is what comes of marrying a professor," he said, when we finally did start. Aunt Virginia's house looked so clean and neat and brave—the servants were so anxious and proud and smiling—we went into the living-room to wait for the hot milk, and there were fresh flowers and a wood fire burning—and Rodney's eyes were anxious too— "If there's anything you want to change," he said, "just start right in tomorrow morning." Even if it hadn't been a nice house, no woman alive could have hurt him by saying it wouldn't do—no woman could ask for anything better than a house warm and worn with kindness and contentment and love—it wasn't good enough for Marcia, though, and that had left its mark on Rodney's soul. The lovely grand piano in the corner, and the way he looked when I sat down at it and played—what was it I played first, I can't remember—but you must remember these things, you must never forget how it was in the beginning—and you must remember how he wakes up, instantly, all there, in focus, with eyes like a child's—and you

239

must remember how he is around the house, hardly making a sound, he never sings or whistles, doors don't bang, things don't drop—when he ties my shoes they never come undone—it's a trick he has with the knot—I must remember all these things, they're terribly important—I suppose I ought to pray, but I can't think of the words—Our Father Which art in Heaven—that's the way it starts—Rodney would know what comes next—Rodney was properly brought up—I know what I'll do if I lose him, though—I'll curse God, and die—

There was a shouting somewhere—strong hands caught her by the shoulders—she reeled, and somebody was holding her up—

"Liz!" cried Charles, and shook her. "What's happened? Liz, *where's Rodney?*"

XXI

Sometime before mid-afternoon Charles had one of his premonitions. The earthquake had done little damage at the Casa Paraiso, beyond cracking a wall in the *sala* and breaking the water connection to the fountain so that its cheerful dribble was absent from the patio. Jamaica started in at once to repair it. Nobody else was able to settle to work, though no actual anxiety could reasonably be felt about the two on a picnic, once it became fairly apparent that the volcano itself wasn't going to act up. Charles wandered rather aimlessly about the house between dark-room and laboratory; Sturgis smoked endless cigarettes and every now and then would go and look up at the sky. The Guerbers were very silent, and brewed a fresh pot of coffee on their private spirit-stove, and the strong, heartening fragrance drifted out on the rising wind. Frank and Sturgis each went and begged a cup. The Guerbers, who were always enchanted to serve anyone coffee at any hour of the day, bustled about to replenish the pot.

When the storm broke in its fury, Charles gave up any pretense of work and stood at a window in the laboratory with his hands in his pockets, staring out into the gray sheets of rain. Skinner ventured the opinion that they ought to send Pedro up to meet Rodney and Elizabeth and bring them safely in.

"I'm going myself," said Charles, staring into the rain. "Pretty soon."

Skinner said that in that case he thought he'd go along.

"Rodney won't try to move through this," said Charles. "He'll shelter somewhere till it slackens. Then we'll go out to meet him,

241

with restoratives. There'll be a lot of stuff down in the trail." And he went off to round up Jamaica and Pedro with their *machetes*, and order thermos bottles of hot coffee, and a brandy-flask..

At last the rain did slacken. Horses were saddled and Charles, Skinner, and Frank set out, wearing oilskins, with the restoratives in their saddle-bags, a *machete* to each man, Pedro and Jamaica going on before.

They had not ridden far, only to the first kink in the trail, when Jamaica and Pedro began to shout excitedly, and Charles saw her coming, weaving drunkenly towards them, but somehow staying on her feet until he caught her and held her up.

"Liz, what's happened? *Where's Rodney?*"

"Back there—under a tree—" she mumbled, pushing up her wet hair with a swollen, bleeding hand. "He's hurt. I'll take you to him."

Frank unscrewed a thermos and held out the cup towards her, full of strong black coffee laced with brandy. Charles poured it down her, scalding hot but bracing. They gave her a horse to hold to on the other side, and she stood gripping the stirrup-leather and shaking her head, fighting for consciousness.

"All right, take your time," said Charles, but his voice was not quite steady. "What happened up there?"

"A tree fell—it's got him across the legs. I couldn't move it. It killed the horse. He—Rodney—didn't answer when I spoke to him—I think his heart's still beating—"

"Where is he?"

"On the other side of the landslip. It came down again, across the trail. I marked the way I came—with bits of rag—I can show you the way—can I have this horse?"

"Now, wait a minute," said Charles. "You can't start back like this. You won't last. Besides, we'd better get a doctor."

"There isn't time—it will get dark—I can't find the way to him after dark—" She tried to mount the horse.

"Easy, now," said Charles, and swung her up, and she grabbed

242

weakly at the pommel. "See what I mean? You've had enough."

"You can't find him without me—I know the way—"

"All right, I'm not going without you. But first we're going back to the house and get some dry things on you and send the car down for the doctor. Then we can start right."

"There isn't time—"

"It's the only way to do it, Liz," he explained patiently. "Pedro and Jamaica will go straight on now, and clear the trail. We're only ten minutes from the house, you know. And if Rodney's badly smashed I don't want to move him without the doctor."

"His legs—might be broken—he didn't answer—" She lurched, and caught at the horse's mane.

"Hold tight, Liz—we'll get him."

Leading the horse which carried her, Charles started back towards the house, formulating his plans. Pedro and Jamaica were working the trail ahead of them. Skinner would drive the car into Santa Rosa and pick up the doctor. Meanwhile he and Mrs. Guerber between them would have to bring Liz round and keep her going somehow. By turning over in his mind the details of his preparations Charles was able to keep his imagination in check with regard to what Rodney himself might be enduring up there alone. To rush off blindly was no good. It wouldn't save time, Liz would collapse on the way, they might never get to Rodney, and if they did they probably couldn't handle him. At the same time, they must get to him before dark. It was pretty hard on Charles.

Skinner went skidding madly down the road towards Santa Rosa in the car, the chains banging against the mudguards. Frank eased the saddle-girths and went to make ready another horse for the doctor and one for Rodney. Rodney would have to come down on a horse somehow, unless— Charles was digging out a hammock, which formed the nucleus of a little heap of first-aid objects accumulating on the laboratory floor. Skinner was to tell the doctor to bring morphine, which was not included in their supplies.

243

Charles was trying to close his mind while he worked, to the need of morphine.

Mrs. Guerber took charge of Elizabeth, who was behaving very well. Docilely she stripped off her soaked clothing and allowed Mrs. Guerber's practiced hands to rub her dry and massage her punished body back to warmth and sensation. Mrs. Guerber worked over her in an enigmatic silence which was neither disapproving nor friendly—gentle and efficient in all she did. Elizabeth submitted as she would have submitted to anything which would help her get back to Rodney. By the time the car was heard groaning up the road again she had drunk a bowl of thick hot soup and another cup of coffee, her arm was tightly bandaged, and she was dressed and waiting in the laboratory beside the oilskins, electric torches, lanterns, ropes, the hammock and first-aid kit. The rain had shrunk to a drizzle and would soon stop.

Skinner was alone and white-faced. The doctor had gone to Santo Tomas, where the quake had been very bad and the hospital was full of casualties. The wires were down. Someone would have to drive to Santo Tomas while the rest of them went to Rodney. The doctor had taken his opiates with him, and Father Joseph had none.

Charles made up his mind.

"Go to Santo Tomas," he told Skinner curtly. "Bring the doctor here if you have to hog-tie him."

Skinner threw in the clutch and was off again, his chains banging.

"Sturgis," said Charles, and Sturgis jumped for a waterproof. "Come on, Liz. Frank, load the stuff on the lead horse."

Pedro and Jamaica had by then cleared the trail of the worst obstructions nearly as far as the landslip, and the horses made fairly good time. There was going to be an angry sort of sunset, which would give them extra light.

At the landslip they all dismounted and started across on foot. It was agonizing work. Elizabeth and Charles went first, the

244

others followed, dragging the willing little horses by the bridles. The wind and rain had demolished some of her landmarks, and sometimes there was a long halt while she cast about wildly with Pedro and Jamaica skirmishing round the edges. Each time the drenched bit of rag or soggy paper was found at last and they inched forward again.

But once they stuck hopelessly.

"It must have been just about here that I made the sharp turn downwards," she said over and over again. "The marker is a piece of Rodney's necktie—quite a large piece—but it would have to be green!" She glanced round at the ring of tense faces which waited on her next move, and made a frenzied, hysterical gesture with her clenched hands. "Don't all stand there staring at me like that! I'm doing the best I can!" She dropped down on a log and buried her face in her arms and began to cry.

Charles looked at Sturgis with despair. Sturgis gave his bridle to Frank and slithered along the muddy slope till he could lay a hand on her shoulder.

"You're doing all right," he said. "What was that crack you made last night about playing Indians?" (She was very still under his hand, listening.) "None of us ever did it better," said Sturgis, and his fingers tightened till they hurt, forcing their way into her exhaustion. "Come on, Daniel Boone, you can't quit now!"

"Who says I'm quitting?" she demanded angrily.

"Not me," said Sturgis in mild surprise. "But we're losing time."

She braced both hands against the log on either side of her and forced herself to rise again, her head hanging, the two damp wings of her hair hiding her face. She froze there, looking down. In the shiny, trampled mud between the feet of one of the horses lay a bit of green rag. She seized it with a cry.

"I've got it! Now I know where I am! I know where I am, Charles! *Come on!*"

And so finally they came to the last stretch of trail between

245

the landslip and the stair. Elizabeth and Charles broke into a stumbling run together, his hand at her elbow.

Rodney lay just as she had left him, face down in the fern, which was now matted and glistening with rain. His soaked shirt stuck to his shoulder blades, the note she had left was pulp in his fingers. Charles slid a capable hand under Rodney's chest.

"Attaboy! The old pump's still on the job!"

"He's not dead?" begged Elizabeth, on her knees beside him.

"Of course he's not dead! It takes more than a one-horse earthquake like that to kill Rodney! Where's Jamaica? All right, boys, lay hold of the tree and see what happens."

They all straddled the tree and laid hold. Their muscles bulged, their faces got red, their veins stood out. It made not a millimeter of difference to the tree.

"That's no good," said Charles. "Let's think, now. The ground is soft underneath him. I don't believe he's crushed at all, I think he's just— Yes, we'll dig him out. With the *machetes* and our hands—it can be done!"

Down on their knees on either side of him, they worked like terriers in the black soil, until Rodney lay in a shallow sort of trench from the waist down.

"That'll do," said Charles, and wiped his face. "It's got to do. Sturgis, take his other side. Watch his feet, Frank, don't let us yank him. Ready, now—you'd never believe what he weighs, for a skinny guy like that—easy—once more—that's doing it—once more—all right, Frank?—once more— Hullo, son, that sounds natural!"

As they hauled him into the clear, Rodney had come to on a gust of plain and fancy swearing which was music to their ears. Its mule-skinner Spanish embellishments made Jamaica grin, and raised it well above Elizabeth's comprehension.

"All right, all right, tell us just what you think of us, we like it!" said Charles affectionately, and his competent hands ran again

246

over Rodney's body. "Where does it hurt? Anywhere above the knees? Give us a lap, Liz, to put his head in. That's better."

Rodney was silent now, his eyes closed. He gripped Elizabeth's ankle as she sat down and slid under him, and buried his face in her lap. Charles bent above him with the brandy-flask.

"Still there, son?"

"Yep, I'm here."

"Have some of this."

Rodney opened his eyes, and closed them again as the whiff of brandy met his nostrils.

"Take it away. If I can pass out again, let me. It's my right leg, mostly. Get on with it."

"Ribs feel all right?"

"Yes."

"Back all right?"

"It's my *leg,* blast you, it wants a splint, are we going to stay here all night? Stop talking and get at it! Where's Liz?"

"I'm here, Rodney."

"Hullo," he said. "What struck us?"

"You pushed me out from under the tree. It hit you." With her futile handkerchief she was wiping at his thick hair, still wet from the rain.

"That's right, I remember. How did Charles get here?"

"I went after him."

"All by yourself? That's pretty cute. Weren't you scared?"

"I was scared you'd die before I got back."

"I'm not one to die of a broken leg, I guess. What's Charles doing?"

"They're cutting down some saplings."

"That's for the splint. Tell 'em to hurry up."

"Oh, Rodney, does it hurt much?"

"It's pretty lively. Don't cry, Liz."

"I'm not c-crying."

"Either you're crying, or the rain around here is salt. Oh, *damn*

247

you, Charles, why didn't you warn me!" He pressed his face deeper into her lap, his fingers bit into her ankle.

Charles was kneeling beside him, working Frank's jacket around the injured leg as a pad. Pedro came up with two long rough-hewn poles and a rope, and Frank was searching out adhesive tape and rolls of bandage.

"Getting him over the saddle is going to be pure hell," said Sturgis in a low voice.

"I can fix that," said Charles. "Might as well now as later." He laid gentle hands on Rodney's shoulders and turned him so that Rodney lay in the bend of his arm. Rodney's eyes unclosed. A look passed between them. "All right, son, let's deal with it," said Charles, and brought his fist up sharply to the point of Rodney's jaw. He replaced the inert weight on Elizabeth's lap and returned to his splint-making. "Now we can work fast," he added. "Let me know the minute he starts to come round, Liz."

She sat with her fingers in Rodney's hair and watched while they wrapped Frank's jacket round the injured leg, laid the poles alongside, and taped and bound them tightly into place. Then Jamaica stooped and lifted Rodney in his arms like a child, with Charles supporting the splinted leg, and hung him on his stomach across the saddle of a horse. And then, with Charles on one side and Sturgis on the other to keep things from hitting him, they began the slow, jolting journey back across the landslip, following Pedro's trail now, which was boldly enough marked to guide them even after they had to light the lanterns.

It was long after dark when they reached the Casa Paraiso, and the doctor still had not arrived. Jamaica and Charles lifted Rodney off the horse and got him into the house and on his bed, which Mrs. Guerber had in readiness. He fainted again when they took him off the horse, and lay quiet while they undressed him, looking very flat and dead. It was not till then that anybody noticed that Elizabeth's teeth were chattering uncontrollably and she was shaking all over as she sat huddled in a chair in a corner of the room.

"Liz has fever," said Sturgis. "She must get to bed at once."

"I'm all right," she insisted, chattering. "I need some brandy, that's all."

"Rum and quinine for you," he told her kindly. "I'll fix it."

He went away, and Mrs. Guerber came to her.

"You are to have Charles's room now, and he will sleep here," she said. "I have moved out his things and Dr. Sturgis's. Come along, I'll help you to bed." She reached down strong, comforting hands, and Elizabeth jerked away from her, crouching back into the chair.

"But I want to be near Rodney—"

"He will want a man to look after him now. Come."

"No! Why can't I stay with Rodney—"

"Because you are no good to him now," said Mrs. Guerber bluntly. "You are going to be ill. You have fever."

"I'm perfectly able to take care of him myself—"

"Even if you were well, you could not nurse him alone. He is too heavy for you. How would you lift and turn him? How would you change him, and put fresh linen on his bed? How about shaving him each morning, how about—"

"Charles could come in and—"

"Nursing a sick man who cannot help himself is not just feeding him broth out of a spoon," said Mrs. Guerber severely. "One must have the strength of a horse and the stomach of a butcher. I have done it and I know! You have finished your part and now you can rest, you have earned it. Come to bed now, and be good."

Elizabeth looked up with amazement into her face and saw that she was smiling, and when she smiled there was a place where a dimple once had been in the leathery cheek. No one had ever seen her smile before. Clinging to the strong, comforting hands of the woman whose husband called her Ernestine, Elizabeth allowed herself to be led away into the room next door. By the time

249

she had been got to bed and dosed with Sturgis's witch's brew of hot rum and quinine she was babbling in feeble delirium.

Skinner finally arrived, bringing the doctor, who had accompanied him without demur, having had, he explained, the pleasure of Señor Monroe's acquaintance for an hour or so three years ago at Tehuantepec; not professionally, of course, merely to have a drink together in the *cantina*. The doctor had been laboring for hours among the casualties of Santo Tomas, and slept exhaustedly while Skinner drove. He stepped out of the car fresh and efficient, with his little bag of tools, and requisitioned Mrs. Guerber at once for the administration of ether.

During her absence, Sturgis was told off to watch beside Elizabeth, who every now and then tried to get out of bed in the belief that Rodney still lay face down under the tree waiting for her to come back to him. While the sweet, sickish odor of ether wafted in from Rodney's room, Sturgis held her down with hands as gentle as a woman's, and tried to reason with her.

"Rodney's safe, child—thanks to you. You saved him, remember?"

"I didn't know what to do—he lay so still—I hadn't anything to give him—I couldn't make him answer—Charles would have known what to do—Charles must never let him out of his sight down here—it was my fault we went on the picnic alone—I wanted Rodney to myself—Charles wouldn't have let him die—"

"He isn't going to die, child—"

"N-not going to die—" she repeated, vaguely comforted.

"Not by a jugful, he's just got a bad leg, remember? He's going to be as good as new in no time. We've all got you to thank for that."

"Not going to die—"

Holding fast to Sturgis with hot dry hands, she seemed to doze.

When Mrs. Guerber came in from Rodney's room and said that all was well, Elizabeth roused again with the same single-minded impulse to finish a task which seemed to her only half done, and

250

tried to get out of bed. Mrs. Guerber bent over her quickly, all tenderness, coaxing, reasoning, reassuring, stroking Elizabeth's hair, patting her scarred, iodine-daubed hands, while Sturgis stared at them in astonishment and awe—

"There, there, lovey," she soothed, over and over again, and Sturgis began to think he was delirious too. "There, there, lovey, don't you fret—your man is safe, all thanks to you—just a bad leg, lovey, it will mend—that's my brave girl—that's my darrling, there, there, hold fast to me, yes, it is all over now, you have only to rest and get well—there, there, nursling, don't you cry—" She turned her head to find Sturgis gaping at her. "It is the shock," she said as though extenuating Elizabeth's loss of control. "Even more than fever, it is the shock, to see the man you love lie help- less—you doubt God. We will need the doctor here, go and fetch him from the other room."

Sturgis went off in a daze to where Charles and the doctor sat by Rodney's bed, waiting for him to come out of the ether—and reported that Mrs. Guerber had gone all soft and motherly in the twinkling of an eye and was calling Liz her nursling.

"The iron woman has melted," said Sturgis, mopping his brow. "You wouldn't know her!"

Charles looked bewildered and said No fooling.

"Women," said the little Spanish doctor, and nodded his head wisely. "Always they understand each other. It leaves us no place!" He went away into Elizabeth's room.

As the night wore on, Rodney wavered back through the mists of anesthetic to pain and the sound of sobbing.

"I didn't know what to do for him—" Elizabeth's pitiful tale ran on and on, and every word had to come in through the open doors. "—he could have had my life, but I didn't know how to give it to him—so I had to leave him there—I *knew* I oughtn't to leave him, but I didn't know what else to do—there was nobody but Charles to save him—I wasn't any good to him, I didn't even know how to pray—I don't know anything—if Rodney dies,

251

Charles has the right to shoot me—I hope he *will* shoot me—oh, I *hope* he will—"

Rodney dragged his eyes open and found Charles beside the bed, watching him.

"It's all right, son," said Charles at once. "Liz is in for a go of fever. The doctor is with her."

"Fever," Rodney whispered, and his head moved restlessly on the pillow. "I was afraid of that. I caught her skipping her quinine."

"No!" said Charles.

"I hoped she'd get by without anything like this, though. I ought to be in there with her—"

"She'll be all right—"

"I want Rodney," said Elizabeth suddenly on a new note. "If Rodney's alive, why isn't he here? You're lying to me, there's something wrong—why doesn't Rodney come?"

"He can't come, lovey, he's got a bad leg—"

"Rodney!" Elizabeth persisted, and then, with the old familiar scream of terror—*"Rodney!!"*

"Sh! Do you want to wake him? Rodney's got to sleep, you mustn't disturb him—"

Rodney struggled up on one elbow.

"Get Jamaica. I'm going in there. I bet Jamaica could carry me—"

"Now, now, take it easy, son, that won't help." Charles stood over him.

"She's scared. You go in and talk to her, then. Tell her I'm all right. She might listen to you."

"She won't, not just now, she doesn't take anything in. It will wear off, and she'll sleep. Now, look, if you start caving round they'll blame me for being a rotten nurse. Here, it's time for your medicine."

Rodney regarded the small white pill with suspicion.

"What is it?"

"Doctor's orders."

252

"I don't want a sedative now, I've got to keep track of things."

"You'll keep track. Come on, son, down it."

Rodney swallowed the pill and lay still, enduring his leg and listening.

"She's scared," he said again. "I was out like a light, it must have been hell for her. No wonder she thinks I'm dead. She never ought to have had a scare like that." And finally, with another weary turn of his head on the pillow—"Oh, my God, isn't there some way to stop her?"

"The doctor's working at it. He's a good little guy and knows his job."

"What sort of temperature is she running?"

"A hundred and four."

"That's pretty tough," said Rodney, and sighed helplessly, and lay there, listening. "I ought to be with her. She counts on me when she's scared. A hundred and four is tough. Two-fifths more, and you hope you die. Four-fifths more, and maybe you do."

"Nobody around here is going to die," Charles said firmly. "Not if I catch 'em at it!"

"She can't understand what they say to her—if I could only get my hands on her she'd be quiet—let me know if it goes on up— she'd listen to me—things are slipping—damn you, Charles, you've doped me—" His eyes closed against his will, and he went under.

"Such love!" sighed the little Spanish doctor enviously, when Elizabeth slept at last, sweating, and a reassuring report could be made to Rodney before they knocked him out with another sedative. "Such love! It is like the cinema!"

XXII

The holocaust had thrown down trees and flooded ravines and damaged or drowned the eggs and fledglings in most of the nests they were watching. Charles and Pedro brought in two young birds which promptly died. So far as the harpy eagle enterprise was concerned, the trip was, Charles said grimly, a washout.

Rodney's disappointment seemed to Elizabeth disproportionate. In her view, Rodney was alive and the hell with eagles, let's go home. But to Rodney it was failure, and he had never before failed on so grand a scale as to find himself helpless with an important part of the job unaccomplished. Rodney was both angry and blue. His leg, which had suffered rough treatment and gone too long untended, was giving him more trouble than was usual, and would be slow in mending. After his first pleasure and relief at seeing Elizabeth like herself again when she was up and about, Rodney refused to cheer up. He said he would have to come back next year for the eagles, and Elizabeth, turning cold, thought Oh, no, never again!

The bond between Mrs. Guerber and Elizabeth strengthened day by day. They were Lisa and Ernestine to each other now, and that surprising dimple in Mrs. Guerber's leathery cheek came and went as they bent their heads together in inconsequential female chatter over mending, needlepoint, or a new magazine in the mail. "She is so happy," Dr. Guerber would point out, almost in tears himself. "Not since years have I seen her like this! It is the girl she never bore—it is the *Mädchen* she prayed for—at last—"

Rodney had a different explanation. "Liz beat her at her own game," he said to Charles.

254

There was some discussion of flying him to the hospital at Panama for treatment as soon as he could be moved. That project was abandoned after some frantic cabling by Andrew, in favor of flying him straight through to New York as directly and quickly as possible. There was an air-field at Santa Ana thirty miles away, which connected with both Tegucigalpa and San José, and thence via Balboa and Miami with New York. Elizabeth and Charles were to leave with him. The rest, under Sturgis's command, would finish the packing and return by boat via Los Angeles.

Elizabeth, who hated to fly, packed her bags and Rodney's with efficient hands, and checked off the remaining days on a calendar. Packing was something a trouper did know how to do, she said with some pride, when Rodney attempted to give directions from his bed. Stand back, and see how it was done. But Rodney's eyes were moody as he watched her, and he insisted on knowing exactly where she was stowing his things, and how. Rodney ill was a Problem Child of the first water.

At last the day came when a rather primitive little motor-ambulance rattled over from Santo Tomas to drive them to Santa Ana, where a rather raffish-looking plane awaited them for the first leg of the journey. Elizabeth eyed it with misgiving, but the pilot was a young and cheerful soul from Brownsville who inspired confidence, and he brought them down safely with a flourish beside the big gray Pan-American plane which was to carry them to Balboa. From there on in it wasn't bad.

Andrew met them at La Guardia Field with an ambulance, a limousine, and an expression of acute anxiety, which latter cleared a little when Elizabeth flung herself round his neck and Rodney greeted him with a rueful smile.

Then the doctors got at Rodney and made his life a misery to him. Elizabeth moved in with Aunt Virginia at the apartment, and spent as much time at the hospital as was allowed. Rodney was not permitted to use his leg, and his state of mind was disheartening. He moped and he brooded.

255

Gradually a feeling of permanent apology towards him damped Elizabeth's spirits. It was all her fault. If he hadn't taken her to the stair on a picnic it would never have happened. *You don't belong in my life,* he had said once. She was to blame for his first real failure in the field. He would never, never forgive her. . . .

And so she in her own way began to brood, which Rodney had once said was fatal. Her guilt seemed to her too obvious to require mentioning—and if Rodney did not hold her responsible for the ruin of his trip, why did he act the way he did? Oh, yes, he seemed glad to see her each day when she came to the hospital. He kissed her hands, and took an interest in the foolish, hopeful offerings she laid on his coverlet—she spent hours combing the town for gifts which might amuse him. But there was no getting round one thing. Even after the pain left, even after he got out of the hospital and came to live at the apartment, Rodney was not himself, and Elizabeth went on feeling penitent and small, so that silences fell with a thud between them now, and something of spontaneity was gone from their companionship.

It was one of those situations which a few sensible words in the right place might have cured. But two highly-strung people tempestuously in love seldom say sensible things. If Elizabeth had only abased herself openly in words, he might have seen what his quite natural depression was doing to her, and then his normal philosophy would have reasserted itself for her protection, as it had not done for his own. But in his unnatural preoccupation with himself, he thought he saw her being bored by his invalidism—he was almighty bored by it himself—and so he only fretted against it the more. Things were getting pretty bad.

Each time Aunt Virginia made a move to vacate the guest room and leave them to themselves, Elizabeth implored her to stay and help amuse Rodney. Aunt Virginia, never having seen much of them together before, was unaware how serious the rift was becoming, but she did feel instinctively that it was high time Rodney pulled himself together. She finally said so, on an afternoon when

256

Elizabeth had gone out to choose some new books for reading aloud, which was one way they filled in their silences now.

"This broody spell of yours," said Aunt Virginia bluntly, "has gone on about long enough. I don't say you haven't got cause—no man can bear to have anything the matter with him, much less one with the physical conceit you've always had. But you're getting on my nerves, young man, and I'm sorry for your wife!"

"So am I," he said meekly, and at his restless movement the cane he used when he walked fell down beside his chair. "I guess I'm on her nerves too."

"Has she told you so?"

"She doesn't have to. I can read Liz like a book."

"Oh, *can* you!" said Aunt Virginia, and her tone was hostile. "Can you, indeed! Well, how about the writing on the wall? Can you read that too?"

He glanced at her with an apprehension quickly veiled.

"I'm not sure," he said. "As a matter of fact, I'm not sure of anything any more."

"That's bad," said Aunt Virginia unsympathetically.

"What do you see written on the wall? Do you think she wants to go back to the stage?"

"Is that what's haunting you?" she asked shrewdly. "Because something is."

"I wish you'd find out if she does," he said. "I can't ask her. It's silly, but every time I try I cave in. She isn't the way she used to be, that's all I know. Something's gone." He put his head in his hands. "It was asking too much of her—what she had to do for me. If I'd dreamed anything like that would happen I'd never have let her go with us at all. Sometimes I wonder if she doesn't hate me for letting her in for a thing like that!"

Aunt Virginia put down her knitting and went and sat on the broad arm of his chair and laid her arm across his shoulders. He leaned against her gratefully, his face hidden.

"I think you're exaggerating," she said.

"It should never have happened to her. I was the guy that was going to make her forget all the ugly things she knew. And look at me, I damned near killed her, that's what it amounts to!"

"She won't hold it against you if you behave yourself now," said Aunt Virginia, her fingers in his hair.

"I've lost her," he said hopelessly.

"Oh, nonsense."

"She only went along because she wanted to be with me—and she almost died of it. That's quite a lot to forgive!"

"All the same, I can't help but feel there's a screw loose somewhere in your thinking," said Aunt Virginia. "I can't prove it to you right now. But I don't think you've read her right side up."

"It's gone," said Rodney, sitting very still.

"What is? Or shouldn't I ask?"

"Whatever we had that was different from everybody else. Maybe we'll get along, somehow—but now we're just any two people who are married to each other, getting along. That's not just time, and custom, and general staleness. It happened to us because of the earthquake. We were all right, I tell you, in spite of everything —till after the earthquake."

"It will come back, my dear, when you're quite well again."

"I don't see how it can. It was in her eyes—it was somewhere inside me, like my heart beating." He slid forward, his arm across her lap and his face hidden. "It's gone," he said.

Elizabeth came out of the shop carrying a parcel of books, and started to signal a taxi. Then, on an impulse too sudden and too instinctive to be anything but a hunch, she turned and walked quickly down the block to the small apartment hotel where Charles was staying in a couple of rooms to be near Rodney, while he worked up notes on the trip and co-ordinated material which Rodney would need when he wrote the book he had not yet had what it took to begin.

She went up in the elevator without being announced and rang

258

the bell. Charles himself opened the door. She had been sure that he would. She smiled her orphan-smile into his surprised face.

"Can I come in? I want to—ask you something where Rodney can't hear."

"Delighted," said Charles, stunned.

She came in and sat down in silence, on the davenport. Charles took the other end, and offered her cigarettes, which was light-headed of him as he knew she didn't smoke.

"No, thanks, I—only want to stay a minute, if you aren't too busy—"

"Why would I be too busy?" he inquired, his kind blue eyes taking in the fact that she was troubled and humble and nervous, his kind heart going out to her in pity as it would have done to anybody in those circumstances. "Can I do something?"

"You can tell the truth," she said.

"Sometimes I can—if I try real hard."

"Well, first of all—Rodney's going to be all right, isn't he? I mean—his leg *will* get well?"

"Oh, sure. By the end of the summer probably he won't even be limping."

"He can ride again, and—do all the things that he's used to?"

"Sure. Don't you worry about that."

"Well, then—now, Charles, I want the truth!"

"All right, I promise."

"Do you think I ought to—clear out?"

Charles stared.

"I don't know what you mean," he said.

"I mean I don't belong in Rodney's life—you may as well admit that, he said so himself while he was still trying not to marry me! I knew I didn't, but I—I wanted him anyhow. Well, I've not done him any good so far, we may as well admit that too. So hadn't I better just—eliminate myself?"

"It's a bit late to do that, isn't it?" said Charles, groping.

259

"I could tell him I wanted to go back to the stage, I thought."

"Do you?"

Her eyes filled.

"No. But that's got nothing to do with it."

"I think it has," said Charles. "In fact, I think that's the answer. If you don't want to leave him—why bring it up?"

"To set him free!" she cried, and began to search desperately in her bag for a handkerchief, and as usual had lost it. "I know that sounds like something out of a Pinero play, but it was all my fault and I just can't bear it any longer! He's much too polite to blame me out loud, but I never should have gone on the trip at all, why did you let me?"

Charles handed her the clean handkerchief from his breast pocket.

"He wanted you to go," he said. "He hoped you'd like it once you got there."

"Well, I didn't. I'm not meant for that sort of thing, and I never pretended to be. He'd be better off without me."

"Now, wait a minute," said Charles. "Have you said anything to him about all this?"

"No, I can't. Rodney's—different. Once I could say anything I liked to him and trust him to understand, but now—"

"Well, you certainly can't walk out on him without—"

"No, no, don't you understand, Charles, it's the *way* I walk out that counts! If he knows I'm just doing it to get out of his way, he'll be so nice about it I'll collapse the way I did when I tried to send him away before we were married. But if I put on an act about wanting to go back to my Career, he'd accept that, wouldn't he? It wouldn't matter to him after a while, and—"

"It would half kill him, that's all," said Charles.

"I wish I could believe that, but—"

"Look, Liz. I had a premonition. I saw all this coming—well, something of the sort, anyway." Charles got up and walked round the room with his hands in his pockets. "If I'd thought less of Rodney—or if I'd been a little more of a heel than I am—well,

260

I'd have been glad to see you drop dead or something before we started. But all that was yesterday. Speaking in the light of what I know now—if you walk out on Rodney for any reason I can think of, up to and including some other guy, I'll shoot you, Liz, by gum I will!"

"Why—why, Ch-*Charles*—!"

"You're a grand gal, Liz, I'm the first to admit that," he said, wandering up and down the room. "But sometimes I wonder what you think you think with, I really do, because it's not brains, it can't be! You are the most sublimely nit-witted thing I ever saw in my life, and for two cents I'd be crazy about you myself, but this is tops, Liz, this beats anything you've ever tossed off before!"

"B-but I don't understand, I thought—"

"Sure you don't, you never do know what it's all about, but there you sit, looking as though you could be eaten with a spoon, and Rodney can't live without you and I'm not sure I could either now, so you want to put on an act and go back to your Career! And for why? Have you got some loony idea Rodney will forget he ever set eyes on you?"

"W-wouldn't he?" she queried, awed.

"No!!" shouted Charles in utter exasperation. "You're not that kind of a woman, worse luck!" He came and sat down beside her and took both her hands in his. "Liz, don't you know *anything?* Rodney's in love with you, gal, you've heard tell of love, it's what makes the world go round."

She was gazing at him with an incredulous kind of hope.

"But he—acts so sort of f-funny now—"

Charles sat looking down at her beautiful, unself-conscious hands between his blunt brown ones, wondering how they had got there. The fragrance of her was in the room, along with the smell of his pipe. Rodney's wife, Rodney's love, the light of Rodney's soul —between his hands. Maybe she didn't belong in their lives, but there was no way to swear off now, as though she was tobacco or hard liquor. She hadn't a lick of sense, she didn't know a bird

261

from a tree, she was always afraid of things, always the wrong things, until she had some real reason to be scared and then she came through like a ton of bricks, she spelt trouble, dalliance, and confusion, they had certainly been better off without her, but now she was theirs, for better or for worse, and God help her.

"You're acting pretty funny yourself," he said slowly, feeling his way. "I don't know why you pick on me for this, I'm no Mr. Fix-it, but I'll tell you one thing, Liz—just one, and after that you're on your own. Never leave him. Not even if he kicks you down a flight of stone steps. See what I mean?"

She gazed at him bewilderedly still, her hands in his.

"Charles."

"Mm-hm?"

"You're awful sweet."

He put her hands back in her lap, and rose, and began to fill his pipe.

"Have you got any fixed ideas about where you spend the summer?" he queried casually.

"Well, that's another thing, of course I w-wanted to go to Maine, but Rodney thinks he'll do better at the farm writing the book now—and Aunt Virginia says to look out because he's sure to find it dull at the farm, and—"

"All right, I know what she means," said Charles hastily. "Now, look, Liz, you go right back home and raise hell about Maine."

?

"Yep, you go back there now and start in on him. Beg, coax, cry, nag, have jim-jams—but hold out for Maine!"

??

"Then tomorrow I'll come in all breezy-like and say, What about Maine, let's make up our minds, are we going to sit around here all night? And Rodney will say, That's funny, Liz has been at me about Maine. And I'll say, Doesn't she want to go? And Rodney will say, Well, as a matter of fact, she wants to start right

262

away. And I'll say, Fine, what are we waiting for?" He spread his hands. "It's so simple," he said, and grinned.

"B-but do you think he'll—"

"A couple of days ago he wrote to Mercer, asking him to take the directorship of the Station this summer," said Charles. "Only I forgot to post the letter. That's called a Coincidence."

"Oh, Charles, you're wonderful!"

"Not at all," said Charles modestly. "I was wondering how the dickens I was going to get round him about this. Heaven sent you here today, Liz. Heaven knows exactly what we're up against. Heaven is well acquainted with these Monroes!"

XXIII

"Wake up," Rodney was saying softly. "It's our anniversary."

Elizabeth woke up, reluctantly as always, and lay a moment with her eyes still closed, assembling herself. A year ago today she had roused to find the room full of a mysterious rosy glow which was the dawn, and had knelt on the window-seat to watch the sun come up out of the sea. A year ago today she had gone for a walk before breakfast and met Rodney.

Now, when she opened her eyes the room would be exactly the same—the comfortable, heavy, unmodern furniture, the faded summer chintzes, the great four-poster bed with a ruffled canopy—her dressing-gown over a chair—Snorky snoozing in his basket in the corner—dawn coming up outside—but now Rodney was raised on one elbow beside her, saying, "Will you wake up? Or must I kiss you?"

She smiled, with her eyes still shut, and he did.

"Ooh," she said then, not too distressfully. "Go and shave!"

"You didn't say *that* a year ago today!" he remarked, and his weight left the bed. "I'll be back," he warned her, and the bathroom door closed behind him.

She burrowed deeper into the pillow, luxuriously. It was darker than last year—earlier. Plenty of time to keep her appointment. She lay still, warm and drowsy with contentment. She and Charles had won. Rodney was himself again. Droll, ardent, busy, and gay again—not even limping any more. Each morning he drove over to the Station, each noon and each evening he drove back to the Old Baxter Place, which he now called home. If only Sam could

264

see him here, she thought—if only Sam could fully appreciate his legacy to her. . . .

In the bathroom the shower had stopped. She sat up, her hands around her knees, and watched the seaward windows brighten. After a few thoughtful minutes—

"Rodney!" she yelled.

The bathroom door opened.

"Hullo?"

"What's over there, across from us?"

"Over where?" He stood in the doorway, wearing a bulky bathrobe of white toweling, lather on his face, a razor in his hand.

"Where the sun is coming from." She pointed through the window.

"Spain," he said. "Even Snorky knows that."

The doorway was empty again.

That's funny, she thought. Spain is so far south. She left the bed and went to sit on the window-seat, hugging her knees, while the light turned golden. Pretty soon Rodney came in, still wearing the white bathrobe, and claimed the kiss which was his morning reward for a smooth chin, and found her half of it a trifle absent-minded.

"Wool-gathering, eh," he remarked, sitting down on the window-seat facing her. "Any luck?"

"Well, I was just thinking—"

"Wait! Let me guess! You were thinking that if you had it all to do again, starting with a year ago this morning, you'd turn over and go back to sleep—but *quick!*"

"If I'd done that, you wouldn't be here now."

"That's the idea, yes."

Her eyes came back from the window to rest on him impersonally. He looked so fresh and rested in the mornings. His hair, still damp from the shower, had been brushed within an inch of its life.

"Trying to think where you've seen me before?" he suggested gently. "I was here last night—remember?"

"How come I married such a *handsome* man?" she murmured.

It was a line he couldn't take, and she knew it. He rose and brought her dressing-gown and slippers—doubtless another evidence of Aunt Virginia's early training—and put her into them, lest she catch cold. Then he sat down again beside her, where she could lean against him, a shielding arm between her and the sill.

"Well, there it is," he said. "Our whole new world, that we got in the blink of an eye. Looks nice and big, doesn't it!"

"Spain," she said thoughtfully, gazing at the horizon. "It used to be so lovely, and so gay." Something like a shiver ran through her, and she nestled back into his arms, which were quick and comforting. "Oh, Rodney, we have so much to lose!"

"What we have already had, we can't altogether lose," he told her. "So each day as it comes—days like this one—must last forever." And a few minutes later—"Now, according to the script," he remarked, "you go and wash your face and get dressed in a brown suit, and we drink orange juice in the kitchen, and then we take the shore-path and you sit down on a log to admire the view—and that's where I come in, flat on my face. Can we skip the fall? I'm out of practice."

"And then you carry me back across the ford—"

"And we have waffles for breakfast."

She twisted in his arms to look up at him.

"Isn't this better than the Casa Paraiso?"

"Unfair."

"Well, but isn't it?"

"Lotus-eating," he sighed, against her hair. "The Song of the Sirens. *Dolce far niente.*"

"But, Rodney—"

"I started something I didn't finish, at the Casa Paraiso. That rankles."

"You started something else up here that you haven't finished yet. You started a marriage."

266

"That's my life," he said simply. "Casa Paraiso was just a job. Got to do my jobs, sooner or later."

And so it was still there, after all, she thought, leaning against him. The cloud no bigger than a man's hand—something he hadn't finished. She had a little lost sight of it, as the placid summer days slipped by and Rodney went on being so entirely himself; his charming, funny, considerate self, with so many odd things going on behind that poker-face of his. She knew that he had committed himself to teach during the fall term, anyway—but how about the spring? How about next summer, when the fledglings hatched again?

Once she had wrought herself up nobly to set him free, but she saw now that she didn't have to leave him to do that. Rodney, like his friend Epictetus, would never be anything but free—he lived as he chose. And because it is always humiliating to see what was intended as a generous gesture look ridiculous, even to oneself, and because humiliation breeds anger, and mostly because she was, after all, Liz Dare, Rodney's innocent imperviousness to the deep, fundamental change in herself became a sort of insult. The long summer days which had knit them closer than ever before in an orderly domestic pattern, in what to her was delicious habit and security in an uncertain world, had not affected his mental routine in the least. To him it was still interlude (*dolce far niente!*) while it had become the whole fabric of her life as she wanted to live it. Never leave him, said Charles, doubtless knowing all along that she was no slightest check on Rodney's freedom, for Rodney, being Rodney, confidently expected to have both her and his freedom too. She mattered as little as that. Rodney could take even Liz Dare in his stride. Then perhaps any other presentable woman would have done just as well?

"I had a job myself," she said, her eyes on the horizon. "I gave it up when I married you."

"I never said you had to."

"I wanted to. I wanted to be with you."

267

"I'm very grateful," he said sincerely.

"But you couldn't do the same for me."

"Now, Liz, you knew perfectly well when you married me—"

"Oh, Rodney, please don't start all over again, I can't bear it!" She jerked herself out of his hold and leaned forward, hiding her face against the rough white sleeve on his arm which lay along the window-sill. "I won't go back there—not in a thousand years!"

"You won't have to," he said equably. "I never expected you to go in the first place. We'll start all over again with the original arrangement."

"Which was what?" she said, against his sleeve.

"Why, I just go and do my jobs when I have to, and—you're here when I get back."

"Am I?"

"Now, Liz—" It had a warning note.

"We aren't at the beginning any more. At least I'm not. I've come a long way. I've found out a lot of things about myself in the past year. I've found out I like being married to you—"

"Surprise!" he crowed softly.

"Well, it is, in a way, when I've spent my life in the theater and was always miserable when I wasn't working! I never meant to retire, Rodney, not even after they had to carry me on and off like Bernhardt! The theater is in my blood and bones, it's all I know, all I ever expected to care about. And now I find that because I'm married to you I don't even miss the theater—"

"Oh, Liz, I'm so glad, I've been afraid—"

"*You're* glad!" she cried, and left the window-seat and began a restless pacing in the room, while he watched her from where he sat, puzzled, but not yet seriously alarmed. "Sure, that's fine, you lay your hand on me and I come up by the roots, like a radish! That makes you feel swell. But what about me? It's a little bit draughty where I am!"

"Well, but, Liz, I don't see—"

"You don't see what I'm kicking about, do you! I won't starve if I never work again, I'm still young and healthy, I caught the boat, I can put *Mrs.* in front of your name! Sure, I wear a ring on the third finger of my left hand! *You* put it there, and you said beautiful words to me in front of a clergyman and your Aunt Virginia! *To have and to hold,* you said, *from this day forward— till death do us part!* Do you still subscribe to that?"

"I do," he said solemnly. "But—"

"But those words don't mean the same thing to you that they do to me, is that it? You think they leave you the right to risk your neck any way you see fit any time you please, without any regard to what becomes of my life if you happen to get killed!"

"Well, at least they don't mean that I have to stay tied to your apron-strings till I die of senile decay!" he objected mildly.

"I can't face it again, Rodney—what I went through thinking you might be dead. I *won't* face it again!"

"Now, look, Liz, I'm the last person to belittle what you did for me. But you must realize that both times my life was in any danger on this trip it was owing to very exceptional circumstances—"

"Exceptional like the weather in California!"

"Well, just don't get any idea that I'm going to certain death if you're not there to protect me, that's all. Because if I go down again after the eagles and mind my own business and don't get involved in any sideshows—"

"Then you *do* feel it was my fault that you failed!"

"Liz, will you for God's sake be reasonable—"

He rose and went towards her, and she faced him defiantly in the middle of the room, her chin up.

"So you mean to go back and finish that job," she said.

"I certainly do, but—"

"And nothing I say will have any effect on your decision."

"Well, let's not make an issue of it, I—"

"Where's the money coming from?"

"I hadn't got around to that yet, I—"

269

"You think Andrew will give it to you, don't you! Well, he won't! I'll see to that!"

"Liz, that's pretty low, I—"

"Sure it's low, I don't have to fight fair, I'm only a woman! Just a wife, supposed to sit down and wait till my lord and master comes home from the wars!" she swept on. "Well, you aren't going to any more wars, Rodney, not these private ones you cook up for your own amusement, not if I can stop you, and believe me, I'm going to try!"

"Honey, you're making entirely too much of this thing," Rodney said sanely. "I know you had a bad scare down there, but there's a thing called the Law of Averages. I never ran into trouble like that on a trip before, and I probably never will again. It just happened that way. Next time I'll stick to the old routine, just Charles and me with our noses to the grindstone, and I'll be back with the birds almost before you know I've gone—"

"All right, *go!*" she cried, suddenly beside herself. "Go where you please, as soon as you please, and never mind about me, I'm only the one that loves you! The world is full of fear and disaster and the peril of war—more men die every day, and more women are left weeping! You and I live in a country where it is still possible to be safe and happy and *together,* but for how long? Perhaps our time will come too for war, and then I'll be no worse off than all the rest of them! But you can't wait for it, you've got to go after harpy eagles *now!* You've got to gamble with whatever time there is left to us, because you want to prove to yourself that you can't fail! All right, *go,* but don't be surprised if things are different here when you get back!" She ran from him, into the bathroom, and shut the door.

He stood a moment, looking after her.

"Liz," he said softly against the panels. "Liz, my darling—"

There was no answer but her sobbing.

Very thoughtfully he dressed and ate breakfast alone in the dining-room, and drove to the Station. He was not angry with her,

270

any more than he was convinced of her viewpoint; for her un-reasoning hatred of the work which was to him so simple and so normal he considered a child's fear of bogeys in the dark. It was unfortunate that the bogeys had once jumped at her and cried *Boo!* but the circumstances were, as he had pointed out, exceptional, and were due, again unfortunately, to her presence on his beat.

After a rather morose morning's work among the students, he drove home for lunch, prepared for almost anything but a table set for one and an envelope in the middle of his plate.

Dear Rodney [she had written]

This is the note on the pin-cushion. I am catching the 10:15. Pete is doing a new show with a South American setting, and has been nagging me for weeks to go into it. I have just rung him up and said I would. It is just the thing for those new routines I learned from Vicente. We will start rehearsing right away, I expect.

Liz

That was all. He stared at it numbly, while something thumped inside his head, preventing him from understanding what she meant. She didn't say what she meant. She was just gone.

When he could see and breathe again, he found his way to the telephone and asked Charles to come over from the Station for lunch. After an aeon or two Charles ran up the front steps and banged the screen door.

"Hullo," he chirped. "What goes on?"

"Be very careful," said Rodney from the corner of the davenport where he was sitting with Elizabeth's note still in his fingers, "or I'll come apart in your hand. My head, for instance, is very loosely fastened on—if at all."

Charles saw at once that it was serious.

"What's the matter?" he asked quietly.

"You know those nightmares everybody has—walking up Fifth Avenue without your pants—or being on a ship at sea whose decks are exactly level with the water—and then one time it isn't a

271

nightmare after all, and you know you'll never wake up again—"

Charles demanded to know what he was talking about.

"Liz. She's left me."

Charles gave a thin, wordless whistle between his front teeth and sat down heavily, casting his mind back over a dozen signs that he had got this thing fixed once and for all. And now she had done the very thing he'd told her never to do.

"Pete is starting a new show," Rodney was saying, "about South America. She is going to do Vicente's routines in it."

"But she didn't want to go back to the stage!"

"I know, but—well, things sort of got out of hand here this morning. I'm not quite clear about what really did happen—something came up about those damned eagles, and the first thing I knew there was a row on. She thought I said it was her fault I didn't get them, or something, and she's got that fool idea I'll get killed the minute I'm out of her sight—and you know as well as I do that I never would have tangled with her friend Bolivar at all if she hadn't gone out and rounded him up, and—"

"I hope to God you didn't say that!" said Charles.

"No," said Rodney vaguely. "I don't think I did. Well, anyway, I wouldn't swear to spend the rest of my life between Maine, New York, and the University, and this is the result. The question is, What do I do now?"

"You go after her," said Charles. "Buckety-buckety, by the first train!"

"Is that the formula?"

"If there is a formula."

But she had a long start. The 10:15 was the one train all day which made good connections, and it would get her to New York in time for dinner. It was too late now to catch the Local at 2:07. The only thing available to Rodney was the milk-train, and so it would be lunch time the following day before he could arrive at the apartment.

That evening, unable to bear inaction any longer, he rang the

New York number, hoping for the best, and of course got Aunt Virginia.

"Where's Liz?" he asked at once.

"Out," said Aunt Virginia, "on the town. Why aren't you on your way here?"

"I am. I mean, I can't start till the train goes. Is she still sore?"

"Whatever did you *do*, Rodney?"

"I wish somebody would tell me!" he said. "It all just blew up out of nowhere. I'll be there about noon tomorrow. You hang on to things till I come."

"How can I do that? She's got into her best gown and gone to dinner with one Stanley."

"Oh-oh. That's the works."

"I thought it was, when I saw him!"

"Well, at least she won't be conscious tomorrow much before I arrive. Don't tell her I'm on the way."

"Why not?"

"I want a chance to talk to her before she can walk out on me again!"

But Elizabeth came in entirely sober about midnight, rose by the alarm-clock—a music-box gadget which played two bars of *Poet and Peasant*—and with her chin very high she went off to an eleven o'clock appointment. When she came home in the middle of the afternoon, Aunt Virginia was nowhere to be seen, and Rodney rose lengthily from the davenport and stood looking at her across the living-room.

"Hullo," he said, almost as though he had been around for weeks.

"*Rodney!*" She threw herself at him with the strangling hug which always softened his bones.

"Glad to see me," he noted with satisfaction. "Imagine that!" And he sat down in the nearest chair with her on his lap.

"Oh, Rodney, I never dreamed you'd come after me!"

"Well—you forgot to kiss me good-by, and—"

273

Elizabeth sat up and with one gloved hand along his cheek looked him straight in the eye.

"Rodney, tell me truthfully, did you really come all this way to New York j-just because of me?"

"Well, great Scott, Liz, why else would I come? You see, I'd never been deserted before, and I figured I'd better do something about it, because— What's the matter now?"

She sat there on his knees, wilting in every line.

"I—I'm afraid I've done the wrong thing," she confessed in a very small voice.

"I wouldn't be surprised. But if you have asked Blaine to start divorce proceedings you can march straight to the phone now and tell him that's all off."

"It's worse than that, Rodney. When I got to Pete's office this morning he had a run-of-the-play contract waiting for me, and— I signed it."

"Well, I'm sorry, but that's off too. You'd better let him know right away."

"I c-can't do that, Rodney, I—"

"You're coming back with me tonight, where you belong. I don't suppose I'll ever know quite what happened up there yesterday morning, but whatever it was—"

"Whatever it was, you'd like to forget about it! It's too late for that now."

"I came as fast as I could. I just missed a plane at Boston."

She rose from his lap and pulled off her hat and gloves and threw them with a gesture of despair at the davenport.

"If only I'd known you were coming—!"

"What difference would that have made?"

"I don't know." She stood looking at him with wide, puzzled eyes. "Maybe none. But it's very *flattering* to have you leave your work and come chasing down here after me at the drop of a hat—"

"Now, look, Liz—" He rose and stood over her. "You knew perfectly well I'd have to come after you—"

274

"I *didn't!*" she cried indignantly. "That makes it sound as though I only came to make you follow me!"

"Instead of which, you really meant to leave me," he said slowly, as it came home to him. "Why?" He waited, and she made no answer, staring down at the floor between them. "What have I done, Liz? It couldn't be just because of that silly row yesterday morning!"

"That wasn't a silly row. It showed me exactly where I stand with you—which is a poor second to a harpy eagle!"

He took her by the elbows and shook her gently.

"Liz, I've told you before you're making too much of a Thing about a few pinfeathers! In any case, I'm not starting out tomorrow! I've promised to teach this year, and I couldn't get out of that if I wanted to. Besides, I have to make plans, I have to find out when Sturgis can get away again, and so on. Now, the sooner you ring up Pete and tell him—"

"Tell him what? That I've changed my mind once more? Don't forget, I stood him up last year on account of you! That's why he had my contract ready this morning, and that's why I signed it without waiting for Andrew's O.K. To show Pete I meant business—I thought!"

"You mean he wouldn't let you off now? You'll have to go on with the show?"

"I just can't ask him to let me off now, that's all. It isn't so much a question of whether he'd sue me—though God knows he'd have a case. Show business is a dirty racket, Rodney, I admit that, but to people like me, born to the racket, a contract is, oddly enough, a contract. Pete smelled a rat yesterday when I rang up, and he got busy. Nobody around here believed I'd last even this long away from Broadway. So Pete dropped another girl like a hot potato when they'd practically settled with her, lined up a lot of story space about my come-back, stirred up a lot more backing on the strength of it—remember Liz Dare? she stood 'em up at

275

the back!—and before the ink was dry on my signature he shot the works. See all the evening papers!"

"But that means the whole winter goes by with you living here and me up at the University!"

"You see!" she pointed out resentfully. "It's different when I'm the one to step out of line, and there aren't any birds involved!"

"It's very different," he agreed promptly, "for the simple reason that because of a problematical two months or so on a trip which I refuse to throw out of the window, you rob us of a whole year at home!"

"We'll have the week-ends, Rodney," she said, a minute later.

"That will be just dandy. From early Sunday morning till Monday afternoon, and I have classes all day Monday. That's fine. And there's another thing. Don't forget that every time you cross Broadway going to rehearsal you risk your life a lot worse than I could ever risk mine going after eagles. But that doesn't count, does it, because you're so much more accustomed to people being run over by trucks than you are to earthquakes!"

"Maybe the show won't run," she said, and twisted away from him and sat down on the davenport.

"Of course it will run! You haven't had a flop since 1934!"

She sighed, and put her head in her hands, her elbows on her knees.

"Well, there we are, Rodney. I've been and gone and done it. And I'm pretty sorry already, if that helps any."

"No, that doesn't get you anywhere at all," he sighed, and walked away to the window. "It wouldn't be so bad if you had really wanted to go back to the theater, I could have understood that and resigned myself to it. But no—this is just a piece of fantastic wrong-headedness that need never have happened to us!"

"If ever you feel like forgiving me—let me know!"

"We seem to be right back where we started from." He stood at the window, staring out across the Park in the summer sunlight. "It was sure nice while it lasted!"

276

There was a long silence in the room. Then she said—

"D-does that mean you want me to get the divorce after all?"

He whirled on her.

"Now, Liz—look—I never said a word about divorce, so help me! You can't hang that on me!" He went to the davenport and sat down beside her and took her into his arms. "Honey, you are probably, the darnedest woman God ever made—but I can't get along without you, that's what I'm squawking about, you know that, don't you!"

She stared at him unbelievingly. This was Rodney, who raised hell when she least expected it, and then when he had good reason to beat her came and made love.

"You—you aren't going to be sore at me?" she quavered.

"Sure I'm sore at you! I could wring your neck with pleasure." His long fingers closed round her throat. His slow, smiling gaze went from her hair to her eyes to her lips. "Some day probably I *will* wring your neck. Kiss me."

XXIV

Right back where they started from, Rodney had said, and it was dismally near the truth. September found Elizabeth living at the apartment in New York, and Aunt Virginia readying the house for Rodney's return to the University. They were not angry with each other any more, but they were not resigned, either. Elizabeth, falling into her big white bed at the end of a nerve-raveling day in the theater, could only remind herself with bitter satisfaction that it was her own damned fault for going off half-cocked and trying to get even with Rodney for having a mind of his own. He didn't see her viewpoint, he never would. But they might have had months and months together before—

It was no satisfaction to Rodney that Liz had brought it on herself, and him, needlessly, and out of willfulness. With so much of deep, abiding happiness behind them, it was quite maddening to return to the barren existence he had dealt with so masterfully a year ago. And now the house was haunted of her—all the things she had left there tugged at his heart-strings, and her clothes still hanging in the wardrobe teased his nostrils with their ghostly fragrance. In vain he promised himself the week-ends and the Christmas Recess, and reminded himself that she hadn't *left* him, not really, that she would be there some of the time, that it was absurd to feel that he had lost her. . . .

But the house was very still in the evenings, which were endless, and with a growing alarm he realized that life was emptier than he had ever known it before. Was it possible that already he had got into a rut? Well, a very elegant, plush-lined rut, with Liz, but

278

a rut, nevertheless. That wouldn't do. Falling as much in love with anybody as he had done with Liz would naturally cause some private upheavals, one could expect that. A certain amount of bachelor peace of mind and singleness of purpose were bound to go. Not that there weren't compensations. To possess Liz was compensation for almost anything. At the same time one must retain one's own identity, one's integrity of spirit, even in love. One must not go soft, one must not, good heavens, *settle down*. Well, not yet.

Love, he decided with great originality during those long evenings without her, was a very dangerous thing. The more you got the more you wanted. It was a sort of delicious dissolution of self. All right, live alone awhile now, and see how you like it. Very useful experience, and from all the signs, just in time. No more distractions. Get a lot of work done, stuff that had piled up. Finish the book. Stop fooling away whole evenings with the accordion, stop seeing so many movies, stop reading frivolous stuff aloud after dinner, stop lotus-eating. For a while. And stop feeling so damned dreary about it, are you a man or a mouse?

Pete wasn't taking any chances this time. The chorus-call went out next day, and Elizabeth began to have long, difficult, complicated conferences with composer and choreographer, while Vicente's intricate steps and Amadeo's vagrant tunes were worked into the pattern of the show—which, to be sure, was called *Pan Americana,* but, said Pete, that was near enough.

Elizabeth was dissatisfied with the results she was getting, and distrusted her memory when it came to scoring some of the new numbers. Finally she rang up Rodney in the middle of the week, catching him just as he came in the door after a particularly heavy day. For once the sound of her voice only depressed him further, emphasizing the distance between them, and the dullness of doing without her.

"Rodney, we can't get that '*No Hay*—!' song right. I've lost the fourth bar. How does it go?"

279

"Fourth bar," he repeated, his mind groping wearily. "Let's see, now— You sing what you've got, and I'll try to remember—"

She sang it.

"No, no, that's wrong," he interrupted.

"I know it is, but how does it go?"

He whistled it. She sang it.

"No!" he barked. "Listen."

He whistled it again. She got it right, a little uncertainly.

"And now where it goes into the chorus with all those accidentals—" she went on, and sang that part.

"That's wrong," he said again.

"I know, but *how?* I can't remember!" She sounded near tears.

"You're all off. I'd better come down and play it to you."

"Oh, Rodney, *would* you? If you start now you could get dinner on the train and spend the night here and get an early train back. Oh, Rodney, *please!*"

"Tonight?"

"Oh, if you only *would!*" And she added, with a little whimper of weariness—"It isn't just the song. I want to see you!"

"All right, I will!" he decided suddenly. "What kind of a life is this, anyway? I've got a ten o'clock class tomorrow, but what the hell!"

"Oh, Rodney, you're *wonderful!* Bring the accordion."

"I'll be there about—let's see, by about nine, I should think. Hold everything!"

Whistling the *"No Hay—!"* ("There Is None—!") song, he ran upstairs and had a shower and a shave and put on a different suit. Aunt Virginia drove him to the station, noticing rather grimly that he wasn't a bit tired any more. He was seldom tired, she knew, unless he was bored.

The apartment, when he reached it, was a blaze of light and seemed to be full of people. Elizabeth opened the door to him, wearing a house-coat and a ribbon around her hair. She kissed him in rapturous welcome, and then led him into the drawing-room and presented him (with visible pride) to Pete, to Jake, who did the score, to Willie, who did the lyrics, and to a pallid young man who sat permanently at the piano with a cigarette in the corner of his mouth. Everybody was cordial to Liz's husband—a little too cordial. Rodney saw in a glance that they were all prepared to be patient and polite to him. His left eyebrow was at a slight angle as he took his accordion from its case, ducked under the strap, and sat down casually on a leather pouf near the piano.

"What's the trouble?" he inquired with modest competence. " 'No Hay—!'?" Effortlessly, without apologies or flourish, he began to play it. When he came to the tricky fourth bar his eyes went to Elizabeth, and he picked out the melody sharply for her benefit. When it went into the chorus he made an emphatic and detailed *retard* on the accidentals, and then picked up the tempo again and sailed to an easy finish.

By that time everybody had forgotten about being patient and polite.

"Well, this is something *like!*" Jake said. "Why didn't we do this long ago? Got it, Buzz?" he inquired of the pianist, who was working at it softly in the treble and appeared to take no notice. When Buzz came to the chorus he fumbled, and Rodney checked him up briskly on his own keyboard. The piano echoed the amendment docilely and tinkled on to the end.

"Try it, Liz," said Rodney then, and began at the beginning.

She came and knelt on the floor beside him, watching his fingers on the keys. Her voice and the piano treble followed him softly, obediently, through verse and chorus. Pete and Jake exchanged glances. They couldn't believe it, but there it was. The fellow was a wizard with the accordion. He had what it took. You couldn't faze him with a brick-bat, either. He had everything. Yes, by God, *everything*. A speculative gleam came into Pete's eye and stayed there.

Jake got his score-paper and fountain pen and drew up a chair on Rodney's other side.

281

"Gimme that again," he said. "Watch it, Buzz. Shut up and watch it. Shut up, Liz. Now—from the beginning—not too fast—"

It went on like that. It went on for hours, and not once did Rodney's good humor sag. At last they broke up, stretching themselves wearily, and highballs went round.

"Well, this is something *like!*" Jake said again. "Now I know where I am! How do you feel, Willie?"

"Yeh," said Willie, who had been scribbling on the back of an old envelope. "I got some ideas."

"Liz, I've been thinking," said Pete very tentatively, looking all ready to dodge. "I've been thinking—now, don't anybody let fly, I got a right to think!—I was only going to say—how about a couple of numbers with the two of you?"

There was a dazed sort of silence. Rodney found everybody looking at him.

"Who, me?" he said, with more amusement than surprise. "You're dreaming."

"Rodney—" said Elizabeth, rather like a prayer, and laid her hand on his sleeve.

"Might make it worth your while," said Pete, that gleam in his eye.

"Well, thanks very much," said Rodney quietly, "but I've got a job."

"R-Rodney—" said Elizabeth again, as though she was begging for her life.

Rodney looked slowly round the circle of waiting faces—one, two, three, four, and the pianist, who was drinking his whiskey in a haze of cigarette smoke at the keyboard.

"You aren't serious about this?" he said, still more amused than anything else.

"I'm talking business," said Pete, and he looked it.

"Well, I'm sorry," said Rodney without hesitation, "but there it is. Who'd teach my classes?"

"We'd hire somebody," said Pete grandly, waving a hand as

though there was a wand in it. "No foolin'. We've got something here."

"He can dance too," said Elizabeth reverently, her hand on Rodney's sleeve. "It's all wasted."

"I think you've all got a touch of the sun," said Rodney, amused. "Or else you're 'way ahead of me with your drinking!"

"How much do you get for teaching whatever it is you teach?" Pete inquired, and without asking anybody's pardon or permission poured out another drink for himself.

"I teach zoology," said Rodney gently.

It lay there.

"Well, I'll double it," said Pete, and squirted soda briefly into his glass before he raised it solemnly against the light. "Here's to Dare & Monroe," he said. "It even *sounds* right—Dare & Monroe —And the Accordion."

Rodney found Elizabeth's eyes fixed on his face. The look which passed between them was long and intimate and sobering.

"Liz, you don't really—" he began, his eyes on hers.

"Oh, *couldn't* you—to please me?"

He turned easily to Pete then, with a friendly, undisconcerted smile.

"Now, see what you've done," he said. "This is a nice spot you've got me on!"

"Rodney, surely it could be arranged somehow—about your classes—"

"It's the middle of the term," he pointed out, as though that settled everything.

"How long do you want?" asked Pete. "We could put somebody else in, and stay on the road awhile. We could wait for you."

"At that rate," said Rodney, smiling, "you'd never get into Town!"

He was sitting between Elizabeth and Pete. Behind him, Elizabeth caught Pete's eyes, and the tilt of her head indicated ever so slightly—the door. Pete got it.

"Well, it seems too bad," he said, and appeared to relinquish the idea. "It would have been a great stunt."

"I also have a very nice hand-stand," said Rodney, still with his disarming smile. "But I don't as a rule do that in public either."

Before long Pete gathered up Jake and Willie and the pianist and they departed. Elizabeth and Rodney stood looking at each other across the empty, brightly lighted room.

"I bet you're tired," he said, and held out his arms. "Are they working you to death?"

She leaned against him, absorbing once more the knowledge of his strength, his height, and his warmth—his unpredictable mixture of insight and imperviousness.

"Rodney. *Is* it such a crazy idea, after all?"

"Is what? Dare & Monroe? I never heard a crazier one!" His arms cradled and upheld her weary body. "Monroe & Monroe, now —that's Something!"

"I'm never one to quibble about the billing," she said.

"Say, was I framed?" he demanded suspiciously, and tried to see her face. "Was that why you rang me up and—"

"Oh, Rodney, *no!*" Her honest eyes met his. "It was Pete's own idea, right on the spur of the moment!"

"All right, I believe you. Has Mary gone to bed?"

"Hours ago."

"You sit down here and put your feet up, and I'll make us some hot milk, how would that be?"

"Heavenly. Rodney, were you born thinking of things like that, or did Aunt Virginia teach you?"

He cocked an eyebrow at her, on his way to the kitchen.

"Aunt Virginia doesn't like hot milk," he said, and was gone.

She sat still on the davenport with her feet up, brooding, until he returned with the milk and a plate of sugar cookies on a tray.

"*Why* is it such a crazy idea?" she greeted him rebelliously, as he set down the tray on the coffee-table in front of the davenport.

284

"Because the only place an amateur has any standing," he said, "is in the more violent forms of sport. Drink your milk." He handed it to her, and sat down beside her with his own.

"After all, it's a way of being together," she muttered, sipping. And when he made no reply— "After all, I went to Central America just to be with you!"

"Is that what's known as female logic?" he queried peaceably.

"I don't know about female. It's certainly logic!"

"That's what you think. Honey, look—I'm supposed to be a scientist and an instructor of the young. How much would I be worth in a professor's chair if I took a flier in musical comedy with a squeeze-box?"

"So the stage is too far beneath you!"

"Now, Liz—"

"Well, you said as much to Pete! You said it would be like standing on your head!"

"I never said anything of the kind! Now, you're spoiling for a fight, I know, but—*no hay!* Pete's idea is out. And it's time you were in bed."

She finished her milk at a gulp and set down the glass on the tray with a click, and rose.

"Mind using the guest bathroom tonight? I'm going to have a long hot soak." And she added, over her shoulder from the doorway, while he was putting out the lights—"I suppose writing books about migration is more dignified than playing the accordion!"

When she emerged from their bathroom some time later, smelling very sweet, with her hair in little damp rings around her ears, Rodney was in bed reading the *New Yorker*. And later still, when the room was dark and quiet, and he was just slipping off with his usual ease into oblivion, he turned his head on the pillow to listen—

"Liz, you're crying!" He gathered her into his arms, and her cheek was wet against his. "Sweetheart, I know it's tough—yes, and you're tired, and you ache all over, and your poor little nerves

285

are all shot to hell—it's a dog's life, I know—there—don't cry, honey, the time will pass somehow, time always does—don't cry, my sweet—"

He soothed and petted and comforted and adored her, until at last she fell asleep, damply, in the hollow of his shoulder. The idea of altering his decision never once crossed his supremely rational mind.

XXV

Pan Americana opened in Baltimore on the Monday before Franksgiving Day, and went from there to Pittsburgh and Philadelphia—three weeks when she never saw him at all, during which time Aunt Virginia found life just a wee mite trying. The dreaded dull patch had overtaken them again. Rodney was bored.

Full of forebodings not confined to the hazards of a Broadway first night, Aunt Virginia accompanied him and Charles to New York for the opening. The ovation which greeted Liz Dare's first entrance brought tears of pride to their eyes. She looked so small under the pitiless applause—so small and shining and precious—so much their own Liz, with her funny pointed smile and that white brow like a child's—

Rodney suffered agonies through her solos—they had keyed *No Hay—!* too high for her—they still had the fourth bar wrong, too—they had mucked up the end of *Paquita*—they lost the whole point of the camellia song, how come she'd let them do that?—Willie, the lyric writer, must be a half-wit—leading-man too fast with his rumba—drag it, man, for God's sake *drag*—oh, Liz, my darling, there never was anything so beautiful as you are—that's my wife up there—and I used to think if I ever so much as met her I'd drop dead—she's mine now—sweetheart, you're flatting—that's better—it's nervousness—orchestra too loud, much too loud—slower, in the name of—she's getting her second wind now, not so scared any more—right in there pitching, aren't you, Liz—look at the way she puts those feet down—don't rush it, Liz, take your time—that's the girl—her low notes are terrific tonight—warmer

287

—richer—that's me—well, it could be—it's not just my imagination, she's lovelier than she's ever been before—the critics will say so, you wait—that's swell—that chorus work is swell—she's never had a better show, I'll say that for it—it's not just because she's mine now. . . .

There was no doubt at the first act interval that the show was a hit. Rodney and Charles and Aunt Virginia, who none of them smoked much, lighted cigarettes in the lobby with unsteady fingers and joined Andrew and Minnie who were doing likewise. Everybody was there, and a critic was even seen to smile. Liz was safe. Liz had a triumph.

After the final curtain-call, the three of them waited in a corner of the dressing-room while Elizabeth worked her charming way through the mob of people who came behind to tell her they knew she'd be back, and better than ever—it will run a year, people said, over and over again, until the words wore a sore spot in Rodney's mind—*it will run a year*—and then when the last well-wisher had gone, Elizabeth put on a fresh make-up and got into a new evening dress and was ready for the party.

The party was at Stanley's pent-house on Park Avenue. It was a large pent-house and a large party—all the principals and about six rows of the orchestra. There was a five-piece dance-band, and a small dance-floor, and a large buffet, and practically all the good champagne left in the world. Stanley, who never bustled his guests, was a smiling, tranquil host, and things had got well under way when they arrived.

Everybody was crazy about the music in the show. Everybody was trying to remember how *No Hay—!* went. Finally somebody suggested that if Liz would only sing it once through to the band they could pick it up.

"I'll get Rodney to play it for us," she said. "Rodney—where are you?—borrow the man's accordion and play *No Hay—!* They want me to sing it again."

288

"Well—" said Rodney, with a rather hunted glance around the crowded room.

"That's the stuff, Liz!" said Pete, who was tucking away champagne and feeling as though he had earned it. "Show 'em what I tried to buy and couldn't! Dare & Monroe—And the Accordion. I *still* think it's a natural!"

"Come on, Rodney, they want to hear it again!"

Rodney set down his glass, excused himself to the blonde beside him, and crossed the floor towards the band, looking Magnificent in white tie and tails. The accordionist surrendered his instrument with a grin, Rodney ducked under the strap and settled himself without any visible embarrassment in a gilt chair at one side of the room.

He ran his fingers over the keyboard, caught Elizabeth's eye, and played the fourth bar at her accusingly.

"Now, don't tell me we've still got that wrong!" she said, and went to him.

"Unless you like it better your way," he nodded.

"Well, I'll be darned! Show me again. Jake, listen to this!"

Jake joined them, while Rodney showed her again. Then he played the opening measures and waited for her to begin.

"You've got it in G," she said, and waited for him to change key.

"Mm-hm. Try it."

She sang it in G. And while the applause was still dying down—

"It's better in G," she said. "Where's Jake? Jake, I want *No Hay—!* in G, do you hear?"

"I heard," said Jake meekly, coming forward.

"You had it too high for her," said Rodney, looking up at him, and grinned. "I never thought she'd make it!"

Everyone who heard him, including Jake, waited dazedly for red flames from hell to consume the man who had uttered such heresy, but Liz only went on smiling, and Jake tottered away for

289

another drink. You had to be married to her to talk like that, but boy, oh, boy, it was something to hear!

While they were doing *Paquita* together, a hand stole under Stanley's elbow where he stood at the opposite edge of the room, and a soft voice said in his ear—

"Somebody's been holding out on me. Just wrap it up and I'll take it with me."

"Look out," he said. "It's already wrapped up."

"Where were you when this happened?"

"I took my eye off her for just two months, and when I looked again—there he was!"

"But this is all wrong," she said. "He goes places and does things. Where does *she* come in?"

Stanley, who knew a woman in love when he saw one, and that was Liz Dare, smiled a cold little smile.

"Never mind that, she *is* in!" he said.

"It won't last," she murmured.

"You hope!" said Stanley rudely. "Now, Nita, take that look off your face! You can't poach here."

"Poaching is for rabbits," she said. "My grandmother was a pirate!"

Later, when the dancing had begun again, Elizabeth was sitting one out between Aunt Virginia and Andrew in order to put away a plateful of Stanley's excellent buffet—she was always ravenous after an opening began to wear off—and Aunt Virginia leaned towards her and said quietly—

"Liz. You remember what I told you about the dull patch. There's what always goes with it!"

She nodded towards the dance-floor and Elizabeth saw Rodney waltzing with a fragile-looking thing whose golden hair was in a soft bang with curls on her neck, and who wore a very bouffant taffeta picture-dress. She was one of those cuddlesome dancers, and her waist-line, under Rodney's hand, was practically non-existent.

"I don't know," said Elizabeth charitably. "She looks like a nice enough girl."

"Nice enough for what?" queried Aunt Virginia.

"Well, maybe nice enough to know her place."

"Rodney's smarter than you are. Look at him!"

His head was bent, her lips were at his ear. When he answered her, briefly, with his slow smile, she tilted up her face and laughed at him, and his arm tightened possessively as he swung her in a spirited pirouette through an open space on the floor.

"I see what you mean," said Elizabeth after a moment. "How long will it last?"

"I'd give it three months—maybe four."

"That's too long. What had I better do?"

"Don't ask me, I'm only his aunt!"

"Andrew," said Elizabeth, turning to him confidentially, "what's that Rodney's got hold of? And I mean got hold of!"

Andrew looked.

"The name is Juanita Donahue," he said, for Andrew always knew what you asked him. "She writes books."

"Oh, Lord," said Elizabeth. "What sort of books?"

"Tripe. All about the pettiness of life as it is lived in the big cities, and the sweet clean air of the wide open spaces where you can throw off the artificial restrictions of civilization and, presumably, do what you bloody well please in the way of thumbing your nose at God and man."

"My, my," she said admiringly. "You seem to know all about it!"

"She sends them to me," he complained. "Autographed. What's more, your friend Stanley publishes them. You really ought to put a stop to that."

"You mean she travels round the wide open spaces and then writes it up?"

"She seems to have a sort of system. She seems to know everybody everywhere and they give her letters of introduction to

291

everybody else, so that she week-ends in Borneo and spends Labor Day in Alaska, and that sort of thing."

"Is Rodney going to fall for it, do you think?"

"Not for the books, no," said Andrew.

Just then Charles came up and made her a little bow and said was she tired or would she go round just once with him in his favorite waltz.

"I'll go round and round," said Elizabeth, the plate being empty, and she rose most willingly. Had Charles seen Rodney? Charles always saw Rodney. One might as well— "Don't look now," she muttered, "but Rodney's picked up something."

"I only know her middle name," said Charles. "Which is Trouble."

"Or what always goes with a dull patch."

"Absolutely."

"Well, I'm new here. What do I do now?"

"Pray."

There was a silence, while they danced. Rodney brushed past them, the golden head close under his chin. He never knew they were there.

"Go on, Charles—say it!"

"Say what?"

"Well, you told me never to leave him, didn't you! And I've an idea that this is where I get kicked down the flight of stone steps."

"Well, now, wait a minute, Liz—after all, things are a little different, aren't they, since you came into his life!"

"Do they look different?"

Charles glanced over his shoulder.

"Not very," he admitted.

Rodney and Miss Donahue were just disappearing through the door of the library, a small paneled room with soft davenports and shaded lights, its walls lined with all the books Stanley had ever published, along with a great many others.

"Didn't anybody tell me your name?" Rodney had inquired, while they were still dancing, and she gave him a wise upward glance.

"I can't remember that we were ever introduced."

"That's the best of these big parties," he said placidly. "You can pick out the people you like the looks of, and get away with it."

"Who picked out whom?"

"Well, you were looking as though you wanted a glass of cham= pagne, and by a curious coincidence I happened to have two. What's your name, I said."

"Donahue."

"Do I have to guess the rest? Or should I know?"

"Juanita—Donahue."

"Juanita? No foolin'?"

"I was born in Mexico. My parents were kind of hypnotized at the time."

"What part of Mexico?"

"My father had a silver mine south of Mexico City. You notice I say *had.*"

"Mexicans took it, I suppose."

"They *acquired* it, by a sort of osmosis. The Germans are sup= posed to have it now. I haven't been there for several years, but I'm going back in the spring."

"Me too," said Rodney.

"Me what?"

"I haven't been there since 1937. And I'm going back as soon as I can manage it."

"So we might meet again—in Mexico!"

"I wouldn't be surprised. Mexico's not so big."

She laughed.

"Why are *you* going to Mexico?" she asked then.

"Harpy eagles, blast 'em."

"I hope to get stuff for another book while I'm there."

"Another book," he repeated thoughtfully. "I must have been missing my cues. How many books have you written?"

"Only five."

"Oh-oh," said Rodney, wincing. "I'm sorry. Just an old fogey buried in a classroom—how would I know? What have you written books about?"

It was then that she led the way into the library. She went straight to the shelves which housed Stanley's own publications and laid a brightly jacketed volume in his hands: *Mexico: The Silver Lining. By Juanita Donahue.*

"Well, well," said Rodney apologetically. "I wonder how I—" Another volume was laid on top. *Borneo: In Search of Wild Men. By Juanita Donahue.* "My goodness," he murmured. "Did you—" A third book slid into place. *Tierra del Fuego: Land of Fire. By Juanita Donahue.* "Great Scott!" said Rodney. "How did you get to it?"

"It's quite simple to get to it," she said modestly. "There is a regular air service from B.A. to Gallego, in Patagonia, and once a week a lovely tri-motor plane flies from there to Rio Grande on the east coast of Tierra del Fuego. I crossed the Strait of Magellan at five thousand feet, sitting up in the pilots' cabin watching the chart. They were awfully nice to me."

"Odd of them," he said. "What does it look like down there?"

"We could see the snow-capped Andes on our right while we flew over the sheep country coming into Rio Grande. There's nothing much there except the packing-house and corrals—and penguins! I went up to one of the hilltops where the penguins go to die. It was kind of pitiful—all bones and feathers—and those awful *carrancha* hawks, just waiting. Then I rode down to Lake Fagnano and crossed the pass to the penal settlement at Ushuaia, and got into really sublime country—sort of like Norway, with glaciers and fjords."

He had opened the book and sat down with it on a sofa.

"Who took the pictures?" he asked.

294

"I did."

"Nice work. What did you use?"

"Those are mostly Leica shots enlarged."

"Tell that to Charles! For years he fought off a Leica and said they weren't any good. We took one on this last trip and he practically slept in it!"

"I had a 16 mm. movie camera too, with color film."

"You did?" His interest was quick and keen. "Is there any way I can see those films some time?"

"I think it could be arranged."

He looked up from the book to find her smiling. There was something in her eyes he had not seen anywhere for a while— something he recognized for exactly what it was, with a familiar stirring of amusement and (we may as well admit it) satisfaction. In Juanita Donahue's wide blue eyes the good old huntress stare was decently veiled with humor and sophistication, but it was there all the same, tribute and challenge to his own spectacular manhood; something shameless, and reckless, and ruthless, and greedy—something he had dealt with many times in the past, one way and another, and knew perfectly well how to handle now if he chose. After the weeks of boredom he had been going through, and because of the weeks of boredom which stretched ahead of him—(*it will run a year!*)—the insurgent Old Adam in him rose to meet the double-dare in her long gaze.

"Where do you show your films?" he asked, dead-pan.

"Well, believe it or not, I'm spending Christmas with the Kennedys, and I'll bring my films with me, of course."

"Dwight Kennedy? Our head man in Modern Languages?"

"Dwight Kennedy and his wife used to spend a lot of time at our place in Mexico when I was a kid, and I lived with them for a while after my father died."

"Well, well, how the Lord does provide!" said Rodney with real astonishment.

295

"I've got some films of Mexico too that I took in 1934 and '37, but they're not in color."

"I'd like to see them. The first time I ever went to Mexico was 1934."

"We'll run them all, in the Kennedys' back parlor!"

"How long can you stretch that Christmas visit? Because I'm going to be in New York for the Recess."

"Oh, I'll stay quite a while, I expect," she said casually. "I want to use Dwight's library before I start off again—he's got dozens of books about Mexico."

"So have I," he remarked, and added without a flicker in his polite gray gaze— "If there's anything Kennedy hasn't got, come and try my library."

"Thanks, I will. When are you going back to Mexico?"

"I'm not sure. Maybe this summer, if I can get away early enough, which I doubt."

"I'll be there this summer."

"Well, that's another inducement."

"I thought I might fly as far as Mexico City this time."

"I've always wanted to try that myself."

"We seem to think along the same lines."

"Then perhaps it has occurred to you too that we ought to go on dancing," said Rodney, and rose, and they slipped again into the music.

When the party broke up at last, Rodney and Elizabeth dropped Charles at his hotel and took Aunt Virginia on to the guest room at the apartment. As he closed the door of their bedroom behind them, Elizabeth said "Phew!" and sat down rather limply on the chaise-longue, and then tipped over on to the cushions, fur wrap and all, in a little heap, with her high-heeled silver slippers waggling pitifully over the edge.

Rodney came at once and knelt to take them off, massaging her feet in his warm hands.

"That feels wonderful," she purred, with her eyes shut.

"How you could go on dancing," he said. "You must be about dead from the knees down." He went into the bathroom and turned on the taps, and then took off his coat and waistcoat and collar and put on a dressing-gown, and bent over the chaise-longue. "Now, then," he said competently, and slid her out of the wrap. "How does this dress undo?—got it—does it have to come off over your head?"

"No, just pull." She dropped it off her shoulders.

"One of your minor mysteries to me," he said, easing the dress down over her feet, "is the way you spend hours in an atmosphere thick with smoke and alcoholic fumes, and come out of it still smelling of flowers."

"And what does that Donahue girl smell of?"

"*L'Heure Bleu,*" he said promptly, without thinking. "Forty dollars a bottle."

Elizabeth raised her head and blinked at him, for the question had been largely rhetorical.

"Did she *tell* you?"

"Nope. I've been around."

"I suppose Marcia used it too."

It was his turn to blink.

"Now, what on earth made you say that?"

"I'm psychic," she told him, with melancholy satisfaction.

"She's been to Tierra del Fuego, of all places," he said, bringing her dressing-gown and helping her into it. "And she was born in Mexico, and was back there taking pictures the same year I went there first."

"Odd you didn't meet."

"Well, no, she was up near Mexico City and I was in— Say, was that a crack?"

"I don't know—was it?" she said, and made for the bathroom.

XXVI

Aunt Virginia saw it coming, of course. So did Charles. Not a word passed between them regarding the apprehension they shared, but each knew that the other was watching in the same state of hypnotized helplessness, for Rodney to run true to form. Rodney was bored, tied by the leg, disorganized and chafing. Liz or no Liz in his life (and there was precious little of her these days) Rodney was looking for trouble.

As usual, it came to his doorstep. But not often, reflected Aunt Virginia bitterly, had it presented itself in such fancy and flawless form. Blondes had happened before. Women who had done things he admired and been places he coveted had happened before. Sudden crushes who possessed (or achieved) connections at the University had happened before. But never all at once. This triple-threat Donahue girl was simply too much of a good thing. The mere fact that her books read like the illegitimate offspring of a cruise booklet and one of the Rover Boys would never put him off, because after about thirty pages he wouldn't read her books, and because she didn't usually talk the way she wrote—and because she looked the way she did.

She had left him no time to forget her, either. She arrived at the Kennedys' for the pre-Christmas-holiday whirl, and went to all the dances and took morning walks on the Green with a little fur hat perched on her golden hair and a powerful police-dog tugging at a leash. By the time Rodney returned from New York in January the University had fallen for her, hook, line and sinker, and when the spring semester began Professor Kennedy was bask-

298

ing complacently with his mousey wife in a popularity they had never dreamed of before. On three separate evenings their drawing-room was packed with an enthralled audience which came to see Juanita Donahue's moving-pictures and hear the amusing, unboastful little lecture which went with them—to such effect that it was finally arranged for her to appear before a much larger audience in the Auditorium. That, too, was a great success.

There was nothing hard, nothing leathery, nothing frightening to masculine self-esteem about this fragile-seeming thing with the soft voice and the big blue eyes under a golden bang, who yet possessed the stamina and courage and enterprise to do things and go places which would have taxed the lustiest of them. They ate it up. They flocked around her. They applied for jobs as camera-man and porter and general provider; they paid her old-fashioned compliments and made modern, uninhibited jokes. She took it all with perfect composure, and gave each of them a small, intimate smile and a lift of her shadowed eyelids to carry away with him and ponder again, for it would seem to set him apart from all the others, during that brief moment when her eyes met his. . . .

Rodney, of course, was present with Aunt Virginia on these evenings in the Kennedys' drawing-room. Once, on a Sunday, Elizabeth was present too, and beheld with respect and a tinge of envy the films and photographs of Juanita's splendid hacienda home in Mexico, where she had spent a fabulous childhood living like a princess, with her own maid-servants and *mozo* and horses, in an apparently secure inheritance of her father's wealth in the silver mines. It was all gone now, she told them in her light, touching voice, with an admirable absence of self-pity. Her father was one of the last to retain his prestige and position, after less popular American interests had been forced out. But he too had found it impossible to hold on against the internal disorders and government restrictions—there were serious ructions in the mines, and finally a shooting affray which resulted in the death of some of their best men in defense of the rights of the owner—it was all very terrible for a little girl to experience—she would never forget how she and her father had fled at night from the insurrectionists and after three days in the wilderness when even food was hard to get, had found refuge with friends at Taxco— (She didn't say which revolution, and Obregon's assassination in 1928 was skillfully embedded in the vague chronology of her eventful childhood.) She had returned to Mexico in 1934, when these pictures were taken, a homeless little ghost haunting the scenes of her former grandeur, and she found them sadly changed. A Mexican family had moved into the hacienda. Some of the old servants were still around, and had been touchingly glad to see their *niña* come back. The mines had known a long period of inactivity, but now the earth was being futilely scratched at again—it took a man like her father to really get results down there, and he had died years ago in exile from the place he had so long called home. The Mexican usurpers seemed prosperous and friendly, and had allowed her to wander about unmolested on her heartbreaking pilgrimages. She had gone back again in 1937, and thought everything looked a little run-down and dreary. And now she had heard that the mines were crawling with German agents. So she meant to go and find out about that for herself in the spring, and get some color-films of *fiestas* and native dances. One could bear the Mexicans, only just, but to think of her lovely hacienda in the hands of Nazis was really too much. . . .

Very well done, Elizabeth was thinking coolly as the pictures faded from the screen and the lights came on again. Very clever, indeed. A teeny bit overplayed, perhaps, but they fell for it, in that voice. Liz, you're up against it, she thought. Not yet, perhaps —no, certainly not yet. Rodney will put up a decent fight. But he's interested. Bound to be. And she's smart, Liz, she's awful smart, she knows better than to rush him. Well, so here's my pet nightmare already—here's a charming, civilized woman who talks his language and belongs in his world. And I brought it on myself, whatever happens. If I was here on the job, every day in the week, she wouldn't matter *that* to him. At least, I don't think she would. But no, I have to make it easy for her! I practically hand him over on a platter! Pete's got to let me off the run-of-the-play. Yes, and what do I say to him, There's a blonde after my husband? Liz, you're on a spot. She's here to use Kennedy's library, is she! And how about Rodney's library, that's full of books about Mexico too! I wonder how soon she's going back there—if he follows her —if he goes to Mexico for the eagles this summer, Liz, we're done for. . . .

On that Monday after lunch Elizabeth walked across the Green with him to a two-o'clock class, before taking the train back to New York. Fifteen more minutes together—they had come to that, in the slow starvation she had let them in for. Fifteen more minutes to tell him things she had forgotten, to hear him say things she could take away to remember. Then, outside the Laboratory, he would raise his hat to her, their fingers would tighten and tear apart, and he would turn away, smiling—

It was a dry, cold, sunny January day, and the children were out with their dogs and roller-skates. Midway across the Green they saw Juanita Donahue coming towards them along the ribbon of cement, her little fur hat cocked over one eye, the big dog stalking beside her. She waved to them, and just as she got within speaking distance a small girl on roller-skates shot past her from behind, careened into the dog, and fell in a heap on the walk between them. Instantly Juanita was on her knees beside the child, who was howling her head off, and Rodney and Elizabeth arrived a few seconds later.

"There, there," Juanita was saying in her pretty voice, mopping at the child's streaming eyes with a lace-edged handkerchief. "Darling, I'm *so* sorry, how *did* it happen, I didn't *see* you at all—"

Rodney knelt down and went after the real difficulty, which was large skinned places on the plump bare knees.

"That's a nasty scrape, Cathie," he was saying sympathetically

301

to the child, who was a daughter of one of the professors. "Let's get the skates off, shall we, you'll want to walk home, I expect—"

"Ugh! My God, she's *bleeding!*" cried Juanita sharply, and stood up with such suddenness that Cathie lost her balance and grabbed at Rodney's shoulder and yelled louder than ever.

"Just a bad scrape," said Rodney, dabbing at the poor little knees with his white handkerchief, which showed red stains in the sunlight, while Elizabeth worked at the skate straps. "But it's full of grit, and wants to be painted with iodine the minute you get home, Cathie, do you hear?"

"Can't you stop it bleeding all over everything?" cried Juanita, and held up a white-gloved hand to shield her eyes from the sight of his handkerchief. "Can't you tie it up?"

"I don't want to tie it up while it's still dirty. Now, look, Cathie, it's all right, it doesn't hurt as much as all that, you go back and tell mother to—"

"I've got to be going," said Juanita, rather breathlessly, her eyes averted, the shielding hand still raised. "I can't look—forgive me, but I—must go on—" And she walked away quickly, the big dog padding at her side.

"She's a bit squeamish, it seems to me, for an intrepid female from the open spaces!" said Elizabeth, with a glance over her shoulder.

"Some people can't bear the sight of blood," he said, and stood Cathie on her feet.

"Does she call that blood?" Elizabeth pointed to his red-dappled handkerchief, and the few little drops which stood out on Cathie's raw knees.

"It's a thing they really can't control," he said, and picked up the skates and handed them to her. "I knew a Varsity football player once who fainted at sight of a nose-bleed. You'd better take Cathie home on your way back, and make sure they've got some iodine in the house. If they haven't, lend them ours!" He raised his hat to her, above the still whimpering child. "Good-by,

302

honey, I'll be there when you get home from the matinée on Saturday."

" 'By, Rodney." Their glances clung. "Do you want to come to the show that night?"

"Sure I want to come to the show!" His forefinger rested a moment beneath her tilted chin. "Just the way I used to!"

He replaced his hat and smiled at her and walked away towards his two-o'clock class. He was pretty sweet, she thought, taking Cathie's hand and turning back with her, carrying the skates. Pretty sweet, to come and sit in the front row all by himself, just for old times' sake. It's going to take some beating, Juanita.

Charles got a nasty shock the first day he came into Rodney's study and found Miss Donahue ensconced at the student's table in the window, with a stack of books about Mexico beside her. Very business-like she was, in a slim dark frock with a white frill, and her blond curls smooth and shining; very busy writing things down in a note-book. Rodney was working at his own desk in the usual way, and Charles drew up a chair at the corner of it and worked on the leaf, in the usual way. The phone rang, Rodney himself called a number, their voices were not unduly hushed— all according to Hoyle and established Monroe custom. And yet, without looking, you knew she was there, you were disturbingly conscious between your shoulder blades of an alien presence. You had, if you were Charles, a premonition. When he had finished all he came to do, he packed up his brief-case and left, in the usual way, closing the study door behind him.

"Ahoy!" said Aunt Virginia inelegantly from the stairs. "Come back to lunch."

"Well, I don't know, I—" He hesitated. His eyes met hers appealingly.

"I said Come back to lunch," she repeated.

"O.K.," said Charles. "If that won't make too many."

"Since when is four too many around here?" asked Aunt Virginia, and he escaped out the door with a grin. Reinforcements signaled for. Aunt Virginia was feeling the strain. Neither of them had glanced once towards the study.

At that luncheon, and many others similar to it, the conversation rolled smoothly along, lit by flashes of laughter and unembarrassed by pauses. Juanita Donahue's attitude towards Aunt Virginia was so completely right that it somehow became monstrously wrong—the attitude of a visiting child anxious to make a good impression. She was afraid of Charles, and it showed in a half-bullying, half-defensive barrage of backchat which drove him almost crazy. With Rodney she kept up an idolatrous formality which was at the same time more intimate than her impudence to Charles. Rodney was the master, she the humble disciple. Charles in his innards writhed and seethed. And Rodney? The same formality was his—the punctilious touch to his good manners, the gravity of gaze, the avoidance of any familiarity in address, the impersonal admiration of a colleague and an equal. Aunt Virginia could have smacked him.

It was a game, as subtle and entrancing as a minuet, and twice as full of innuendo. They played it alone in the study as well as at lunch—till the air of the quiet room tingled with unspoken words and glances duly bereft of double meanings. Rodney had, he thought, a grip on things, since that first reflex response to a familiar challenge. An occasional chance encounter, a brief crossing of foils now and then, would have been one thing—this heedless invasion of territory which was, after all, Liz's home ground, was not so good. He was, above all else, a fastidious creature. In the rooms which had embraced his daily life with Liz it was impossible for him to behave otherwise than as though that life was still going on as usual.

And so Miss Donahue found herself at arm's length, and schooled herself wisely to a graceful submission to his masculine notions about the things one did and did not do. Her eyes, with their upward look, her small white hands tugging at a heavy book, her sweet, confiding voice with its unfinished phrases and tactful evasions—these she could not, presumably, help. And the things she said, and the things she left unsaid, were as carefully timed and selected inside her busy head as the moves of a chess game.

She would have denied, even to her mirror, that she was deliberately setting out to take Rodney away from his wife. But she and Rodney had so much in common, so much more (she was sure) than existed between him and the woman he had married, and it was in her power to give him something of what he so obviously lacked of understanding and companionship, and—he would be wonderful in the field. She wasn't really trying to steal him from Liz Dare. That is—she meant to give him back. And as for Liz Dare, well, who was she to complain! Everybody knew that she and Stanley . . .

They spoke very little during those hours between classes when Rodney sat working in the same book-lined room. She was scrupulous not to interrupt him in his own absorption with the examination-papers or note-books on his desk. He himself rarely broke their silence. But silence itself is intimate, and inevitably a feeling of old acquaintance and solidarity developed between them. If his entrance or departure found her at her table she would look up, the good scholar, from her books, and then a little conversation might ensue.

Thus the days slid past towards the Spring Recess, which would give him a fortnight's holiday to spend with Liz in New York. He was looking forward to it more than he could believe. The game with Juanita Donahue was wearing him down. Insurgent impulses ruthlessly strangled were telling on his peace of mind. One careless moment now might land them in a disastrous situation from which there could be no retreat save undignified flight. Danger and uncertainty lent as usual a certain fascination—but at the same time he would be very glad of Liz, with whom one could relax, thank God, let down all barriers, and know exactly where one was. Well, there it was again. With Liz one settled down, ceased to strive, ceased (perhaps) to accomplish. But with Liz one knew what peace could be.

"You'll have this place to yourself for a while," he said on an afternoon in March. "I'm going down to New York tonight for the whole of Spring Recess."

Juanita gave him that upward look beneath her shadowed eye-lids, and her small, sad smile.

"I expect I'll be gone when you get back," she said. "I've nearly finished here. And I want to be at Cuernavaca for Easter. The Alisons have asked me to stay, and there will be stuff to photograph all round there."

"Well, I'll miss you," he said, an idle pen in his hand. "What's more, I'll envy you. Are you flying down?"

"Not this time. I have friends in Santa Fe where I'll pick up a car, and drive in through Laredo. There's a grand road now, straight to Mexico City—not like the old days!"

"Mm-hm." He was correcting Freshman note-books, his pen poised above the page. "You sure have my blessing. That empty place in the back seat is me wishing I was there."

"Why don't you come along?" she said.

There was a silence, during which the little traveling clock on his desk ticked loudly.

"I work here," he said at last, and made a mark on the drawing before him. "Believe it or not."

"What would happen if you just walked out?"

"I'd get fired." His eyes met hers across the width of the room. "More ways than one."

"Good thing if you did. You don't belong here."

"I'm doin' all right here," he said, and his pen began to draw little useless squiggles on the blotter.

"Are you happy?"

"Perfectly."

"That's a lie."

"I know it is, but it's the right answer all the same."

"Why don't you admit that you're the loneliest soul in the world?"

Rodney, who like most men wouldn't have known his own lonely soul if he fell over it, eyed her warily.

"Well, I—don't—think I—"

"You're wasting your life sitting behind a desk correcting exercises, and going to faculty meetings!" she cried. "You're no more meant for this artificial, circumscribed life you lead here than your eagles are meant to be caged!"

"I expect to live through it, though," he murmured, and smiled.

"You oughtn't to have to just live through things! You ought to be free!"

"I'm free from June till September, which is more than a lot of people can say."

"You ought to be able to pack a bag and go wherever you like at a moment's notice, without waiting for the end of the term!"

"That's Utopia," he smiled.

"For you it's only common sense! The first thing you know you'll be in such a rut you'll be *satisfied* to live here like this, with less than three months of the year to call your own! And soon after that you'll lose your waistline and your sense of direction, and turn into just another college professor, narrow-minded and conventional and—*civilized!*"

"Well, I was brought up civilized, don't forget. I only reverted to the jungle after I graduated."

"Because you were driven by something free and splendid inside you to find your right environment, which is *away* from all this! You don't belong in a collar and tie behind a stack of exams! You belong on the deck of a ship, or the back of a horse, or in the cockpit of a plane, with the wind in your face! You don't belong in New York for the Spring Recess, you—"

"Liz didn't belong in Central America either, but she stuck it out, and saved my life into the bargain," he said sharply, for Juanita had made a mistake with that reference to his New York

307

plans. "And while we're on the subject, I don't belong, at Easter, in Mexico with you."

"I wasn't suggesting that you did," she recovered herself with quick humility. "I'm sorry if I gave the impression that I—thought that was anything more than an impossible shining sort of dream, I— You see, I have a bad habit of telling myself fairy stories— I suppose all lonely children learn to do that—and I *have* dreamed of showing you the house I used to live in, and the places I love so much—" Her golden head was bent, her small hands twisted a lace-edged handkerchief in her lap.

"I'd like very much to see them." He laid down his pen and rose, and went to sit on the corner of the table above her. "Perhaps I can see them sometime. I still want those eagles, you know."

She raised her head hopefully, with starry, worshiping eyes.

"If only I can find you Manuel, my old *mozo*—he knows all that country like his own pocket, and it would cut your time and trouble in half to have him with you. Is there any chance of your coming down this summer in case I do find him?"

"Well, I don't know about that. I want to, of course, but—"

"You could fly down to Mexico City the minute school closes and come on as far as Taxco by motor. I'll be there, or somewhere near it. Our place is a full day's hard riding into the mountains, and Manuel could take you up into the eagle country from there."

"I'm afraid, even if I could get away the minute final exams end in June, it would be pretty late for fledglings by then—"

"Not at that altitude! Oh, *please* say you'll come!" She laid her hand on his sleeve, her face upturned to his. "It needn't take long, if you fly both ways. You could be back here in a matter of weeks, and you'll have practically no expenses except fares. Charles could run that place in Maine till you—"

"Charles would have to come with me," he said, and looked her in the eyes. "I never go anywhere without him and the accordion, it's bad luck. Does that cancel your invitation?"

308

"Why, no, of course not!" she cried, all innocence. "But surely you can find someone to run the Station till you get back?"

"I expect so."

"Then—you *will* come?"

There was a moment's silence.

"Yes—I think I will," he said, his eyes on hers.

Instead of reaching for him, which would have been fatal, she relaxed into her chair, and her hand fell away from his sleeve with the weariness of a battle won.

"It makes me so happy I could cry!" she whispered. "It's the thing I want most in the world—to be with you when you see that part of the country. You'll love it, I know—just as much as I do."

"Not much doubt about that," he said matter-of-factly, and went back to his desk and began to stack up note-books preparatory to departing for a class.

"Then the next time we meet will be at Mexico City! I'll drive up to the airport to meet you."

"That's fine. Leave an address where I can wire you when we start."

"Oh, you'll be hearing from me!" she said lightly. "As soon as I get there I'll write you exactly what the situation is. One never knows down there, from one week to the next!"

"O.K.," he said, just as lightly, and picked up his hat and came to her, his hand out. "Till the end of June!"

"Till Mexico!" she said, her fingers soft and lingering in his.

When the door had closed behind him she sat a long while, her chin in her hand. He had made his decision so easily, when the time came; made it independently, and without reservations, a man who was unaccustomed to being interfered with in his decisions. Charles would come with him and Liz Dare could lump it. He was going to her for his holidays with a clear conscience, and when he returned full of renewed virtue—Juanita was a realist —he would find the study empty except for the promise of June.

It was taking a big risk to leave him like this. It was taking a bigger one to stay and let something happen which might scare him off for good. Now was the time to go, while he still thought he had everything well in hand.

If he broke the news to Liz as soon as he got to New York it might somewhat color their time together. And if he saved it till the last day, they might end on a row. Unless Liz didn't really care what he did while she was tied up with a show—or unless she put fantastic faith in Charles as a gooseberry. . . .

Three months, one would have to get along without seeing him. But there was a great deal to do, in Mexico, before he came.

XXVII

As it turned out, he didn't tell Liz till the last evening. The fortnight together had drawn them close again, in spite of the fact that Rodney had his choice of spending the evenings at the theater or alone or with friends who didn't seem to fill in the time very well—and he had his mornings to himself too, because in a heavy role and a long run Elizabeth always slept late. The rest of the time—except for matinées—they had with each other. And it was enough to prove, if they had needed proof, that all the old enchantment was still there.

They had been counting on that last evening, which was a Sunday. He would be leaving early Monday morning for a class. The delicate matter of his proposed flying trip to Mexico had not weighed too heavily on his mind, because now that the time element had been reduced to a minimum he felt that the main objection—the only valid objection—had been removed. If Mercer opened the Station, he would be back in time to take over. And if Liz could only close her beastly show, there was their summer again, practically intact. The trouble with closing the show while business was still good was that it meant wantonly throwing sixty-seven people out of work, most of whom needed it very badly. Liz had the trouper's contempt for the star who got tired of doing eight performances a week and sat back on a bank-account while the little people started hunting another job. Half the people in the show were only now catching up on debts and doctors' bills, and eating regularly was still new to some of them. But if Liz Dare broke or bought up her contract, the show would fold.

Sitting on the davenport with her, round about hot-milk time that last evening, Rodney drew a long breath and cautiously opened the subject.

"This sort of thing is sure easy to take," he remarked. "I could do with a lot more of the same."

Elizabeth stirred gratefully and murmured assent. She was leaning against him with her feet up on the davenport and her eyes shut while he read her things from the Sunday papers, which they had only just got round to look at. (She loved being read to. Nobody had ever done it but Rodney. Even if she wasn't interested in what he read—and usually she was—she listened like a purring cat to the sound of his low voice, savoring his mere presence, as though she basked in the sun.) The *Book Review* slid to the floor, his hand cupped her chin, crept gently round her throat.

"Are you going to close the show this summer?" he said. "Or shall I choke all the sing out of you right now?"

"If it isn't closed by the first of July, you can choke me then," she promised, nestling.

"Honest?"

"Honest."

Rodney was boomeranged.

"Give it till the first of August," he said. "I'm going to fly to Mexico the minute exams are over and fly back with the birds. Then we'll go to Maine."

It was out. Elizabeth sat very still, his hand on her throat.

"Since when?" she said.

"Since a couple of weeks ago."

"Juanita Donahue," she said.

"Nope. Eagles."

"I suppose they grow in her back yard down there!"

"Well, practically. She's going to hunt up her old *mozo* to help me get 'em, which will simplify things for me quite a lot."

"She'll be there."

"Thereabouts, perhaps. But so will Charles!" he added, and grinned above her head. "And probably Sturgis too. I've written him. So you see I'll be thoroughly chaperoned."

"Does she know they're coming too?"

"Certainly."

"That ought to cramp her style—but not very much!"

"Now, look, Liz—"

She shook off his hand and sat up, swinging her feet to the floor.

"What does Charles say to all this?"

"Nothing," he replied, recalling the ominous lack of enthusiasm with which Charles had received the project. It had not been mentioned between them again.

"Charles is pretty well trained by now, I guess!" she said bitterly. "I've learned not to expect much from Charles."

"Liz, I give you my word, Juanita Donahue will be nothing but a means to an end. With her help I think I can get my birds easily, quickly, and without too much expense. I can finance it myself this way, and then we can forget it. I hope."

"And what's she going to be doing all that time?"

"I don't know. I don't care. That's up to her. She asked me to come, she offered to help, and I accepted at its face value. If she's got anything more in mind, it's just too bad." With the words on his lips, he believed them. "So will you please be reasonable about this thing—"

"That's just what I mean to be. I know when I'm licked." She rose, straight and slender in her long house-gown, her chin very high. "Well—thanks for the ride!" she said, and turned away.

"Now, wait, Liz—" He was on his feet too. "You've got it all wrong. How you can possibly object to my spending two or three weeks in Mexico, entirely surrounded by Charles and Sturgis—"

"Don't forget the eagles!"

"Yes, *and* the eagles!"

"And Miss Donahue's old *mozo,* don't forget him!"

313

"Well, there you are!" He spread his hands. "What in blazes are you kicking about?"

"I'm not kicking. It's just happened a little sooner than I—expected, that's all. I'm trying to be nice about it, Rodney, give me credit for that!"

"Nice about it!" he exclaimed.

"I'm trying not to hang round your neck and snivel because you're leaving me. I'm trying to let you go gracefully, as I promised myself I would, when the time came. Because I knew it would come. I know the signs, if you don't! Maybe you're not in love with Juanita Donahue now, this minute, because you're still here, with me. But you will be in love with her when you come back from Mexico, and Charles is a mere—technicality!"

"This is the sort of thing that got us where we are now," he reminded her grimly. "You went haywire once before, remember? That time you signed a contract. Then you saw the light—too late. Well, I'm warning you, Liz, if you start a divorce suit over this trip I'll fight it, here or in Reno, or anywhere you like! Unless, of course, you really prefer a husband who sits behind a nice mahogany desk in a New York office every day in the year, like your friend Stanley!"

"You leave Stanley out of this!" she cried furiously.

"I'd like to," he said, and his eyes were cool and watchful. "I'm trying to be reasonable too. But I'll play Stanley against Juanita Donahue if I have to, which will make very nice reading on the campus, won't it!"

"Rodney, how *dare* you say such a thing!"

"Because I'm trying to make you see sense this time, and because—"

"Even if it were true, you couldn't afford a scandal like that in your position!"

"The hell with my position! If you smash up our marriage now, I'll resign anyway, there's nothing to keep me here!"

"*I* certainly won't try to keep you here, when you'd rather be

314

free! Juanita Donahue, or somebody like her, was bound to happen to us some day, I took that risk with my eyes open. And don't try to fool yourself that she isn't out to kill, I know her kind and so do you! Either you see her game quite clearly and don't care, or else you're a lot stupider than I think you are, so don't stand there looking innocent!"

"All right, for the sake of argument, suppose she has a game? Was I born yesterday? Why do you think I'm taking Charles and Sturgis?"

"To make it look better!"

"You're wrong! To get the birds! And when I've got 'em, I leave. Maybe she doesn't think I can. Apparently, neither do you! What will you bet, Liz? The rest of our lives together, against my being back here in July *with* the birds?"

"If you go," she said quietly, "you needn't come back here."

She left the room with her head up, and a few moments later the door of her bedroom closed.

So Rodney went to bed in the guest room where, fortunately, he kept a lot of spare parts in a drawer of the chiffonier. And they slept that night with a closed door between them, which was a thing that had never happened in their marriage before.

It never occurred to Rodney to try if the door was locked. The way Rodney had been brought up, if a lady closed her door against you, you were definitely out in the cold till she opened it again, and no pounding on the panels and demanding admittance. There was just enough guilt in his relationship with Juanita Donahue to complicate things. He honestly believed that he could handle it and come away. But he knew that not even Charles agreed with him. He knew that even Aunt Virginia expected him to backslide. Well, if they were all so convinced that he was the world's prize heel . . .

Elizabeth, on the other side of the door, waited breathlessly when she heard him coming down the passage to bed—waited for him to lay his hand on the knob and discover that she had not turned

315

the key. What would happen then, she didn't quite know. A little firmness from him might have brought her tearfully into his arms. After all, it was their last evening together. . . .

When Rodney went to bed in the guest room she pulled the covers over her head and lay there in a little heap, too miserable to cry. This was the end.

He had gone to his early train before she was awake in the morning. There was a note on her breakfast tray:

Darling Liz—

In case you can forgive me for all that I haven't yet done, I will come down next Saturday if you will let me. Don't let's fight through the mails.

Rodney

She read it once and then wadded it up and threw it across the room. Snorky, who was always bored and dejected for a day after Rodney left, trotted busily after it and brought it back in his mouth, and got cuffed for his pains, and then was cried over.

It was typical of Liz Dare that she never once dreamed of confiding in any of her women friends. People like Caroline Jones, she knew, would exhort her not to stand any nonsense. Minnie Blaine would no doubt assure her philosophically that all men were a little that way. Ernestine Guerber, in whose eyes Rodney could do no wrong, would probably never speak to her again anyway. Aunt Virginia—but one couldn't very well consult Aunt Virginia behind Rodney's back. She thought of Charles, who was already overdue on his promise to shoot her. She thought of Stanley, because he was always a bulwark to her self-esteem—but pride forbade her to admit to him that she couldn't hold her own against Juanita Donahue. She thought of Andrew, and laid her hand on the phone and took it away again. No. One couldn't go squealing to Andrew, he thought very highly of Rodney.

It would have to come out some time, of course, that Juanita had won. But not yet. Not till the show closed and she was able to go away and hide. Hide where? Reno? Maybe if she didn't get a divorce right away no one would have to know quite how it happened. But of course she would have to get a divorce, Rodney couldn't traipse about the world with the Donahue girl unless he married her. . . . But perhaps if he wasn't free to marry her . . . You aren't as low as that, Liz. And it's no good crying any more —you'll look your age if you do.

When Rodney got her note to say that he had better not come down on Saturday as there didn't seem to be anything more to say, he was seized by a highly unscientific impulse to throw the eagles overboard forever and call the whole thing off. It surprised him, but there it was. Let the eagles go. Give in to Liz. Never see Juanita Donahue again. Yellow, eh?

The old battle was on again, between his job as he saw it and his love—and he hated to think that there was not room in his life for both. Liz held him with silken bonds stronger than iron. He had once prophesied truly that without her he would never know peace again. But Juanita had planted one devilish sentence in his mind that summed up all his secret forebodings and crystallized his problem: *The first thing you know, you'll be satisfied to live here like this—*

With Liz back in the house, yes. With Liz he had a life full of gracious possibilities he had never seriously contemplated before—things he had thought he could do without—things that had begun to look worth having. If he lost Liz now he was maimed for life, he knew that. But he didn't mean to lose her. She had come round before, and bitterly regretted the contract with Pete. If he was careful, and clever, she would come round again—in July. The bet was now definitely on with himself that he would be back in July with the birds—and with nothing on his conscience. That would show them. And then—well, then perhaps it would be time to relax a little.

317

So the first week-end passed that they did not spend together. On the Monday Rodney wrote again:

Liz, darling—

I'm pretty miserable, thanks, and how are you? Suppose I am willing to swear off after this trip—would that do? And how if I come down next Saturday? Even if you say No I can always buy a ticket the way I used to do!
                                                                    Rodney

Her answer did not arrive till Saturday morning.

Dear Rodney—

I have written this letter a dozen times, but the answer always comes out the same—No. So I'll just let it go at that, I guess. If you came, I'd only howl and make a fool of myself. I can't change my mind, any more than you can change yours. It will be easier if we don't see each other again. I'll do my best to handle the divorce as quietly as possible.
                                                                    Liz

Rodney took an afternoon train to New York, got a ticket to *Pan Americana* with some difficulty, put on a dinner-jacket, and saw the show from the fifth row. To his searching eyes she looked tired, but her performance did not falter. Liz was trouping.

After the final curtain he went out to the drug-store on the corner and drank a cup of coffee. When the right amount of time had elapsed he went back to the theater and stood in the shadows under the darkened marquee, watching the blind alley which led to the stage door. If she came out alone he was going to speak to her. If not—he didn't know. The limousine at the curb was not hers, so presumably someone was taking her out to supper. He waited in the soft spring air, his heart like lead.

She came out with Stanley. They were in evening dress. Her face was upturned, and she smiled, and his hand held her elbow possessively. He put her into the car and it drove away with them.

318

A long time later Rodney found himself back at Grand Central, getting into a train. He never knew quite how he got there.

Elizabeth sat looking at Stanley across the table, while the dance-music drummed in her ears. His eyes as he looked back at her were puzzled and affectionate.

"Well, maybe I shouldn't have told you about it," he was saying. "But I can't help wanting to get to the bottom of this. It wasn't just curiosity. I—had to know how you felt." He waited. "I always have cherished a secret yen to break his neck. If you go on looking like that, I shall go and do it! Liz, my angel—where does it hurt?"

She blinked as though he had thrown cold water in her face, and passed a hand across her eyes in a blind sort of way.

"It's—my fault, not his," she said automatically. "I'm not much good to him. But what did she *say*? Could I see the letter?"

"I tore it up. It had already been read by my private secretary!"

"Please tell me exactly what she said."

"First that she had taken a house there, and expected Rodney to join her in June."

"Yes—what else?"

"Then she said, 'Whether he gets the birds or not is of course immaterial and very much beside the point!'"

"Yes—I see—what else?"

"Then there were three words underlined: 'Now's your chance!'" He waited, with a rueful smile. She was silent, staring bleakly at the dance-floor. "I'm sorry, Liz, I had no idea it would hit you as hard as this. I thought—"

Her eyes came back to him slowly.

"Well, what did you think?"

"Good riddance!" he suggested. "After all, it wasn't the kind of a marriage that could be expected to last, was it!"

"No," she said passively, without resentment. "It couldn't last, of course. I loved him, that's all."

"Why, Liz—my poor dear—"

319

"Poor Liz, yes. But poor Rodney too. I had my limitations, but at least I had a sense of common decency. Rodney's going to come to, you know—some time. And when he does, he'll find he's been smeared, and he won't like that."

"And then poor Juanita—we hope!"

"Yes, then she'll get what's coming to her—if there is a God!"

"It's time," he said. "It's high time. That girl's got quite a record."

"How do you mean?"

"Some very odd things have happened on her trips."

"Odd? You mean scandals?"

"Oh, yes—but odder than that. She turns up minus a porter—or she doesn't turn up at all where she is due but some other place entirely—always with a water-tight explanation, of course. Native servants who have worked for her once won't hire on again. She very seldom goes back to a place a second time, I've noticed that."

"But—what are you driving at?"

"There are ugly stories, Liz, none of them substantiated, most of them hard to prove. She is supposed to be utterly unscrupulous, utterly selfish and hard. She'll use anybody, and squeeze them dry, and throw them away. Nothing stops her from getting what she wants—not even a life."

"It's difficult to believe that. She looks so sort of—of—"

"Exactly!"

"But surely if these things are known—"

"They aren't known, generally, and they aren't going to be, if I can prevent it. I got most of it out of an Englishman who was passing through here—he had met up with her in Borneo. He seemed surprised that she was on my Spring List—he opened the book and read in it here and there—I could see him getting madder by the minute—but you know how those fellows are, before I could pin him down to anything he went back into his shell and wouldn't talk about her at all."

"Well, w-why do you go on publishing her stuff?"

"It sells!" He shrugged. "Put her picture on it, looking frail and courageous with a rifle in her hand and a wild animal or a black man beside her, and it sells!"

"Do you think Rodney knows about—about the ugly stories?"

"If he doesn't, I wouldn't care to warn him!"

"No," she said thoughtfully. "You're right about that. Nobody could tell him—"

"Not without being knocked down, I should think."

"And if *I* tried, he'd only say I'd been listening to malicious gossip. He has a contempt for talk of that kind, without proof. He wouldn't listen. He'd be all the surer to go—just to prove to himself that there was nothing in it."

"Well, nothing much can happen this time," Stanley consoled her. "This house of hers seems to be somewhere near Taxco, and that's bang on the tourist route now. He'll be safe enough, even if—"

"I could have borne losing him to somebody worth while," she said, and passed her hand across her eyes again in that pitiful gesture of pain and confusion. "But to have her write letters to people *bragging* about it—!"

"Nita has no delicacy about such things," he grinned. "You ought to see what we've had to cut out of her manuscripts!"

Elizabeth stared at him in horror.

"My God, will she write about *Rodney?*"

"Probably. Leave that to me. I'll squash it. Liz, I'm sorry in a way that I worried you with this. I hoped you'd think it was funny. Are you going to divorce him?"

"What else can I do? This summer, after the show closes."

"That's all pretty beastly, isn't it! Reno?"

"I suppose so." Her shoulders sagged, and she tried to smile at him. "All right—you said it would be Reno, didn't you! That day in the office."

"I asked you that day to remember that I didn't!"

"Well, anyway, you were right," she conceded foolishly.

321

"I hesitate to say this," he began, with something less than his usual assurance. "It may be too soon. On the other hand, it may be of some use to you now. I've been learning a very hard lesson, Liz. I've been learning what it is to be without the sight of you—without the hope of you—for months on end. It's hell, Liz. Forget Rodney Monroe, and give me a chance to marry you. I'll be around."

Her eyes filled helplessly under his sympathetic gaze.

"That's awfully n-nice of you—"

"I'm not saying it just to be nice. I'm no altruist, Liz. I'm thinking of Stanley. I want you."

She gave him a teary smile.

"It makes me feel kind of good to hear you say so," she said.

Juanita's air-mail letter, which had missed the Saturday delivery outside New York, reached Rodney on Monday morning.

Dear Rodney—

I hope you will approve when I tell you that I have taken the most divine house, with room for all of us, even the Sturgis man if you bring him. It belongs to some friends of mine who are going to the States for a round of visits until the autumn. I practically pushed them out when I found there was a chance of our getting it! You, as the Chief, can have a superb east room with a private study leading off it where you can lock yourself in and work to your heart's content. Or if you prefer to look towards the town, whose dear little red roofs go tumbling down the mountain to the adorable pink church, there is a sort of suite in the other wing which you could share with Charles, with a sitting-room between—though if all three of you come, it will be ideal for him and Sturgis. When you hear what one pays for all this luxury, you just won't believe it.

We can get riding horses, and dear faithful Manuel is already here and at your service. He says it is a late season all round, and

322

there will be plenty of fledglings, and he has already disappeared for three days scouting for nests in his mysterious way. You will have to camp out a few nights, of course, but I am seeing to all that in advance so there will be no time lost. You asked about a place to keep the birds. Manuel can build any kind of cages you want, and they can be housed in one of the empty servants' rooms —most of the staff are to be given leave to visit their own people while the family is away. I am keeping the cook on, as she is too marvelous, and I have my own little Indian maid, the cutest thing you ever saw. Her mother was my laundress when I was little.

The Nazis are here, just as I was told they would be, bringing trouble as they always do. The oil people have suffered the worst from their operations, but apparently they consider that silver is not to be sneezed at, and our mine has had at least one bad strike and a good deal of internal disorder to follow. Everybody is hoping the soldiers won't·be sent in, as that will mean shooting, and once that starts down here anything can happen, as you very well know.

I am getting some wonderful pictures, and I do so long for you to arrive and see the color and the beauty of it all. Please remember me to your aunt, and give Charles my regards.

As always,

J. D.

Well, was there anything wrong with that? To prove that there wasn't, he handed it over bodily to Charles, remarking that there was no sense in his trying to rehash it, Charles might as well see for himself. Charles read it gravely, said it sounded fine, and laid it down again on the desk.

"Sturgis will meet us at Brownsville," said Rodney.

Charles said that was fine.

"Look, Charles—you may as well say it, with the face you've got on! *Must* you be so down on this trip?"

323

"It's not the trip, son, it's just—"

"I know! Liz. Well, nothing can save that now, so what the hell!"

"Nothing?"

"Nothing I can think of," said Rodney wearily.

"You mean if you called this trip off now she wouldn't come back?" Charles was gazing at him as though he suspected that Rodney was out of his mind.

"That's what I mean."

"I don't believe it," said Charles flatly.

"All right, call me a liar!" cried Rodney, his temper flaring as it sometimes did when he was raw inside. "Maybe I pushed her out into the snow! Maybe I don't love her any more! Maybe I prefer blondes!" He put his head in both hands, his elbows on the desk.

Looking pinched and white around the mouth, Charles came and sat down at the corner of the desk and waited till he could speak steadily.

"Is there anything I can do?" he asked then.

"You can let me forget her," said Rodney without moving. "If I can."

"I suppose I couldn't talk to her?" suggested Charles, and Rodney's head came up slowly between his hands until their eyes met.

"If ever I catch you pleading my cause with Liz," he said deliberately, "I'll knock your front teeth back into your tonsils."

"Well, I only thought—"

"Charles, can you understand plain English? Liz is gone. We're through. It won't work. I've got my life to live and—she's living hers. She's back where she belongs, where I should have left her, and I'll soon be out of a job. If you're going to philosophize, and catechize, and agonize, you're out of a job too. On the other hand, if you want to string along with me and do a little beachcombing while I live through this, I'll be glad to have you. Now, where's that Pan American Airways folder? It was here yesterday."

324

"I've heard there's a right nice beach near Taxco," said Charles, producing the folder, and Rodney's glance flickered towards him, for they both knew well that Taxco lay five thousand feet up in the heart of the Mexican mountains.

"That's where I mean to start," he said evenly. "Let's see, now, we can leave Brownsville—oh, hell, they use a twenty-four-hour clock in this time-table!—leave Brownsville at fourteen o'clock and arrive Mexico City at 16:45. That's easy enough—we'll be wherever we're going just about in time for a sun-downer!"

XXVIII

Juanita was waiting for them with a car at the Mexico City airport. She was delighted to see them all. She greeted Charles like an old chum with a rowdy smack on the cheek, tiptoed prettily for a subdued peck at Rodney, and at once assumed a fond and daughterly manner towards Sturgis—who had received the briefest possible private résumé of the situation from Charles and was still a little befogged. Sturgis was a simple soul. He had seen Rodney and Elizabeth together at the Casa Paraiso only a year ago, and to be told now that he was not to mention Liz nor ask why she had not come just didn't add up. Juanita Donahue didn't add up either. Rodney was looking thin and tired. Charles looked as though something had aged him overnight. Sturgis sat silent in the back seat of the car and wondered what the world was coming to.

He soon had no mental leisure left, however, in which to contemplate the state of Rodney's private life. The car, with Juanita behind the wheel, plunged into the whirligig traffic of the town, narrowly missing overcrowded buses and the policemen on their little boxes at the corners. Juanita's driving was fast, skillful, and imaginative. In no time at all it had Charles and Sturgis gripping either side of the back seat convulsively, with apprehensive eyes fixed on the road ahead.

They zoomed across the Zócalo and into the Avenida 5 de Febrero, and out past the Country Club. By that time the hard daily shower was on, but Juanita drove straight through it, remarking that once they started to climb they would soon be above it, and anyhow she knew every inch of the way. The closed

326

car was heavy and kept the road, the windshield-wiper sang merrily. While she drove she chattered to Rodney, who sat beside her relaxed and at his ease and who showed no sign of sharing Charles's mounting desire to snatch the wheel and get his foot on the brake. His brief comments and questions always came aptly, and he seemed to follow her rather rhapsodic narrative with the keenest interest.

She had seen the Tiger Dance performed, she told them enthusiastically, for the first time since her childhood, and had got color films of it. That and the Dance of the Little Roosters, which she still hoped to photograph, lasted them as far as Tlalpam, where the road started its sharp ascent towards the 9,000-foot summit, and Juanita began to tell Rodney about a mountain-top citadel she wanted to show him, where in the midst of a cornfield you came upon cut stone and masonry, obsidian utensils, carved gods of fertility, and the plumed serpent motif.

When they reached La Cima at the top, the sky was blue with ragged dark storm clouds far below them, and it was very cold; and Juanita was apologizing to Rodney for her Spanish which, she was afraid, had Indian terminations because of a nurse she had had when she was little. Her father, who had been locally known as *El Patron Grande,* could speak the purest Castilian, but that was no good at the mines, and he had been master of any number of obscure dialects as well. It had been a matter of great pride among his workmen and house-servants that *El Patron Grande* always spoke to each one of them in his or her own childhood tongue. Charles and Sturgis, trying to swallow their ears and enjoy the scenery, were disturbingly aware of the narrowness of the road and the way the back end of the car seemed to whip out over sheer space at the turns.

"Why so quiet back there?" Juanita broke off to inquire, and while she didn't actually take her eyes off the road, it seemed as though for an appreciable number of seconds she drove with the back of her head. "Seasick?"

327

Charles said they were admiring the view.

"Am I driving too fast for you?" she queried, which was of course so absurd that she didn't even wait for a reply. "Pretty soon we'll come to the place where Serrano was shot in 1927," she went on. "Well do I remember! Of course I was only a kiddie at the time, but—"

And so forth, until suddenly Cuernavaca lay below them, with Popocatepetl mounting guard over it and his sleeping wife. The road was sliding down the mountain now, and Charles and Sturgis braced their feet against the floor of the car and began silently to pray. Juanita was telling Rodney about Borda and the first silver mines, and how she was hot on the trail of a rumor that some pages of manuscript written in his own hand were hidden in a village shrine somewhere down Iguala way, and she meant to have them for her very own if it was humanly possible, but the trouble was that now even in the most out-of-the-way places people were beginning to have some idea of the actual value of such things—

Their descent in the late light into the lovely valley of Morelos was made at catapulting speed. There were sunny patches of bananas now among the dark foliage of mangoes and coffee bushes, and sometimes a bright field of sugar cane far below. The mountains all round them seemed to be covered with soft green plush, and the distant peaks were snow-capped.

"Feel better now?" she called cheerily into the back seat, as the car flashed through Cuernavaca's little round plaza with the palms and bougainvillea and the simple, dripping fountain.

Charles said they did.

"There's the Palace," she said. "And the Borda Gardens."

Both lay behind them as she spoke, and she let the car out again on the Taxco road, where rain began to fall, bringing a sudden darkness with it and a cold almost as penetrating as at La Cima on the summit. Juanita said it was a great pity, but after all it was the rainy season, wasn't it, and now they couldn't see Taxco until tomorrow morning. Charles doubted if he would see tomorrow morning anywhere this side of Paradise, but not being able to distinguish anything at all outside the car windows gave him a fatalistic repose. He was dozing inside his coat-collar when the car stopped with a jerk and Juanita said here they were, and weren't they all dying for a drink.

Sturgis, who had been a little air-sick to begin with, had by now relapsed into a coma, and was with difficulty extricated from the luggage, which seemed to have slid about a bit. The rain was still streaming down. They dodged under a colonnade into a lighted *zaguán,* which gave, through arches, a view of the vast *sala* beyond, bright with a log fire and the sharp, precise patterns of Indian rugs and *sarapes.* Manuel, a stringy, discouraged-looking Indian with tragic eyes, attached himself to Rodney's bags and started off with them.

"Just follow Manuel, Rodney, he'll see that you have everything you want," said Juanita, the perfect hostess. "I've put you in the east room with the study. Charles, you and Dr. Sturgis are down this way, I'll show you myself, and your things will come right along. We'll all take time to wash and change, shall we, and then foregather in front of the fire for cocktails, I'm sure you're all starved—" She led Charles and Sturgis off in the opposite direction to the one in which Manuel had now disappeared with Rodney's bags.

"Are you the eagle *mozo?*" Rodney inquired, overtaking Manuel at the door of his room.

"*Sí, señor,* I have seen the eagles."

"Can you take me to them?"

"*Sí, señor.*" He put down the bags and turned. His sad eyes ran over Rodney with respect and a kind of appeal. "It is a hard ride," he said.

"We don't mind that, do we?"

"They will not live, *señor.* Parakeets, now—or even clarínas—"

"I know," said Rodney kindly. "We'll go into that."

"Sí, señor," Manuel acquiesced, and d⌣parted, closing the door behind him.

Rodney looked round the room with approval. Everything was in the best of taste, in the Spanish style. It was colorful, massive, and visibly clean. Two doors stood open in the wall against which the bed head stood. One led into a tiled bathroom, the other into a small, book-lined study. There was a third door, closed, in the opposite wall. It had no key in the lock.

He unpacked a few things, had a shower, and put on a different suit. As he was about to leave the room his eye fell again on the third door, and he stood still, looking at it. It fascinated and re-pelled him. He had found all he required beyond the other two. It was no business of his where a third door led.

He crossed the room with his noiseless tread, and laid his hand on the knob.

The door opened away from him, and he stood on the threshold of another bedroom, the twin to his own. Juanita turned from the wardrobe at the sound of the latch, a dress on a hanger in each hand. She was wearing a soft pink house-gown. Her eyes were frank and unsurprised, as though it was not the first time he had walked into her bedroom.

"Hullo," she said in her dainty voice. "I was trying to decide which of these to put on." And she held out the two dresses for his inspection, one in each hand.

He leaned against the jamb of the open door, at his ease. Their eyes met in a long look of complete understanding—Juanita on familiar ground, Rodney wrought upon by all the devils in hell, winding up a dull patch. His smile was small and bitter.

"So I fell for it!" he said.

Her orderly-work had been perfect, in all directions. There was no time to be lost if the birds were to be brought in young enough to be reared in captivity according to Sturgis's plans. Rodney was able to set out on the second day following, with Charles, Sturgis, and Manuel, and full camping equipment for several nights in the mountains. They returned after four days with three young birds, one of which died.

It was in half plumage, and Rodney decided to preserve the skin. He borrowed a table from the kitchen, put it in the patio, spread newspapers on it, brought out his shiny tools, and set to work. Charles, who dearly loved to skin birds and seldom got a chance, drew up a chair to watch Rodney enviously at his delicate task of handling skin like wet tissue paper.

Rodney made the first deft incision down the breast-line, eased the insides out with a simple twist of the wrist, and was patiently working the head free with a good deal of muttering, when Juanita came out of the house. Shading her eyes with a pretty hand, she demanded to know what he had got there.

Rodney looked up guiltily as she approached, but Charles said— "Hurry up, you're just in time for the best part!"

She stopped abruptly beside the fountain and stood there, paralyzed with horror and staring at the thing on the table.

"My God, it's a bird!" she cried. "Rodney, there's *blood* on your hands! How *dare* you do such a thing in my lovely house!"

"I'm sorry, Juanita, I should have warned you—"

"You *know* I can't bear the sight of blood, and you go and bring a ghastly, filthy, dripping thing like that into my own patio! You've got it all over your beautiful hands, in sickening red smears —*go and wash your hands!*" She turned and fled into the house. A door banged behind her.

"My mistake," said Rodney, placidly returning to work at the head. "I forgot she had a phobia. Lay hold just here with the forceps, will you—he whiffs some, doesn't he!"

They worked on, their heads together, in an absorbed and companionable silence.

The two remaining birds, still in the pinfeather and gaper stage, soon lost their fear, accepted Sturgis's diet, and appeared willing to thrive. Cages were built to travel them in, according to Sturgis's

331

specifications. Rodney sat up nights with them, fed them on schedule, supervised their daily exercise, behaved generally like a broody hen. Quite suddenly one evening, after a consultation with Sturgis in the nursery, he gave the order to pack up.

Juanita heard him with incredulity, reminding him that he hadn't been down to see her hacienda yet. And why had he come to Mexico if not to see her hacienda?

"I came for the eagles," he reminded her.

Without any further warning Juanita lost her temper. She stood there, erect and slender in the bright, precise room, the firelight making a nimbus of her hair, and in a voice which never once lost its musical quality gave him such a tongue-lashing as not one of those three pampered males had ever dreamed of. The general gist of it was that he was an inconsiderate, selfish, egotistical brute, who had battened on her innocent hospitality and then callously refused to do the one little thing she asked of him in return; the one small, kind-hearted, generous thing he might do to repay her own boundless favors to him; the one transcendent thing he knew she had counted on from the beginning—which was to make with her the pilgrimage to her childhood home in order that she might take pictures of him in its famous garden.

Just as Charles was beginning to feel that he couldn't bear another second of it without crawling out of the room on his hands and knees under the furniture, Rodney said half a dozen quiet words which produced an instantaneous silence.

"How long will it take?" he said.

She stood there, looking like an angry angel, fair and delicate in the firelight.

"One day down, a couple of days there, one day back."

"Four days," he said, with none of his usual graciousness. "Can we start tomorrow morning?"

Suddenly she was angry no longer. Her delightful smile broke, showing teeth white as a little cat's in her honey-tanned face.

"Oh, Rodney, you devil, you were only teasing all the time, and

332

I thought you meant it!" she cried fondly. "We'll start *mañanita*—at the crack of dawn! After all, what's a few more days, Rodney?" Her wide blue gaze embraced them all, one by one, in disarming confidence. "Charles and Sturgis will watch your precious baby birds night and day, won't you, Charles, darling? And you won't grudge Rodney and me this little holiday all to ourselves, will you, after he's worked so hard!" And she went away to give her orders to the servants.

Rodney found two pairs of questioning eyes upon him.

"Well," he said, "my reputation is now in your hands! Like the birds."

"Look, son, I don't know that I altogether subscribe to this—" Charles began cautiously.

"I'm sorry you're not invited," said Rodney, with an old perversity and gleam which Charles knew only too well. "But after all, we do owe her something for her hospitality, don't we! Of course it's really you she needs, Charles, if she only knew it, you'd be such a help with the color camera!"

Charles stood up.

"Are you regular on the loose?" he demanded, and Rodney threw up a defensive elbow, behind which his eyes were dark and dangerous.

"I'm stuck with it, that's all," he said ungallantly. "You have things ready to pull out of here early on Thursday morning. The plane leaves Mexico City about one—at 13:20, to be exact!"

Juanita had got her way, but at the price of Rodney's utter disenchantment. He felt smeared. She had shown him up before Charles and Sturgis, as well as betraying herself, for until now the decencies, even the delicacies, had been preserved. Now there could be no doubt left in anybody's mind as to how things stood between them. She had made him very angry. Worse, she had embarrassed him before his peers. She had presumed. It is a thing no woman can afford to do.

In order to end the scene he agreed to go. But he was going on

333

his own terms. He would find a certain satisfaction in teaching her a lesson, by behaving from now on as formally as before he came to Mexico. It would infuriate her, he knew, and he looked forward to that. There was nothing she could do about it. He could still enjoy himself, a little, by thwarting her when she thought she had won. A daemonic interest in her reactions to his intended attitude of impersonal good manners was about all the trip could promise, but it would do. And when the four days were over, he could climb into that blissful, heavenly plane which would take him out of here, even though it could not take him back to Liz—and then he need never see Juanita Donahue again.

The next morning when he went out into the brisk bright air just before sunrise to where Manuel and the horses were waiting, he was surprised to learn that Manuel was not going with them. Juanita had breakfasted in her bedroom and so had not yet appeared. The old Indian sidled close to him and pretended to be busy with the stirrup-leather of the horse which was to carry him.

"The Señorita is very brave," he murmured, "but a little headstrong. There is trouble at the mine."

"What kind of trouble?"

"The kind it is best to stay out of," said Manuel, fumbling at the strap, his head bent.

"Does the Señorita know there is trouble?"

"We have all tried to make her see wisdom, señor. My brother rode in from there two days ago. He says the soldiers are coming."

"Well, it ought to be safe enough if the military are in charge," said Rodney.

"They are not in charge—yet."

"What seems to be going on up there?"

"They say the men steal—they say the yield is not enough, and that therefore a portion of it *must* be stolen—they say—"

"Who are 'they'?"

"The new owners."

"Are they German owners?"

"I have not seen them," said Manuel evasively. "They speak Spanish, the better to corrupt honest men like my brother."

"How did they get control of the mine?"

"*¿Quien sabe?* They arrived. They brought machinery—fine machinery. They seem always to expect bonanzas. Then they are disappointed. Then they say the men steal. The search is very strict—the penalty—" He shook his head, working with unsteady fingers at the strap.

"How many of them are there?"

"Enough."

"You mean they brought workmen with them too?"

"*Sí—sí*—many workmen up from the coast—all armed. There is much talk of exploitation, and increase-in-production—the mine was very rich once, in *El Patron Grande's* day. It had a reputation. They cannot believe the yield is now so small. They do not realize that without *El Patron Grande*—" Manuel glanced over his shoulder towards the door, and laid a brown claw briefly on Rodney's sleeve. "*Señor*—I am an old man—I have seen many things—do not go with her today."

Before Rodney could draw breath, Juanita came out of the house, looking fresh and smart in her well-cut riding clothes and a gay sombrero.

"What's this about trouble at the mine?" Rodney queried.

"Hogwash!" she said easily. "Manuel is an alarmist. He'll scare you to death if you listen to him!"

"Mightn't he know what he's talking about?"

"Are you afraid?" she asked, with her upward look.

"I want to leave here on time Thursday morning, that's all."

"Well, I won't let them kidnap you!" She swung into the saddle unassisted.

"It's you they'd kidnap," he remarked, and mounted also.

"Oh, nonsense, Rodney, these are my own people, I know how to handle them! Even if there *was* a little trouble we'd be perfectly safe at the hacienda."

335

"Are you pals with all the soldiers too—and the new owners?"

"Why, I do believe you're nervous!" she laughed. "Shall we get Charles out of bed and take him along to protect you?"

"It might not be a bad idea to take Manuel."

"Oh, Rodney, don't be absurd! I know the way, I couldn't lose it if I tried, we needn't go near the mine, the hacienda stands quite separate, we'll be there before dark, and Innocencio has four stalwart sons to defend us!"

"O.K.," he said cheerfully, smiling at Manuel's dark, discouraged face, and they rode out together with one pack-mule to carry food for the journey and their overnight bags.

Manuel stood a long moment looking after them. He had tried —because he had grown very attached to this Americano who treated one as though one was, after all, a man. But it was not a thing one could speak straight out about, when the daughter of *El Patron Grande* had made up her mind. He and his brother had shaken anxious heads over the Señorita's orders which had been forwarded to Innocencio at the hacienda. When the Señorita and her lover reached the hacienda, the orders ran, all the horses were to be stolen—presumably by the military—and hidden up at the mine. Thus the Señor's return by Thursday morning would be rendered impossible. To Manuel and his brother it seemed madness, in view of the conditions at the mine, to isolate oneself from fresh, reliable horses. Besides—although this was, of course, no business of theirs—force was not the way to hold a man's heart.

XXIX

The trip was a grueling one, through very wild country, and Rodney wondered anew at her endurance and spirits as the day drew on.

They began with a two-hour steady exhausting climb till they came to where they could look back towards the cliffs of black bare rock round Cuernavaca where Popo watched above recumbent Ixtacihuatl in the hazy distance. Juanita said the road was once infested by bandits, and supposedly fabulous riches had been cached in the hills roundabout—silver buttons, priceless embroidered saddles, swords set with jewels, inlaid firearms—"I always carried my own little pearl-handled pistol when I was a child," she said. "It was a birthday present from my father. I knew how to use it, too!"

They paused to breathe the horses, looking down on the vast velvet folds of the Sierras, which held little villages in their pockets, and the tiny opalescent rivers at the bottom of the winding *barrancas*. Juanita remarked on how just by crossing one of the razor-backed ridges you could change the terrain from lava and cactus and *guaje* trees to palms (stunted by altitude but still palms) and sugar cane—from raw, brutal rock set on edge to all the softness and beauty of the tropics and none of their discomforts, because of this perfect climate which was Mexico.

Rodney rode on beside her in receptive silence, his long body loose and easy in the roomy Mexican saddle. The beautiful, terrible desolation of the heights suited his mood. He felt between worlds, equidistant from adventure and regret; somber, pliant, submissive to a willful destiny. It seemed to matter very little any more what he did or didn't do.

337

The road led through a rocky pass, a mere slit in the mountain-wall, to a country where nothing grew but prickly pear, a country bleak as Rodney's soul. And then, following a rough track whose surface alternated loose stones with solid lava ridges, they crossed a spiny waste where orchids and cactus grew side by side, until, descending always, their way was edged with moss and giant fern and shiny castor-oil plants, and flowers by the armload—unrecognizable orchids, and fantastic, nameless, scented lily-growths.

Juanita seemed not to mind his silence nor to notice his pre-occupation. Her pretty voice ran on tirelessly, a comforting human sound in the nightmarish drift of his consciousness—he was grateful for it, in a way, though only bits of what she said really penetrated his comprehension—

"When I was little I used to set scorpions on to fight each other," she was saying against the strong, sweet song of a cañon wren which reached his ear more clearly than her words. "They're like cocks for fighting, did you know? But no blood comes of it—I hate blood—my nurse was shocked at such a game, but she thought nothing of cleaning a fowl for my dinner—I couldn't do that if I was starving. . . . I'm not afraid of live things, though—like *coralillo* snakes, for instance, they're absolutely deadly but I think they're beautiful, I'd like to *wear* one—tarantulas are beautiful too, like black velvet—and the flight of a *zopilote* in the blue sky above the patio is one of the loveliest sights in the world—I always had pet birds when I was little, *zenzontls,* mostly—that's the mocking-bird with the white breast—I always used the Aztec names for my pets, I spoke Aztec with our gardener—he always wore a different flower behind his ear each day while he worked—it was amazing how seldom he had to repeat himself. . . . Indians always tell you what they think you want them to say, but I suppose you can't call it lying, really. . . . You drink the *tequila* straight, and suck a quarter of a lime afterwards—everybody gets tight on their saint's day, so nobody could blame him, I don't suppose he was even jailed. . . . Mexicans always try to appear as poor as possible, on account

338

of the tax-collector. The *Presidente* of this next village is a pal of mine, do you mind if we stop and chin awhile? He has the most amusing parrot that sits and screams *'Muy bien'* at you. . . ."

They drank warm beer with the *Presidente,* who was the village store-keeper as well as its mayor, and smoked the cheap *Tigres* cigarettes which he sold singly from the packet to his Mexican customers and bestowed on his Americano visitors with high courtesy. He had been a handsome man once, and he swaggered rather pathetically in his infatuation with the Señorita, who had obviously led him on in their previous encounters. Rodney emerged sufficiently from his mental inertia to conceive a certain distaste for Don Epifanio's cordialities.

They paused for lunch in a deep ravine beside the sound of dripping water, which mitigated a little the immense silence in which they had moved since leaving the village *Presidente*. The walls of the ravine were covered with cactus, its trees were festooned with honeysuckle and mistletoe. Vermilion fly-catchers and little flocks of orange-and-black orioles were recorded by Rodney's observant sub-conscious.

After lunch Juanita, lying back on her elbows with her boots crossed, was running on about how Mexico would always be for her the land of dreams, where everything came true, where nothing was surprising, and anything wonderful could always happen. "*Abandono,*" she crooned, with lazy eyes on him. "Surrender—let the world wag. *Mañana.* The very days of the week lose their identity here—market day is often Sunday—any day can be a feast-day—there are no fire alarms in Mexico—no ambulance sirens, not even telephone bells—nothing to deny the gospel of leisure they live by—the luxury of timelessness—the fine art of lotus-eating—"

The word struck his heart like a hammer on a gong. It was a word which belonged to Liz, to an era of peace and contentment he had forever forfeited. And for what? For a brace of gangling, ungrateful, sickly birds in little wicker cages, who might die and be damned if only he could get back that moment on the window-seat and Liz in his arms saying, "Isn't this better than the Casa Paraiso?" He felt all the idle quiescence of the morning ride fade before sudden sharp crowding thoughts of things he had put behind him. This was not lotus-eating, this sticky interlude with a romanticizing woman who babbled platitudes. There was a word for it, though, and she knew what it was, and so did he. So did Charles, whose honest, troubled eyes would be hard to meet in the usual way on Thursday. Feeling rather sick, Rodney rose abruptly.

"How about making a slight effort to get off this trail before dark?" he said.

Juanita sighed as she rose, and said there was plenty of time.

New corn was up several inches high in fields enclosed by walls of lava in that valley. Burros crowded past them in the narrow trail cut into the winding *barrancas,* loaded with charcoal, barbed wire of all things, casks of liquor, and sometimes bags of ore; Indians in pink and lavender shirts and white *calzones,* their faces like Aztec masks; women in blue or black *rebozos. Adiós,* they said gently in greeting and eternal farewell, as they passed. *Adiós, señorita. . . .*

Sometimes Juanita sang as she rode, in a clear, sweet pipe rather like a canary. The songs, such as *Mama Ines,* and the bawdy *Tu Ya No Soplas,* were all too big for her, and Rodney wished she wouldn't, whereas only the day before he might have joined in as he was expected to, with certain verses of his own.

At last they edged round a sharp shoulder of rock with a sheer drop on the left, down, down, hundreds of feet down to tree-tops which looked like bushes at the bottom of the *barranca* where the silver thread of a stream wound. From there she pointed out, beyond the rise of another sharp ridge, the pale hacienda walls among the green.

"That's it!" she said proudly. "The going from here on in is simply frightful. People who can't bear heights just have to shut their eyes and trust their horses. Lots of our visitors used to arrive

340

limp with fright, and had to be lifted down and given restoratives in the courtyard. I like it that way, myself—heaven should be hard to get to, and mine is! Or should I say *ours?*"

The sun was dropping towards the west when they reached the hacienda she had once called home. It lit up with sharp golden light the long red scars of the mine-workings on the slope of the mountain which rose close behind the house, and the graceful curve of an old aqueduct stood out against the green foliage. They rode through the great open gates into a paved courtyard. Beyond a second superb arch draped in bougainvillea an alluring green patio showed.

No one came to meet them. There was no one in sight at all.

"This is certainly a palace," he said as they dismounted. "I don't wonder you're proud of it. It seems to go on and on."

"Forty rooms!" she said. "We used them all, too! Most of them are closed off now. I wonder where everybody is. Innocencio!" Her voice was swallowed up by the blank vast walls of the courtyard. "Well, that's funny," she said. "Let's go in."

They passed under the second arch into the inner patio where the fountain was, amid a pageant of well-tended bloom. Still there was no sign of the family.

"Inez!" Juanita called with a growing urgency. "Innocencio!"

"Not a soul," said Rodney. "Looks as if they weren't expecting us."

"Well, they wouldn't just *leave*—" she cried, and led the way into the grand *sala,* whose tiled floor echoed to their booted footsteps. "Inez! Ramon!"

"All right, so you fixed it this way," said Rodney knowingly. "Why bother?"

"I did not!" Her blue eyes were bright with indignation. "Why would I fix it so we have to get our own dinner? Something's happened. Let's try the kitchen."

The kitchen was tidy and full of food, but deserted. Even fresh vegetables had been brought in that morning, and the antiquated

341

electric refrigerator was switched on and making ice. At least they would not starve.

"I simply don't understand it," she kept repeating. "It looks as though they had expected to have dinner here— Rodney, I think there's something very queer. Nine or ten people live in this house, counting the servants. Well, where are they?"

"Could they have gone up to the mine?"

"But *why*? Unless—"

"Well?"

"Well, there's a refuge at the mine," she said slowly. "We hid there for two days once ourselves, from brigands. But surely if they'd had some sort of alarm they'd have locked things up, they'd have made some effort to—to—" Her eyes went round the well-stocked kitchen. "And if they'd been kidnapped or anything like that there'd be some signs of struggle, the place would have been looted, or—"

"How's this for a sign?" he asked, looking out into the kitchen patio.

She came quickly to his side and then recoiled. The body of a dead soldier lay on the tiled floor outside, between the kitchen door and an arch covered with a climbing white rose through which the stables could be seen.

"What does it *mean*?" she gasped.

"Means the military have come. Means the shooting has started. Means maybe Manuel was right, and it's not so healthy around here."

"But Innocencio had nothing to do with the mine any more— or with the soldiers. All he ever wanted was to live here in peace. What's become of the family?"

"Well, if one of the family killed the soldier—especially as he's been shot in the back—"

"Oh, that's impossible! What shall we do? Don't just stand there looking at it! Let's get out of here before anyone sees us!"

"I've no desire to tackle that trail after dark," he said, "even if we had fresh horses, which we haven't. We'll feed our beasts, and get some rest ourselves, and start the minute it's light."

"You mean—*spend the night here anyhow?*"

"What else?"

"But suppose they come back for him—out there."

"They probably will. Wait, now, there's no need to panic about that—"

"But they might think we killed him!"

"I don't know why they should think that. We aren't armed, and we've no interest in what goes on at the mine." He looked at her with sudden suspicion. "Or have we?" he said.

"Well, I—only a sentimental one."

"Have you been mixing into this?" he demanded sternly.

"Why, no, of course not! Except that the last time I was here Innocencio was complaining about the way he was treated, and I tried to make them all see that he mustn't take it lying down— that he must stand up for his rights here, and not let himself be over-run or jockeyed out by either side—"

"So he shot the soldier in the back," Rodney said reflectively.

"Oh, *no*—I—"

"Innocencio got mixed up, and did the wrong thing," he went on, working it out. "And either they've all been taken into custody, or they're hiding. Why did you have to give him bad advice like that, it was no business of yours!"

"Well, after all, you're only guessing, we've no proof that Innocencio killed him!"

"Yes, I'm only guessing," he admitted. "That seemed to be about the least embarrassing guess I could make. On the other hand, the new owners may have shot the soldier in order to pin it on Innocencio, which would eventually give them possession of his house if things worked out according to plan—that's the way it's worked before, isn't it, on a slightly larger scale—"

"Oh, Rodney, they've been *trying* to get the house—"

"Sure they have! They want it for the *Herr Aufseher,* or the

343

Herr Inspektor or whatever they call him. Now, it might be just as well not to show a light here, beyond a pocket-torch. And it'll be dark soon. So I'll go out and see to the horses while—"

"I'll come with you."

"You'd better stay here and collect some food while you can see to find your way around. There's enough left over from lunch still in the saddle-bags to see us through tomorrow, and I'll just leave it there. I think I'll leave our bags there too, in case we want to leave in a hurry."

"Oh, Rodney, now I won't get a picture of you in my lovely garden!" she cried tragically.

"I'm afraid you won't!" he agreed from the doorway, and disappeared.

Horses had waited in the stable patio recently, he noticed as he led his own tired beasts in. The stalls, however, were clean and empty. He took off the saddles and the pack, fed and watered the three animals, and returned to the house just as the sinking sun was turning the highest peaks in the distance a rosy pink. He paused a moment under the arch where the white rose climbed, and stood looking up towards the mine-shaft. There were perhaps a dozen men with rifles lounging about in plain view. Work seemed to have stopped. There was not a soldier in sight, except the dead one. But Rodney, who like most of his kind had developed a sixth sense, felt a prickle of nerves along his spine as he stepped round the body on his way back to the kitchen. All quiet. For how long?

Juanita had found a cold chicken and avocados and a pineapple in the ice-box, and was struggling to open a bottle of sherry. He drew the cork for her, and they carried the meal on a tray into the *sala,* which was still lit by the last long rays of the sun.

"Well, here's to vanished splendor!" she said, and raised her sherry glass, but her eyes were frightened.

Vanished splendor. He carried his glass to the wide door which stood open on to the colonnaded patio and leaned there, looking

344

out at the fountain and the bougainvillea and the magnificent towering mountain range behind. From here too he had a view of the main shaft and the group of casual-seeming men with rifles, although with the setting sun in their eyes, they could hardly see into the hacienda. There was no indication that they had any interest in the hacienda.

"You're sorry you came," she said, watching him from where she sat inside the room.

"I'm sorry about quite a lot of things."

"But you don't blame *me,* Rodney," she pleaded prettily.

"You?" he said without moving. "You had nothing to do with it."

"I see! You mean anybody else would have done just as well as me, to show her you didn't care! I just happened to be around!"

"I wasn't trying to show her anything. I did care. She knew that."

"Then why—"

"Why did I come to Mexico? I keep telling you—for the eagles."

"That's your story!"

"And I'm stuck with it," he said, smiling. *"How* I'm stuck with it! I'm sorry, Nita—" For the first time he looked at her, from the doorway. Revenge was not so sweet, no matter what the books said. His ingrowing, native chivalry irked him, now that he came to teach her that lesson. She was frail and small, and she had been very sweet once—once or twice. She was without scruples or morals or good taste, and she had just about wrecked his life. But she was after all female, and therefore pretty helpless, and she had got them into a nice jam, and now she was frightened. "Don't take any notice of anything I say," he added, from the doorway. "Just—think nothing of it at all."

"Well, love is a wonderful thing!" she jibed, for the eagles always made her savage. "I wish I could believe in it! And I ought to be able to, after what I go through with you!"

345

"I'm sorry," he repeated.. "I've said the wrong thing, as usual. But I'm very grateful to you, all the same."

"For the birds!" she said, and looked at him piteously, her blue eyes swimming with tears. "You don't love me any more," she accused.

He stared at her, unable to believe his own ears that people really said such things. And she meant it. It was the way she actually talked. Beautiful in the fading light, her tanned skin seeming darker than her fine, fair hair, her head drooping on its long, delicate neck, she sat with tears in her eyes demanding of him a love-scene—now—with all the trimmings. It was tactless, and cheap, and—worst of all—it was embarrassing.

He was angry with her again, as angry as he had ever been, but his incorrigible fastidiousness, which tended to avoid rows, restrained him from giving way to a shout of cruel and raucous laughter.

"We won't go into that," he said briefly.

"Oh, Rodney, I only wanted four days more—I only—"

"And you were going to get 'em," he told her grimly. "But not the way you thought!"

"I don't know what you mean," she said, with a studied desolation.

"No, and now you never will—which is a pity, because you had it coming to you!"

"I suppose you've got an attack of conscience!" she suggested bitterly. "A trifle late!"

"It's not conscience," he denied in an even tone. "It's just a rush of sense to the head. Late, I grant you."

"You wish you hadn't come!" she asserted tensely. "Not just here. You wish you hadn't come to Mexico at all! You may as well admit it! You may as well throw it in my face that I'm nothing to you, nothing at all, and if Liz Dare crooked her finger you'd walk out on me forever!"

"She hasn't crooked her finger," he said gently, "but I'm walking out on you, all the same. Tomorrow."

"Oh, you would, would you!" she cried in a fury. "And for what? Do you flatter yourself that she'd take you back now, if you crawled to her on your stomach? She's through with you, why can't you see that, everybody else can! Why don't you get wise to things? You horned in and took her away from Stanley, and now he's got her back again! Why can't you just write it off?"

He moved towards her then, setting down his glass on the way. His eyes were bright and narrow.

"Why, you blabbing little hussy," he said deliberately. "I ought to break you in two!" He seized her wrist and jerked her to her feet, spilling the sherry she held. "Stand up and tell me you lied! Because it *is* a lie, I know that, and so do you!"

"Everybody in New York—" she was beginning defiantly, when a volley of shots rang out on the hillside behind the house, doubled by an echo from the patio walls. *"What's that?"* she whispered, and began to tremble as he dropped her arm and went back to the door.

Before he could speak there was the shattering roar of an explosion which rattled everything in the room. More shots followed.

"There goes the mine!" he said. "They've blown something sky-high, and it's on fire. They're coming this way now—what's left of them."

"Well, let's do something, don't let's *stand* here—"

"What can we do?" he asked calmly. "We can't leave. If it gets too hot we'll just lie flat and hope for the best. It's not our war, after all."

"We can't just stay here and be *shot* at—"

"Easy, now, they aren't shooting at us."

"I'm going to get away from here! Let's run for the horses—" She darted out of the room towards the kitchen and the stables.

"Nita!" He ran after her. "Come back, you fool, it will be dark in half an hour! *Nita!*" She moved like greased lightning,

347

but he caught her in the kitchen patio, just short of the rose-clad arch leading to the stables. "You're crazy!" he said, while she wriggled and twisted in his grasp. "They're on both sides of the house now, the army's moving in from below! If you try to get to the stables you'll run straight through a cross-fire!"

"Let me go—*I want to get out of here—let me go!*"

"Go where? We can't make that trail after dark, we'll ride bang over the edge into the *barranca!* We'll be all right here, Nita, how about the cellar—"

She bent swiftly and sank her teeth into his hand. As his hold automatically relaxed an instant, she wrenched away from him and flashed across the open space between the wall of the kitchen patio and the stables. A bullet nicked the ground near her feet as she ran, another struck the wall beside the arch where he stood and ricocheted.

Rodney swore, then made a dash for the stables himself. Just as he reached their shelter he stumbled and caught at his right shoulder, and swore again.

Juanita had got the saddle on her horse, and was working feverishly at buckles and straps.

"Nita, will you listen to reason?" he panted, leaning against the inner wall in the semi-darkness of the stables which was lit now by a red glow from the fire at the mine-shaft on the mountain behind the house. "They aren't after us—we only have to wait till things quiet down—"

"You can do as you like, but I'm leaving! I'd rather take a chance on the trail than stay here and be murdered!"

"You can't go now, I'm afraid—I'll have to have some help, I— I'm hit—"

She stared at him where he sagged against the wall, his left hand gripping his right shoulder. Then she came towards him, leading her horse by the bridle.

"Rodney—you aren't—*wounded*—!"

"Find some cloths," he gasped. "Get some linen out of the bags

348

over there—my pajamas—shirt—we'll have to make some sort of bandage—*will you please hurry*—"

"You're bleeding!" she cried in horror, and backed away from him, into the horse.

"I told you there was a cross-fire—now, I know this is going to be hard on you, Nita, but you've got to pull yourself together—I can't manage—alone—"

"No, no, I won't touch it—I've got to get out of here—keep away from me—you're *bleeding*—"

With a quick spring she was in the saddle, and he lurched forward and caught her arm.

"Nita, you've lost your head—nobody could stay on that trail at night—"

"*Take your hands off me!*" she screamed, and struck at him blindly. "*There is blood on your hands!*"

The horse lunged into motion as she dug her heels into its sides, ripping free from his hold, so that he staggered and fell to the ground. The thud of the galloping hooves was drowned out by a new burst of firing from the hillside.

Rodney lay still, trying to keep a grip on consciousness. Then with a great effort he crawled to where the luggage lay on the stable floor, got his bag open, got a handful of linen to staunch the wound. Finally, in darkness lit by the red glare from the mine and punctuated by rifle-fire, he dragged himself into an empty stall, collapsed on the straw, pulled a horse blanket over him, and waited for the merciful oblivion which was sure to come.

After dinner the following day, Manuel approached Charles in the *sala* and said that his brother had had word of a shooting at the mine, and would the Señores care to listen. Charles said they would.

Manuel's brother Atanasio was fetched, and told a vague, rambling tale of meeting a man in a *cantina* whose sister's husband had been brought in at sundown with a bullet in his leg which he had got in a running fight two days ago between the new workmen and the men whose fathers and grandfathers had worked for *El Patron Grande* in the old days—so then the soldiers had been sent for—there was an explosion at the mine, and a fire —then there was more fighting—but yes, of course near the hacienda, it lay in the line of fire, with the mine just behind it— the family, which had small children, were said to have fled to a village in the valley when the soldiers came in—presumably there was no longer anyone in residence—well, possibly a servant or two, but they would have no love for the soldiers—no, he had heard nothing of the Señorita and the Señor Doctor, though starting yesterday morning they would doubtless have arrived before the explosion occurred—there was no reason to suppose, however, that the hacienda itself had been damaged—

Charles and Sturgis looked at each other, and Sturgis nodded his head. Charles swung back to where the two old Indians waited, their eyes turned on the ground.

"We'll start at dawn tomorrow," he said.

Their eyes came up to him respectfully.

"For the hacienda, *señor?*"

"For the hacienda."

"*Sí, señor. Buenas noches, señores.*"

Manuel and his brother melted away.

"Maybe we're just a couple of old wives," said Sturgis at last, into the silence.

"Maybe you'd better stay with the birds," said Charles. "Then only one of us is wrong."

"I might miss some fun."

"You might. But if anything happens to those damned birds now, we may as well go jump in the lake."

"How true!" sighed Sturgis.

"I had a premonition," said Charles. "This is it. Let's go to bed."

So Charles set out at dawn with Manuel and Atanasio—wonder-

350

ing all the way if he was behaving like an interfering busybody or a man with second-sight; wondering what he was going to say if at the end of his journey he encountered two very surprised and not very cordial people; wondering what he would do if he found nobody at all at the hacienda. . . .

After hours of grueling travel, the shadows began to lengthen. The three of them were strung out single file where the trail edged along the mountain side, between sharp, jutting rock and a sheer drop. Charles, who hated heights but had always contrived to keep even Rodney from suspecting it, rode with his eyes fixed on Manuel's back some yards ahead of him. Atanasio brought up the rear.

Charles saw Manuel rein in and look down into the *barranca* which fell away abruptly on the left, its bare side dotted with cactus and shrub, to tree-tops several hundred feet below. Then Atanasio shouted, and Manuel dismounted and began to uncoil the rope from his saddle-horn. Charles rode up and swung out of the saddle with a certain caution.

"What is it?" he said, and reluctantly looked down.

Snagged against a sturdy thorn-bush which grew at an angle half way down the steep *barranca*-side, was a khaki-colored bundle. Another hundred feet below it, piled up against a rock ledge, its stiffening legs in the air, was the horse. *Zopilotes* circled boldly overhead.

"My God!" said Charles, and took a hasty step forward, and Manuel caught his arm, while a small cascade of rock rippled down the slope from Charles's boot.

"Wait for the rope, *señor,*" said Manuel, and Atanasio ran up with his own, which they knotted to Manuel's and made the end fast to Manuel's saddle-horn. *"Con permiso, señor—*I go down myself. She is dead," said Manuel sadly, and lowered himself along the rope.

Atanasio followed him, the younger man, putting less strain on the rope. Together, while the *zopilotes* watched, they brought

351

back the broken body of Juanita Donahue and laid it gently across Atanasio's saddle and covered it carefully with his *sarape*.

"The hacienda is just over the next ridge, *señor*," said Manuel, unfastening his rope and returning Atanasio's. "We will go on, with the *señor's* permission."

"What about the Señor Doctor?" Once more Charles's eyes searched flinchingly among the tree-tops at the bottom of the *barranca*. He felt sick and helpless. "Oughtn't we to look for—another horse?"

"I think the Señorita was alone, or she would not have been killed like that. I think we find the Señor Doctor further along —perhaps at the hacienda."

They rode on again, hurrying now, gaining fast on Atanasio, who came behind, leading his horse.

It was an hour before sunset when they passed through the open gates of the hacienda, a splendid desolation still. Smoke curled sluggishly from the deserted pit-head on the hill. There was not a workman or a soldier in sight. Manuel dismounted silently and Charles followed him towards the *sala*.

The spacious room was all askew, and had been tramped through by many feet. Rodney's hat and Juanita's gay sombrero lay side by side on the polished mahogany bench before the fireplace; two sherry glasses sat on the table beside the tray which was now stripped of its chicken and its pineapple.

"He was here," said Charles, and picked up Rodney's hat. "We're on his trail!"

The long refectory table in the dining-room was a shambles of broken food and dirty crockery and overturned glasses, where the soldiery had made a meal. The kitchen, where the meal had been prepared, was worse. All empty now.

Charles and Manuel turned back and went methodically through the rest of the rooms, where doubtless some pilfering had gone on, and loose objects had been pocketed. But the rooms were empty and mute and cryptic. Somewhere a clarína in a cage

352

whistled idyllically. The fountain tinkled in the patio. Charles stood beside it, still carrying Rodney's hat and looking very white around the mouth.

"Where next?" he asked Manuel. "There must be cellars. Or shall we go up to the mine?"

They searched the cellars. Then Manuel led the way across the kitchen patio and through the arch where the white rose climbed, and they came to the stables, which were empty too. The contents of the two overnight-bags had been turned out on the floor, the saddle-bags, the horses, and the mule were gone. Manuel shook his head.

"No hay," he said sadly.

Charles walked past him, casting about like a puzzled bird-dog —glanced into a couple of empty stalls, came to the disheveled luggage and stood looking down at it. He stooped suddenly, and peered at the light inner lining of Rodney's bag, which was daubed with blood. On the floor near by lay a folded handkerchief, also with red stains. Charles stood up. He turned, and walked on down the line of empty stalls beyond the heap of luggage—and then he saw the horse-blanket on the floor of the end stall, and under it, very still, was Rodney.

"Got him," said Charles, on his knees in the straw. "All right, son—what have they done to you?" he queried, though Rodney could not hear, and drew away the blood-soaked wad against the wound. "That's bad, isn't it—that's a nasty one—thank God, you knew enough to lie still and not bleed to death! Manuel, bring my saddle-bags! No, we won't move him, he stays right here. Bring some clean towels from the house—sheets, anything—bring some blankets too—put water on to boil—hurry up!"

"Sí, señor." Manuel was gone.

"Well, you damned near made it this time, didn't you, son!" Charles resumed affectionately, cutting away Rodney's shirt with his pen-knife. "That is one beauty of a bullet-hole, what were you trying to do, stop the whole army? Let's figure, now, what hap-

353

pened, anyway—how come you're left like this with no first aid? —how come you let her go at all, unless—"

He was still puzzling at it when Manuel returned with his arms full. He had even brought a pillow from the house. He dumped down his load and went back for the hot water. When he arrived with it, Charles was scribbling a message to Sturgis on the back of an old letter.

"You start back now," he said to Manuel. "Take my horse as well as your own, they can rest each other—keep going as long as you can see to move—crawl on your hands and knees, but *keep going*— Give this message to Señor Doctor Sturgis—it's all there, I think—stretcher to move him into the house to a bed— anti-tetanus—best doctor in town to come back with you—and send for the Señorita. And you get me that doctor here before tomorrow night, *sabe?*"

"*Sí, señor.*"

"And, Manuel—don't talk! Say nothing of how we found the Señorita, so far from the hacienda, nor of the Señor Doctor— here. There was shooting—the Señorita was killed, the Señor Doctor has a gunshot wound. That's all you know, *sabe?*"

"*Sí, señor.*"

Manuel evaporated into the shadows, and Charles went back to the dreary and frightening task of cleansing the wound and trying to bring Rodney to.

XXX

Elizabeth woke to Gertrude's hand on her shoulder, and Gertrude's soft voice saying—

"Mr. Blaine is here, Miss Elizabeth. He says you must see him. Mr. Blaine is here—"

"What?" said Elizabeth, blinking. "*Who?* What's he want?"

"He says tell you you must see him." Gertrude was holding a dressing-gown inexorably.

"What time is it?" Elizabeth climbed into the dressing-gown, and went to the mirror and passed a powder-puff over her face and picked up a lipstick.

"It's only ten after nine. But he said—"

"Said I must see him!" repeated Elizabeth, around the lipstick. "The man's mad. Bring my orange-juice into the drawing-room." She picked up a comb. Then suddenly she met her own eyes in the mirror—laid down the comb and went quickly out of the room.

Andrew's face as he turned towards her was grave.

"It's Rodney," she said, without a greeting, and reached for Andrew's hand. "Never mind breaking it gently, what's happened?"

"I don't know the details yet. But he has a gunshot wound and the Donahue girl has been killed."

She leaned against him a moment. Then—

"Let's sit down to this," she said quietly, and moved towards the davenport, still holding his hand. "How did you hear?"

355

"Because they knew I had financed his last trip, the AP rang up to find out if I was connected with this one. There's a paragraph in the morning papers, and I wanted to get to you before you saw it."

"Thank goodness you did. Show me." She held out her hand for the paper.

AMERICAN CASUALTIES IN MEXICO. *Mystery surrounds the death of Juanita Donahue, well-known traveler and author of several books . . . local disorders in a silver mine once owned by her father. . . . Dr. Monroe sustained a serious gunshot wound which may prove fatal . . . two other members of the party were uninjured. . . . Nothing is known of the circumstances. . . . Dr. Monroe unable to give any account. . . .*

"I thought you might want me to telegraph Charles," Andrew was saying.

"I don't know where they were staying. Stanley does. Get Stanley on the phone."

Stanley had not yet arrived at his office. Andrew called his home, and the line was busy. The instant he put down the receiver Elizabeth's telephone rang and it was Stanley. He knew nothing beyond what was in the paper and the AP call he had received as Juanita Donahue's publisher. Andrew wrote down the address which Stanley gave him. Stanley himself was on the point of telegraphing for details, but agreed to leave that to Andrew—they also agreed that the story must be played down, at least till Charles was heard from—and that Liz must be kept out of it as far as possible. Stanley said he'd get busy on that angle right away, and they hung up.

Andrew wrote out a telegram to Charles, and paused as he was about to telephone it in.

"Do you want to fly down there?" he queried.

"Yes," said Elizabeth. "But how can I? Oh, Lord, I don't mean the show, I'd put the understudy on! But I can't just swoop down and snatch back my husband the minute she's dead! Can I! Besides, it puts Rodney on a spot. He may be nearly out of his mind about her, where would I come into that? And how would it make him look to the people there if— No, Andrew, I've got to stay here and kick my heels and go crazy!"

"Let's put it to Charles, then, in the telegram."

"All right, do that! *'Can Liz fly down?'* Charles will love that!"

Andrew wrote it in, and sent the telegram.

When he turned back to her she was· sitting rigid in the grip of a new idea.

"Andrew—have you ever *heard* things about her?"

"Why, yes, one hears things," he said normally. "What sort of things do you mean?"

"Ugly things. That she sacrificed other people to what she wanted. That there were—accidents—on her trips."

"Accidents?" He seemed puzzled.

"Stanley said she daren't go back to Borneo. He said nothing had ever been proved but— Andrew, what *happened* down there at the mine? Rodney doesn't just go out and cheerfully get himself shot all for nothing. People who are—are in Rodney's protection don't get killed unless—unless he can't save them."

"He might have been disabled first," he pointed out.

"Yes—yes, of course, and she might have given her life trying to—" She picked up the paper and read the paragraph again. "It doesn't say that she was shot too," she muttered. "It doesn't say how she died."

"We'll know soon, when we hear from Charles," said Andrew, as Gertrude came in with a glass of orange-juice on a tray. "Drink that—and will you please ask me to breakfast? I haven't had any."

"Oh, Andrew, you're wonderful—will you stay with me till Charles's answer comes?"

357

Sturgis, nursing the eagles alone and waiting for a courier from the hacienda, opened Andrew's message when it came, and after considerable mental anguish sent off his reply:

CHARLES IN MOUNTAINS WITH RODNEY STOP SHOT IN RIGHT SHOULDER CONDITION GRAVE BUT LOTS OF STAMINA TO FIGHT INFECTION AND LOSS OF BLOOD STOP GOOD DOCTOR FROM MEXICO CITY REACHES RODNEY TOMORROW STOP FURTHER REPORT WITHIN SEVENTY-TWO HOURS STOP TELL LIZ AWAIT ORDERS STOP TWO BIRDS OK
STURGIS

"So he got the birds!" said Elizabeth, when Andrew handed it to her. "Darling Sturgis, to put that in!"

It somehow made a difference in the way she felt about things, that he had got the birds.

When the second message came it was briefer:

RODNEY WILL RECOVER TRANSPORT DIFFICULT DONT LET LIZ COME
STURGIS

"What did I tell you!" she said miserably, and went off to the theater.

When days had passed without further news in any form, she wrote to Aunt Virginia, very humbly, at the address she had once called home, asking for news of Rodney. And after some days more had passed, Aunt Virginia replied to say that she had had a rather unsatisfactory letter from Charles at last, and as a consequence knew very little herself—except that Rodney was alive and would not lose his arm, and would be flown home as soon as it was safe to move him. He had lost a great deal of blood, and there was an infection, but Charles had confidence in the doctor in charge. Charles himself still did not know exactly what had happened because Rodney said he could not remember, which was of course nonsense, and only made it more suspicious. And Aunt Virginia promised in the friendliest way to send word again when

358

she had seen Rodney herself, and she was *As always, Affectionately.*

The show ran on and on and there was no reason now to stop it. Pete offered Elizabeth a week's lay-off and she refused. Might as well be working, it kept your mind off things. But finally the leading-man got real fidgets about Hollywood, and a heat-wave set in, and the notice went up.

When Elizabeth came back to her dressing-room at the end of the last mid-week matinée the doorman handed her a folded note: *I must see you. Ernestine Guerber.*

Elizabeth said to bring her in, and got into a dressing-gown. The only thing she could think was that they needed money very badly—or that Dr. Guerber had been taken ill—or—but surely they wouldn't come to her for news of Rodney—or possibly—but no, how *could* they know anything more when Aunt Virginia had promised— She wondered if Ernestine hated her and blamed her for smashing up Rodney's life—or if Ernestine had pitied her when they heard about Juanita. She had always wondered about that.

At sight of the timid little figure in mussy brown with the dimple in its smile, she opened welcoming arms.

"Ernestine! How nice of you to come and see me!" she cried, and they kissed.

Mrs. Guerber sat down on the edge of the chaise-longue and went straight to the point.

"I come as a traitor," she said, in her simple, exact English. "I come to betray a trust."

"My goodness," said Elizabeth, smiling at her.

"They all made me promise not to tell," said Mrs. Guerber, with a crafty look. "I promised. Now I tell."

Elizabeth had stopped smiling.

"Rodney—?" she whispered, and Mrs. Guerber nodded.

"He is here. And the birds are safe at the Zoo, thriving. So he is satisfied."

359

Elizabeth sat down weakly beside her on the chaise-longue and laid hold of the knotted hands in Mrs. Guerber's lap.

"Where is he? You're holding something back, I don't care about the birds, *tell me about Rodney!*"

"Aha! I knew you still love him!"

"Of course I do! Whoever said I didn't? Ernestine, have a heart, you've seen him, what have you come to tell me?"

"He is in the hospital. I have just come from there. I come straight, while I still believe I am right."

"H-hospital. Then his wound—didn't heal—?"

"It healed. There was an infection. That too is finished. But—they say he will never use his arm again."

"It's—*gone?*"

"No, no, it is there—but it hangs. He cannot lift it. He cannot even bend the elbow."

With a little sound, Elizabeth hid her face against Mrs. Guerber's shoulder.

"Now, now—" Mrs. Guerber patted the tense hands in hers. "Now, now, Lisa—that is not the way to do. But you see now why you have heard nothing. He has made them all swear—he made me swear too when I went in to see him—but I am only a woman, I have no sense of honor, and it does not matter if my soul is damned. So I come to tell you. He is still a sick man, he does not think straight yet—often the mind stays sick after the body is made well. And so he has a horror that if you know about his maiming you will return to him out of pity—and he does not want that."

Elizabeth raised her head.

"Is that the only reason they haven't sent for me?"

"That is the only one. Charles says it is as much as his life is worth to suggest it."

"But—but what *becomes* of him, what will they—"

"He says he can still teach."

Their eyes met.

360

"Will you take me to him?" Elizabeth asked.

"Now, Lisa, wait. It will be difficult. You must be patient with him, you must use discretion, and remember he still thinks crooked."

"But you saw him today! Oh, darling, *tell* me, what did he say to you, how does he look, how ill is he—"

"He sits up in a chair. He looks just the same—a little thinner—"

"He *couldn't* be thinner!"

"Yes, he is too, thinner! But he smiled at me in the old wicked way, and—and—" Mrs. Guerber very nearly simpered. "—and he called me *Ernestine!*"

"Well, go on—what else? What was he doing when you got there, reading?"

The light left Mrs. Guerber's face, and she looked away from Elizabeth's eager eyes.

"He was writing—trying to write—with his left hand." Her voice broke. "He tried to hide the paper from me, but I saw—the letters—the poor words—like a child's—" She wept softly into her hands.

Elizabeth stood up and snatched off her dressing-gown.

"You're going to take me to him. *Now.*" A dress went on over her head. She snatched up a hat and jammed it on, stage make-up and all. "Come on, Ernestine, pull yourself together, the car's outside. Where do we go?"

In the car Mrs. Guerber blew her nose and straightened her hat.

"Be sure to tell him I did it," she said with a certain pride. "Else he will kill Charles all for nothing. If a woman breaks her word it is no matter. God does not expect much."

Elizabeth sat looking out of the window, praying that she would not start to cry now and ruin her make-up. Mind your mascara, Liz, she was saying to herself with a kind of dizzy firmness. You can't go to him all smeared and drippy, you've got to look your best. Mind your mascara. . . .

"What happened—when he was hurt?" she asked at last, to see if her voice was quite steady, and it was.

"Ah! We would like to know that!"

"You mean he's never *told?*"

"He says he does not know what happened. He says the fever wiped out his memory. That might be true if it did not look so fishy to start with. We *think* she tried to get away and save herself—*after* he was helpless."

"*Deserted* him? Why, the dirty, yellow, double-crossing little ——!" Elizabeth's vocabulary seemed to fail her.

"*Scheissweib*," nodded Mrs. Guerber, which would have horrified her husband, and Elizabeth, even though she had no idea what a vulgar word it was, was satisfied.

There was silence again in the car while it worked its tedious way uptown through the six o'clock traffic.

"Then he doesn't—grieve for her," said Elizabeth, voicing a secret dread that gnawed.

"Before God, Lisa—no."

"And—is there any pain now?"

"Not since the infection cleared. He is cured."

"Except that his arm won't work."

"He thinks it won't."

"But you s-said—"

"I know. The doctors give up. They have done all they can. He gives up too. That is not like him."

"But you think if he did things like exercising it—and had massage—and some kind of treatments—"

"He has had all that."

"Well, then, but how—"

"He must care more. He must persist."

"You mean I must make him try to use it—try to write with it—things like that? Ernestine, I'm no good at illness, I don't know anything about it, I— You'll come and talk to him sometimes, and show me what to do?"

362

"You won't need me."

"But I *will,* Ernestine, remember at the Casa Paraiso, how you—"

The car stopped in front of the hospital.

Mrs. Guerber guided her into the elevator and down a long shining corridor to where a door stood ajar with a screen across the opening. Not a sound came from within. Mrs. Guerber pointed and stood aside.

"Wish me luck!" Elizabeth whispered, and kissed her swiftly and stepped round the screen.

Rodney sat alone in a big chair by the window in the late light, wearing a dressing-gown, with a rug over his knees and a lap-board. He was patiently pushing a pencil across a sheet of paper with his left hand.

He looked up and saw her standing just inside the screen. When their eyes met she went to him silently, slipped to her knees beside his chair, and felt his left arm close strongly round her shoulders. The lap-board fell down beside the chair, the pencil rolled out across the floor. Silently they held to each other. At last—

"How on earth did you get here?" he said quietly. "I made Charles swear on a stack of Bibles—"

"It wasn't Charles. It was Ernestine. She said God didn't expect a woman to keep her word of honor. Rodney, what's the idea of holding out on me like this?"

"For a while I kept hoping somebody would get a brain-wave that might solve things. When nobody did, I—quit hoping."

"About your arm, you mean."

"Well, yes, you see—"

"What's the matter with it?"

"Well, you see, it—" He was staring at his right arm, which now lay close around her as she leaned against his knees. "It— *moved!*" he said incredulously.

"Well, sure it moved, what do you expect, you needed both

363

of them, didn't you?" She tried hard to keep her voice steady and casual.

"Liz, I give you my word, it—"

His eyes came back to her face, which was so smiling—so casual. It almost seemed as though he had been dreaming and that there never had been anything wrong with his arm. He looked at it again, and a sort of fear crept into his eyes. She spoke quickly, before it could lodge there.

"You're going to want that arm from now on," she said. "How are you going to play the accordion for me without it? And you're going to have to play the accordion, or I'll have nothing to sing to, because the show is closing on Saturday."

"I'd like to see it again," he said, but his eyes still rested on the arm that lay against her.

"All right, come on! Positively your last chance to see me from the front row! I've retired. I married a professor, remember?"

Something relaxed in him. She could almost feel it let go, like an overcoiled spring released, though only his eyes changed.

"Now, watch this," he said. "Watch this very closely—"

Slowly, a little uncertainly, but obedient to his will, his right hand slid along her shoulder—paused there—and went on, until his forefinger rested beneath her tilted chin.